Praise for Ted Chi

EXHALATION

"There are books so jammed with brilliant, mind-exploding ideas it's like the author packed fireworks between the covers, all strung together on a very short fuse. There are others that take a single fascinating notion and walk all the way around it. . . . To read Ted Chiang is to do both at the same time."

—NPR

"Exciting as hell. . . . [Chiang's] stories brim with wonder and horror. . . . His work has a profound richness."   —*The Nation*

"Humane, skillfully assembled stories, populated by vivid and memorable characters. . . . Boast[s] a beguiling mix of compassion and awe. . . . An immensely pleasing book."

—*San Francisco Chronicle*

"Chiang . . . masterfully confront[s] the anxieties of modern life through tales of technology and science, inspiring us to reconsider reality."   —*Time*

"Through lean, thought-provoking prose, Chiang manages to render stories about machines deeply felt—and deeply human."

—*Esquire*

"A stunning achievement in speculative fiction, from an author whose star will only continue to rise."

—*Los Angeles Review of Books*

"Chiang's prose is liquid and seductive, and his emotional entanglements create subtle agony. His writing shows how crucial written fiction still is." —*New York Journal of Books*

"An instant classic. . . . Visionary speculative stories that will change the way readers see themselves and the world around them: This book delivers in a big way."
—*Kirkus Reviews* (starred review)

"Exquisitely crafted. . . . Chiang is an entertaining, empathetic writer first, before being one of contemporary sci-fi's intellectual powerhouses. . . . One of the most exciting voices in his field." —*BookPage* (starred review)

"These stories are brilliant experiments, and [Chiang's] commitment to exploring deep human questions elevates them to among the very best science fiction."
—*Publishers Weekly* (starred review)

Ted Chiang

EXHALATION

Ted Chiang's fiction has won four Hugo, four Nebula, and four Locus awards and has been featured in *The Best American Short Stories*. His debut collection, *Stories of Your Life and Others*, has been translated into twenty-one languages. He was born in Port Jefferson, New York, and currently lives near Seattle, Washington.

ALSO BY TED CHIANG

Stories of Your Life and Others

EXHALATION

EXHALATION

TED CHIANG

VINTAGE BOOKS

A DIVISION OF PENGUIN RANDOM HOUSE LLC

NEW YORK

FIRST VINTAGE BOOKS EDITION, JUNE 2020

Copyright © 2019 by Ted Chiang

All rights reserved. Published in the United States
by Vintage Books, a division of Penguin Random House LLC,
New York, and distributed in Canada by Penguin Random House
Canada Limited, Toronto. Originally published in hardcover
in the United States by Alfred A. Knopf, a division of
Penguin Random House LLC, New York, in 2019.

Page 353 constitutes an extension of this copyright page.

The Library of Congress has cataloged the Knopf edition as follows:
Name: Chiang, Ted, author.
Title: Exhalation / Ted Chiang.
Description: First edition. | New York : Alfred A. Knopf, 2019.
Identifiers: LCCN 2018030957
ISBN Classification: LCC PS3603.H53 A6 2019 | DDC 813/.6—dc23
LC record available at https://lccn.loc.gov/2018030957

Vintage Books Trade Paperback ISBN: 978-1-101-97208-3
eBook ISBN: 978-1-101-94790-6

Book design by Betty Lew

www.vintagebooks.com

Printed in the United States of America
20 19 18 17 16 15 14 13 12 11

TO MARCIA

The Merchant and the Alchemist's Gate   3

Exhalation   37

What's Expected of Us   58

The Lifecycle of Software Objects   62

Dacey's Patent Automatic Nanny   173

The Truth of Fact, the Truth of Feeling   185

The Great Silence   231

Omphalos   237

Anxiety Is the Dizziness of Freedom   270

Story Notes   341

Acknowledgments   351

EXHALATION

THE MERCHANT AND THE ALCHEMIST'S GATE

O MIGHTY CALIPH AND COMMANDER OF THE FAITHFUL, I am humbled to be in the splendor of your presence; a man can hope for no greater blessing as long as he lives. The story I have to tell is truly a strange one, and were the entirety to be tattooed at the corner of one's eye, the marvel of its presentation would not exceed that of the events recounted, for it is a warning to those who would be warned and a lesson to those who would learn.

My name is Fuwaad ibn Abbas, and I was born here in Baghdad, City of Peace. My father was a grain merchant, but for much of my life I have worked as a purveyor of fine fabrics, trading in silk from Damascus and linen from Egypt and scarves from Morocco that are embroidered with gold. I was prosperous, but my heart was troubled, and neither the purchase of luxuries nor the giving of alms was able to soothe it. Now I stand before you without a single dirham in my purse, but I am at peace.

Allah is the beginning of all things, but with Your Majesty's permission, I begin my story with the day I took a walk through the district of metalsmiths. I needed to purchase a gift for a man I had to do business with, and had been told he might appreciate a tray made of silver. After browsing for half an hour, I noticed that one of the largest shops in the market had been taken over by a new merchant. It was a prized location that must have been expensive to acquire, so I entered to peruse its wares.

Never before had I seen such a marvelous assortment of goods. Near the entrance there was an astrolabe equipped with seven plates inlaid with silver, a water clock that chimed on the hour, and a nightingale made of brass that sang when the wind blew. Farther inside there were even-more-ingenious mechanisms, and I stared at them the way a child watches a juggler, when an old man stepped out from a doorway in the back.

"Welcome to my humble shop, my lord," he said. "My name is Bashaarat. How may I assist you?"

"These are remarkable items that you have for sale. I deal with traders from every corner of the world, and yet I have never seen their like. From where, may I ask, did you acquire your merchandise?"

"I am grateful to you for your kind words," he said. "Everything you see here was made in my workshop, by myself or by my assistants under my direction."

I was impressed that this man could be so well versed in so many arts. I asked him about the various instruments in his shop and listened to him discourse learnedly about astrology, mathematics, geomancy, and medicine. We spoke for more than an hour, and my fascination and respect bloomed like a flower warmed by the dawn, until he mentioned his experiments in alchemy.

"Alchemy?" I said. This surprised me, for he did not seem the sort to make such a sharper's claim. "You mean you can turn base metal into gold?"

"I can, my lord, but that is not in fact what most seek from alchemy."

"What do most seek, then?"

"They seek a source of gold that is cheaper than mining ore from the ground. Alchemy does describe a means to make gold, but the procedure is so arduous that, by comparison, digging beneath a mountain is as easy as plucking peaches from a tree."

I smiled. "A clever reply. No one could dispute that you are a learned man, but I know better than to credit alchemy."

Bashaarat looked at me and considered. "I have recently built something that may change your opinion. You would be the first person I have shown it to. Would you care to see it?"

"It would be a great pleasure."

"Please follow me." He led me through the doorway in the rear of his shop. The next room was a workshop, arrayed with devices whose functions I could not guess—bars of metal wrapped with enough copper thread to reach the horizon, mirrors mounted on a circular slab of granite floating in quicksilver—but Bashaarat walked past these without a glance.

Instead he led me to a sturdy pedestal, chest high, on which a stout metal hoop was mounted upright. The hoop's opening was as wide as two outstretched hands, and its rim so thick that it would tax the strongest man to carry. The metal was black as night but polished to such smoothness that, had it been a different color, it could have served as a mirror. Bashaarat bade me stand so that I looked upon the hoop edgewise, while he stood next to its opening.

"Please observe," he said.

Bashaarat thrust his arm through the hoop from the right side, but it did not extend out from the left. Instead, it was as if his arm were severed at the elbow, and he waved the stump up and down, and then pulled his arm out intact.

I had not expected to see such a learned man perform a conjuror's trick, but it was well done, and I applauded politely.

"Now wait a moment," he said as he took a step back.

I waited, and behold, an arm reached out of the hoop from its left side, without a body to hold it up. The sleeve it wore matched Bashaarat's robe. The arm waved up and down and then retreated through the hoop until it was gone.

The first trick I had thought a clever mime, but this one seemed far superior, because the pedestal and hoop were clearly too slender to conceal a person. "Very clever!" I exclaimed.

"Thank you, but this is not mere sleight of hand. The right side of the hoop precedes the left by several seconds. To pass through the hoop is to cross that duration instantly."

"I do not understand," I said.

"Let me repeat the demonstration." Again he thrust his arm through the hoop, and his arm disappeared. He smiled and pulled back and forth as if playing tug-a-rope. Then he pulled his arm out again and presented his hand to me with the palm open. On it lay a ring I recognized.

"That is my ring!" I checked my hand and saw that my ring still lay on my finger. "You have conjured up a duplicate."

"No, this is truly your ring. Wait."

Again, an arm reached out from the left side. Wishing to discover the mechanism of the trick, I rushed over to grab it by the hand. It was not a false hand but one fully warm and alive as mine. I pulled on it, and it pulled back. Then, as deft as a pickpocket, the hand slipped the ring from my finger, and the arm withdrew into the hoop, vanishing completely.

"My ring is gone!" I exclaimed.

"No, my lord," he said. "Your ring is here." And he gave me the ring he held. "Forgive me for my game."

I replaced it on my finger. "You had the ring before it was taken from me."

At that moment an arm reached out, this time from the right side of the hoop. "What is this?" I exclaimed. Again I recognized it as his by the sleeve before it withdrew, but I had not seen him reach in.

"Recall," he said, "the right side of the hoop precedes the left." And he walked over to the left side of the hoop and thrust his arm through from that side, and again it disappeared.

Your Majesty has undoubtedly already grasped this, but it was only then that I understood: whatever happened on the right side of the hoop was complemented, a few seconds later, by an event on the left side. "Is this sorcery?" I asked.

"No, my lord, I have never met a djinni, and if I did, I would not trust it to do my bidding. This is a form of alchemy."

He offered an explanation, speaking of his search for tiny pores in the skin of reality, like the holes that worms bore into wood, and how upon finding one he was able to expand and stretch it the way a glassblower turns a dollop of molten glass into a long-necked pipe, and how he then allowed time to flow like water at one mouth while causing it to thicken like syrup at the other. I confess I did not really understand his words and cannot testify to their truth. All I could say in response was "You have created something truly astonishing."

"Thank you," he said, "but this is merely a prelude to what I intended to show you." He bade me follow him into another room, farther in the back. There stood a circular doorway whose massive frame was made of the same polished black metal, mounted in the middle of the room.

"What I showed you before was a Gate of Seconds," he said. "This is a Gate of Years. The two sides of the doorway are separated by a span of twenty years."

I confess I did not understand his remark immediately. I imagined him reaching his arm in from the right side and waiting twenty years before it emerged from the left side, and it seemed a very obscure magic trick. I said as much, and he laughed. "That is one use for it," he said, "but consider what would happen if you were to step through." Standing on the right side, he gestured for me to come closer, and then pointed through the doorway. "Look."

I looked and saw that there appeared to be different rugs and pillows on the other side of the room than I had seen when I had entered. I moved my head from side to side and realized that when I peered through the doorway, I was looking at a different room from the one I stood in.

"You are seeing the room twenty years from now," said Bashaarat.

I blinked, as one might at an illusion of water in the desert, but what I saw did not change. "And you say I could step through?" I asked.

"You could. And with that step, you would visit the Baghdad of twenty years hence. You could seek out your older self and have a conversation with him. Afterward, you could step back through the Gate of Years and return to the present day."

Hearing Bashaarat's words, I felt as if I were reeling. "You have done this?" I asked him. "You have stepped through?"

"I have, and so have numerous customers of mine."

"Earlier you said I was the first to whom you showed this."

"This Gate, yes. But for many years I owned a shop in Cairo, and it was there that I first built a Gate of Years. There were many to whom I showed that Gate, and who made use of it."

"What did they learn when talking to their older selves?"

"Each person learns something different. If you wish, I can tell you the story of one such person." Bashaarat proceeded to tell me a story, and if it pleases Your Majesty, I will recount it here.

THE TALE OF THE FORTUNATE ROPE-MAKER

There once was a young man named Hassan who was a maker of rope. He stepped through the Gate of Years to see the Cairo of twenty years later, and upon arriving he marveled at how the city had grown. He felt as if he had stepped into a scene embroidered on a tapestry, and even though the city was no more and no less than Cairo, he looked on the most common sights as objects of wonder.

He was wandering by the Zuweyla Gate, where the sword dancers and snake charmers perform, when an astrologer called to him, "Young man! Do you wish to know the future?"

Hassan laughed. "I know it already," he said.

"Surely you want to know if wealth awaits you, do you not?"

"I am a rope-maker. I know that it does not."

"Can you be so sure? What about the renowned merchant Hassan al-Hubbaul, who began as a rope-maker?"

His curiosity aroused, Hassan asked around the market for others who knew of this wealthy merchant and found that the name was well known. It was said he lived in the wealthy quarter near the Birkat al-Fil so Hassan walked there and asked people to point out his house, which turned out to be the largest one on its street.

He knocked at the door, and a servant led him to a spacious and well-appointed hall with a fountain in the center. Hassan waited while the servant went to fetch his master, but as he looked at the polished ebony and marble around him, he felt that he did not belong in such surroundings and was about to leave when his older self appeared.

"At last you are here!" the man said. "I have been expecting you!"

"You have?" said Hassan, astounded.

"Of course, because I visited my older self just as you are visiting me. It has been so long that I had forgotten the exact day. Come, dine with me."

The two went to a dining room, where servants brought chicken stuffed with pistachio nuts, fritters soaked in honey, and roast lamb with spiced pomegranates. The older Hassan gave few details of his life: he mentioned business interests of many varieties, but did not say how he had become a merchant; he mentioned a wife, but said it was not time for the younger man to meet her. Instead, he asked young Hassan to remind him of the pranks he had played as a child, and he laughed to hear stories that had faded from his own memory.

At last the younger Hassan asked the older, "How did you make such great changes in your fortune?"

"All I will tell you right now is this: when you go to buy hemp from the market, and you are walking along the Street of Black Dogs, do not walk along the south side as you usually do. Walk along the north."

"And that will enable me to raise my station?"

"Just do as I say. Go back home now; you have rope to make. You will know when to visit me again."

Young Hassan returned to his day and did as he was instructed, keeping to the north side of the street even when there was no shade there. It was a few days later that he witnessed a maddened horse run amok on the south side of the street directly opposite him, kicking several people, injuring another by knocking a heavy jug of palm oil onto him, and even trampling one person under its hooves. After the commotion had subsided, Hassan prayed to Allah for the injured to be healed and the dead to be at peace and thanked Allah for sparing him.

The next day Hassan stepped through the Gate of Years and sought out his older self. "Were you injured by the horse when you walked by?" he asked him.

"No, because I heeded my older self's warning. Do not forget, you and I are one; every circumstance that befalls you once befell me."

And so the elder Hassan gave the younger instructions, and the younger obeyed them. He refrained from buying eggs from his usual grocer, and thus avoided the illness that struck customers who bought eggs from a spoiled basket. He bought extra hemp, and thus had material to work with when others suffered a shortage due to a delayed caravan. Following his older self's instructions spared Hassan many troubles, but he wondered why his older self would not tell him more. Whom would he marry? How would he become wealthy?

Then one day, after having sold all his rope in the market and carrying an unusually full purse, Hassan bumped into a boy while walking on the street. He felt for his purse, discovered it missing, and turned around with a shout to search the crowd for the pickpocket. Hearing Hassan's cry, the boy immediately began running through the crowd. Hassan saw that the boy's tunic was torn at the elbow, but then quickly lost sight of him.

For a moment Hassan was shocked that this could happen with no warning from his older self. But his surprise was soon replaced by anger, and he gave chase. He ran through the crowd, checking the elbows of boys' tunics, until by chance he found the pickpocket crouching beneath a fruit wagon. Hassan grabbed him and began shouting to all that he had caught a thief, asking them to find a guardsman. The boy, afraid of arrest, dropped Hassan's purse and began weeping. Hassan stared at the boy for a long moment, and then his anger faded, and he let him go.

When next he saw his older self, Hassan asked him, "Why did you not warn me about the pickpocket?"

"Did you not enjoy the experience?" asked his older self.

Hassan was about to deny it, but stopped himself. "I did enjoy it," he admitted. In pursuing the boy, with no hint of whether he'd succeed or fail, he had felt his blood surge in a way it had not for many weeks. And seeing the boy's tears had reminded him of the Prophet's teachings on the value of mercy, and Hassan had felt virtuous in choosing to let the boy go.

"Would you rather I had denied you that, then?"

Just as we grow to understand the purpose of customs that seemed pointless to us in our youth, Hassan realized that there was merit in withholding information as well as in disclosing it. "No," he said, "it was good that you did not warn me."

The older Hassan saw that he had understood. "Now I will tell you something very important. Hire a horse. I will give you directions to a spot in the foothills to the west of the city. There you will find within a grove of trees one that was struck by lightning. Around the base of the tree, look for the heaviest rock you can overturn, and then dig beneath it."

"What should I look for?"

"You will know when you find it."

The next day Hassan rode out to the foothills and searched until he found the tree. The ground around it was covered in rocks, so Hassan overturned one to dig beneath it, and then another, and then another. At last his spade struck something besides rock and soil. He cleared aside the soil and discovered a bronze chest, filled with gold dinars and assorted jewelry. Hassan had never seen its like in all his life. He loaded the chest onto the horse and rode back to Cairo.

The next time he spoke to his older self, he asked, "How did you know where the treasure was?"

"I learned it from myself," said the older Hassan, "just as you did. As to how we came to know its location, I have no explanation except that it was the will of Allah, and what other explanation is there for anything?"

"I swear I shall make good use of these riches that Allah has blessed me with," said the younger Hassan.

"And I renew that oath," said the older. "This is the last time we shall speak. You will find your own way now. Peace be upon you."

And so Hassan returned home. With the gold he was able to purchase hemp in great quantity and hire workmen and pay them a fair wage and sell rope profitably to all who sought it. He married a beautiful and clever woman, at whose advice he began trading in other goods, until he was a wealthy and respected merchant. All the while he gave generously to the poor and lived as an upright man. In this way Hassan lived the happiest of lives until he was overtaken by death, breaker of ties and destroyer of delights.

· · ·

"That is a remarkable story," I said. "For someone who is debating whether to make use of the Gate, there could hardly be a better inducement."

"You are wise to be skeptical," said Bashaarat. "Allah rewards those he wishes to reward and chastises those he wishes to chastise. The Gate does not change how he regards you."

I nodded, thinking I understood. "So even if you succeed in avoiding the misfortunes that your older self experienced, there is no assurance you will not encounter other misfortunes."

"No, forgive an old man for being unclear. Using the Gate is not like drawing lots, where the token you select varies with each turn. Rather, using the Gate is like taking a secret passageway in a palace, one that lets you enter a room more quickly than by walking down the hallway. The room remains the same, no matter which door you use to enter."

This surprised me. "The future is fixed, then? As unchangeable as the past?"

"It is said that repentance and atonement erase the past."

"I have heard that, too, but I have not found it to be true."

"I am sorry to hear that," said Bashaarat. "All I can say is that the future is no different."

I thought on this for a while. "So if you learn that you are dead twenty years from now, there is nothing you can do to avoid your death?" He nodded. This seemed to me very disheartening, but then I wondered if it could not also provide a guarantee. I said, "Suppose you learn that you are alive twenty years from now. Then nothing could kill you in the next twenty years. You could then fight in battles without a care, because your survival is assured."

"That is possible," he said. "It is also possible that a man who would make use of such a guarantee would not find his older self alive when he first used the Gate."

"Ah," I said. "Is it then the case that only the prudent meet their older selves?"

"Let me tell you the story of another person who used the Gate, and you can decide for yourself if he was prudent or not." Bashaarat proceeded to tell me the story, and if it pleases Your Majesty, I will recount it here.

THE TALE OF THE WEAVER WHO STOLE FROM HIMSELF

There was a young weaver named Ajib who made a modest living as a weaver of rugs, but yearned to taste the luxuries enjoyed by the wealthy. After hearing the story of Hassan, Ajib immediately stepped through the Gate of Years to seek out his older self, who, he was sure, would be as rich and as generous as the older Hassan.

Upon arriving in the Cairo of twenty years later, he proceeded to the wealthy Birkat al-Fil quarter of the city and asked people for the residence of Ajib ibn Taher. He was prepared, if he met someone who knew the man and remarked on the similarity of their features, to identify himself as Ajib's son, newly arrived from Damascus. But he never had the chance to offer this story, because no one he asked recognized the name.

Eventually he decided to return to his old neighborhood and see if anyone there knew where he had moved to. When he got to his old street, he stopped a boy and asked him if he knew where to find a man named Ajib. The boy directed him to Ajib's old house.

"That is where he used to live," Ajib said. "Where does he live now?"

"If he has moved since yesterday, I do not know where," said the boy.

Ajib was incredulous. Could his older self still live in the same house, twenty years later? That would mean he had never become wealthy, and his older self would have no advice to give him, or at least none Ajib would profit by following. How could his fate differ so much from that of the fortunate rope-maker? In hopes that the boy was mistaken, Ajib waited outside the house, and watched.

Eventually he saw a man leave the house, and with a sinking heart recognized it as his older self. The older Ajib was followed by a woman that he presumed was his wife, but he scarcely noticed her, for all he could see was his own failure to have bettered himself. He stared with dismay at the plain clothes the older couple wore until they walked out of sight.

Driven by the curiosity that impels men to look at the heads of the executed, Ajib went to the door of his house. His own key still fit the lock, so he entered. The furnishings had changed, but were simple and worn, and Ajib was mortified to see them. After twenty years, could he not even afford better pillows?

On an impulse, he went to the wooden chest where he normally kept his savings and unlocked it. He lifted the lid and saw the chest was filled with gold dinars.

Ajib was astonished. His older self had a chest of gold, and yet he wore such plain clothes and had lived in the same small house for twenty years! What a stingy, joyless man his older self must be, thought Ajib, to have wealth and not enjoy it. Ajib had long known that one could not take one's possessions to the grave. Could that be something that he would forget as he aged?

Ajib decided that such riches should belong to someone who appreciated them, and that was himself. To take his older self's wealth would not be stealing, he reasoned, because it was he himself who would receive it. He heaved the chest onto his shoulder, and with much effort was able to bring it back through the Gate of Years to the Cairo he knew.

He deposited some of his newfound wealth with a banker, but always carried a purse heavy with gold. He dressed in a Damascene robe and Cordovan slippers and a Khurasani turban bearing a jewel. He rented a house in the wealthy quarter, furnished it with the finest rugs and couches, and hired a cook to prepare him sumptuous meals.

He then sought out the brother of a woman he had long desired from afar, a woman named Taahira. Her brother was an apothecary, and Taahira assisted him in his shop. Ajib would occasionally purchase a remedy so that he might speak to her. Once he had seen her veil slip, and her eyes were as dark and beautiful as a gazelle's. Taahira's brother would not have consented to her marrying a weaver, but now Ajib could present himself as a favorable match.

Taahira's brother approved, and Taahira herself readily consented, for she had desired Ajib, too. Ajib spared no expense for their wedding. He hired one of the pleasure barges that floated in the canal south of the city and held a feast with musicians and dancers, at which he presented her with a magnificent pearl necklace. The celebration was the subject of gossip throughout the quarter.

Ajib reveled in the joy that money brought him and Taahira, and for a week the two of them lived the most delightful of lives. Then one day Ajib came home to find the door to his house broken open and the interior ransacked of all silver and gold items. The terrified cook emerged from hiding and told him that robbers had taken Taahira.

Ajib prayed to Allah until, exhausted with worry, he fell asleep. The next morning he was awoken by a knocking at his door. There was a stranger there. "I have a message for you," the man said.

"What message?" asked Ajib.

"Your wife is safe."

Ajib felt fear and rage churn in his stomach like black bile. "What ransom would you have?" he asked.

"Ten thousand dinars."

"That is more than all I possess!" Ajib exclaimed.

"Do not haggle with me," said the robber. "I have seen you spend money like others pour water."

Ajib dropped to his knees. "I have been wasteful. I swear by the name of the Prophet that I do not have that much," he said.

The robber looked at him closely. "Gather all the money you have," he said, "and have it here tomorrow at this same hour. If I believe you are holding back, your wife will die. If I believe you to be honest, my men will return her to you."

Ajib could see no other choice. "Agreed," he said, and the robber left.

The next day he went to the banker and withdrew all the money that remained. He gave it to the robber, who gauged the desperation in Ajib's eyes and was satisfied. The robber did as he promised, and that evening Taahira was returned.

After they had embraced, Taahira said, "I didn't believe you would pay so much money for me."

"I could not take pleasure in it without you," said Ajib, and he was surprised to realize it was true. "But now I regret that I cannot buy you what you deserve."

"You need never buy me anything again," she said.

Ajib bowed his head. "I feel as if I have been punished for my misdeeds."

"What misdeeds?" asked Taahira, but Ajib said nothing. "I did not ask you this before," she said. "But I know you did not inherit all the money you gained. Tell me: Did you steal it?"

"No," said Ajib, unwilling to admit the truth to her or himself. "It was given to me."

"A loan, then?"

"No, it does not need to be repaid."

"And you don't wish to pay it back?" Taahira was shocked. "So you are content that this other man paid for our wedding? That he paid my ransom?" She seemed on the verge of tears. "Am I your wife, then, or this other man's?"

"You are my wife," he said.

"How can I be, when my very life is owed to another?"

"I would not have you doubt my love," said Ajib. "I swear to you that I will pay back the money, to the last dirham."

And so Ajib and Taahira moved back into Ajib's old house and began saving their money. Both of them went to work for Taahira's brother the apothecary, and when he eventually became a perfumer to the wealthy, Ajib and Taahira took over the business of selling remedies to the ill. It was a good living, but they spent as little as they could, living modestly and repairing damaged furnishings instead of buying new. For years, Ajib smiled whenever he dropped a coin into the chest, telling Taahira that it was a reminder of how much he valued her. He would say that even after the chest was full, it would be a bargain.

But it is not easy to fill a chest by adding just a few coins at a time, and so what began as thrift gradually turned into miserliness, and prudent decisions were replaced by tightfisted ones. Worse, Ajib's and Taahira's affections for each other faded over time, and each grew to resent the other for the money they could not spend.

In this manner the years passed and Ajib grew older, waiting for the second time that his gold would be taken from him.

. . .

"What a strange and sad story," I said.

"Indeed," said Bashaarat. "Would you say that Ajib acted prudently?"

I hesitated before speaking. "It is not my place to judge him," I said. "He must live with the consequences of his actions, just as I must live with mine." I was silent for a moment, and then said, "I admire Ajib's candor, that he told you everything he had done."

"Ah, but Ajib did not tell me of this as a young man," said Bashaarat. "After he emerged from the Gate carrying the chest, I did not see him again for another twenty years. Ajib was a much-older man when he came to visit me again. He had come home and found his chest gone, and the knowledge that he had paid his debt made him feel he could tell me all that had transpired."

"Indeed? Did the older Hassan from your first story come to see you as well?"

"No, I heard Hassan's story from his younger self. The older Hassan never returned to my shop, but in his place I had a different visitor, one who shared a story about Hassan that he himself could never have told me." Bashaarat proceeded to tell me that visitor's story, and if it pleases Your Majesty, I will recount it here.

THE TALE OF THE WIFE AND HER LOVER

Raniya had been married to Hassan for many years, and they lived the happiest of lives. One day she saw her husband dine with a young man, whom she recognized as the very image of Hassan when she had first married him. So great was her astonishment that she could scarcely keep herself from intruding on their conversation. After the young man left, she demanded that Hassan tell her who he was, and Hassan related to her an incredible tale.

"Have you told him about me?" she asked. "Did you know what lay ahead of us when we first met?"

"I knew I would marry you from the moment I saw you," Hassan said, smiling, "but not because anyone had told me. Surely, Wife, you would not wish to spoil that moment for him?"

So Raniya did not speak to her husband's younger self, but only eavesdropped on his conversation and stole glances at him. Her pulse quickened at the sight of his youthful features; sometimes our memories fool us with their sweetness, but when she beheld the two men seated opposite each other, she could see the fullness of the younger one's beauty without exaggeration. At night, she would lie awake, thinking of it.

Some days after Hassan had bid farewell to his younger self, he left Cairo to conduct business with a merchant in Damascus. In his absence Raniya found the shop that Hassan had described to her and stepped through the Gate of Years to the Cairo of her youth.

She remembered where he had lived back then, and so was easily able to find the young Hassan and follow him. As she watched him, she felt a desire stronger than she had felt in years for the older Hassan, so vivid were her recollections of their youthful lovemaking. She had always been a loyal and faithful wife, but here was an opportunity that would never be available again. Resolving to act on this desire, Raniya rented a house, and in subsequent days bought furnishings for it.

Once the house was ready, she followed Hassan discreetly while she tried to gather enough boldness to approach him. In the jewelers' market, she watched as he went to a jeweler, showed

him a necklace set with ten gemstones, and asked him how much
he would pay for it. Raniya recognized it as one Hassan had
given to her in the days after their wedding; she had not known
he had once tried to sell it. She stood a short distance away and
listened, pretending to look at some rings.

"Bring it back tomorrow, and I will pay you a thousand dinars,"
said the jeweler. Young Hassan agreed to the price, and left.

As she watched him leave, Raniya overheard two men talking nearby:

"Did you see that necklace? It is one of ours."

"Are you certain?" asked the other.

"I am. That is the bastard who dug up our chest."

"Let us tell our captain about him. After this fellow has sold
his necklace, we will take his money, and more."

The two men left without noticing Raniya, who stood with
her heart racing but her body motionless, like a deer after a tiger
has passed. She realized that the treasure Hassan had dug up
must have belonged to a band of thieves, and these men were two
of its members. They were now observing the jewelers of Cairo
to identify the person who had taken their loot.

Raniya knew that since she possessed the necklace, the young
Hassan could not have sold it. She also knew that the thieves
could not have killed Hassan. But it could not be Allah's will for
her to do nothing. Allah must have brought her here so that he
might use her as his instrument.

Raniya returned to the Gate of Years, stepped through to her
own day, and at her house found the necklace in her jewelry box.
Then she used the Gate of Years again, but instead of entering it
from the left side, she entered it from the right, so that she visited
the Cairo of twenty years later. There she sought out her older
self, now an aged woman. The older Raniya greeted her warmly

and retrieved the necklace from her own jewelry box. The two women then rehearsed how they would assist the young Hassan.

The next day, the two thieves were back with a third man, whom Raniya assumed was their captain. They all watched as Hassan presented the necklace to the jeweler.

As the jeweler examined it, Raniya walked up and said, "What a coincidence! Jeweler, I wish to sell a necklace just like that." She brought out her necklace from a purse she carried.

"This is remarkable," said the jeweler. "I have never seen two necklaces more similar."

Then the aged Raniya walked up. "What do I see? Surely my eyes deceive me!" And with that she brought out a third identical necklace. "The seller sold it to me with the promise that it was unique. This proves him a liar."

"Perhaps you should return it," said Raniya.

"That depends," said the aged Raniya. She asked Hassan, "How much is he paying you for it?"

"A thousand dinars," said Hassan, bewildered.

"Really! Jeweler, would you care to buy this one, too?"

"I must reconsider my offer," said the jeweler.

While Hassan and the aged Raniya bargained with the jeweler, Raniya stepped back just far enough to hear the captain berate the other thieves. "You fools," he said. "It is a common necklace. You would have us kill half the jewelers in Cairo and bring the guardsmen down upon us." He slapped their heads and led them off.

Raniya returned her attention to the jeweler, who had withdrawn his offer to buy Hassan's necklace. The older Raniya said, "Very well. I will try to return it to the man who sold it to me." As the older woman left, Raniya could tell that she smiled beneath her veil.

Raniya turned to Hassan. "It appears that neither of us will sell a necklace today."

"Another day, perhaps," said Hassan.

"I shall take mine back to my house for safekeeping," said Raniya. "Would you walk with me?"

Hassan agreed and walked with Raniya to the house she had rented. Then she invited him in and offered him wine, and after they had both drunk some, she led him to her bedroom. She covered the windows with heavy curtains and extinguished all lamps so that the room was as dark as night. Only then did she remove her veil and take him to bed.

Raniya had been flush with anticipation for this moment, and so was surprised to find that Hassan's movements were clumsy and awkward. She remembered their wedding night very clearly; he had been confident, and his touch had taken her breath away. She knew Hassan's first meeting with the young Raniya was not far away, and for a moment did not understand how this fumbling boy could change so quickly. And then of course the answer was clear.

So every afternoon for many days, Raniya met Hassan at her rented house and instructed him in the art of love, and in doing so she demonstrated that, as is often said, women are Allah's most wondrous creation. She told him, "The pleasure you give is returned in the pleasure you receive," and inwardly she smiled as she thought of how true her words really were. Before long, he gained the expertise she remembered, and she took greater enjoyment in it than she had as a young woman.

All too soon, the day arrived when Raniya told the young Hassan that it was time for her to leave. He knew better than to press her for her reasons, but asked her if they might ever see each other again. She told him, gently, no. Then she sold the furnishings to the house's owner and returned through the Gate of Years to the Cairo of her own day.

When the older Hassan returned from his trip to Damascus, Raniya was home waiting for him. She greeted him warmly, but kept her secrets to herself.

. . .

I was lost in my own thoughts when Bashaarat finished this story, until he said, "I see that this story has intrigued you in a way the others did not."

"You see clearly," I admitted. "I realize now that, even though the past is unchangeable, one may encounter the unexpected when visiting it."

"Indeed. Do you now understand why I say the future and the past are the same? We cannot change either, but we can know both more fully."

"I do understand; you have opened my eyes, and now I wish to use the Gate of Years. What price do you ask?"

He waved his hand. "I do not sell passage through the Gate," he said. "Allah guides whom he wishes to my shop, and I am content to be an instrument of his will."

Had it been another man, I would have taken his words to be a negotiating ploy, but after all that Bashaarat had told me, I knew that he was sincere. "Your generosity is as boundless as your learning," I said, and bowed. "If there is ever a service that a merchant of fabrics might provide for you, please call upon me."

"Thank you. Let us talk now about your trip. There are some matters we must speak of before you visit the Baghdad of twenty years hence."

"I do not wish to visit the future," I told him. "I would step through in the other direction, to revisit my youth."

"Ah, my deepest apologies. This Gate will not take you there. You see, I built this Gate only a week ago. Twenty years ago, there was no doorway here for you to step out of."

My dismay was so great that I must have sounded like a forlorn child. I said, "But where does the other side of the Gate lead?" and walked around the circular doorway to face its opposite side.

Bashaarat circled the doorway to stand beside me. The view through the Gate appeared identical to the view outside it, but when he extended his hand to reach through, it stopped as if it met an invisible wall. I looked more closely and noticed a brass lamp set on a table. Its flame did not flicker but was as fixed and unmoving as if the room were trapped in clearest amber.

"What you see here is the room as it appeared last week," said Bashaarat. "In some twenty years' time, this left side of the Gate will permit entry, allowing people to enter from this direction and visit their past. Or," he said, leading me back to the side of the doorway he had first shown me, "we can enter from the right side now and visit them ourselves. But I'm afraid this Gate will never allow visits to the days of your youth."

"What about the Gate of Years you had in Cairo?" I asked.

He nodded. "That Gate still stands. My son now runs my shop there."

"So I could travel to Cairo, and use the Gate to visit the Cairo of twenty years ago. From there I could travel back to Baghdad."

"Yes, you could make that journey, if you so desire."

"I do," I said. "Will you tell me how to find your shop in Cairo?"

"We must speak of some things first," said Bashaarat. "I will not ask your intentions, being content to wait until you are ready to tell me. But I would remind you that what is made cannot be unmade."

"I know," I said.

"And that you cannot avoid the ordeals that are assigned to you. What Allah gives you, you must accept."

"I remind myself of that every day of my life."

"Then it is my honor to assist you in whatever way I can," he said.

He brought out some paper and a pen and inkpot and began writing. "I shall write for you a letter to aid you on your journey." He folded the letter, dribbled some candle wax over the edge, and pressed his ring against it. "When you reach Cairo, give this to my son, and he will let you enter the Gate of Years there."

A merchant such as myself must be well versed in expressions of gratitude, but I had never before been as effusive in giving thanks as I was to Bashaarat, and every word was heartfelt. He gave me directions to his shop in Cairo, and I assured him I would tell him all upon my return. As I was about to leave his shop, a thought occurred to me. "Because the Gate of Years you have here opens to the future, you are assured that the Gate and this shop will remain standing for twenty years or more."

"Yes, that is true," said Bashaarat.

I began to ask him if he had met his older self, but then I bit back my words. If the answer was no, it was surely because his older self was dead, and I would be asking him if he knew the date of his death. Who was I to make such an inquiry, when this man was granting me a boon without asking my intentions? I saw from his expression that he knew what I had meant to ask, and I bowed my head in humble apology. He indicated his acceptance with a nod, and I returned home to make arrangements.

The caravan took two months to reach Cairo. As for what occupied my mind during the journey, Your Majesty, I now tell you what I had not told Bashaarat. I was married once, twenty years before, to a woman named Najya. Her figure swayed as gracefully as a willow bough, and her face was as lovely as the moon, but it was her kind and tender nature that captured my heart. I had just begun my career as a merchant when we married, and we were not wealthy, but did not feel the lack.

We had been married only a year when I was to travel to Basra to meet with a ship's captain. I had an opportunity to profit by trading in slaves, but Najya did not approve. I reminded her that the Koran does not forbid the owning of slaves as long as one treats them well, and that even the Prophet owned some. But she said there was no way I could know how my buyers would treat their slaves, and that it was better to sell goods than men.

On the morning of my departure, Najya and I argued. I spoke harshly to her, using words that it shames me to recall, and I beg Your Majesty's forgiveness if I do not repeat them here. I left in anger, and never saw her again. She was badly injured when the wall of a mosque collapsed, some days after I left. She was taken to the *bimaristan*, but the physicians could not save her, and she died soon after. I did not learn of her death until I returned a week later, and I felt as if I had killed her with my own hand.

Can the torments of hell be worse than what I endured in the days that followed? It seemed likely that I would find out, so near to death did my anguish take me. And surely the experience must be similar, for like infernal fire, grief burns but does not consume; instead, it makes the heart vulnerable to further suffering.

Eventually my period of lamentation ended, and I was left a hollow man, a bag of skin with no innards. I freed the slaves I had bought and became a fabric merchant. Over the years I became wealthy, but I never remarried. Some of the men I did business with tried to match me with a sister or a daughter, telling me that the love of a woman can make you forget your pains. Perhaps they are right, but it cannot make you forget the pain you caused another. Whenever I imagined myself marrying another woman, I remembered the look of hurt in Najya's eyes when I last saw her, and my heart was closed to others.

I spoke to a mullah about what I had done, and it was he who told me that repentance and atonement erase the past. I repented and atoned as best I knew how; for twenty years I lived as an upright man, I offered prayers and fasted and gave alms to those less fortunate and made a pilgrimage to Mecca, and yet I was still haunted by guilt. Allah is all-merciful, so I knew the failing to be mine.

Had Bashaarat asked me, I could not have said what I hoped to achieve. It was clear from his stories that I could not change what I knew to have happened. No one had stopped my younger self from arguing with Najya in our final conversation. But the tale of Raniya, which lay hidden within the tale of Hassan's life without his knowing it, gave me a slim hope: perhaps I might be able to play some part in events while my younger self was away on business.

Could it not be that there had been a mistake, and my Najya had survived? Perhaps it was another woman whose body had been wrapped in a shroud and buried while I was gone. Perhaps I could rescue Najya and bring her back with me to the Baghdad of my own day. I knew it was foolhardy; men of experience say, "Four things do not come back: the spoken word, the sped arrow, the past life, and the neglected opportunity," and I understood the truth of those words better than most. And yet I dared to

hope that Allah had judged my twenty years of repentance sufficient and was now granting me a chance to regain what I had
lost.

The caravan journey was uneventful, and after sixty sunrises
and three hundred prayers, I reached Cairo. There I had to navi-
gate the city's streets, which are a bewildering maze compared
with the harmonious design of the City of Peace. I made my way
to the Bayn al-Qasrayn, the main street that runs through the
Fatimid quarter of Cairo. From there I found the street on which
Bashaarat's shop was located.

I told the shopkeeper that I had spoken to his father in Baghdad, and gave him the letter Bashaarat had given me. After reading it, he led me into a back room, in whose center stood another
Gate of Years, and he gestured for me to enter from its left side.

As I stood before the massive circle of metal, I felt a chill and
chided myself for my nervousness. With a deep breath I stepped
through and found myself in the same room with different furnishings. If not for those, I would not have known the Gate to be
different from an ordinary doorway. Then I recognized that the
chill I had felt was simply the coolness of the air in this room,
for the day here was not as hot as the day I had left. I could feel
its warm breeze at my back, coming through the Gate like a sigh.

The shopkeeper followed behind me and called out, "Father,
you have a visitor."

A man entered the room, and who should it be but Bashaarat,
twenty years younger than when I'd seen him in Baghdad. "Welcome, my lord," he said. "I am Bashaarat."

"You do not know me?" I asked.

"No, you must have met my older self. For me, this is our first
meeting, but it is my honor to assist you."

Your Majesty, as befits this chronicle of my shortcomings, I must confess that, so immersed was I in my own woes during the journey from Baghdad, I had not previously realized that Bashaarat had likely recognized me the moment I stepped into his shop. Even as I was admiring his water clock and brass songbird, he had known that I would travel to Cairo, and likely knew whether I had achieved my goal or not.

The Bashaarat I spoke to now knew none of those things. "I am doubly grateful for your kindness, sir," I said. "My name is Fuwaad ibn Abbas, newly arrived from Baghdad."

Bashaarat's son took his leave, and Bashaarat and I conferred; I asked him the day and month, confirming that there was ample time for me to travel back to the City of Peace, and promised him I would tell him everything when I returned. His younger self was as gracious as his older. "I look forward to speaking with you on your return, and to assisting you again twenty years from now," he said.

His words gave me pause. "Had you planned to open a shop in Baghdad before today?"

"Why do you ask?"

"I had been marveling at the coincidence that we met in Baghdad just in time for me to make my journey here, use the Gate, and travel back. But now I wonder if it is perhaps not a coincidence at all. Is my arrival here today the reason that you will move to Baghdad twenty years from now?"

Bashaarat smiled. "Coincidence and intention are two sides of a tapestry, my lord. You may find one more agreeable to look at, but you cannot say one is true and the other is false."

"Now as ever, you have given me much to think about," I said.

I thanked him and bid farewell. As I was leaving his shop, I passed a woman entering with some haste. I heard Bashaarat greet her as Raniya, and stopped in surprise.

From just outside the door, I could hear the woman say, "I have the necklace. I hope my older self has not lost it."

"I am sure you will have kept it safe, in anticipation of your visit," said Bashaarat.

I realized that this was Raniya from the story Bashaarat had told me. She was on her way to collect her older self so that they might return to the days of their youth, confound some thieves with a doubled necklace, and save their husband. For a moment I was unsure if I were dreaming or awake, because I felt as if I had stepped into a tale, and the thought that I might talk to its players and partake of its events was dizzying. I was tempted to speak and see if I might play a hidden role in that tale, but then I remembered that my goal was to play a hidden role in my own tale. So I left without a word and went to arrange passage with a caravan.

It is said, Your Majesty, that Fate laughs at men's schemes. At first it appeared as if I were the most fortunate of men, for a caravan headed for Baghdad was departing within the month, and I was able to join it. In the weeks that followed, I began to curse my luck, because the caravan's journey was plagued by delays. The wells at a town not far from Cairo were dry, and an expedition had to be sent back for water. At another village, the soldiers protecting the caravan contracted dysentery, and we had to wait for weeks for their recovery. With each delay, I revised my estimate of when we'd reach Baghdad and grew increasingly anxious.

Then there were the sandstorms, which seemed like a warning from Allah, and truly caused me to doubt the wisdom of my actions. We had the good fortune to be resting at a caravanserai west of Kufa when the sandstorms first struck, but our stay was prolonged from days to weeks as, time and again, the skies became clear, only to darken again as soon as the camels were reloaded. The day of Najya's accident was fast approaching, and I grew desperate.

I solicited each of the camel drivers in turn, trying to hire one to take me ahead alone, but could not persuade any of them. Eventually I found one willing to sell me a camel at what would have been an exorbitant price under ordinary circumstances, but which I was all too willing to pay. I then struck out on my own.

It will come as no surprise that I made little progress in the storm, but when the winds subsided, I immediately adopted a rapid pace. Without the soldiers that accompanied the caravan, however, I was an easy target for bandits, and sure enough, I was stopped after two days' ride. They took my money and the camel I had purchased, but spared my life, whether out of pity or because they could not be bothered to kill me I do not know. I began walking back to rejoin the caravan, but now the skies tormented me with their cloudlessness, and I suffered from the heat. By the time the caravan found me, my tongue was swollen and my lips were as cracked as mud baked by the sun. After that I had no choice but to accompany the caravan at its usual pace.

Like petals dropping one by one from a fading rose, my hopes dwindled with each passing day. By the time the caravan reached the City of Peace, I knew it was too late, but the moment we rode through the city gates, I asked the guardsmen if they had heard of a mosque collapsing. The first guardsman I spoke to had not, and for a heartbeat I dared to hope that I had misremembered the date of the accident, and that I had in fact arrived in time.

Then another guardsman told me that a mosque had indeed collapsed just yesterday in the Karkh quarter. His words struck me with the force of the executioner's ax. I had traveled so far, only to receive the worst news of my life a second time.

I walked to the mosque and saw the piles of bricks where there had once been a wall. It was a scene that had haunted my dreams for twenty years, but now the image remained even after I opened my eyes, and with a clarity sharper than I could endure. I turned away and walked without aim, blind to what was around me, until I found myself before my old house, the one where Najya and I had lived. I stood in the street in front of it, filled with memory and anguish.

I do not know how much time had passed when I became aware that a young woman had walked up to me. "My lord," she said, "I'm looking for the house of Fuwaad ibn Abbas."

"You have found it," I said.

"Are you Fuwaad ibn Abbas, my lord?"

"I am, and I ask you, please leave me be."

"My lord, I beg your forgiveness. My name is Maimuna, and I assist the physicians at the *bimaristan*. I tended to your wife before she died."

I turned to look at her. "You tended to Najya?"

"I did, my lord. I am sworn to deliver a message to you from her."

"What message?"

"She wished me to tell you that her last thoughts were of you. She wished me to tell you that while her life was short, it was made happy by the time she spent with you."

She saw the tears streaming down my cheeks and said, "Forgive me if my words cause you pain, my lord."

"There is nothing to forgive, child. Would that I had the means to pay you as much as this message is worth to me, because a lifetime of thanks would still leave me in your debt."

"Grief owes no debt," she said. "Peace be upon you, my lord."

"Peace be upon you," I said.

She left, and I wandered the streets for hours, crying tears of release. All the while I thought on the truth of Bashaarat's words: past and future are the same, and we cannot change either, only know them more fully. My journey to the past had changed nothing, but what I had learned had changed everything, and I understood that it could not have been otherwise. If our lives are tales that Allah tells, then we are the audience as well as the players, and it is by living these tales that we receive their lessons.

Night fell, and it was then that the city's guardsmen found me, wandering the streets after curfew in my dusty clothes, and asked who I was. I told them my name and where I lived, and the guardsmen brought me to my neighbors to see if they knew me, but they did not recognize me, and I was taken to jail.

I told the guard captain my story, and he found it entertaining but did not credit it, for who would? Then I remembered some news from my time of grief twenty years before, and told him that Your Majesty's grandson would be born an albino. Some days later, word of the infant's condition reached the captain, and he brought me to the governor of the quarter. When the governor heard my story, he brought me here to the palace, and when your lord chamberlain heard my story, he in turn brought me here to the throne room, so that I might have the infinite privilege of recounting it to Your Majesty.

Now my tale has caught up to my life, coiled as they both are, and the direction they take next is for Your Majesty to decide. I know many things that will happen here in Baghdad over the next twenty years, but nothing about what awaits me now. I have no money for the journey back to Cairo and the Gate of Years there, yet I count myself fortunate beyond measure, for I was given the opportunity to revisit my past mistakes, and I have learned what remedies Allah allows. I would be honored to relate everything I know of the future, if Your Majesty sees fit to ask, but for myself, the most precious knowledge I possess is this:

Nothing erases the past. There is repentance, there is atonement, and there is forgiveness. That is all, but that is enough.

EXHALATION

IT HAS LONG BEEN SAID THAT AIR (WHICH OTHERS CALL argon) is the source of life. This is not in fact the case, and I engrave these words to describe how I came to understand the true source of life and, as a corollary, the means by which life will one day end.

For most of history, the proposition that we draw life from air was so obvious that there was no need to assert it. Every day we consume two lungs heavy with air; every day we remove the empty ones from our chest and replace them with full ones. If a person is careless and lets his air level run too low, he feels the heaviness of his limbs and the growing need for replenishment. It is exceedingly rare that a person is unable to get at least one replacement lung before his installed pair runs empty; on those unfortunate occasions where this has happened—when a person is trapped and unable to move, with no one nearby to assist him—he dies within seconds of his air running out.

But in the normal course of life, our need for air is far from our thoughts, and indeed many would say that satisfying that need is the least important part of going to the filling stations.

For the filling stations are the primary venue for social conversation, the places from which we draw emotional sustenance as well as physical. We all keep spare sets of full lungs in our homes, but when one is alone, the act of opening one's chest and replacing one's lungs can seem little better than a chore. In the company of others, however, it becomes a communal activity, a shared pleasure.

If one is exceedingly busy, or feeling unsociable, one might simply pick up a pair of full lungs, install them, and leave one's emptied lungs on the other side of the room. If one has a few minutes to spare, it's simple courtesy to connect the empty lungs to an air dispenser and refill them for the next person. But by far the most common practice is to linger and enjoy the company of others, to discuss the news of the day with friends or acquaintances and, in passing, offer newly filled lungs to one's interlocutor. While this perhaps does not constitute air sharing in the strictest sense, there is camaraderie derived from the awareness that all our air comes from the same source, for the dispensers are but the exposed terminals of pipes extending from the reservoir of air deep underground, the great lung of the world, the source of all our nourishment.

Many lungs are returned to the same filling station the next day, but just as many circulate to other stations when people visit neighboring districts; the lungs are all identical in appearance, smooth cylinders of aluminum, so one cannot tell whether a given lung has always stayed close to home or whether it has traveled long distances. And just as lungs are passed between persons and districts, so are news and gossip. In this way one can receive news from remote districts, even those at the very edge of the world, without needing to leave home, although I myself enjoy traveling. I have journeyed all the way to the edge of the world, and seen the solid chromium wall that extends from the ground up into the infinite sky.

It was at one of the filling stations that I first heard the rumors that prompted my investigation and led to my eventual enlightenment. It began innocently enough, with a remark from our district's public crier. At noon of the first day of every year, it is traditional for the crier to recite a passage of verse, an ode composed long ago for this annual celebration, which takes exactly one hour to deliver. The crier mentioned that on his most recent performance, the turret clock struck the hour before he had finished, something that had never happened before. Another person remarked that this was a coincidence, because he had just returned from a nearby district where the public crier had complained of the same incongruity.

No one gave the matter much thought beyond the simple acknowledgment that seemed warranted. It was only some days later, when there arrived word of a similar deviation between the crier and the clock of a third district, that the suggestion was made that these discrepancies might be evidence of a defect in the mechanism common to all the turret clocks, albeit a curious one to cause the clocks to run faster rather than slower. Horologists investigated the turret clocks in question, but on inspection they could discern no imperfection. In fact, when compared against the timepieces normally employed for such calibration purposes, the turret clocks were all found to have resumed keeping perfect time.

I myself found the question somewhat intriguing, but I was too focused on my own studies to devote much thought to other matters. I was and am a student of anatomy, and to provide context for my subsequent actions, I now offer a brief account of my relationship with the field.

Death is uncommon, fortunately, because we are durable, and fatal mishaps are rare, but it makes difficult the study of anatomy, especially since many of the accidents serious enough to cause death leave the deceased's remains too damaged for study. If lungs are ruptured when full, the explosive force can tear a body asunder, ripping the titanium as easily as if it were tin. In the past, anatomists focused their attention on the limbs, which were the most likely to survive intact. During the very first anatomy lecture I attended a century ago, the lecturer showed us a severed arm, the casing removed to reveal the dense column of rods and pistons within. I can vividly recall the way, after he had connected its arterial hoses to a wall-mounted lung he kept in the laboratory, he was able to manipulate the actuating rods that protruded from the arm's ragged base, and in response the hand would open and close fitfully.

In the intervening years, our field has advanced to the point where anatomists are able to repair damaged limbs and, on occasion, attach a severed limb. At the same time we have become capable of studying the physiology of the living; I have given a version of that first lecture I saw, during which I opened the casing of my own arm and directed my students' attention to the rods that contracted and extended when I wiggled my fingers.

Despite these advances, the field of anatomy still had a great unsolved mystery at its core: the question of memory. While we knew a little about the structure of the brain, its physiology is notoriously hard to study because of the brain's extreme delicacy. It is typically the case in fatal accidents that, when the skull is breached, the brain erupts in a cloud of gold, leaving little besides shredded filament and leaf from which nothing useful can be discerned. For decades the prevailing theory of memory was that all of a person's experiences were engraved

on sheets of gold foil; it was these sheets, torn apart by the force
of the blast, that were the source of the tiny flakes found after
accidents. Anatomists would collect the bits of gold leaf—so thin
that light passes greenly through them—and spend years trying
to reconstruct the original sheets, with the hope of eventually
deciphering the symbols in which the deceased's recent experiences were inscribed.

I did not subscribe to this theory, known as the inscription
hypothesis, for the simple reason that if all our experiences are in
fact recorded, why is it that our memories are incomplete? Advo-
cates of the inscription hypothesis offered an explanation for
forgetfulness—suggesting that over time the foil sheets become
misaligned from the stylus which reads the memories, until the
oldest sheets shift out of contact with it altogether—but I never
found it convincing. The appeal of the theory was easy for me to
appreciate, though; I too had devoted many an hour to examining flakes of gold through a microscope and can imagine how
gratifying it would be to turn the fine-adjustment knob and see
legible symbols come into focus.

More than that, how wonderful would it be to decipher the
very oldest of a deceased person's memories, ones that he himself had forgotten? None of us can remember much more than a
hundred years in the past, and written records—accounts that we
ourselves inscribed but have scant memory of doing so—extend
only a few hundred years before that. How many years did we
live before the beginning of written history? Where did we come
from? It is the promise of finding the answers within our own
brains that makes the inscription hypothesis so seductive.

I was a proponent of the competing school of thought, which
held that our memories were stored in some medium in which
the process of erasure was no more difficult than recording:

perhaps in the rotation of gears, or the positions of a series of switches. This theory implied that everything we had forgotten was indeed lost, and our brains contained no histories older than those found in our libraries. One advantage of this theory was that it better explained why, when lungs are installed in those who have died from lack of air, the revived have no memories and are all but mindless: somehow the shock of death had reset all the gears or switches. The inscriptionists claimed the shock had merely misaligned the foil sheets, but no one was willing to kill a living person, even an imbecile, in order to resolve the debate. I had envisioned an experiment which might allow me to determine the truth conclusively, but it was a risky one, and deserved careful consideration before it was undertaken. I remained undecided for the longest time, until I heard more news about the clock anomaly.

Word arrived from a more distant district that its public crier had likewise observed the turret clock striking the hour before he had finished his new year's recital. What made this notable was that his district's clock employed a different mechanism, one in which the hours were marked by the flow of mercury into a bowl. Here the discrepancy could not be explained by a common mechanical fault. Most people suspected fraud, a practical joke perpetrated by mischief-makers. I had a different suspicion, a darker one that I dared not voice, but it decided my course of action; I would proceed with my experiment.

The first tool I constructed was the simplest: in my laboratory I fixed four prisms on mounting brackets and carefully aligned them so that their apexes formed the corners of a rectangle. When they were arranged thus, a beam of light directed at one of the lower prisms was reflected up, then backward, then down, and then forward again in a quadrilateral loop. Accordingly, when I sat with my eyes at the level of the first prism, I obtained a clear view of the back of my own head. This solipsistic periscope formed the basis of all that was to come.

A similarly rectangular arrangement of actuating rods allowed a displacement of action to accompany the displacement of vision afforded by the prisms. The bank of actuating rods was much larger than the periscope but still relatively straightforward in design; by contrast, what was attached to the end of these respective mechanisms was far more intricate. To the periscope I added a binocular microscope mounted on an armature capable of swiveling side to side or up and down. To the actuating rods I added an array of precision manipulators, although that description hardly does justice to those pinnacles of the mechanician's art. Combining the ingenuity of anatomists and the inspiration provided by the bodily structures they studied, the manipulators enabled their operator to accomplish any task he might normally perform with his own hands, but on a much smaller scale.

Assembling all of this equipment took months, but I could not afford to be anything less than meticulous. Once the preparations were complete, I was able to place each of my hands on a nest of knobs and levers and control a pair of manipulators situated behind my head and use the periscope to see what they worked on. I would then be able to dissect my own brain.

The very idea must sound like pure madness, I know, and had I told any of my colleagues, they would surely have tried to stop me. But I could not ask anyone else to risk themselves for the sake of anatomical inquiry, and because I wished to conduct the dissection myself, I would not be satisfied by merely being the passive subject of such an operation. Auto-dissection was the only option.

I brought in a dozen full lungs and connected them with a

manifold. I mounted this assembly beneath the worktable that I would sit at and positioned a dispenser to connect directly to the bronchial inlets within my chest. This would supply me with six days' worth of air. To provide for the possibility that I might not have completed my experiment within that period, I had scheduled a visit from a colleague at the end of that time. My presumption, however, was that the only way I would not have finished the operation in that period would be if I had caused my own death.

I began by removing the deeply curved plate that formed the back and top of my head; then the two, more shallowly curved plates that formed the sides. Only my faceplate remained, but it was locked into a restraining bracket, and I could not see its inner surface from the vantage point of my periscope; what I saw exposed was my own brain. It consisted of a dozen or more sub-assemblies, whose exteriors were covered by intricately molded shells; by positioning the periscope near the fissures that separated them, I gained a tantalizing glimpse at the fabulous mechanisms within their interiors. Even with what little I could see, I could tell it was the most beautifully complex engine I had ever beheld, so far beyond any device man had constructed that it was incontrovertibly of divine origin. The sight was both exhilarating and dizzying, and I savored it on a strictly aesthetic basis for several minutes before proceeding with my explorations.

It was generally hypothesized that the brain was divided into an engine located in the center of the head which performed the actual cognition, surrounded by an array of components in which memories were stored. What I observed was consistent with this theory, since the peripheral subassemblies seemed to resemble one another, while the subassembly in the center appeared to be different, more heterogeneous and with more moving parts.

However, the components were packed too closely for me to see much of their operation; if I intended to learn anything more, I would require a more intimate vantage point.

Each subassembly had a local reservoir of air, fed by a hose extending from the regulator at the base of my brain. I focused my periscope on the rearmost subassembly and, using the remote manipulators, I quickly disconnected the outlet hose and installed a longer one in its place. I had practiced this maneuver countless times so that I could perform it in a matter of moments; even so, I was not certain I could complete the connection before the subassembly had depleted its local reservoir. Only after I was satisfied that the component's operation had not been interrupted did I continue; I rearranged the longer hose to gain a better view of what lay in the fissure behind it: other hoses that connected it to its neighboring components. Using the most slender pair of manipulators to reach into the narrow crevice, I replaced the hoses one by one with longer substitutes. Eventually, I worked my way around the entire subassembly and replaced every connection it had to the rest of my brain. I was now able to unmount this subassembly from the frame that supported it and pull the whole section outside of what was once the back of my head.

I knew it was possible I had impaired my capacity to think and was unable to recognize it, but performing some basic arithmetic tests suggested that I was uninjured. With one subassembly hanging from a scaffold above, I now had a better view of the cognition engine at the center of my brain, but there was not enough room to bring the microscope attachment itself in for a close inspection. In order for me to really examine the workings of my brain, I would have to displace at least half a dozen subassemblies.

Laboriously, painstakingly, I repeated the procedure of substituting hoses for other subassemblies, repositioning another one farther back, two more higher up, and two others out to the sides, suspending all six from the scaffold above my head. When I was done, my brain looked like an explosion frozen an infinitesimal fraction of a second after the detonation, and again I felt dizzy when I thought about it. But at last the cognition engine itself was exposed, supported on a pillar of hoses and actuating rods leading down into my torso. I now also had room to rotate my microscope around a full three hundred and sixty degrees and pass my gaze across the inner faces of the subassemblies I had moved. What I saw was a microcosm of auric machinery, a landscape of tiny spinning rotors and miniature reciprocating cylinders.

As I contemplated this vista, I wondered where my body was. The conduits which displaced my vision and action around the room were in principle no different from those which connected my original eyes and hands to my brain. For the duration of this experiment, were these manipulators not essentially my hands? Were the magnifying lenses at the end of my periscope not essentially my eyes? I was an everted person, with my tiny, fragmented body situated at the center of my own distended brain. It was in this unlikely configuration that I began to explore myself.

I turned my microscope to one of the memory subassemblies and began examining its design. I had no expectation that I would be able to decipher my memories, only that I might divine the means by which they were recorded. As I had predicted, there were no reams of foil pages visible, but to my surprise neither did I see banks of gearwheels or switches. Instead, the subassembly seemed to consist almost exclusively of a bank of air tubules. Through the interstices between the tubules, I was able to glimpse ripples passing through the bank's interior.

With careful inspection and increasing magnification, I discerned that the tubules ramified into tiny air capillaries, which were interwoven with a dense latticework of wires on which gold leaves were hinged. Under the influence of air escaping from the capillaries, the leaves were held in a variety of positions. These were not switches in the conventional sense, for they did not retain their position without a current of air to support them, but I hypothesized that these were the switches I had sought, the medium in which my memories were recorded. The ripples I saw must have been acts of recall, as an arrangement of leaves was read and sent back to the cognition engine.

Armed with this new understanding, I then turned my microscope to the cognition engine. Here too I observed a latticework of wires, but they did not bear leaves suspended in position; instead the leaves flipped back and forth almost too rapidly to see. Indeed, almost the entire engine appeared to be in motion, consisting more of lattice than of air capillaries, and I wondered how air could reach all the gold leaves in a coherent manner. For many hours I scrutinized the leaves, until I realized that they themselves were playing the role of capillaries; the leaves formed temporary conduits and valves that existed just long enough to redirect air at other leaves in turn, and then disappeared as a result. This was an engine undergoing continuous transformation, indeed modifying itself as part of its operation. The lattice was not so much a machine as it was a page on which the machine was written, and on which the machine itself ceaselessly wrote.

My consciousness could be said to be encoded in the position of these tiny leaves, but it would be more accurate to say that it was encoded in the ever-shifting pattern of air driving these leaves. Watching the oscillations of these flakes of gold, I saw that air does not, as we had always assumed, simply provide power to the engine that realizes our thoughts. Air is in fact the very medium of our thoughts. All that we are is a pattern of air flow. My memories were inscribed, not as grooves on foil or even the position of switches, but as persistent currents of argon.

In the moments after I grasped the nature of this lattice mechanism, a cascade of insights penetrated my consciousness in rapid succession. The first and most trivial was understanding why gold, the most malleable and ductile of metals, was the only material out of which our brains could be made. Only the thinnest of foil leaves could move rapidly enough for such a mechanism, and only the most delicate of filaments could act as hinges for them. By comparison, the copper burr raised by my stylus as I engrave these words and brushed from the sheet when I finish each page is as coarse and heavy as scrap. This truly was a medium where erasing and recording could be performed rapidly, far more so than any arrangement of switches or gears.

What next became clear was why installing full lungs into a person who has died from lack of air does not bring him back to life. These leaves within the lattice remain balanced between continuous cushions of air. This arrangement lets them flit back and forth swiftly, but it also means that if the flow of air ever ceases, everything is lost; the leaves all collapse into identical pendent states, erasing the patterns and the consciousness they represent. Restoring the air supply cannot re-create what has evanesced. This was the price of speed; a more stable medium for storing patterns would mean that our consciousnesses would operate far more slowly.

It was then that I perceived the solution to the clock anomaly. I saw that the speed of these leaves' movements depended on their being supported by air; with sufficient air flow, the leaves could move nearly frictionlessly. If they were moving more slowly, it was because they were being subjected to more friction, which could occur only if the cushions of air that supported them were thinner, and the air flowing through the lattice was moving with less force.

It is not that the turret clocks are running faster. What is happening is that our brains are running slower. The turret clocks are driven by pendulums, whose tempo never varies, or by the flow of mercury through a pipe, which does not change. But our brains rely on the passage of air, and when that air flows more slowly, our thoughts slow down, making the clocks seem to us to run faster.

I had feared that our brains might be growing slower, and it was this prospect that had spurred me to pursue my auto-dissection. But I had assumed that our cognition engines—while powered by air—were ultimately mechanical in nature, and some aspect of the mechanism was gradually becoming deformed through fatigue, and thus responsible for the slowing. That would have been dire, but there was at least the hope that we might be able to repair the mechanism and restore our brains to their original speed of operation.

But if our thoughts were purely patterns of air rather than the movement of toothed gears, the problem was much more serious, for what could cause the air flowing through every person's brain to move less rapidly? It could not be a decrease in the pressure from our filling stations' dispensers; the air pressure in our lungs is so high that it must be stepped down by a series of regulators before reaching our brains. The diminution in force, I saw, must arise from the opposite direction: the pressure of our surrounding atmosphere was increasing.

How could this be? As soon as the question formed, the only possible answer became apparent: our sky must not be infinite in height. Somewhere above the limits of our vision, the chromium walls surrounding our world must curve inward to form a dome; our universe is a sealed chamber rather than an open well. And air is gradually accumulating within that chamber, until it equals the pressure in the reservoir below.

This is why, at the beginning of this engraving, I said that air is not the source of life. Air can neither be created nor destroyed; the total amount of air in the universe remains constant, and if air were all that we needed to live, we would never die. But in truth the source of life is *a difference in air pressure,* the flow of air from spaces where it is thick to those where it is thin. The activity of our brains, the motion of our bodies, the action of every machine we have ever built, are driven by the movement of air, the force exerted as differing pressures seek to balance one another out. When the pressure everywhere in the universe is the same, all air will be motionless and useless; one day we will be surrounded by motionless air and unable to derive any benefit from it.

We are not really consuming air at all. The amount of air that I draw from each day's new pair of lungs is exactly as much as seeps out through the joints of my limbs and the seams of my casing, exactly as much as I am adding to the atmosphere around me; all I am doing is converting air at high pressure to air at low. With every movement of my body, I contribute to the equalization of pressure in our universe. With every thought that I have, I hasten the arrival of that fatal equilibrium.

Had I come to this realization under any other circumstance,

I would have leapt up from my chair and run into the streets, but in my current situation—body locked in a restraining bracket, brain suspended across my laboratory—doing so was impossible. I could see the leaves of my brain flitting faster from the tumult of my thoughts, which in turn increased my agitation at being so restrained and immobile. Panic at that moment might have led to my death, a nightmarish paroxysm of simultaneously being trapped and spiraling out of control, struggling against my restraints until my air ran out. It was by chance as much as by intention that my hands adjusted the controls to avert my periscopic gaze from the latticework, so all I could see was the plain surface of my worktable. Thus freed from having to see and magnify my own apprehensions, I was able to calm down. When I had regained sufficient composure, I began the lengthy process of reassembling myself. Eventually I restored my brain to its original compact configuration, reattached the plates of my head, and released myself from the restraining bracket.

At first the other anatomists did not believe me when I told them what I had discovered, but in the months that followed my initial auto-dissection, more and more of them became convinced. More examinations of people's brains were performed, more measurements of atmospheric pressure were taken, and the results were all found to confirm my claims. The background air pressure of our universe was indeed increasing, and slowing our thoughts as a result.

There was widespread panic in the days after the truth first became widely known, as people contemplated for the first time the idea that death was inevitable. Many called for the strict curtailment of activities in order to minimize the thickening of our atmosphere; accusations of wasted air escalated into furious brawls and, in some districts, deaths. It was the shame of having caused these deaths, together with the reminder that it would be many centuries yet before our atmosphere's pressure became equal to that of the reservoir underground, that enabled the panic to subside. We are not sure precisely how many centuries it will take; additional measurements and calculations are being performed and debated. In the meantime, there is much discussion over how we should spend the time that remains to us.

One sect dedicated itself to the goal of reversing the equalization of pressure and found many adherents. The mechanicians among them constructed an engine that took air from our atmosphere and forced it into a smaller volume, a process they called compression. Their engine restored air to the pressure it originally had in the reservoir, and these Reversalists excitedly announced that it would form the basis of a new kind of filling station, one that would—with each lung it refilled—revitalize not only individuals but the universe itself. Alas, closer examination of the engine revealed its fatal flaw. The engine itself was powered by air from the reservoir, and for every lungful of air that it produced, the engine consumed not just a lungful but slightly more. It did not reverse the process of equalization but, like everything else in the world, exacerbated it.

Although some of their adherents left in disillusionment after this setback, the Reversalists as a group were undeterred and began drawing up alternate designs in which the compressor was powered instead by the uncoiling of springs or the descent of weights. These mechanisms fared no better. Every spring that is wound tight represents air released by the person who did the winding; every weight that rests higher than ground level represents air released by the person who did the lifting. There is no source of power in the universe that does not ultimately derive from a difference in air pressure, and there can be no engine whose operation will not, on balance, reduce that difference.

The Reversalists continue their labors, confident that they will one day construct an engine that generates more compression than it uses, a perpetual power source that will restore to the universe its lost vigor. I do not share their optimism; I believe that the process of equalization is inexorable. Eventually, all the air in our universe will be evenly distributed, no denser or more rarefied in one spot than in any other, unable to drive a piston, turn a rotor, or flip a leaf of gold foil. It will be the end of pressure, the end of motive power, the end of thought. The universe will have reached perfect equilibrium.

Some find irony in the fact that a study of our brains revealed to us not the secrets of the past but what ultimately awaits us in the future. However, I maintain that we have indeed learned something important about the past. The universe began as an enormous breath being held. Who knows why, but whatever the reason, I am glad that it did, because I owe my existence to that fact. All my desires and ruminations are no more and no less than eddy currents generated by the gradual exhalation of our universe. And until this great exhalation is finished, my thoughts live on.

So that our thoughts may continue as long as possible, anatomists and mechanicians are designing replacements for our cerebral regulators, capable of gradually increasing the air pressure within our brains and keeping it just higher than the surrounding atmospheric pressure. Once these are installed, our thoughts will continue at roughly the same speed even as the air thickens around us. But this does not mean that life will continue unchanged. Eventually the pressure differential will fall to such a level that our limbs will weaken and our movements will grow sluggish. We may then try to slow our thoughts so that our physical torpor is less conspicuous to us, but that will also cause external processes to appear to accelerate. The ticking of clocks will rise to a chatter as their pendulums wave frantically; falling objects will slam to the ground as if propelled by springs; undulations will race down cables like the crack of a whip.

At some point our limbs will cease moving altogether. I cannot be certain of the precise sequence of events near the end, but I imagine a scenario in which our thoughts will continue to operate, so that we remain conscious but frozen, immobile as statues. Perhaps we'll be able to speak for a while longer, because our voice boxes operate on a smaller pressure differential than our limbs, but without the ability to visit a filling station, our every utterance will reduce the amount of air left for thought and bring us closer to the moment when our thoughts cease altogether. Will it be preferable to remain mute to prolong our ability to think, or to talk until the very end? I don't know.

Perhaps a few of us, in the days before we cease moving, will be able to connect our cerebral regulators directly to the dispensers in the filling stations, in effect replacing our lungs with the mighty lung of the world. If so, those few will be able to remain conscious right up to the final moments before all pressure is equalized. The last bit of air pressure left in our universe will be expended driving a person's conscious thought.

And then, our universe will be in a state of absolute equilibrium. All life and thought will cease and, with them, time itself.

But I maintain a slender hope.

Even though our universe is enclosed, perhaps it is not the only air chamber in the infinite expanse of solid chromium. I speculate that there could be another pocket of air elsewhere, another universe besides our own that is even larger in volume. It is possible that this hypothetical universe has the same air pressure as ours or even higher, but suppose that it had a much lower air pressure than ours, perhaps even a true vacuum?

The chromium that separates us from this supposed universe is too thick and too hard for us to drill through, so there is no way we could reach it ourselves, no way to bleed off the excess atmosphere from our universe and regain motive power that way. But I fantasize that this neighboring universe has its own inhabitants, ones with capabilities beyond our own. What if they were able to create a conduit between the two universes and install valves to release air from ours? They might use our universe as a reservoir, running dispensers with which they could fill their own lungs, and use our air as a way to drive their own civilization.

It cheers me to imagine that the air that once powered me could power others, to believe that the breath that enables me to engrave these words could one day flow through someone else's body. I do not delude myself into thinking that this would be a way for me to live again, because I am not that air, I am the pattern that it assumed, temporarily. The pattern that is me, the patterns that are the entire world in which I live, would be gone.

But I have an even fainter hope: not only that those inhabitants use our universe as a reservoir, but that once they have emptied it of its air, they might one day be able to open a passage and actually enter our universe as explorers. They might wander our streets, see our frozen bodies, look through our possessions, and wonder about the lives we led.

Which is why I have written this account. You, I hope, are one of those explorers. You, I hope, found these sheets of copper and deciphered the words engraved on their surfaces. And whether or not your brain is impelled by the air that once impelled mine, through the act of reading my words, the patterns that form your thoughts become an imitation of the patterns that once formed mine. And in that way I live again, through you.

Your fellow explorers will have found and read the other books that we left behind, and through the collaborative action of your imaginations, my entire civilization lives again. As you walk through our silent districts, imagine them as they were: with the turret clocks striking the hours, the filling stations crowded with gossiping neighbors, criers reciting verse in the public squares, and anatomists giving lectures in the classrooms. Visualize all of these the next time you look at the frozen world around you, and it will become, in your minds, animated and vital again.

I wish you well, explorer, but I wonder: Does the same fate that befell me await you? I can only imagine that it must, that the tendency toward equilibrium is not a trait peculiar to our universe but inherent in all universes. Perhaps that is just a limitation of my thinking, and your people have discovered a source of pressure that is truly eternal. But my speculations are fanciful enough already. I will assume that one day your thoughts too will cease, although I cannot fathom how far in the future that might be. Your lives will end just as ours did, just as everyone's must. No matter how long it takes, eventually equilibrium will be reached.

I hope you are not saddened by that awareness. I hope that your expedition was more than a search for other universes to use as reservoirs. I hope that you were motivated by a desire for knowledge, a yearning to see what can arise from a universe's exhalation. Because even if a universe's life span is calculable, the variety of life that is generated within it is not. The buildings we have erected, the art and music and verse we have composed, the very lives we've led: none of them could have been predicted, because none of them was inevitable. Our universe might have slid into equilibrium emitting nothing more than a quiet hiss. The fact that it spawned such plenitude is a miracle, one that is matched only by your universe giving rise to you.

Though I am long dead as you read this, explorer, I offer to you a valediction. Contemplate the marvel that is existence, and rejoice that you are able to do so. I feel I have the right to tell you this because, as I am inscribing these words, I am doing the same.

WHAT'S EXPECTED OF US

THIS IS A WARNING. PLEASE READ CAREFULLY.

By now you've probably seen a Predictor; millions of them have been sold by the time you're reading this. For those who haven't seen one, it's a small device, like a remote for opening your car door. Its only features are a button and a big green LED. The light flashes if you press the button. Specifically, the light flashes one second before you press the button.

Most people say that when they first try it, it feels like they're playing a strange game, one where the goal is to press the button after seeing the flash, and it's easy to play. But when you try to break the rules, you find that you can't. If you try to press the button without having seen a flash, the flash immediately appears, and no matter how fast you move, you never push the button until a second has elapsed. If you wait for the flash, intending to keep from pressing the button afterward, the flash never appears. No matter what you do, the light always precedes the button press. There's no way to fool a Predictor.

The heart of each Predictor is a circuit with a negative time delay; it sends a signal back in time. The full implications of the technology will become apparent later, when negative delays of greater than a second are achieved, but that's not what this warning is about. The immediate problem is that Predictors demonstrate that there's no such thing as free will.

There have always been arguments showing that free will is an illusion, some based on hard physics, others based on pure logic. Most people agree these arguments are irrefutable, but no one ever really accepts the conclusion. The experience of having free will is too powerful for an argument to overrule. What it takes is a demonstration, and that's what a Predictor provides.

Typically, a person plays with a Predictor compulsively for several days, showing it to friends, trying various schemes to outwit the device. The person may appear to lose interest in it, but no one can forget what it means; over the following weeks, the implications of an immutable future sink in. Some people, realizing that their choices don't matter, refuse to make any choices at all. Like a legion of Bartleby the scriveners, they no longer engage in spontaneous action. Eventually, a third of those who play with a Predictor must be hospitalized because they won't feed themselves. The end state is akinetic mutism, a kind of waking coma. They'll track motion with their eyes, and change position occasionally, but nothing more. The ability to move remains, but the motivation is gone.

Before people started playing with Predictors, akinetic mutism was very rare, a result of damage to the anterior cingulate region of the brain. Now it spreads like a cognitive plague. People used to speculate about a thought that destroys the thinker, some unspeakable Lovecraftian horror, or a Gödel sentence that crashes the human logical system. It turns out that the disabling thought is one that we've all encountered: the idea that free will doesn't exist. It just wasn't harmful until you believed it.

Doctors try arguing with the patients while they still respond to conversation. We had all been living happy, active lives before, they reason, and we hadn't had free will then either. Why should anything change? "No action you took last month was any more freely chosen than one you take today," a doctor might say. "You can still behave that way now." The patients invariably respond, "But now I know." And some of them never say anything again.

Some will argue that the fact the Predictor causes this change in behavior means that we do have free will. An automaton can't become discouraged, only a freethinking entity can. The fact that some individuals descend into akinetic mutism while others don't just highlights the importance of making a choice.

Unfortunately, such reasoning is faulty; every form of behavior is compatible with determinism. One dynamic system may fall into a basin of attraction and wind up at a fixed point, while another exhibits chaotic behavior indefinitely, but both are completely deterministic.

I'm transmitting this warning to you from just over a year in your future; it's the first lengthy message received when circuits with negative delays in the megasecond range are used to build communication devices. Other messages will follow, addressing other issues. My message to you is this: Pretend that you have free will. It's essential that you behave as if your decisions matter, even though you know they don't. The reality isn't important; what's important is your belief, and believing the lie is the only way to avoid a waking coma. Civilization now depends on self-deception. Perhaps it always has.

And yet I know that, because free will is an illusion, it's all predetermined who will descend into akinetic mutism and who won't. There's nothing anyone can do about it; you can't choose the effect the Predictor has on you. Some of you will succumb and some of you won't, and my sending this warning won't alter those proportions. So why did I do it?

Because I had no choice.

THE LIFECYCLE OF SOFTWARE OBJECTS

1

HER NAME IS ANA ALVARADO, AND SHE'S HAVING A BAD day. She spent all week preparing for a job interview, the first one in months to reach the videoconference stage, but the recruiter's face barely appeared on-screen before he told her that the company has decided to hire someone else. So she sits in front of her computer, wearing her good suit for nothing. She makes a half-hearted attempt to send queries to some other companies and immediately receives automated rejections. After an hour of this, Ana decides she needs some diversion: she opens a Next Dimension window to play her current favorite game, Age of Iridium.

The beachhead is crowded, but her avatar is wearing the coveted mother-of-pearl combat armor, and it's not long before some players ask her if she wants to join their fireteam. They cross the combat zone, hazy with the smoke of burning vehicles, and for an hour they work to clear out a stronghold of mantids; it's the perfect mission for Ana's mood, easy enough that she can be confident of victory but challenging enough that she can derive satisfaction from it. Her teammates are about to accept another mission when a phone window opens up in the corner of Ana's video screen. It's a voice call from her friend Robyn, so Ana switches her microphone over to take the call.

"Hey Robyn."

"Hi, Ana. How's it going?"

"I'll give you a hint: right now I'm playing AoI."

Robyn smiles. "Had a rough morning?"

"You could say that." Ana tells her about the canceled interview.

"Well, I've got some news that might cheer you up. Can you meet me in Data Earth?"

"Sure, just give me a minute to log out."

"I'll be at my place."

"Okay, see you soon."

Ana excuses herself from the fireteam and closes her Next Dimension window. She logs on to Data Earth, and the window zooms in to her last location, a dance club cut into a giant cliff face. Data Earth has its own gaming continents—Elderthorn, Orbis Tertius—but they aren't to Ana's taste, so she spends her time here on the social continents. Her avatar is still wearing a party outfit from her last visit; she changes to more conventional clothes and then opens a portal to Robyn's home address. A step through and she's in Robyn's virtual living room, on a residential aerostat floating above a semicircular waterfall a mile across.

Their avatars hug. "So what's up?" says Ana.

"Blue Gamma is up," says Robyn. "We just got another round of funding, so we're hiring. I showed your résumé around, and everyone's excited to meet you."

"Me? Because of my vast experience?" Ana has only just completed her certificate program in software testing. Robyn taught an introductory class, which is where they met.

"Actually, that's exactly it. It's your last job that's got them interested."

Ana spent six years working at a zoo; its closure was the only reason she went back to school. "I know things get crazy at a start-up, but I'm sure you don't need a zookeeper."

Robyn chuckles. "Let me show you what we're working on. They said I could give you a peek under NDA."

This is a big deal; up until now, Robyn hasn't been able to give any specifics about her work at Blue Gamma. Ana signs the NDA, and Robyn opens a portal. "We've got a private island; come take a look." They walk their avatars through.

Ana's half expecting to see a fantastical landscape when the window refreshes, but instead her avatar shows up in what looks at first glance to be a day-care center. On second glance, it looks like a scene from a children's book: there's a little anthropomorphic tiger cub sliding colored beads along a frame of wires; a panda bear examining a toy car; a cartoon version of a chimpanzee rolling a foam-rubber ball.

The on-screen annotations identify them as digients, digital organisms that live in environments like Data Earth, but they don't look like any that Ana's seen before. These aren't the idealized pets marketed to people who can't commit to a real animal; they lack the picture-perfect cuteness, and their movements are too awkward. Neither do they look like inhabitants of Data Earth's biomes: Ana has visited the Pangaea archipelago, seen the unipedal kangaroos and bidirectional snakes that evolved in its various hothouses, and these digients clearly didn't originate there.

"This is what Blue Gamma makes? Digients?"

"Yes, but not ordinary digients. Check it out." Robyn's avatar walks over to the chimp rolling the ball and crouches down in front of it. "Hi, Pongo. Whatcha doing?"

"Pongo pliy bill," says the digient, startling Ana.

"Playing with the ball? That's great. Can I play too?"

"No. Pongo bill."

"Please?"

The chimp looks around and then, never letting go of the ball, toddles over to a scattering of wooden blocks. It nudges one of them in Robyn's direction. "Robyn pliy blicks." It sits back down. "Pongo pliy bill."

"Okay then." Robyn walks back over to Ana. "What do you think?"

"That's amazing. I didn't know digients had come so far."

"It's all pretty recent; our dev team hired a couple of PhDs after seeing their conference presentation last year. Now we've got a genomic engine that we call Neuroblast, and it supports more cognitive development than anything else currently out there. These fellows here"—she gestures at the day-care-center inhabitants—"are the smartest ones we've generated so far."

"And you're going to sell them as pets?"

"That's the plan. We're going to pitch them as pets you can talk to, teach to do really cool tricks. There's an unofficial slogan we use in-house: 'All the fun of monkeys, with none of the poop throwing.'"

Ana smiles. "I'm starting to see where an animal-training background would be handy."

"Yeah. We aren't always able to get these guys to do what they're told, and we don't know how much of that is in the genes and how much is just because we aren't using the right techniques."

Ana watches as the panda-shaped digient picks up the toy car with one paw and examines the underside; with its other paw it cautiously bats at the wheels. "How much do these digients start out knowing?"

"Practically nothing. Let me show you." Robyn activates a video screen on one wall of the day-care center; it displays footage of a room decorated in primary colors with a handful of digients lying on the floor. Physically they're no different from the ones in the day-care center now, but their movements are random, spasmodic. "These guys are newly instantiated. It takes them a few months subjective to learn the basics: how to interpret visual stimuli, how to move their limbs, how solid objects behave. We run them in a hothouse during that stage, so it all takes about a week. When they're ready to learn language and social interaction, we switch to running them in real time. That's where you would come in."

The panda pushes the toy car back and forth across the floor a few times, and then makes a braying sound, *Mo mo mo.* Ana realizes that the digient is laughing.

Robyn continues, "I know you studied primate communication in school. Here's a chance to put that to use. What do you think? Are you interested?"

Ana hesitates; this is not what she envisioned for herself when she went to college, and for a moment she wonders how it has come to this. As a girl she dreamed of following Fossey and Goodall to Africa; by the time she got out of grad school, there were so few apes left that her best option was to work in a zoo; now she's looking at a job as a trainer of virtual pets. In her career trajectory you can see the diminution of the natural world, writ small.

Snap out of it, she tells herself. It may not be what she had in mind, but this is a job in the software industry, which is what she went back to school for. And training virtual monkeys might actually be more fun than running test suites, so as long as Blue Gamma is offering a decent salary, why not?

.   .   .

His name is Derek Brooks, and he's not happy with his current assignment. Derek designs the avatars for Blue Gamma's digients, and normally he enjoys his job, but yesterday the product managers asked him for something he considers a bad idea. He tried to tell them that, but the decision is not his to make, so now he has to figure out how to do a decent job of it.

Derek studied to be an animator, so in one respect creating digital characters is right up his alley. In other respects, his job is very different from that of a traditional animator. Normally he'd design a character's gait and its gestures, but with digients those traits are emergent properties of the genome; what he has to do is design a body that manifests the digients' gestures in a way that people can relate to. These differences are why a lot of animators—including his wife, Wendy—don't work on digital life-forms, but Derek loves it. He feels that helping a new life-form express itself is the most exciting work an animator could be doing.

He subscribes to Blue Gamma's philosophy of AI design: experience is the best teacher, so rather than try to program an AI with what you want it to know, sell ones capable of learning and have your customers teach them. To get customers to put in that kind of effort, everything about the digients has to be appealing: their personalities need to be charming, which the developers are working on, and their avatars need to be cute, which is where Derek comes in. But he can't simply give the digients enormous eyes and short noses. If they look like cartoons, no one will take them seriously. Conversely, if they look too much like real animals, their facial expressions and ability to speak become disconcerting. It's a delicate balancing act, and he has spent countless hours watching reference footage of baby animals, but he's managed to design hybrid faces that are endearing but not exaggeratedly so.

His current assignment is a bit different. Not satisfied with cats, dogs, monkeys, and pandas, the product managers have decided that there needs to be more variety among the avatars, something other than baby animals. They suggest robots.

The idea makes no sense to Derek. Blue Gamma's entire strategy relies on people's affinity for animals. The digients learn through positive reinforcement, the way animals do, and their rewards include interactions like being scratched on the head or receiving virtual food pellets. These make perfect sense with an animal avatar, but with a robot avatar they look comical and forced. If they were selling physical toys, robots would have the advantage of being cheaper to build than plausible animals, but production costs don't matter in the virtual realm, and animal faces are more expressive. Providing robotic avatars seems like offering imitations at the same time that you're selling the real thing.

His train of thought is interrupted by a knock at his doorway; it's Ana, the new member of the testing team.

"Hey Derek, you should watch the video of this morning's training session. They were pretty funny."

"Thanks, I'll check them out."

She's about to leave, but then stops. "You look like you're having a bad day."

Derek thinks hiring a former zookeeper was a good idea. Not only did she devise a training program for the digients, she had a great suggestion about improving their food.

Other digient vendors provide a limited variety of digient food pellets, but Ana suggested that Blue Gamma radically open up the forms that digient food takes; she pointed out that a varied diet keeps zoo animals happier and makes feeding time more fun for visitors. Management agreed, and the development team edited the digients' basic reward map to recognize a wide range of virtual foods; they couldn't actually simulate different chemical compounds—Data Earth's physics simulation is nowhere near good enough for that—but they added parameters to stand in for a food's taste and texture and designed an interface for the food-dispensing software allowing users to concoct their own recipes. It's turned out to be a big success; the individual digients each have their own favorites, and the beta testers report that they love catering to their digient's preferences.

"Management decided that the animal avatars aren't enough," says Derek. "They want robot avatars, too. Can you believe it?"

"That sounds like a good idea," says Ana.

He's surprised. "You really think so? I'd have thought you'd prefer the animal avatars."

"Everyone here thinks of the digients as animals," she says. "The thing is, the digients don't behave like any real animal. They've got this nonanimal quality to them, so it feels like we're dressing them in circus costumes when we try to make them look like monkeys or pandas."

It hurts a little to hear his carefully crafted avatars compared to circus costumes. His face must give him away, because she adds, "Not that the average person would notice. It's just that I've spent a lot more time with animals than most people."

"That's okay," he says. "I appreciate hearing a different perspective."

"Sorry. The avatars look great, honestly. I like the tiger cub especially."

"It's fine. Really."

She gives an apologetic wave and walks down the hall while Derek thinks about what she said.

Perhaps he's gotten too wrapped up in the animal avatars, so much so that he's begun thinking of the digients as something they're not. Ana's right, of course, that the digients aren't animals any more than they're traditional robots, and who's to say that either analogy is more accurate than the other? If he works from the premise that a robotic avatar is just as good a way for this new life-form to express itself as an animal avatar, then perhaps he'll be able to design an avatar he's happy with.

. . .

A year later, and Blue Gamma is days away from its big product launch. Ana is at work in her cubicle, across the aisle from Robyn's; they sit with their backs to each other, but right now both of their video screens are displaying Data Earth, where their avatars stand side by side. Nearby, a dozen digients scamper around a playground, chasing one another over a tiny bridge or under it, climbing up a short flight of steps, and sliding down a ramp. These digients are the release candidates; in a few days, they—or close approximations thereof—will be available for purchase to customers throughout the overlapping realms of the real world and Data Earth.

Rather than teach the digients any new behaviors at this late date, Ana and Robyn are supposed to keep the digients in practice with what they've already learned. They're in the middle of a session when Mahesh, one of the cofounders of Blue Gamma, walks past their cubicles. He pauses to watch. "Don't mind me; keep doing what you're doing. What's today's skill?"

"Shape identification," says Robyn. She instantiates a scattering of colored blocks on the ground in front of her avatar. To one of the digients, she says, "Come here, Lolly." A lion cub toddles over from the playground.

Meanwhile Ana calls over Jax, whose avatar is a neo-Victorian robot made of polished copper. Derek did a great job designing it, from the proportions of the limbs to the shape of the face; Ana thinks Jax is adorable. She likewise instantiates a selection of colored blocks with different shapes and directs Jax's attention to them.

"See the blocks, Jax? What shape is the blue one?"

"Tringle," says Jax.

"Good. What shape is the red one?"

"Squir."

"Good. What shape is the green one?"

"Circle."

"Good job, Jax." Ana gives him a food pellet, which he devours with enthusiasm.

"Jax smirt," says Jax.

"Lolly smirt too," Lolly volunteers.

Ana smiles and rubs them on the backs of their heads. "Yes, you're both very smart."

"Both smirt," says Jax.

"That's what I like to see," says Mahesh.

The release candidates are the final distillation of countless trials, the cream of the crop in terms of teachability. It's partly been a search for intelligence, but just as much it's been a search for temperament, the personality that won't frustrate customers. One element of that is the ability to play well with others. The development team has tried to reduce hierarchical behavior in the digients—Blue Gamma wants to sell a pet that owners won't need to continually reassert their dominance over—but that doesn't mean competition never arises. The digients love attention, and if one notices that Ana's giving praise to another, it tries to get in on the action. Most of the time this is fine, but whenever a digient seemed particularly resentful of its peers or of Ana, she would flag it, and its specific genome would be excluded from the next generation. The process has felt a bit like breeding dogs, but more like working in an enormous test kitchen, baking endless batches of brownies and sampling each one's toothsomeness to find the perfect recipe.

The current instances of the release candidates will be kept as mascots, and copies will be available for purchase, but the expectation is that most people will buy younger digients, when they're still prelinguistic. Teaching your digient how to talk is half the fun; the mascots primarily serve as examples of the kind of results you can expect. Selling prelinguistic digients also allows them to be sold in non-English-speaking markets, even though Blue Gamma only has enough staff to raise mascots in English.

Ana sends Jax back to the playground and calls over a panda-bear digient named Marco. She's about to start testing his shape recognition when Mahesh points to one corner of her video screen. "Hey, look at that." A couple of digients are on the hill next to the playground, rolling down the slope.

"Hey, cool," she says. "I've never seen them do that before." She walks her avatar over to the hill, with Jax and Marco following and then joining the rest of the digients. The first time Jax tries it, he stops rolling almost immediately, but after a little practice he's able to make it all the way down the hill. He does that a few times and then runs back to Ana.

"Ana watch?" asks Jax. "Jax spinning lying din!"

"Yes, I saw you! You were rolling down the hill!"

"Rilling din hill!"

"You did great." She rubs him on the back of his head again.

Jax runs back and resumes rolling. Lolly has also taken to the new activity with enthusiasm. Once she's reached the bottom of the hill, she keeps rolling across the flat ground, and then hits one of the playground bridges.

"Eeh, eeh, eeh," Lolly says. "Fuck."

Suddenly everyone's attention is on Lolly. "Where did she learn that?" asks Mahesh.

Ana toggles her microphone off and walks her avatar over to comfort Lolly. "I don't know," she says. "She must have overheard it."

"Well, we can't sell a digient that says 'fuck.'"

"I'm on it," says Robyn. In a separate window on her own screen, she brings up the archives of their training sessions and runs a search on the audio track. "Looks like that's the first time any of the digients has said it. As for when any of us has said it . . ." The three of them watch as search results accumulate in the window; it appears that the culprit is Stefan, one of the trainers from Blue Gamma's Australian office. Blue Gamma has people working in Australia and England to train the digients when the West Coast office is closed; the digients don't need to sleep—or, more precisely, the integration processing that's their analog to sleep can be run at high speed—so they can be trained twenty-four hours a day.

They review the video footage of every time Stefan said the word "fuck" during a training session. The most dramatic outburst is from three days ago; it's hard to be sure from watching his Data Earth avatar, but it sounds like he banged his knee against his desk. There are previous examples going weeks back, but none as loud or prolonged.

"What do you want us to do?" asks Robyn.

The trade-off is apparent. This close to the release date, they don't have time to repeat weeks of training; should they gamble that the earlier utterances didn't make an impression on the digients? Mahesh thinks for a moment, and then decides. "Okay. Roll them back three days and pick up from there."

"All of them?" says Ana. "Not just Lolly?"

"We can't take the chance; roll them all back. And I want a keyword flagger running on every training session from now on. The next time any of you curses, roll all of them back to the last checkpoint."

So the digients lose three days of experience. Including the first time they rolled down a hill.

2

Blue Gamma's digients are a hit. Within the first year of release, a hundred thousand customers buy them and—more important—keep them running. Blue Gamma is gambling on a razor-and-blades business model, because just selling the digients wouldn't recoup the development costs; instead, the company charges customers each time they make digient food, and thus maintains a revenue stream for as long as the digients remain entertaining to their owners. And so far, the customers are finding them enormously entertaining, keeping them running all day long. It's common for customers to run the integration processing slowly so the digients sleep the entire night, but some run it at high speed, so their digients are awake almost all the time; they share their digients in cooperation with people in other time zones, enabling them to mature more rapidly. Scores of digient playgrounds and day-care centers appear across Data Earth's social continents, and public-events calendars become dotted with group playdates, training classes, and talent contests. Some owners even bring their digients to the racing zones and let them ride in their vehicles. The virtual world acts as a global village for raising the digients, a social fabric into which a new category of pet is woven.

Half of the digients that Blue Gamma sells are one-offs, having a genome that's randomly generated while remaining within the parameters chosen during the breeding process. The other half are copies of the mascots, but the company takes pains to remind buyers that each copy will develop differently depending on its environment. As an illustration of this, Blue Gamma's sales team points to Marco and Polo, two of the company's mascots. Both are instances of the exact same genome and both have panda-bear avatars, but they have distinctly different personalities. Marco was two years old when Polo was instantiated, and Polo latched on to him as a kind of older brother; the two are inseparable now, but Marco is more outgoing while Polo is more cautious, and no one expects that Polo will turn into Marco anytime soon.

Blue Gamma's mascots are the oldest Neuroblast digients

running, and management originally hoped they would provide the test team with a preview of digient behavior before customers encountered it. In practice, it hasn't worked out that way; it's impossible to predict how digients raised in a thousand different settings will turn out. In a very real sense, each digient owner is exploring new territory, and they turn to one another for help. Online forums for digient owners spring up, filled with anecdotes and discussions, advice sought and given.

Blue Gamma has a customer liaison whose job is to read the forums, but Derek sometimes follows the forums on his own, after work. Sometimes customers talk about the digients' facial expressions, but even when they don't, Derek enjoys reading the anecdotes.

....

From: Zoe Armstrong

You won't believe what my Natasha did today! We were at the playground, and another digient hurt himself when he fell and was crying. Natasha gave him a hug to make him feel better, and I praised her to high heaven. Next thing I know, she pushes over another digient to make him cry, hugs him, and looks to me for praise!

....

The next post he reads attracts his attention:

....

From: Andrew Nguyen

Are some of the digients just not as smart as others? My digient doesn't respond to my commands the way I've seen other people's do.

....

He looks at the customer's public profile, and sees that the avatar is an endless shower of gold coins; the coins bounce off one another so that their trajectories suggest a highly abstract human figure. It's a dazzling piece of animation, but Derek suspects that the user hasn't read Blue Gamma's recommendations on raising the digients. He posts a reply:

....

From: Derek Brooks

When you're playing with your digient, are you wearing the avatar that's displayed in your profile? If you are, one problem is that your avatar doesn't have a face. Set your camera to track your facial expressions and wear an avatar that can display them, and you'll get a much better response from your digient.

....

He continues to browse. A minute later, he sees another question that he finds interesting:

....

From: Natalie Vance

My digient Coco is a Lolly, a year and a half old. Lately she's been really naughty. Never does what I tell her to, driving me crazy. She was an absolute doll a few weeks ago, so I tried restoring her from a checkpoint, but it doesn't last. I've tried it twice now, and she still ends up with the same naughty attitude. (It took a little longer the second time, though.) Has anyone had a similar experience? I'm especially interested if you have a Lolly. How far did you need to roll back to get around the problem?

....

There are several replies in which people suggest ways to isolate what specifically triggered Coco's change in mood and then work around it. He's about to post a reply of his own, to the effect that a digient is not a video game that you replay until you get a perfect score, when he sees a response from Ana:

....

From: Ana Alvarado

I can sympathize, because I've seen the exact same thing. It's not specific to the Lollys, it's something that a lot of digients go through. You can keep trying to work around episodes like this, but I suspect they're unavoidable, and you'll just wind up spending months on a digient that never gets any older. Or you can push through the rough patch and have a more mature digient when you come out the other side.

....

He's heartened to read this. The practice of treating conscious beings as if they were toys is all too prevalent, and it doesn't just happen to pets. Derek once attended a holiday party at his brother-in-law's house, and there was a couple there with an eight-year-old clone. He felt sorry for the boy every time he looked at him. The child was a walking bundle of neuroses, the result of growing up as a monument to his father's narcissism. Even a digient deserves more respect than that.

He sends Ana a private message, thanking her for her post. Then he notices that the customer with the faceless avatar has responded to his suggestion.

....

From: Andrew Nguyen
   The hell with that. I paid good money for this avatar,
and I bought it specifically to wear when I'm on the social
continents. I'm not going to stop wearing it for a digient.

....

Derek sighs; there's probably no chance of changing the man's mind, but hopefully he'll just suspend his digient rather than do a bad job of raising it. Blue Gamma has done what it can to minimize abuses; all the Neuroblast digients are equipped with pain circuit breakers, which render them immune to torture and thus unappealing to sadists. Unfortunately, there's no way to protect the digients from things like simple neglect.

.   .   .

Over the next year, other companies begin marketing their own genomic engines that support language learning. None of them can match Neuroblast's popularity on the Data Earth platform, although on other platforms the situation is different. On Next Dimension, the Origami engine becomes dominant; on Anywhere, it's an engine called Fabergé. Fortunately, Blue Gamma has inspired companies to offer complementary products as well as competing ones.

Today half of the company's employees are crowded into the reception area: managers, developers, testers, designers. They're here because a highly anticipated delivery has finally arrived: a shipping carton the size of a large suitcase sits in front of the receptionist's desk.

"Let's open it up," says Mahesh.

Ana and Robyn pull the tabs on the shipping carton, separating it into eight blocks of cellulose foam that hinge open. The resident of this custom sarcophagus is a robot body, newly arrived from the fabrication facility. The robot is humanoid in shape but small, less than three feet in height, to keep the inertia of its limbs low and allow it a moderate amount of agility. Its skin is glossy black and its head is disproportionately large, with a surface mostly occupied by a wraparound display screen.

The robot is from SaruMech Toys. A number of companies have sprung up to offer services targeting digient owners, but SaruMech is the first one with a hardware product instead of software. They've sent an example of their product to Blue Gamma in hopes of an endorsement.

"Which mascot got the high score?" asks Mahesh. He's referring to the agility trials. Last week all the digients were given test avatars whose weight distribution and range of motion matched the robot body's; they've spent some time each day wearing the avatars, practicing moving around in them. Yesterday Ana scored the digients on their ability to lie on their backs and then rise to their feet, ascend and descend stairs, balance on one leg and then the other. It was like conducting a sobriety test for a bunch of toddlers.

"That was Jax," says Ana.

"Okay, get him ready."

The receptionist relinquishes his workspace to Ana, who logs in to Data Earth from there and calls Jax over. Jax is lucky because the test avatar isn't radically different from his own; it's bulkier, but the limbs and torso have similar proportions. By contrast, the digients who grew up wearing panda-bear and tiger-cub avatars have been having more difficulty.

Robyn checks the diagnostics panel on the robot. "Looks like we're good to go."

Ana opens a portal in the gymnasium on-screen and gestures to Jax. "Okay, Jax, come on in."

On-screen, Jax steps through the portal, and in the reception area the little robot comes alive. The robot's head lights up to display Jax's face, turning the oversize head into a bubble helmet he's wearing. The design is a way of maintaining the resemblance to the digient's original avatar without having to produce custom bodies. Jax looks like a copper robot wearing a suit of obsidian armor.

Jax turns around to take in the entire room. "Wow." He stops turning. "Wow wow. Sound different. Wow wow wow."

"It's okay, Jax," says Ana. "Remember, I told you your voice might sound different in the outside world." The information packet from SaruMech had warned about this; a metal-and-plastic chassis conducts sound in a way that avatars in Data Earth don't.

Jax looks up to face Ana, and she marvels at the sight of him. She knows that he's not really *in* the body—Jax's code is still being run on the network, and this robot is just a fancy peripheral—but the illusion is perfect. And even after all their interaction in Data Earth, it's thrilling to have Jax stand in front of her and look her in the eye.

"Hi, Jax," she says. "It's me, Ana."

"You wear different avatar," Jax says.

"In the outside world, we call it a body, not an avatar. And people don't switch their bodies here; we can only do that in Data Earth. Here we always wear the same body."

Jax pauses to consider that. "You look this always?"

"Well, I can wear different clothes. But yes, this is the way I look."

Jax walks over for a closer view, and Ana squats, elbows on

knees, so they're almost the same height. Jax peers at her hands and then her forearms; she's wearing short sleeves. He brings his head closer, and Ana can hear the faint whir of the robot's camera eyes refocusing. "Little hairs on your arms," he says.

She laughs; her avatar has arms as smooth as a baby's. "Yes, there are."

Jax brings up a hand and extends a thumb and forefinger to grab some of the hairs. He makes a couple of attempts, but like the pincers of a claw vending machine, his fingers keep slipping off. Then he pinches her skin and pulls back.

"Ow. Jax, that hurts."

"Sorry." Jax scrutinizes Ana's face. "Little little holes all over your face."

Ana can feel the amusement of the others in the room. "Those are called pores," she says, standing. "We can talk about my skin later. Right now, why don't you take a look around the room?"

Jax turns and slowly walks around the lobby, a miniature astronaut exploring an alien world. He notices the window looking out onto the parking lot and heads toward it.

Afternoon sunlight slants through the glass. Jax steps into the sunbeam and abruptly backs out of it. "What that?"

"That's the sun. It's just like the one in Data Earth."

Jax cautiously steps into the light again. "Not like. This sun bright bright bright."

"That's true."

"Sun not need be bright bright bright."

Ana laughs. "I suppose you're right."

Jax walks back over to her and looks at the fabric of her pants. Tentatively, she rubs the back of his head. The tactile sensors in the robot body are obviously working, because Jax leans into her hand; she can feel the weight of him, the dynamic resistance of his actuators. Then Jax hugs her around her thighs.

"Can I keep him?" she says to the others. "He followed me home."

Everyone laughs. "You say that now," says Mahesh, "but wait until he flushes your hand towels down the toilet."

"I know, I know," says Ana. There were many reasons Blue Gamma targeted the virtual realm instead of the real one—lower cost, ease of social networking—but one was the risk of property damage; they couldn't sell a pet that might tear down your actual venetian blinds or make mayonnaise castles on your actual rug. "I just think it's cool to see Jax this way."

"You're right, it is. For SaruMech's sake, though, I hope the experience translates well onto video." SaruMech Toys doesn't plan to sell the robot bodies but to rent them for a few hours at a time. Digients will be given use of bodies at a facility outside of Osaka and taken on a field trip into the real world, while the owners watch via cameras mounted on micro-zeppelins. Ana feels a sudden urge to go work for them; seeing Jax this way reminds her of how much she misses the physical part of working with animals, and why working with the digients through a video screen just isn't the same.

Robyn asks Mahesh, "Do you want all the mascots to have a turn in the robot?"

"Yes, but only after they've passed the agility test. If we break this one, SaruMech isn't going to give us another one for free."

Now Jax is playing with her sneakers, tugging on the end of a shoelace. It's not often that Ana wishes she were rich, but right now, feeling her shoelace grow taut from Jax's pulling, that is exactly what she's wishing. Because if she could afford it, she would buy one of these robots in a heartbeat.

. . .

Various employees take turns showing mascots the real world; Derek usually takes Marco or Polo. His first idea is to take them outside, around the office park where Blue Gamma is head-quartered, and show them the strips of grass and shrubbery that divide the parking lot. He points out the crablike robot that tends to the landscaping, product of an earlier venture in bring-ing digients into the real world. The robot is equipped with a stiletto-like trowel for pulling weeds, and its toil is purely instinct driven; it's descended from generations of winners in an evolu-tionary gardening competition conducted in Data Earth hot-houses. Derek's curious about how the mascots will react upon hearing the story of the weed-pulling robot, wondering if they'll identify with it as a fellow émigré from Data Earth, but they don't show the slightest interest.

Instead, it turns out that the mascots are fascinated by tex-tures. Surfaces in Data Earth have a lot of visual detail but no tactile qualities beyond a coefficient of friction; very few play-ers use controllers that convey tactition, so most vendors don't bother implementing texture for their environmental surfaces. Now that the digients can feel surfaces in the real world, they find novelty in the simplest things. When Marco returns from his turn in the robot body, he can't stop talking about the carpets and furniture upholstery; when Polo is wearing the body, he spends all his time feeling the gritty nonskid treads in the build-ing's stairwells. Not surprisingly, the sensor pads in the robot's fingers are the first components that need replacement.

The next thing Marco notices is how Derek's mouth differs from his own. Digient mouths bear only a superficial resemblance to human mouths; although their lips move when they talk, the digients' speech generators aren't physics-based. Marco wants to learn about the mechanics of speech and keeps asking to put his fingers in Derek's mouth when he talks. Polo is astonished to discover that food actually passes down Derek's throat when he swallows, rather than simply vanishing the way digient food does. Derek had feared that the digients might be distressed to learn the boundaries of their physicality, but instead they just find it funny.

An unexpected benefit of seeing the digients in a robot body is that it provides a closer view of their faces than is common when watching them in Data Earth. As a result, the work that Derek has put in on the digients' facial expressions is easier to appreciate. One day Ana comes to his cubicle and says, excited, "You are amazing!"

"Er . . . thanks?"

"I just saw Marco make the most hilarious expressions. You've got to see them. May I?" Ana gestures at his keyboard, and Derek rolls his chair back from his desk so she can reach it. She opens a couple of video windows on his screen: one is a recording of the robot body's camera, showing the digient's point of view, while the other is a recording of what the helmet screen was displaying. Judging by the former, they were out in the parking lot again.

"He went on one of SaruMech's field trips last week," explains Ana, "and of course he loved it, so now he's bored with the office park."

On the screen, Marco says, *"Want go park we go field trip."*

"You can have just as much fun here." On the screen, Ana gestures for Marco to follow her.

The image swings back and forth as Marco shakes his head. *"Not same fun. Park more fun. Show you."*

"We can't go to that park. It's very far away; we would have to travel a long time to get there."

"Just open portal."

"Sorry, Marco, I can't open portals here in the outside world."

"Now watch his face," says Ana.

"You try. Try hard please please." Marco forms his panda-bear face into a pleading expression; Derek hasn't seen it before, and it makes him laugh in surprise.

Ana laughs, too, and says, "Keep watching."

On the screen she says, *"It doesn't matter how hard I try, Marco; the outside world doesn't have portals. Only Data Earth has portals."*

"Then we go Data Earth, open portal there."

"That would work for you if there's a body there for you to wear, but I can't wear a different body, I'd have to move this one, and that would take a long time."

Marco thinks about that, and Derek's delighted to see that the digient's face actually suggests his incredulity. *"Outside world dumb,"* the digient announces.

Derek and Ana burst out into laughter. She closes the windows and says, "You did some terrific work there."

"Thanks. And thanks for showing that to me; it made my day."

"Glad to do it."

It's nice to be reminded that his earlier work is bearing fruit, because most of Derek's recent assignments aren't nearly as interesting. The Origami and Fabergé digients have begun to pop up in a wider variety of avatars, such as baby dragons, gryphons, and other mythological creatures, so Blue Gamma wants to offer similar avatars for the Neuroblast digients. The new avatars are straightforward modifications of the existing ones, requiring nothing new in terms of their facial expressions.

In fact, his newest assignment requires him to create an avatar with no facial expressions at all. A group of artificial-life hobbyists was impressed by the potential of the Neuroblast genome and, rather than wait for real intelligence to evolve on its own in the biomes, commissioned Blue Gamma to design an intelligent alien species for them. The developers engineered a personality taxon that was miles away from the breeds that Blue Gamma sells, and Derek's designing an avatar with three legs, a pair of tentacles instead of arms, and a prehensile tail. Some of the hobbyists want an even stranger body plan, as well as an environment with different physics, but he reminded them that they'll have to wear the avatars themselves when raising the digients, and controlling tentacles will be difficult enough.

The hobbyists have named their new species Xenotherians and set up a private continent called Data Mars on which they intend to create an alien culture from scratch. Derek's curious about it but hasn't been able to visit, because the only language allowed in the presence of the digients is a custom dialect of the artificial language Lojban. He wonders how long the hobbyists will be able to stick with their project. Aside from the enormous barrier to entry, raising the Xenotherians won't offer pleasures like the one that he and Ana just got from watching Marco. The rewards will be purely intellectual, and over the long term, will that be enough?

3

Over the course of the following year, the forecast for Blue Gamma's future changes from sunny to decidedly cloudy. Sales to new customers have slowed down, but worse than that, the revenue generated by the food-dispensing software has fallen: more and more of the existing customers are suspending their digients.

The problem is that as the Neuroblast digients leave infancy behind, they're growing too demanding. In breeding them Blue Gamma aimed for a combination of smart and obedient, but with the unpredictability inherent in any genome, even a digital one, it turns out the developers missed their target. As in an overly difficult game, the balance of challenge and reward that the digients provide is tilting beyond what most people consider fun, and so they suspend them. But unlike dog owners who bought a breed they were unprepared for, Blue Gamma's customers can't be blamed for not having done their homework; the company itself didn't know that the digients would evolve in this way.

Some volunteers have begun maintaining rescue shelters, accepting unwanted digients in hopes of matching them with new owners. These volunteers practice a variety of strategies; some keep the digients running without interruption, while others restore the digients from their last checkpoint every few days, to keep them from developing abandonment issues that might make it harder for them to get adopted. Neither strategy is enormously successful at attracting prospective owners. There is occasionally a person who wants to try a digient without having to raise one from infancy, but these adoptions never last for long, and the shelters essentially become digient warehouses.

Ana's not happy about this trend, but she's familiar with the realities of animal welfare: she knows you can't save them all. She'd prefer to shield Blue Gamma's mascots from what's happening, but the phenomenon is too widespread for that to be practical. Again and again she has taken them to a playground and one of the digients realizes that a regular playmate is absent.

Today's trip to a playground is different and brings a pleasant surprise. Even before all the mascots are through the portal, Jax and Marco notice another digient wearing a robot avatar. They simultaneously exclaim "Tibo!" and run over to him.

Tibo is one of the oldest digients aside from the mascots, owned by a beta tester named Carlton. He suspended Tibo about a month ago; Ana's glad to see that it wasn't permanent. As the digients chatter, she walks her avatar over to Carlton's and talks with him; he explains that he just needed a break and now is feeling ready to give Tibo the attention he's been demanding

Later on, after she's brought the mascots back from the playground to Blue Gamma's island, Jax tells her about his conversation with Tibo. "Tell him about fun we do time he gone. Tell him about field trip zoo fun fun."

"Was he sad he missed it?"

"No he instead argue. He said field trip was mall not zoo. But that trip last month."

"That's because Tibo was suspended the whole time he's been gone," Ana explains, "so he thinks last month's trip was yesterday."

"I say that," says Jax, surprising her with his understanding, "but he not believe. He argue until Marco and Lolly too tell him. Then he sad."

"Well, I'm sure there'll be other trips to the zoo."

"Not because missed zoo. Sad missed month."

"Ah."

"I not want be suspended. Not want miss month."

Ana does her best to sound reassuring. "You don't have to worry about that, Jax."

"You not suspend me, right?"

"Right."

To her relief, Jax seems satisfied by this; he hasn't encountered the idea of extracting a promise, and she's embarrassingly glad that she didn't have to make him one. She takes comfort in the knowledge that if they suspend the mascots for any period of time, they'll almost certainly suspend all of them, so at least there won't be experiential discrepancies within the group. The same would be true if they ever roll the mascots back to a younger age. Restoring an early checkpoint is one of Blue Gamma's suggestions for customers who find their digients too demanding, and there's been talk that the company should do this with its own mascots to endorse the strategy.

Ana notices the time and begins instantiating some games for the mascots to play on their own; it's time for her to train the digients in Blue Gamma's new product line. In the years since creating the Neuroblast genome, the developers have written more sophisticated tools for analyzing the interactions of its various genes, and they understand the genome's properties better. Recently they've created a taxon with less cognitive plasticity, resulting in digients that should stabilize more quickly and stay docile forever. The only way to know for certain is to let customers raise them for years and see what happens, but the developers' confidence is high. This is a significant departure from the company's original goal of digients that become ever more sophisticated, but drastic situations call for drastic measures. Blue Gamma is counting on these new digients to stanch the loss of revenue, so Ana and the rest of the test team are intensively training them.

She has the mascots sufficiently well trained that they wait for her permission before they start playing the games. "All right, everyone, go ahead," she says, and the digients all rush over to their favorites. "I'll see you all later."

"No," says Jax. He stops and walks back to her avatar. "Don't want play."

"What? Sure you do."

"No playing. Want job."

Ana laughs. "What? Why do you want to get a job?"

"Get money."

She realizes that Jax isn't happy when he says this; his mood is glum. More seriously, she asks him, "What do you need money for?"

"Don't need. Give you."

"Why do you want to give me money?"

"You need," he says, matter-of-factly.

"Did I say I need money? When?"

"Last week ask why you play with other digients instead me. You said people pay you play with them. If have money, can pay you. Then you play with me more."

"Oh, Jax." She's momentarily at a loss for words. "That's very sweet of you."

. . .

After another year has gone by, it becomes official: Blue Gamma is shutting down its operations. Not enough customers were willing to take a chance on the perpetually docile digients. Internally there were many proposals discussed, including a breed of digient that understands language but can't speak, but it was too late. The customer base has stabilized to a small community of hard-core digient owners, and they don't generate enough revenue to keep Blue Gamma afloat. The company will release a no-fee version of the food-dispensing software so those who want to can keep their digients running as long as they like, but otherwise, the customers are on their own.

Most of the other employees have been through company collapses before, so while they're unhappy, for them this is just another episode of life in the software industry. For Ana, however, Blue Gamma's folding reminds her of the closure of the zoo, which was one of the most heartbreaking experiences of her life. Her eyes still tear up when she thinks about the last time she saw her apes, wishing that she could explain to them why they wouldn't see her again, hoping that they could adapt to their new homes. When she decided to retrain for the software industry, she was glad that she'd never have to face another such farewell in her new line of work. Now here she is, against all expectation, confronted with a strangely reminiscent situation.

Reminiscent, but not the same. Blue Gamma doesn't actually need to find new homes for its dozen mascots; it can just suspend them, with none of the implications that euthanasia would have. Ana herself has suspended thousands of digients during the breeding process, and they aren't dead or feeling abandoned. The only suffering created by suspending the mascots would be on the part of the trainers; Ana has spent time with the mascots every day for the last five years, and she doesn't want to say goodbye to them. Fortunately, there's an alternative: any employee can afford to keep a mascot as a pet in Data Earth, whereas keeping an ape in her apartment hadn't even been a possibility.

Given how easy it is, Ana's surprised that more of the employees don't want to adopt a mascot. She knows she can count on Derek to take one—he cares about the digients just as much as she does—but the trainers are unexpectedly reluctant. They're all fond of the digients, but most feel that keeping one as a pet now would be like doing their job after they've stopped being paid. Ana is sure that Robyn will take one, but Robyn preempts her with news of her own at lunch.

"We weren't going to tell anyone yet," Robyn confides, "but . . . I'm pregnant."

"Really? Congratulations!"

Robyn grins. "Thanks!" She releases a flood of pent-up information: the options that she and her partner, Linda, considered, the ova-fusion procedure they gambled on, their fabulous luck at having the first attempt succeed. Ana and Robyn discuss issues of job hunting and parental leave. Eventually they get back to the topic of adopting the mascots.

"Obviously you're going to have your hands full," says Ana, "but what do you think about adopting Lolly?" It would be fascinating to see Lolly's reaction to a pregnancy.

"No," says Robyn, shaking her head. "I'm past digients now."

"You're past them?"

"I'm ready for the real thing, you know what I mean?"

Carefully, Ana says, "I'm not sure that I do."

"People always say that we're evolved to want babies, and I used to think that was a bunch of crap, but not anymore." Robyn's facial expression is one of transport; she's no longer speaking to Ana exactly. "Cats, dogs, digients, they're all just substitutes for what we're supposed to be caring for. Eventually you start to understand what a baby means, what it *really* means, and everything changes. And then you realize that all the feelings you had before weren't—" Robyn stops herself. "I mean, for me, it just put things in perspective."

Women who work with animals hear this all the time: that their love for animals must arise out of a sublimated child-rearing urge. Ana's tired of the stereotype. She likes children just fine, but they're not the standard against which all other accomplishments should be measured. Caring for animals is worthwhile in and of itself, a vocation that need offer no apologies. She wouldn't have said the same about digients when she started at Blue Gamma, but now she realizes it might be true for them, too.

4

The year following Blue Gamma's closure involves many changes for Derek. He gets a job at the firm that employs his wife, Wendy, animating virtual actors for television. He's fortunate to work on a series with good writing, but no matter how quick-witted and nonchalant the dialogue sounds, every word of it, every nuance and intonation, is painstakingly choreographed. During the animation process he hears the lines delivered a hundred times, and the final performance seems glossy and sterile in its perfection.

By contrast, life with Marco and Polo is a never-ending stream of surprises. He adopted both of them because they didn't want to be separated, and while he can't spend as much time with them as when he worked for Blue Gamma, owning a digient now is actually more interesting than it's ever been. The customers who kept their digients running formed a Neuroblast user group to keep in touch; it's a smaller community than before, but the members are more active and engaged, and their efforts are bearing fruit.

Right now it's the weekend, and Derek is driving to the park;

in the passenger seat is Marco, wearing a robotic body. He's standing upright on the seat—restrained by the seat belt—so he can see out the window; he's looking for anything that he's seen before only in videos, things that aren't found in Data Earth.

"Firi hidrint," says Marco, pointing.

"Fire hydrant."

"Fire hydrant."

"That's right."

The body Marco's wearing is the one that Blue Gamma owned. Group field trips came to an end because SaruMech Toys closed shortly after Blue Gamma did, so Ana—who got a job testing software used in carbon-sequestration stations—bought the robot body at a discount for Jax to use. She let Derek borrow the body last week so Marco and Polo could play in it, and now he's returning it. She's going to spend the day in the park, letting other owners' digients have a turn in the body.

"I make fire hydrant next craft time," says Marco. "Use cylinder, use cone, use cylinder."

"That sounds like a good idea," says Derek.

Marco's talking about the craft sessions that the digients now have every day. These began a few months ago, after an owner wrote software that allowed a few of Data Earth's on-screen editing tools to be operated from within the Data Earth environment itself. By manipulating a console of knobs and sliders, a digient can now instantiate various solid shapes, change their color, and combine and edit them in a dozen different ways. The digients are in heaven; to them it seems as if they've been granted magical powers, and given the way the editing tools circumvent Data Earth's physics simulation, in a sense they have. Every day after work when Derek logs in to Data Earth, Marco and Polo show him the craft projects they've made.

"Then can show Polo how—park! Park already?"

"No, we're not there yet."

"Sign says BURGERS AND PARKS." Marco points out a sign that they're driving past.

"It says BURGERS AND SHAKES. 'Shakes,' not 'parks.' We've still got a little way to go."

"Shakes," Marco says, watching the sign recede in the distance.

Another new activity for the digients has been reading lessons. Marco or Polo never paid much attention to text before—there isn't a lot of it in Data Earth aside from on-screen annotations, which aren't visible to digients—but one owner successfully taught his digient to recognize commands written on flash cards, prompting a number of other owners to give it a try. Generally speaking, the Neuroblast digients recognize words reasonably well but have trouble associating individual letters with sounds. It's a variety of dyslexia that appears to be specific to the Neuroblast genome; according to other user groups, Origami digients learn letters readily, while Fabergé digients remain frustratingly illiterate no matter what instruction method is used.

Marco and Polo take a reading class with Jax and a few others, and they seem to enjoy it well enough. None of the digients was raised on bedtime stories, so text doesn't fascinate them the way it does human children, but their general curiosity—along with the praise of their owners—motivates them to explore the uses that text can be put to. Derek finds it exciting and laments the fact that Blue Gamma didn't stay in business long enough to see these things come to pass.

They arrive at the park; Ana sees them and walks over as Derek parks the car. Marco gives Ana a hug as soon as Derek lets him out of the car.

"Hi Ana."

"Hi, Marco," replies Ana; she rubs the back of the robot's head. "You're still in the body? You had a whole week. Wasn't that enough?"

"Wanted ride in car."

"Did you want to play in the park for a bit?"

"No, we go now. Wendy not want us stay. Bye Ana." By now Derek has gotten the charging platform for the robot out of the back seat. Marco steps onto the charging platform—they've trained the digients to return to it whenever they return to Data Earth—and the robot's helmet goes dark.

Ana uses her handheld to get the first digient ready to enter the robot. "So you have to go, too?" she asks Derek.

"No, I don't have to be anywhere."

"So what did Marco mean?"

"Well . . ."

"Let me guess: Wendy thinks you spend too much time with digients, right?"

"Right," says Derek. Wendy was also uncomfortable with the amount of time he's been spending with Ana, but there's no point in mentioning that. He assured Wendy that he doesn't think of Ana that way, that they're just friends who share an interest in digients.

The robot's helmet lights up to display a jaguar-cub face; Derek recognizes him as Zaff, who's owned by one of the beta testers. "Hi Ana hi Derek," says Zaff, and immediately runs toward a nearby tree. Derek and Ana follow.

"So seeing them in the robot body didn't win her over?" asks Ana.

Derek stops Zaff from picking up some dog turds. To Ana,

he says, "Nope. She still doesn't understand why I don't suspend them whenever it's convenient."

"It's hard to find someone who understands," Ana says. "It was the same when I worked at the zoo; every guy I dated felt like he was coming in second. And now when I tell a guy that I'm paying for reading lessons for my digient, he looks at me like I'm crazy."

"That's been an issue for Wendy, too."

They watch as Zaff sorts through the leaf litter, extracts a leaf decayed to near transparency, and holds it up to his face to look through it, a mask of vegetable lace. "Although I guess I shouldn't really blame them," says Ana. "It took me a while to understand the appeal myself."

"Not me," says Derek. "I thought digients were amazing right away."

"That's true," agrees Ana. "You're a rare one."

Derek watches her with Zaff, admires her patience in guiding him. The last time he felt so much in common with a woman was when he met Wendy, who shared his excitement at bringing characters to life through animation. If he weren't already married, he might ask Ana out, but there's no point in speculating about that now. The most they can be is friends, and that's good enough.

.   .   .

It's a year later, and Ana is spending the evening at her apartment. On her computer she has a window open to Data Earth, where her avatar is at a playground, supervising a group playdate that Jax has with a handful of other digients. The number of digients continues to shrink—Tibo, for example, hasn't been around in months—but Jax's regular group has merged with another one recently, so he still has the opportunity to make new friends. A few of the digients are up in the climbing equipment, others play with toys on the ground, while a couple watch a virtual television.

In another window, Ana browses through the user-group discussion forums. The topic du jour is the latest action by the Information Freedom Front, an organization that lobbies for the end of privately owned data. Last week it publicized techniques for cracking many of Data Earth's access-control mechanisms, and in recent days people have been seeing rare and expensive items from their game inventories being handed out like flyers on a downtown street corner. Ana hasn't been to a game continent in Data Earth since the problem began.

In the playground, Jax and Marco have decided to play a new game. They both get down on all fours and begin crawling around. Jax waves to get her attention, and she walks her avatar over to him. "Ana," he says, "you know ants talk each other?"

They've been watching nature videos on the television. "Yes, I've heard that," she says.

"You know we know what they saying?"

"You do?"

"We talk ant language. Like this: *Imp fimp deemul weetul.*"

Marco replies, *"Beedul jeedul lomp womp."*

"And what does that mean?"

"Not tell you. Only we know."

"We and ants," adds Marco. And then Jax and Marco both laugh, *Mo mo mo,* and Ana smiles. The digients run off to play something else, and she goes back to browsing the forums.

....

From: Helen Costas

Do you think we need to worry about our digients being copied?

....

From: Stuart Gust

Who would bother? If there were a big demand for digients, Blue Gamma wouldn't have gone out of business. Remember what happened with the shelters? You literally couldn't give a digient away. And it's not as if they've gotten any more popular since then.

....

In the playground, Jax exclaims, "I win!" He's been playing some vaguely defined game with Marco. He rocks side to side in triumph.

"Okay," says Marco, "your turn." He sorts through the toys around him until he finds a kazoo and then hands it to Jax.

Jax puts one end of the kazoo in his mouth. He gets on his knees and uses the kazoo to rhythmically poke at Marco's midsection, around where his navel would be if he had one.

Ana asks, "Jax, what are you doing?"

Jax takes the kazoo from his mouth. "Make Marco blowjob."

"What? Where did you see a blowjob?"

"On TV yesterday."

She looks at the television; right now it's showing a child's cartoon. The television is supposed to draw its content from a children's video repository; someone is probably inserting adult material using the IFF hack. She decides not to make a big deal of it to the digients. "Okay," she says, and Jax and Marco resume their mime. She posts a note about the video tampering to the forums and continues reading.

A few minutes later, Ana hears an unfamiliar chittering sound and sees that Jax has gone to watch television; all of the digients are watching it. She moves her avatar so she can see what's drawn their attention.

On the virtual television, a person wearing a clown avatar is holding down a digient wearing a puppy avatar and hitting the digient's legs repeatedly with a hammer. The digient's legs can't break because its avatar wasn't designed to account for that, and it probably can't scream for similar reasons, but the digient must be in agony, and the chittering sounds are the only way it can express that.

Ana turns the virtual television off.

"What happen?" asks Jax, and several of the other digients repeat the question, but she doesn't answer. Instead she opens a window on her physical screen to read the description accompanying the video that was playing. It's not an animation but a recording of a griefer using the IFF hack to disable the pain circuit breakers on a digient's body. Even worse, the digient isn't an anonymous new instantiation but someone's beloved pet, illicitly copied using the IFF hack. The digient's name is Nyyti, and Ana realizes that he's a classmate in Jax's reading lessons.

Whoever copied Nyyti could have a copy of Jax, too. Or he could be making a copy of Jax right now. Given Data Earth's distributed architecture, Jax is vulnerable if the griefer is anywhere on the same continent as the playground.

Jax is still asking about what they saw on the television. Ana opens a window listing all the Data Earth processes running under her account, finds the one that represents Jax, and suspends it. In the playground, Jax freezes in midsentence and then vanishes.

"What happen Jax?" asks Marco.

Ana opens another window for Derek's processes—they granted each other full privileges for their accounts—and suspends Marco and Polo. She doesn't have full privileges for the other digients, though, and she's not sure what to do next. She can see that they're agitated and confused. They don't have the fight-or-flight response that animals have, nor do they have any reactions triggered by smelling pheromones or hearing distress calls, but they do have an analog of mirror neurons. It helps them learn and socialize, but it also means they're distressed by what they saw on the television.

Everyone who brought their digient to the playdate granted Ana permission to make the digients take a nap, but their processes would still be running even if they were asleep, meaning they'd still be at risk of being copied. She decides to move the digients to a small island, away from the major continents, in hopes that there's less chance that a griefer will be scanning processes there.

"Okay, everybody," she announces, "we're going to the zoo." She opens a portal to the visitor's center of the Pangaea archipelago and ushers the digients through it. The visitor's center appears to be empty, but she's not taking any chances. She forces the digients to sleep and then sends messages to all their owners, telling them where they can pick up their digients. She keeps her avatar with them while she goes on the forums to warn everyone else.

Over the next hour the other owners arrive to pick up their digients while Ana watches the discussion on the forums bloom like algae. There's outrage and threats of lawsuits against various parties. Some gamers take the position that digient owners' complaints should take a back seat to their own because digients have no monetary value, igniting a flame war. Ana ignores most of it, looking for information about the response from Daesan Digital, the company that runs the Data Earth platform. Eventually there's solid news:

....

From: Enrique Beltran
    Daesan has an upgrade to Data Earth's security architecture that they say will fix the breach. It was going to be part of next year's update, but they're bumping it up because of what's been happening. They can't give us a schedule for when it'll be done. Until it is, everyone better keep your digients suspended.

....

From: Maria Zheng
    There's another option. Lisma Gunawan is setting up a private island, and she's only going to allow approved code to run on it. You won't be able to use anything you've bought recently, but Neuroblast digients will run fine. Contact her if you want to be put on the visitor list.

....

Ana sends a request to Lisma and gets an automated reply promising news when the island is ready. Ana's not set up to run a local instance of the Data Earth environment herself, but she does have another option. She spends an hour configuring her system to run a completely local instance of the Neuroblast engine; without a Data Earth portal, she has to load Jax's saved state manually, but eventually she's able to get Jax running with the robot body.

"—turn off television?" He stops, realizing his surroundings have changed. "What happen?"

"It's okay, Jax."

He sees the body he's wearing. "I in outside world." He looks at her. "You suspend me?"

"Yes, I'm sorry. I know I said I wouldn't, but I had to."

Plaintively, he asks, "Why?"

Ana's embarrassed by how hard she's hugging the robot body. "I'm trying to keep you safe."

.   .   .

A month later, Data Earth gets its security upgrade. The IFF disclaims any responsibility for what griefers do with the information they published, saying that every freedom has the potential to be abused, but they shift their attention to other projects. For a while, at least, the public continents in Data Earth are safe for digients again, but the damage has been done. There's no way to track down copies that are being run privately, and even if no one releases videos of digient torture anymore, many Neuroblast owners can't bear the thought that such things are going on; they suspend their digients permanently and leave the user group.

At the same time, other people are excited by the availability of copied digients, particularly of digients who've been taught to read. Members of an AI research institute have wondered whether digients could form their own culture if left in a hothouse, but they never had access to digients who could read, and they weren't interested in raising any themselves. Now the researchers assemble copies of as many text-literate digients as they can, mostly Origami digients, since they have the best reading skills, but they mix in a few Neuroblast ones as well. They put them on private islands furnished with text and software libraries and start running the islands at hothouse speeds. The discussion forums teem with speculation about cities in a bottle, microcosms on a tabletop.

Derek thinks the idea is ridiculous—a bunch of abandoned children aren't going to become autodidacts no matter how many books they're left with—so he's not surprised to read about the results: every test population eventually goes feral. The digients don't have enough aggression in them to descend into *Lord of the Flies*-style savagery; they simply divide into loose, nonhier-archical troops. Initially, each troop's daily routines are held together by force of habit—they read and use eduware when it's time for school; they go to the playgrounds to play—but with-out reinforcement these rituals unravel like cheap twine. Every object becomes a toy, every space a playground, and gradually the digients lose what skills they had. They develop a kind of culture of their own, perhaps what wild digient troops would demonstrate if they'd evolved on their own in the biomes.

As interesting as that is, it's a far cry from the nascent civiliza-tion that the researchers were seeking, so they try redesigning the islands. They try to increase the variety of the test popula-tions, asking owners of educated digients to donate copies; to Derek's surprise, they actually receive a few from owners who have grown tired of paying for reading lessons and are satisfied that the feral digients aren't suffering. The researchers devise various incentives—all automated, so no real-time interaction is required—to keep the digients motivated. They impose hard-ships so that indolence has a cost. While a few of the revised test populations avoid going feral, none ever begins the climb toward technological sophistication.

The researchers conclude that there's something missing in the Origami genome, but as far as Derek's concerned, the fault lies with them. They're blind to a simple truth: complex minds can't develop on their own. If they could, feral children would be like any others. And minds don't grow the way weeds do, flourishing under indifferent attention; otherwise all children in orphanages would thrive. For a mind to even approach its full potential, it needs cultivation by other minds. That cultivation is what he's trying to provide for Marco and Polo.

Marco and Polo occasionally get into arguments, but they don't stay angry for very long. A few days ago, however, the two of them got into a fight over whether it was fair that Marco had been instantiated earlier than Polo, and for some reason it escalated. The two digients have hardly spoken to each other since, so Derek's relieved when they approach him as a pair.

"It's nice to see you two together again. Have you guys made up?"

"No!" says Polo. "Still angry."

"I'm sorry to hear that."

"Both us want your help," says Marco.

"Okay, what can I do?"

"Want you roll back us last week, before big fight."

"What?" This is the first time he's ever heard of a digient requesting to be restored from a checkpoint. "Why would you want that?"

"I want not remember big fight," says Marco.

"I want be happy, not angry," says Polo. "You want us be happy, right?"

Derek opts not to get into a discussion about the difference between their current instantiations and instantiations restored from a checkpoint. "Of course I do, but I can't just roll you back every time you have a fight. Just wait awhile, and you won't be so angry."

"Have waited, and still angry," says Polo. "Fight big big. Want it never happen."

As soothingly as he can, Derek says, "Well, it did happen, and you're going to have to deal with it."

"No!" shouts Polo. "I angry angry! Want you fix it!"

"Why you want us stay angry forever?" demands Marco.

"I don't want you to stay angry forever; I want you to forgive each other. But if you can't, then we'll all have to live with that, me included."

"Now angry at you too!" says Polo.

The digients storm off in different directions, and he wonders if he's made the right decision. It hasn't always been easy raising Marco and Polo, but he's never rolled them back to an earlier checkpoint. This strategy has worked well enough so far, but he can't be certain it will keep working.

There are no guidebooks on raising digients, and techniques intended for pets or children fail as often as they succeed. The digients inhabit simple bodies, so their voyage to maturity is free from the riptides and sudden squalls driven by an organic body's hormones, but this doesn't mean that they don't experience moods or that their personalities never change; their minds are continuously edging into new regions of the phase space defined by the Neuroblast genome. Indeed, it's possible that the digients will never reach "maturity"; the idea of a developmental plateau is based on a biological model that doesn't necessarily apply. It's possible their personalities will evolve at the same rate for as long as the digients are kept running. Only time will tell.

Derek wants to talk about what just happened with Marco and Polo; unfortunately, the person he wants to talk to isn't his wife. Wendy understands the possibilities for the digients' growth and recognizes that Marco and Polo will become more and more capable the longer they're cared for; she simply can't generate any enthusiasm about that prospect. Resentful of the time and attention he devotes to the digients, she would consider their request to be rolled back the perfect opportunity to suspend them for an indefinite period.

The person he wants to talk to is, of course, Ana. What once seemed a groundless fear of Wendy's has come true; he has definitely developed feelings for her beyond friendship. It's not the cause of the problems he's having with Wendy; if anything, it's a result. The time he spends with Ana is a relief, a chance for him to enjoy the digients' company unapologetically. When he's angry he thinks it's Wendy's fault for driving him away, but when he's calm he realizes that's unfair.

The important thing is that he hasn't acted on his feelings for Ana, and he doesn't plan to. What he needs to focus on is reaching an accord with Wendy regarding the digients; if he can do that, the temptation that Ana poses should pass. Until then, he ought to reduce the amount of time he spends with Ana. It's not going to be easy: given how small the digient-owner community is, interaction with Ana is inevitable, and he can't let Marco and Polo suffer because of this. He's not sure what to do, but for now, he refrains from calling Ana for advice and posts a question to the forum instead.

5

Another year passes. Currents within the mantle of the marketplace change, and virtual worlds undergo tectonic shifts in response: a new platform called Real Space, implemented using the latest distributed-processing architecture, becomes the hotspot of digital terrain formation. Meanwhile Anywhere and Next Dimension stop expanding at their edges, cooling into a stable configuration. Data Earth has long been a fixture in the universe of virtual worlds, resistant to growth spurts or sharp downturns, but now its topography begins to erode; one by one, its virtual landmasses disappear like real islands, vanishing beneath a rising tide of consumer indifference.

Meanwhile, the failure of the hothouse experiments to produce miniature civilizations has caused general interest in digital life-forms to dwindle. Occasionally curious new fauna are observed in the biomes, a species demonstrating an exotic body plan or a novel reproductive strategy, but it's generally agreed that the biomes aren't run at a high-enough resolution for real intelligence to evolve there. The companies that make the Origami and Fabergé genomes go into decline. Many technology pundits declare digients to be a dead end, proof that embodied AI is useless for anything beyond entertainment, until the introduction of a new genomic engine called Sophonce.

Sophonce's designers wanted digients that could be taught via software instead of needing interaction with humans; toward that end, they've created an engine that favors asocial behavior and obsessive personalities. The vast majority of the digients generated with the engine are discarded for their psychological malformations, but a tiny fraction prove capable of learning with minimal supervision: give them the right tutoring software, and they'll happily study for weeks of subjective time, meaning that they can be run at hothouse speeds without going feral. Some hobbyists demonstrate Sophonce digients that outperform Neuroblast, Origami, and Faberge digients on math tests, despite having been trained with far less real-time interaction.

There's speculation that, if their energies can be aimed in a practical direction, Sophonce digients could become useful workers within a matter of months. The problem is that they're so charmless that few people want to engage in even the limited amounts of interaction that the digients require.

. . .

Ana has brought Jax along with her to Siege of Heaven, the first new game continent to appear in Data Earth in a year. She shows him around the Argent Plaza, where players congregate and socialize in between missions; it's a massive courtyard of white marble, lapis lazuli, and gold filigree located on top of a cumulonimbus cloud. Ana has to wear her game avatar, a kestrel-cherub, but Jax keeps his traditional copper robot avatar.

As they're strolling among the other gamers, Ana sees the on-screen annotation for a digient. His avatar is a hydrocephalic dwarf, the standard avatar for a Drayta: a Sophonce digient who's skilled at solving the logic puzzles found on the gaming continents. The original Drayta's owner trained him using a puzzle generator pirated from the Five Dynasties continent on the Real Space platform and then released copies to the public domain. Now so many game players take a Drayta with them on their missions that game companies are considering major redesigns.

Ana directs Jax's attention to the other digient. "See the guy over there? He's a Drayta."

"Really?" Jax has heard about Draytas, but this is the first one he's met. He walks over to the dwarf. "Hi," he says. "I'm Jax."

"Wanna solve puzzles," says Drayta.

"What kind puzzles you like?"

"Wanna solve puzzles." Drayta is getting anxious; he runs around the waiting area. "Wanna solve *puzzles.*"

A nearby gamer wearing an osprey-seraph avatar pauses in his conversation to point a finger at Drayta; the digient freezes in midstep, shrinks to an icon, and snaps into one of the gamer's belt compartments as if pulled by an elastic.

"Drayta weird," says Jax.

"Yes, he was, wasn't he?"

"All Draytas like that?"

"I think so."

The seraph walks over to Ana. "What kind of digient have you got? Haven't seen his sort before."

"His name's Jax. He runs on the Neuroblast genome."

"Don't know that one. Is it new?"

One of the seraph's teammates, wearing a Nephilim avatar, comes by. "Nah, it's old, last generation."

The seraph nods. "Is he good at puzzles?"

"Not really," says Ana.

"So what does he do?"

"I like singing," volunteers Jax.

"Really? Let's have a song, then."

Jax doesn't need further encouragement; he launches into one of his favorites, "Mack the Knife" from *Threepenny Opera*. He knows all the words, but the tune he sings is at best a rough approximation of the actual melody. At the same time he performs an accompanying dance that he choreographed himself, mostly a series of poses and hand gestures borrowed from an Indonesian hip-hop video he likes.

The other gamers laugh all through his performance. Jax finishes with a curtsy, and they applaud. "That's brilliant," says the seraph.

Ana says to Jax, "That means he likes it. Say thanks."

"Thanks."

To Ana, the seraph says, "Not going to be much help in the labyrinths, is he?"

"He keeps us entertained," she says.

"I'll bet he does. Send me a message if he ever learns to solve puzzles; I'll buy a copy." He sees that his entire team has assembled. "Well, off to our next mission. Good luck on yours."

"Good luck," says Jax. He waves as the seraph and his teammates take flight and dive in formation toward a distant valley.

Ana's reminded of that encounter a few days later, when she's reading a discussion on the user-group forums:

....

From: Stuart Gust
     Last night I played SoH with some people who take a Drayta on their missions, and while he wasn't much fun, he was definitely useful to have around. It made me wonder if it has to be one or the other. Those Sophonce digients aren't any better than ours. Couldn't our digients be both fun *and* useful?

....

From: Maria Zheng
     Are you hoping to sell copies of yours? You think you can raise a better Andro?
....

Maria's referring to a Sophonce digient named Andro, trained by his owner, Bryce Talbot, to act as his personal assistant. Talbot demonstrated Andro to VirlFriday, maker of appointment-management software, and got the company's executives interested. The deal fell through after the executives got demonstration copies; what Talbot hadn't realized was that Andro was, in his own way, as obsessive as Drayta. Like a dog forever loyal to its first owner, Andro wouldn't work for anyone else unless Talbot was there to give orders. VirlFriday tried installing a sensory-input filter so each new Andro instantiation perceived his new owner's avatar and voice as Talbot's, but the disguise never worked for more than a couple of hours. Before long, all the executives had to shut down their forlorn Andros, who kept looking for the original Talbot.

As a result, Talbot wasn't able to sell the rights to Andro for anywhere near what he'd hoped. Instead, VirlFriday bought the rights to Andro's specific genome and a complete archive of his checkpoints, and they've hired Talbot to work for them. He's part of a team that's restoring earlier checkpoints of Andro and retraining them, attempting to create a version that has the same personal-assistant skills and is also willing to accept a new owner.

....

From: Stuart Gust

No, I don't mean selling copies. I'm just thinking about Zaff doing work the way dogs guide the blind or sniff out drugs. My goal isn't to make money, but if there's something the digients can do that people are willing to pay for, it would prove to all the skeptics out there that digients aren't just for entertainment.

....

Ana posts a reply:

....

From: Ana Alvarado

I just want to make sure we're clear about our motivations. It'd be terrific if our digients learned practical skills, but we shouldn't think of them as failures if they don't. Maybe Jax can make money, but Jax isn't *for* making money. He's not like the Draytas, or the weedbots. Whatever puzzles he might solve or work he might do, those aren't the reason I'm raising him.

....

From: Stuart Gust

Yes, I agree with that completely. All I meant was that our digients might have untapped skills. If there's some kind of job they'd be good at, wouldn't it be cool for them to do that job?

....

From: Maria Zheng

But what can they do? Dogs were bred to be good at specific things, and Sophonce digients are so single-minded that they only want to do one thing, whether they're good at it or not. Neither is true for Neuroblast digients.

....

From: Stuart Gust

We could expose them to lots of different things and see what they have an aptitude for. Give them a liberal arts education instead of vocational training. (I'm only half kidding.)

....

From: Ana Alvarado

That's actually not as silly as it might sound. Bonobos have learned to do everything from making stone-cutting tools to playing computer games when they were given the chance. Our digients might be good at things that it hasn't occurred to us to train them for.

....

From: Maria Zheng

Just what are we talking about? We've already taught them to read. Are we going to give them lessons in science and history? Are we going to teach them critical-thinking skills?

....

From: Ana Alvarado

I really don't know. But I think that if we do this, it's important to have an open mind and not be skeptical. Low expectations are a self-fulfilling prophecy. If we aim high, we'll get better results.

....

Most of the user-group members are content with their digients' current education—an improvised mixture of homeschooling, group tutoring, and eduware—but there are some who are excited by the idea of going further. This latter group begins a discussion with their digients' tutors about expanding the curriculum. Over the course of months, various owners read up on pedagogical theory and try to determine how the digients' learning style differs from that of chimps or human children, and how to design lesson plans that best accommodate it. Most of the time the owners are receptive to all suggestions, until the question arises of whether the digients might make faster progress if their tutors assigned them homework.

Ana prefers that they find activities that develop skills but which the digients enjoy enough to do on their own. Other owners argue that the tutors ought to give the digients actual assignments to be completed. She's surprised to read a forum post from Derek in which he supports the idea. She asks him about it the next time they talk.

"Why would you want to make them do homework?"

"What's wrong with that?" says Derek. "Is this because you once had a mean teacher when you were a kid?"

"Very funny. Come on, I'm serious."

"Okay, seriously: What's so bad about homework?"

She hardly knows where to begin. "It's one thing for Jax to have ways to keep himself entertained outside of class," she says. "But to give him assignments and tell him he has to finish them even if he doesn't enjoy it? To make him feel bad if he doesn't do it? That goes against every principle of animal training."

"A long time ago, you were the one who told me that digients weren't like animals."

"Yes, I did say that," she allows. "But they're not tools either. And I know you know that, but what you're talking about, it sounds like you're preparing them to do work that they wouldn't want to do."

He shakes his head. "It's not about making them work, it's about getting them to learn some responsibility. And they might be strong enough to take feeling bad once in a while; the only way to know is to try."

"Why take the chance of making them feel bad at all?"

"It was something I thought of when I was talking with my sister," he says. Derek's sister teaches children born with Down syndrome. "She mentioned that some parents don't want to push their kids too much, because they're afraid of exposing them to the possibility of failure. The parents mean well, but they're keeping their kids from reaching their full potential when they coddle them."

It takes her a little time to get used to this idea. Ana's accustomed to thinking of the digients as supremely gifted apes, and while in the past people have compared apes to children with special needs, it was always more of a metaphor. To view the digients more literally as special-needs children requires a shift in perspective. "How much responsibility do you think the digients can handle?"

Derek spreads his hands. "I don't know. In a way it's like Down syndrome; it affects every person differently, so whenever my sister works with a new kid, she has to play it by ear. We have even less to go on, because no one's ever raised digients for this long before. If it turns out that the only thing we're accomplishing with homework assignments is making them feel bad, then of course we'll stop. But I don't want Marco and Polo's potential to be wasted because I was afraid of pushing them a little."

She sees that Derek has a very different idea of high expectations than she has. More than that, she realizes that his is actually the better one. "You're right," she says, after a pause. "We should see if they can do homework."

.   .   .

It's a year later, and Derek is finishing up some work before he meets Ana for lunch on a Saturday. For the last couple of hours he's been testing an avatar modification that would change the proportions of the digients' bodies and faces to make them look more mature. Among those owners who have opted to further their digients' education, more and more are commenting on the incongruity between the digients' eternally cute avatars and their increasing competence. This add-on is intended to correct that and make it easier for the owners to think of the digients as more capable.

Before leaving, he checks his messages and is puzzled to see a couple from strangers accusing him of running some kind of scam. The messages seem legitimate, so he reads them more closely. The senders are complaining about a digient approaching them in Data Earth and asking for money.

Derek realizes what must have happened. He recently began giving Marco and Polo an allowance, which they usually spend on game subscriptions or virtual toys; they've asked for more, but he's held the line. They must have decided to ask people in Data Earth at random for money and been rebuffed, but since the digients are running under Derek's Data Earth account, people assumed that he had trained them to beg for money.

He'll send complete apologies to these people later on, but right now he tells Marco and Polo to enter their robot bodies immediately. Fabrication technology has reached the point where he was able to afford two robot bodies of his own, customized to complement Marco and Polo's avatars. A minute later, their panda-bear faces appear in the robots' helmets, and Derek reprimands them for asking strangers for money. "I thought you would know better," he says.

Polo is apologetic. "Yes, know better," he says.

"So why did you do it?"

"My idea, not Polo's," says Marco. "Knew they wouldn't give money. Knew they'd message you."

Derek's astonished. "You were trying to get people angry at me?"

"This happen because we on your account," says Marco. "Not happen if we have own accounts, like Voyl."

Now he understands. The digients have been hearing about a Sophonce digient named Voyl. Voyl's owner—a lawyer named Gerald Hecht—filed papers to create the Voyl Corporation, and Voyl now runs under a separate Data Earth account registered to that corporation. Voyl pays taxes and is able to own property, enter into contracts, file lawsuits, and be sued; in many respects he is a legal person, albeit one for whom Hecht technically serves as director.

The idea has been around for a while. Artificial-life hobbyists all agree on the impossibility of digients ever getting legal protection as a class, citing dogs as an example: human compassion for dogs is both deep and wide, but the euthanasia of dogs in pet shelters amounts to an ongoing canine holocaust, and if the courts haven't put a stop to that, they certainly aren't going to grant protection to entities that lack a heartbeat. Given this, some owners believe the most they can hope for is legal protection on an individual basis: by filing articles of incorporation on a specific digient, an owner can take advantage of a substantial body of case law that establishes rights for nonhuman entities. Hecht is the first one to have actually done it.

"So you were trying to make a point," says Derek.

"People say being corporation great," says Marco. "Can do whatever want."

A number of human adolescents have complained that Voyl has more rights than they do; obviously the digients have seen their comments. "Well, you're *not* incorporated, and you definitely *cannot* do anything you want."

"We sorry," says Marco, suddenly appreciating the trouble he's in. "Just want be corporations."

"I told you before: you're not old enough."

"We older Voyl," says Polo.

"Me especially," says Marco.

"Voyl's not old enough for it, either. His owner made a mistake."

"So you not let us be corporations ever?"

Derek gives them a stern look. "Maybe one day, when you're much older; we'll see. But if you two try a stunt like this again, there are going to be serious repercussions. You understand?"

The digients are glum. "Yes," says Marco.

"Yes," says Polo.

"Okay. I've got to go; we'll talk about this more later." Derek scowls at them. "You two get back into Data Earth now."

As he drives to the restaurant, Derek again thinks about what Marco is asking for. A lot of people are skeptical about the idea of digients becoming corporations; they view Hecht's actions as nothing more than a stunt, an impression Hecht only reinforces by issuing press releases about his plans for Voyl. Right now Hecht essentially runs the Voyl Corporation, but he's training Voyl in business law and insists that someday Voyl will make all the decisions himself; the role of director, whether filled by Hecht or by someone else, will be nothing but a formality. In the meantime, Hecht invites people to put Voyl's status as a legal person to the test. Hecht has the resources for a court battle, and he's itching for a fight. So far no one has taken him up on it, but Derek hopes that someone will; he wants the precedents to be well established before he'll consider incorporating Marco and Polo.

Whether Marco or Polo would ever be intellectually capable of becoming corporations is another question, and to Derek's mind a more difficult one to answer. The Neuroblast digients have shown that they can do homework on their own, and he's confident that their attention spans for independent tasks will increase steadily over time, but even if they become able to do sizable projects without supervision, that's still a far cry from being able to make responsible decisions about one's future. And he's not even sure if that level of independence is something he should encourage Marco and Polo to have as a goal. Turning Marco and Polo into corporations opens the door to keeping them running after Derek himself has passed away, which is a worrisome prospect: for Down syndrome individuals, there are organizations that provide assistance to people living on their own, but similar support services don't exist for incorporated digients. It might be better to ensure that Marco and Polo are suspended in the event that Derek can't take care of them.

Whatever he decides to do, he'll have to do it without Wendy; they've decided to file for divorce. The reasons are complicated, of course, but one thing is clear: raising a pair of digients is not what Wendy wants from life, and if Derek wants a partner in this endeavor, he'll have to find someone else. Their marriage counselor has explained that the problem isn't the digients per se, it's the fact that Derek and Wendy can't find a way to accommodate their having different interests. Derek knows the counselor's right, but surely having common interests would have helped.

He doesn't want to get ahead of himself, but he can't stop thinking that getting divorced offers him an opportunity to be more than just friends with Ana. Surely she's considered the possibility, too; after all the time they've known each other, how could she not have? The two of them would make a great team, working together for what's best for their digients.

Not that he plans to declare his feelings at lunch; it's too soon for that, and he knows Ana is seeing someone right now, a guy named Kyle. But their relationship is fast approaching the six-month mark, which is usually when the guy realizes that Jax isn't just a hobby but the major priority in her life; it probably won't be long before the breakup follows. Derek figures that in telling Ana about his divorce, he'll be reminding her that there are other options, that not every guy will think of digients as competition for her attention.

He looks around for Ana in the restaurant, sees her, and waves; she gives him a big grin. When he reaches the table, he says, "You won't believe what Marco and Polo just did." He tells her what happened, and her jaw drops.

"That's amazing," she says. "God, I'll bet Jax has heard the same things they have."

"Yeah, you might want to have a conversation with him when you get home." This leads to talking about the benefits and drawbacks of giving the digients access to social forums. The forums offer richer interaction than the owners can supply by themselves, but not all the influences the digients receive are positive ones.

After they've discussed digients for a while, Ana asks, "So aside from that, what's new with you?"

Derek sighs. "I might as well tell you: Wendy and I are getting divorced."

"Oh no. Derek, I'm so sorry." Her sympathy is genuine, and it warms him.

"It's been a long time coming," he says.

She nods. "Still, I'm sorry it's happening."

"Thanks." He talks for a while about what he and Wendy have agreed upon, how they'll sell the condo and split the proceeds. Thankfully the process is mostly amicable.

"At least she doesn't want copies of Marco and Polo," says Ana.

"Yeah, thank goodness for that," agrees Derek. A spouse can almost always make a copy of a digient, and when a divorce isn't amicable, it's all too easy to use one to get back at one's ex. They've seen it happen on the forums many times.

"Enough of that," says Derek. "Let's talk about something else. What's happening with you?"

"Nothing, really."

"You looked like you were in a good mood until I started talking about Wendy."

"Well, yeah, I was," she admits.

"So is there something in particular that's got you feeling so upbeat?"

"It's nothing."

"Nothing's got you in a good mood?"

"Well, I have some news, but we don't have to talk about it now."

"No, don't be silly, it's fine. If you've got good news, let's hear it."

Ana pauses and then, almost apologetically, says, "Kyle and I have decided to move in together."

Derek is stunned. "Congratulations," he says.

6

Two more years pass. Life goes on.

Occasionally Ana, Derek, and the other education-minded owners have their digients take some standardized tests, to see how they compare with human children. The results vary. The Fabergé digients, being illiterate, can't take written tests, but they seem to be developing well according to other metrics. Among the Origami digients, there's a curious split in the test results, with half continuing to develop over time and half hitting a plateau, possibly due to a quirk in the genome. The Neuroblast digients do reasonably well if they're permitted the same allowances in testing that dyslexic humans are given; while there's variation between the individual digients, as a group their intellectual development continues apace.

What's harder to gauge is their social development, but one encouraging sign is that the digients are socializing with human adolescents in various online communities. Jax becomes interested in tetrabrake, a subculture focused on virtual dance choreography for four-armed avatars; Marco and Polo have each joined a fan club for a serial game drama, and each regularly tries to convince the other of the superiority of his choice. Even though Ana and Derek don't really understand the appeal of these communities, they like the fact that their digients have become part of them. The adolescents who dominate these communities seem unconcerned with the fact that the digients aren't human, treating them as just another kind of online friend they are unlikely to meet in person.

Ana's relationship with Kyle has its ups and downs, but is generally good. They occasionally go out with Derek and whomever he's dating; Derek sees a series of women, but nothing ever becomes serious. He tells Ana that it's because the women he dates don't share his interest in digients, but the truth is that his feelings for Ana refuse to go away.

The economy goes into a recession after the latest flu pandemic, prompting changes in the virtual worlds. Daesan Digital, the company that created the Data Earth platform, makes a joint announcement with Viswa Media, creator of the Real Space platform: Data Earth is becoming part of Real Space. All Data Earth continents will be replaced by identical Real Space versions added to the Real Space universe. They're calling it a merger of two worlds, but it's just a polite way of saying that, after years of upgrades and new versions, Daesan can no longer afford to keep fighting the platform wars.

For most customers, all this means is that they can travel between more virtual locations without logging out and in again. Over the last few years, almost all of the companies whose software runs on Data Earth have created versions that run on Real Space. Gamers who play Siege of Heaven or Elderthorn can simply run a conversion utility, and their inventories of weapons and clothing will be waiting for them on the Real Space versions of the game continents.

One exception, though, is Neuroblast. There isn't a Real Space version of the Neuroblast engine—Blue Gamma folded before the platform was introduced—which means that there's no way for a digient with a Neuroblast genome to enter the Real Space environment. Origami and Fabergé digients experience the migration to Real Space as an expansion of possibilities, but for Jax and the other Neuroblast digients, Daesan's announcement essentially means the end of the world.

.   .   .

Ana is getting ready for bed when she hears the crash. She hurries out to the living room to investigate.

Jax is wearing the robot body, examining his wrist. One of the tiles on the wall display next to him is cracked. He sees Ana enter and says, "I sorry."

"What were you doing?" she asks.

"I very sorry."

"Tell me what you were doing."

Reluctantly, Jax says, "Cartwheel."

"And your wrist gave way and you hit the wall." Ana takes a look at the robot body's wrist. As she feared, it will require replacement. "I don't make these rules because I don't want you to have fun. But this is what happens when you try dancing in the robot body."

"I know you said. But I try little dancing, and body fine. I try little more, and body still fine."

"So you tried a little more, and now we have to buy a new wrist, and a new display tile." She briefly wonders how quickly she can replace them, if she can keep Kyle—who is out of town on business—from finding out about this. A few months ago Jax damaged a piece of sculpture that Kyle loved, and it might be better not to remind him of that incident.

"I very very sorry," says Jax.

"Okay, back to Data Earth." Ana points to the charging platform.

"I admit was mistake—"

"Just go."

Jax dutifully heads over. Just before he steps on the platform, he says quietly, "It not Data Earth." Then the robot body's helmet goes dark.

Jax is complaining about the private version of Data Earth that the Neuroblast user group has set up, duplicating many of the continents from the original. In one respect it's much better than the private island they used as a refuge from the IFF hack, because now processing power is so cheap that they can run dozens of continents. In another respect it's much worse, because those continents are almost entirely devoid of inhabitants.

The problem is not just that all the humans have moved to Real Space. The Origami and Fabergé digients have gone to Real Space, too, and Ana can hardly blame their owners; she'd have done the same, given the opportunity. Even more distressing is that most of the Neuroblast digients are gone as well, including many of Jax's friends. Some members of the user group quit when Data Earth closed; others took a wait-and-see approach but grew discouraged after they saw how impoverished the private Data Earth was, choosing to suspend their digients rather than raise them in a ghost town. And more than anything else, that's what the private Data Earth resembles: a ghost town the size of a planet. There are vast expanses of minutely detailed terrain to wander around in, but no one to talk to except for the tutors who come in to give lessons. There are dungeons without quests, malls without businesses, stadiums without sporting events; it's the digital equivalent of a postapocalyptic landscape.

Jax's human friends from the tetrabrake scene used to log in to the private Data Earth just to visit Jax, but their visits have grown increasingly infrequent; all the tetrabrake events happen on Real Space now. Jax can send and receive choreography recordings, but a major part of the scene is live gatherings where choreography is improvised, and there's no way for him to participate in those. Jax is losing most of his social life in the virtual world, and he can't find one in the real one: his robot body is categorized as an unpiloted free-roaming vehicle, so he's restricted from public spaces unless Ana or Kyle is there to accompany him. Confined to their apartment, he becomes bored and restless.

For weeks Ana tried having Jax sit at her computer in his robot body and log in to Real Space that way, but he refuses to do it anymore. There were difficulties with the user interface— his inexperience with using an actual computer, compounded by the camera's suboptimal tracking of gestures performed by a robot body—but she believes they could have overcome them. The bigger problem is that Jax doesn't want to control an avatar remotely: he wants to *be* the avatar. For him, the keyboard and screen are a miserable substitute for being there, as unsatisfying as a jungle video game would be to a chimpanzee taken from the Congo.

All the remaining Neuroblast digients are having similar frustrations, making it clear that a private Data Earth is only a temporary fix. What's needed is a way to run the digients on Real Space, allowing them to move freely and interact with its objects and inhabitants. In other words, the solution is to port the Neuroblast engine—to rewrite it to run on the Real Space platform. Ana has persuaded Blue Gamma's former owners to release the source code for Neuroblast, but it will take experienced developers to do the rewriting. The user group has posted announcements on open-source forums in an attempt to attract volunteers.

The sole advantage of Data Earth's obsolescence is that their digients are safe from the dark side of the social world. A company called Edgeplayer markets a digient torture chamber on the Real Space platform; to avoid accusations of unauthorized copying, they use only public-domain digients as victims. The user group has agreed that once they get the Neuroblast engine ported, their conversion procedure will include full ownership verification; no Neuroblast digient will ever enter Real Space without someone committed to taking care of it.

. . .

It's two months later, and Derek is browsing the user-group forum, reading the responses to an earlier post of his on the status of the Neuroblast port. Unfortunately, the news was not good; the attempts to recruit developers for the project haven't met with much success. The user group has held open-house events in their private Data Earth so that people could meet the digients, but there have been very few takers.

The problem is that genomic engines are old news. Developers are drawn to new, exciting projects, and right now that means working on neural interfaces or nanomedical software. There are scores of genomic engines languishing in various states of incompletion on the open-source repositories, all in need of volunteer programmers, and the prospect of porting the dozen-year-old Neuroblast engine to a new platform may be the least exciting of them all. Only a handful of students is contributing to the Neuroblast port, and considering how little time they're able to devote, the Real Space platform will itself be obsolete before the port is finished.

The other alternative is to hire professional developers. Derek has talked to some developers with experience in genomic engines and requested quotes on how much it would cost to port Neuroblast. The estimates he's received are reasonable given the complexity of the project, and for a company with several hundred thousand customers, it would make perfect sense to go ahead with it. For a user group whose membership has dwindled down to about twenty people, however, the price is staggering.

Derek reads the latest comments on the discussion forum and then calls up Ana. Having the digients confined to a private Data Earth has definitely been hard, but for him there's also been a silver lining: he and Ana have reason to talk every day now, whether it's about the status of the Neuroblast port or trying to organize activities for their digients. Over the last few years Marco and Polo had drifted away from Jax as they all pursued their own interests, but now the Neuroblast digients have only one another for company, so he and Ana try to find things for them to do as a group. He no longer has a wife who might complain about this, and Ana's boyfriend, Kyle, doesn't seem to mind, so he can call her up without recrimination. It's a painful sort of pleasure to spend this much time with her; it might be healthier for him if they interacted less, but he doesn't want to stop.

Ana's face appears in the phone window. "Have you seen Stuart's post?" Derek asks. Stuart pointed out what each person would have to pay if they divided the cost evenly, and asked how many of the members could afford that much.

"I just read it," says Ana. "Maybe he thinks he's being helpful, but all he's doing is getting people anxious."

"I agree," he says. "But until we come up with a good alternative, the per-person cost is what everyone will be thinking about. Have you met with that fund-raiser yet?" Ana was going to talk to a friend of a friend, a woman who has run fund-raising campaigns for wildlife sanctuaries.

"As a matter of fact, I just got back from lunch with her."

"Great! What did you find out?"

"The bad news is she doesn't think we can qualify for non-profit status, because we're only trying to raise money for a specific set of individuals."

"But anyone could use the new engine—" He stops. It's true that there are probably millions of snapshots of Neuroblast digients stored in archives around the world. But the user group can't honestly claim to be working on their behalf; without someone willing to raise them, none of those digients would benefit from a Real Space version of the Neuroblast engine. The only digients the user group is trying to help are its own.

Ana nods without him saying a word; she must have had the

exact same thought earlier. "Okay," says Derek, "we can't be a nonprofit. So what's the good news?"

"She says we can still solicit contributions outside of the nonprofit model. What we need to do is tell a story that generates sympathy for the digients themselves. That's the way some zoos pay for things like surgeries on elephants."

He considers that for a moment. "I guess we could post some videos about the digients, try tugging on people's heartstrings."

"Exactly. And if we can build up enough popular sentiment, we might get contributions of time as well as money. Anything that raises the profiles of the digients will increase our chances of getting volunteers from the open-source community."

"I'll start going through my videos for footage of Marco and Polo," he says. "There's plenty of cute stuff from when they were young; I'm not so sure about the more recent stuff. Or do we need heartrending stuff?"

"We should talk about what would work best," says Ana. "I'll post a message on the forum asking everyone else."

This reminds Derek of something. "By the way, I got a call yesterday that might help us out. It's kind of a long shot, though."

"Who was it?"

"Do you remember the Xenotherians?"

"Those digients that were supposed to be aliens? Is that project still going on?"

"Sort of." He explains that he was contacted by a young man named Felix Radcliffe, who is one of the last participants in the Xenotherian project. Most of the original hobbyists gave up years ago, exhausted by the difficulty of inventing an alien culture from scratch, but there remains a small group of devotees who have become almost monomaniacal. From what Derek has been able to determine, most of them are unemployed and rarely leave their bedrooms in their parents' homes; they live their lives in Data Mars. Felix is the only member of the group willing to initiate contact with outsiders.

"And people call us fanatics," says Ana. "So why did he contact you?"

"He heard we were trying to get Neuroblast ported and wants to help. He recognized my name because I was the one who designed the avatars for them."

"Lucky you," she says, smiling, and Derek makes a face. "Why would he care if Neuroblast gets ported? I thought the whole point of Data Mars was to keep the Xenotherians isolated."

"Originally it was, but now he's decided they're ready to meet human beings, and he wants to conduct a first-contact experiment. If Data Earth were still running, he'd let the Xenotherians send an expedition to the main continents, but that's no longer an option. So Felix is in the same boat as us; he wants Neuroblast ported so his digients can enter Real Space."

"Well . . . I guess I can understand that. And you said he might be able to help with funding?"

"He's trying to generate interest among anthropologists and exobiologists. He thinks they'll want to study the Xenotherians so much they'll pay for the port."

Ana looks dubious. "Would they really pay for something like that?"

"I doubt it," says Derek. "It's not as if the Xenotherians are actually aliens. I think Felix would have better luck with game companies who need aliens to populate their worlds, but it's his decision. I figure that as long as he doesn't approach any of the people we're contacting, he won't hurt our chances, and there's a possibility he can help."

"But if he's as awkward as he sounds, how likely is it he can persuade anyone?"

"Well, it wouldn't be with his salesmanship. He's got a video of the Xenotherians that he shows anthropologists, to whet their appetites. He let me see a little bit of it."

"And?"

He shrugs, raises his hands. "I could've been looking at a hive of weedbots for all that I understood."

Ana laughs. "Well, maybe that's good. Maybe the more alien they are, the more interesting they'll be."

Derek laughs, too, imagining the irony: after all the work they did at Blue Gamma to make digients appealing, what if it turns out that the alien ones are what people are more interested in?

7

Another two months go by. The user group's attempts at fund-raising don't meet with much success; the charitably inclined are growing fatigued of hearing about natural endangered species, let alone artificial ones, and digients aren't nearly as photogenic as dolphins. The flow of donations has never risen above a trickle.

The stress of being confined to Data Earth is definitely taking a toll on the digients; the owners try to spend more time with them to keep them from getting bored, but it's no substitute for a fully populated virtual world. Ana also tries to shield Jax from the problems surrounding the Neuroblast port, but he's aware of them nonetheless. One day when she comes home from work, she logs in to find him visibly agitated.

"Want ask you about porting," he says, with no prelude.

"What about it?"

"Before thought it just another upgrade, like before. Now think it much bigger. More like uploading, except with digients instead people, right?"

"Yes, I suppose it is."

"You seen video with mouse?"

Ana knows the one Jax is referring to: newly released by an uploading research team, it shows a white mouse being flash-frozen and then vaporized, one micrometer at a time, into curls of smoke by a scanning electron beam, and then instantiated in a test scape where it's virtually thawed and awakened. The mouse immediately has a seizure, convulsing piteously for a couple of subjective minutes before it dies. It's currently the record holder for longest survival time for an uploaded mammal.

"Nothing like that will happen to you," she assures him.

"You mean I not remember if happens," says Jax. "I only remember if transition successful."

"No one's going to run you, or anyone else, on an untested engine. When Neuroblast has been ported, we'll run test suites on it and fix all the bugs before we run a digient. Those test suites don't feel anything."

"Researchers ran test suites before they uploaded mice?"

Jax is good at asking the tough questions. "The mice were the test suites," Ana admits. "But that's because no one has the source code to organic brains, so they can't write test suites that are simpler than real mice. We have the source code for Neuroblast, so we don't have that problem."

"But you don't have money afford port."

"No, not right now, but we're going to get it." She hopes she sounds more confident than she feels.

"How I help? How I make money?"

"Thanks, Jax, but right now there isn't a way for you to make money," she says. "For now your job is to just keep studying and do well in your classes."

"Yes, know that: now study, later do other things. What if now I get loan, then pay back later when earn money?"

"Let me worry about that, Jax."

Jax looks glum. "Okay."

In fact, what Jax suggests is almost exactly what the user group has attempted recently by looking for corporate investors. It's an avenue opened up by VirlFriday's success in selling digients as personal assistants. It took several years, but Talbot finally managed to raise an instance of Andro that would work for anyone; VirlFriday has sold hundreds of thousands of copies. It's the first demonstration that a digient can actually be profitable, and several other companies are looking to duplicate Talbot's achievement.

One of those companies is called Polytope, which has announced plans for launching an enormous breeding program to create the next Andro. The user group contacted them and offered them a stake in the Neuroblast digients' future: in exchange for paying to port the Neuroblast engine, Polytope would get a percentage of any income generated by the digients in perpetuity. The group was more hopeful than it had been in months, but the company's answer was no; the only digients that Polytope is interested in are Sophonce digients, whose obsessive focus is a necessity if they're going to replace conventional software.

The user group has briefly discussed the possibility of paying for the port out of their own pockets, but it's clearly not feasible. As a result, some members are considering the unthinkable:

....

From: Stuart Gust

I hate being the one to bring this up, but someone has to. What about temporarily suspending the digients for a year or so, until we've raised the money for the port?

....

From: Derek Brooks

You know what happens when anyone suspends their digient. Temporary becomes indefinite becomes permanent.

....

From: Ana Alvarado

I couldn't agree more. It's just too easy to get into perpetual postponement mode. Have you ever heard of anyone restarting a digient that they'd suspended for more than six months? I haven't.

....

From: Stuart Gust

But we're not like those people. They suspended their digients because they were tired of them. We'll miss our digients every day that they're suspended; it'll be an incentive for us to raise the money.

....

From: Ana Alvarado

If you think suspending Zaff will increase your motivation, go ahead. Keeping Jax awake is what keeps me motivated.

....

Ana has no doubts when she posts her reply on the forum, but the conversation is more difficult when, a few days later, Jax brings up the issue himself. The two of them are in the private Data Earth, where she is showing him around a new game continent. It's a classic, one that Ana enjoyed years ago, and it's recently been released for free, so the user group instantiated a copy for the digients. She tries to convey her enthusiasm for it, pointing out what distinguishes it from the other game continents that the digients have grown bored with, but Jax sees the continent for what it is: yet another attempt to keep him occupied while they wait for Neuroblast to be ported.

As they walk through a deserted medieval town square, Jax says, "Sometimes wish I just be suspended, not have to wait more. Restarted when I can enter Real Space, feel like no time passed."

The comment catches Ana off guard. None of the digients has access to the user-group forums, so Jax must have come up with the idea on his own. "Do you really want that?" she asks.

"Not really. Want stay awake, know what happening. But sometimes get frustrated." Then he asks, "You sometimes wish you don't have take care me?"

She makes sure Jax is looking her in the face before she replies. "My life might be simpler if I didn't have you to take care of, but it wouldn't be as happy. I love you, Jax."

"Love you too."

· · ·

Driving home from work, Derek gets a message from Ana saying that she'd been contacted by someone at Polytope, so as soon as he gets home he calls her. "So what happened?" he asks.

Ana looks bemused. "It was a very strange call."

"Strange how?"

"They're offering me a job."

"Really? Doing what?"

"Training their Sophonce digients," she says. "Because of all my previous experience, they want me to be the team leader. They offered a great salary, three years guaranteed employment, and a signing bonus that's, frankly, fabulous. There's a catch, though."

"Well? Don't keep me in suspense."

"All their trainers are required to use InstantRapport."

Derek's eyes widen. "You're kidding," he says. InstantRapport is one of the smart transdermals, a patch that delivers doses of an oxytocin-opioid cocktail whenever the wearer is in the presence of a specific person. It's used to strengthen rocky marriages and strained parent-child relationships, and it's recently become available without a prescription. "What the hell for?"

"They figure that affection will produce better results, and the only way trainers will feel affection for Sophonce digients is with pharmaceutical intervention."

"Oh, I get it. It's a way to increase employee productivity." He knows plenty of people who take nootropics or use transcranial magnetic stimulation to boost their performance at work, but so far no employer has made it a requirement. He shakes his head in disbelief. "If their digients are so hard to love, you would think they'd take a hint and switch to Neuroblast digients."

"I said something similar to them, but they weren't interested. I had an idea, though." Ana leans forward. "I might be able to change their minds if I go work for them."

"How do you figure?"

"It'd be an opportunity to show Jax to Polytope's management on an ongoing basis. I could log in to our private Data Earth from work, maybe even bring him in wearing the robot body. What better way to demonstrate how versatile the Neuroblast engine is? And once they realize that, they'll port it to Real Space."

Derek considers it. "Assuming they don't forbid you from spending time with Jax during work hours—"

"Give me some credit. I wouldn't give them the hard sell; I'd be subtle about it."

"It might work," he says. "But they'd make you wear the InstantRapport patch. Is the chance worth that?"

Ana gives a frustrated shrug. "I don't know. It sure as hell isn't my first choice. But sometimes we have to take a chance, right? Push things a little."

He isn't sure what to say. "What does Kyle think about it?"

She sighs. "He's totally against it. He doesn't like the idea of me taking InstantRapport, and he definitely doesn't think the chances are good enough to justify it." She pauses, and then says, "But he doesn't feel the same way about digients that you or I do, so of course he'd say that. For him, the payoff doesn't seem that big."

Ana's clearly expecting support and he obliges, but privately his thoughts are more conflicted. He has reservations about what she's proposing, but he's hesitant about saying so.

He hates that he has such thoughts, but on the occasions that Ana has mentioned having difficulties with Kyle, he daydreams about the two of them splitting up. He's told himself that he would never do anything to drive them apart, but if Kyle doesn't share Ana's commitment to the digients, Derek isn't doing anything wrong by showing that he does. If that suggests to Ana that he's a better match for her than Kyle, he can't be blamed for that.

The question is whether he really thinks it's a good idea for

Ana to accept Polytope's job offer. He's not sure he does, but until he's sure, he's going to be supportive.

After he gets off the phone, Derek logs on to the private Data Earth to spend time with Marco and Polo. They're playing a game of zero-G racquetball, but descend from the court when they see him.

"Met nice visitors today," says Marco.

"Really? Do you know who they were?"

"Person name Jennifer, and person name Roland."

Derek checks the visitor log and is dismayed by what he sees: Jennifer Chase and Roland Michaels are employees of a company called Binary Desire, maker of sex dolls both virtual and physical.

This isn't the first time the user group has received an inquiry from someone wanting to use the digients for sex. The vast majority of sex dolls are still controlled by conventional software to enact scripted scenarios, but for as long as there have been digients, there have been people trying to have sex with them; the typical procedure is to copy a public-domain digient and reconfigure its reward map so that it enjoys whatever its owner finds arousing. Critics consider it the equivalent of having a dog lick peanut butter off your genitals, and it's not an unfair comparison, either in terms of the intelligence of the digients or the sophistication of the training. Certainly there aren't any digients remotely as person-like as Marco or Polo available for sex right now, so the user group gets occasional inquiries from sex-doll makers interested in purchasing copies of the digients. Everyone in the group has agreed that they should ignore such inquiries.

But according to the log, Chase and Michaels were escorted in by Felix Radcliffe.

Derek tells Marco and Polo to resume their game and then

calls Felix. "What the hell were you thinking? Bringing in Binary Desire?"

"They did not attempt to sex the digients."

"I can see that." He has the recording of their visit playing at double speed in another window.

"They had conversation with them."

Talking to Felix sometimes feels like addressing an alien. "We had an understanding about sex-doll makers. Do you remember that?"

"These people are not like the others. I like the way they think."

He's afraid to ask what that means. "If you like them, bring them to Data Mars and show them your Xenotherians."

"I did show them," says Felix. "They were not interested."

Of course they weren't, Derek realizes; the demand for sex with Lojban-speaking tripods would be microscopic. But he sees that Felix is being honest, that it wouldn't bother him to prostitute the Xenotherians if it would help finance his first-contact experiment. Felix may be eccentric, but he's not a hypocrite.

"Then that should have been the end of it," he says. "We may have to ban you from Data Earth."

"You should talk to these people."

"No, we shouldn't."

"They will pay you for listening to them. They will send a message containing the specifics."

Derek almost laughs. Binary Desire must be pretty desperate if they're paying people to listen to a sales pitch. "Messages are fine. But I'm putting those people on the ban list, and I don't want you bringing in anyone else from a sex-doll maker. Is that clear?"

"That is clear," says Felix, and hangs up.

Derek shakes his head. Normally he wouldn't consider listening to such a sales pitch, even for money, because he doesn't want to give the impression that he'd be willing to sell Marco and Polo as sex objects.

But right now the user group needs every dollar it can get. If listening to one company's presentation could encourage other companies to pay for the same opportunity, then it might be worthwhile. He restarts the video of the visitors' meeting with the digients and watches it at regular speed.

8

The user group has gathered to listen to Binary Desire's presentation via videoconferencing; Binary Desire has made a payment to an escrow service, and the funds will be released after the meeting. Seated at the focus of her wraparound screen, Ana looks around her; everyone's video feeds are integrated so that the user group appears to be gathered in a virtual auditorium, each sitting in a tiny private balcony. Derek's sitting in the balcony to her left, and Felix in turn is to his left. At the podium onstage is Binary's representative Jennifer Chase. Her image on-screen is blond and beautiful and tastefully dressed, and because the parties have agreed to use authenticated video, Ana knows this is how Chase actually looks. She wonders if Binary Desire assigns Chase to do all their negotiations; the woman is probably very good at getting what she asks for.

Felix stands up in his seat and starts to say something in Lojban before catching himself. "You will like what she will say," he says.

"Thank you, Felix, but let me take it from here," says Chase. Felix sits back down, and Chase addresses the group.

"Thank you for agreeing to meet with me. Typically when I meet with a prospective business partner, I talk about how Binary Desire can help them reach a wider market than they can themselves, but I'm not going to do that with you. My goal for this meeting is to assure you that your digients will be treated with respect. We don't want pets that have been sexualized through simple operant conditioning. We want beings that engage in sex at a higher, more personal level."

Stuart calls out, "How do you expect to get that when our digients are completely asexual?"

Chase doesn't miss a beat. "With two years of training, minimum."

Ana's surprised. "That's a major investment," she says. "I thought digient sex dolls were usually trained for a couple of weeks."

"That's because they're usually Sophonce digients, and they don't become better sex partners in two years than they do in two weeks. I don't know if you've seen the results, but if you're curious, I can tell you where you can find a harem of Draytas dressed in Marilyn Monroe avatars, all bleating *Wanna suck dick*. It's not pretty."

Ana laughs despite herself, as do several others in the group. "No, it doesn't sound like it."

"That's not what Binary Desire is looking for. Anyone can take a public-domain digient and reconfigure its reward map. We want to offer sex partners with real personality, and we're willing to invest the effort needed to create that."

"So what would your training entail?" asks Helen Costas, from the back.

"First off, sexual discovery and exploration. We'd give the digients anatomically correct avatars and let them get accustomed to having erogenous zones. We'd encourage the digients to begin sexual experimentation with one another, so they can get some practice as sexual beings and choose a gender they're comfortable with. Since much of the learning during that phase will occur purely among themselves, there may be periods when the digients can be run at faster than real time. Once they've acquired a reasonable amount of experience, we'll begin bonding them with compatible human partners."

"What makes you so sure they'll bond with a specific human?" asks Derek.

"Our developers have examined some of the digients in the shelters; they're too young for our purposes, but they've developed emotional attachments, and our developers have done enough analysis that they believe they can induce similar attachments in older digients. As the digient gets to know a human, we'll enhance the emotional dimension of their interactions, both sexual and nonsexual, so they'll generate love in the digient."

"Like a Neuroblast version of InstantRapport," says Ana.

"Something like that," says Chase, "but more effective and specific, because it'll be custom tuned. For the digient, it will be indistinguishable from falling in love spontaneously."

"That custom tuning doesn't sound like something you'll be able to get right on the first try," says Ana.

"No, of course not," says Chase. "We expect that it will take months for a digient to fall in love; throughout that period we'll be working with the customer, rolling the digient back to checkpoints and trying different adjustments until the emotional bond is firmly established. It'll be like the breeding program you managed when you worked at Blue Gamma; we're just tailoring it for the individual customer."

Ana's about to say that it's very different, but decides not to. All she needs to do is listen to the woman's sales pitch, not refute it. "I can see what you mean," she says.

Derek says, "Even if you can make them fall in love, none of our digients is going to be a convincing Marilyn Monroe."

"No, but that's not our goal. The avatars we'd give them would be humanoid, but not human. You see, we're not trying to duplicate the experience of sex with a human being; we want to provide nonhuman partners that are charming, affectionate, and genuinely enthusiastic about sex. Binary Desire believes this is a new sexual frontier."

"A new sexual frontier?" says Stuart. "You mean popularizing a kink until it becomes mainstream."

"You could call it that," says Chase. "But try looking at it another way: our ideas of what constitutes healthy sex have always broadened over time. People used to think homosexuality, BDSM, and polyamory were all symptoms of psychological problems, but there's nothing intrinsic about those activities that's incompatible with a loving relationship. The problem was having one's desires stigmatized by society. We believe that in time, digient sex will likewise be accepted as a valid expression of sexuality. But that requires being open and honest about it, and not pretending that a digient is a human."

An icon appears on-screen indicating that Chase has transmitted a document to the group. "I'm sending you a copy of the contract we're proposing," she says, "but let me give you a summary. Binary Desire will cover the costs of porting Neuroblast to Real Space in exchange for nonexclusive rights to your digients. You retain the right to make and sell copies of your digients as long as they don't compete with ours. If your digients sell well, we'll also pay royalties. And your digients will enjoy what they do."

"Okay, thank you," Ana says. "We'll take a look at the contract and let you know. Is that all?"

Chase smiles. "Not quite. Before I release the funds, I'd like the chance to address any concerns you might have; I assure you I won't be offended. Is it the sexual aspect that you have reservations about?"

Ana hesitates, and then says, "No, it's the coercion."

"There wouldn't be any coercion. The bonding process ensures the digients will enjoy it as much as their owners."

"But you're not giving them any choice about what they enjoy."

"Is it so different for humans? When I was a little girl, the idea of kissing a boy was completely uninteresting, and if it'd been up to me, that would never have changed." Chase gives a slight, coy smile, as if to suggest how much she enjoys kissing now. "We become sexual beings whether we want to or not. The modifications Binary Desire would make to the digients aren't any different. In fact, they'll be better. Some people get saddled with sexual proclivities that cause them a lifetime of grief. That's not going to happen to the digients. As far as each digient is concerned, it's going to be paired up with a perfectly compatible sex partner. That's not coercion; that's ultimate sexual fulfillment."

"But it's not real," Ana blurts out, and immediately regrets it.

It's precisely the opening Chase was looking for. "How is it not?" she asks. "Your feelings for your digients are real; their feelings for you are real. If you and your digient can have a non-sexual connection that's real, why should a sexual connection between a human and a digient be any less real?"

Ana's at a loss for words momentarily, and Derek steps in. "We could argue philosophy forever," he says. "The bottom line is we didn't spend years raising our digients to have them become sex toys."

"I realize that," says Chase. "And making this deal won't prevent copies of your digients from going on to other things. But right now your digients, amazing as they are, have no marketable job skills, and you can't predict when they'll get any. How else are you going to raise the money you need?"

How many women have asked themselves the same question, Ana wonders. "So it's the oldest profession."

"That's one way to put it, but let me again point out that the digients won't be subjected to any coercion, not even economic coercion. If we wanted to sell faked sexual desire, there are cheaper ways we could do it. The whole point of this enterprise is to create an alternative to fake desire. We believe that sex is better when both parties enjoy it; better as an experience, and better for society."

"That all sounds very noble. What about people who are into sexual torture?"

"We don't condone any nonconsensual sex acts, and that includes sex with digients. The contract I've sent you guarantees that Binary Desire will retain the circuit breakers that Blue Gamma initially installed, enforced with state-of-the-art access control. As I said, we believe sex is better when both parties enjoy it. We're committed to that."

"You approve, correct?" Felix says to the group. "They anticipate all possibilities."

Several of the user-group members glare at him, and even Chase's expression indicates that she'd rather do without Felix's help.

"I know that this wasn't what you were hoping for when you began looking for investors," says Chase. "But if you can see past your initial reaction, I think you'll agree that what we're proposing will be to everyone's advantage."

"We'll think about it and get back to you," says Derek.

"Thank you for listening to my presentation," says Chase. A window pops up on-screen, indicating that the funds have been released from escrow. "Let me say one last thing. If you're approached by another company, be sure to look at the fine print. It will probably include a clause that our lawyers wanted us to include, one that gives them the right to resell your digients to another company, with the circuit breakers disabled. I expect you know what that means?"

Ana nods; it meant that the digients might get resold to a company like Edgeplayer for use as torture victims. "Yes, we do."

"Binary Desire overruled our lawyers' recommendation on that. Our contract guarantees that the digients won't be used for anything but noncoercive sex, ever. See if anyone else will make you that same guarantee."

"Thank you," says Ana. "We'll be in touch."

. . .

Ana went into the meeting with Binary Desire with the attitude that it was purely pro forma, a way to make some money by listening to a sales pitch. Now, having heard the pitch, she finds that she's thinking about it a lot.

She hasn't paid attention to the world of virtual sex since she was in college, when a college boyfriend spent a semester abroad. They bought the peripherals together before he left, discreet hard-shell accessories with hilarious silicone interiors, and digitally locked each device with the other's serial number, a fidelity guarantee for their virtual genitals. Their first few sessions were unexpectedly fun, but it didn't take long for the novelty to wear off and the shortcomings of the technology to become blatant. Sex without kissing was woefully incomplete, and she missed having her face an inch away from his, feeling the weight of his body, smelling his musk; seeing each other on a video screen couldn't replace that, no matter how close the camera was. Her skin hungered for his in a way that no peripheral could satisfy; by semester's end she felt like she was going to burst at the seams. The technology has undoubtedly improved since then, but it's still an impoverished medium for intimacy.

Ana remembers how much of a difference it made the first time she saw Jax wearing a physical body. If a digient were inhabiting a doll, would that make the idea of sex more appealing? No. She's had her face right up against Jax's face, cleaning smudges off his lenses or inspecting scratches, and it's nothing like being close to a person; with a digient there's no feeling of a personal space being entered, not even the trust signified when a dog lets you rub its belly. At Blue Gamma they'd chosen not to put that kind of physical self-protectiveness into the digients—it didn't make sense for their product—but what does physical intimacy mean if there aren't those barriers to overcome? She doesn't doubt that it's possible to give a digient an arousal response close enough to human that both parties' mirror neurons would kick in. But could Binary Desire teach a digient about the vulnerability that came with being naked, and what you were telling someone with your willingness to be naked in their presence?

But maybe none of that matters. Ana replays the recording of the videoconference, listens to Chase saying that it's a new frontier, sex with a nonhuman partner. It's not supposed to be the same as sex with another person, it'll be a different kind of sex, and maybe it'll be accompanied by a different kind of intimacy.

She thinks of an incident that took place when she worked at the zoo, when one of the female orangutans passed away. Everyone was heartbroken, but the orangutan's favorite trainer was particularly inconsolable. Eventually he confessed that he'd been having sex with her, and shortly afterward the zoo fired him. Ana was shocked, of course, but even more so because he wasn't the creepy pervert she imagined a zoophile would be; his grief was as deep and genuine as that of anyone who had lost a lover. He'd been married once, too, which surprised her; she'd assumed such people couldn't get a date, but then she realized she was buying into the stereotype about zookeepers: that they spent time with animals because they couldn't get along with people. As she did at the time, Ana again tries to pin down exactly why nonsexual relationships with animals can be healthy while sexual ones can't, why the limited consent that animals can give is sufficient to keep them as pets yet not to have sex with them. Again she can't articulate an argument that isn't rooted in personal distaste, and she's not sure that's a good enough reason.

As for the question of digients having sex with each other, the topic has occasionally been discussed in the past, and Ana has always felt that the owners are fortunate not to have to deal with it, because sexual maturity is when a lot of animals become difficult to handle. There isn't even the guilt that might be associated with neutering Jax surgically, because she's not depriving him of a fundamental aspect of his nature. But now there's a thread on the discussion forum that is making her reconsider things:

....

From: Helen Costas

I don't like the idea of anyone having sex with my digient, but then I remember that parents never want to think about their kids having sex, either.

....

From: Maria Zheng

That's a false analogy. Parents can't stop their children from becoming sexual, but we can. There's no intrinsic need for digients to emulate that aspect of human development. Don't go overboard with the anthropomorphic projection.

....

From: Derek Brooks

What's intrinsic? There was no intrinsic need for digients to have charming personalities or cute avatars, but there was still a good reason for it: they made people more likely to spend time with them, and that was good for the digients.

I'm not saying we should accept Binary Desire's offer. But I think what we need to ask ourselves is, If we make the digients sexual, would that encourage other people to love them in a way that's good for the digients?

....

Ana wonders if Jax's asexuality means he's missing out on things that would be beneficial for him to experience. She likes the fact that Jax has human friends, and the reason she wants Neuroblast ported to Real Space is so he can maintain those relationships, strengthen them. But how far could that strengthening

go? How close a relationship could one have before sex became
an issue?

Later that evening, she posts a reply to Derek's comment:

....

From: Ana Alvarado

Derek raises a good question. But even if the answer
is yes, that doesn't mean we should accept Binary Desire's
offer.

If a person is looking for a masturbatory fantasy, he
can use ordinary software to get it. He shouldn't buy
a mail-order bride and slap a dozen InstantRapport
patches on her, but that's essentially what Binary Desire
wants to give its customers. Is that the kind of life we want
our digients to have? We could dose them with so much
virtual endorphin that they'd be happy living in a closet
in Data Earth, but we care about them too much to do
that. I don't think we should let someone else treat them
with less respect.

I admit the idea of sex with a digient bothered me initially, but I guess I'm not opposed to the idea in principle.
It's not something I can imagine doing myself, but I don't
have a problem if other people want to, so long as it's not
exploitative. If there's some degree of give-and-take, then
maybe it could be like Derek said: good for the digient as
well as the human. But if the human is free to customize
the digient's reward map, or keep rolling him back until
he finds a perfectly tweaked instantiation, then where's
the give-and-take? Binary Desire is telling its customers
that they don't have to accommodate their digients' pref-

erences in any way. It doesn't matter whether it involves sex or not; that's not a real relationship.

....

. . .

Any member of the user group is free to accept Binary Desire's offer individually, but Ana's argument is persuasive enough that no one does so for the time being. A few days after the meeting, Derek tells Marco and Polo about Binary Desire's offer, figuring that they deserve to be kept informed of what's going on. Polo is curious about the modifications Binary Desire wants to make; he knows he has a reward map but has never thought about what it would mean to edit it.

"Might be fun editing my reward map," says Polo.

"You not able edit your reward map when you working for someone else," says Marco. "You only able do that when you corporation."

Polo turns to Derek. "That true?"

"Well, that's not something I would let you do even when you are a corporation."

"Hey," protests Marco. "You said when we corporations, we make all our own decisions."

"I did say that," admits Derek, "but I hadn't thought about you editing your own reward map. That could be very dangerous."

"But humans able edit own reward maps."

"What? We can't do anything like that."

"What about drugs people take for sex? Ifridisics?"

"Aphrodisiacs. Those are just temporary."

"InstantRapport temporary?" asks Polo.

"Not exactly," says Derek, "but a lot of the time when people take that, they're making a mistake." Especially, he thinks, if a company is paying them to take it.

"When I corporation, I free make own mistakes," says Marco. "That whole point."

"You're not ready to be a corporation yet."

"Because you not like my decisions? Ready mean always agree with you?"

"If you're planning on editing your own reward map as soon as you're a corporation, you're not ready."

"I not said want," says Marco emphatically. "I don't want. I said when corporation, I free do that. That different."

Derek stops for a moment. It's easy to forget, but this is the same conclusion the user group came to during forum discussions about incorporating the digients: if legal personhood is to be more than a form of wordplay, it has to mean granting a digient some degree of autonomy. "Yes, you're right. When you're a corporation, you'll be free to do things that I think are mistakes."

"Good," says Marco, satisfied. "When you decide I ready, it not because I agree you. I can be ready even if I not agree you."

"That's right. But please, tell me you don't want to edit your own reward map."

"No, I know dangerous. Might make mistake that stop self from fixing mistake."

He's relieved. "Thank you."

"But let Binary Desire edit my reward map, that not dangerous."

"No, it's not dangerous, but it's still a bad idea."

"I not agree."

"What? I don't think you understand what they want to do."

Marco gives him a look of frustration. "I do. They make me like what they want me like, even if I not like it now."

Derek realizes Marco does understand. "And you don't think that's wrong?"

"Why wrong? All things I like now, I like because Blue Gamma made me like. That not wrong."

"No, but that was different." He thinks for a moment to explain why. "Blue Gamma made you like food, but they didn't decide what specific kind of food you had to like."

"So what? Not very different."

"It *is* different."

"Agree wrong if they edit digients not want be edited. But if digient agree before be edited, then not wrong."

Derek feels himself growing exasperated. "So do you want to be a corporation and make your own decisions, or do you want someone else to make your decisions? Which one is it?"

Marco thinks about that. "Maybe I try both. One copy me become corporation, second copy me work for Binary Desire."

"You don't mind having copies made of you?"

"Polo copy of me. That not wrong."

At a loss, Derek brings the discussion to a close and sends the digients off to do work on their studies, but he can't easily dismiss what Marco has said. On the one hand Marco made some good arguments, but on the other Derek remembers his college years well enough to know that skill at debate isn't the same as maturity. Not for the first time, he thinks of how much easier it would be if there were a legally mandated age of majority for digients; without one, it will be entirely up to him to decide when Marco is ready to be a corporation.

Derek's not alone in having disagreements in the wake of Binary Desire's offer. The next time he talks to Ana, she complains about a recent fight with Kyle.

"He thinks we should accept Binary Desire's offer," she says.

"He said it's a much better option than me taking the job at Polytope."

It's another opportunity to be critical of Kyle; how should he handle it? All he says is "Because he thinks modifying the digients isn't that big a deal."

"Exactly." She fumes a bit, and then continues. "It's not as if I think wearing the InstantRapport patch is no big deal. Of course it is. But there's a big difference between me using InstantRapport voluntarily and Binary Desire just imposing their bonding process on the digients."

"A huge difference. But you know, that raises an interesting question." He tells her about his conversation with Marco and Polo. "I'm not sure if Marco was just arguing for the sake of arguing, but it made me think. If a digient volunteers to undergo the changes that Binary Desire wants to make, does that make a difference?"

Ana looks thoughtful. "I don't know. Maybe."

"When an adult chooses to use an InstantRapport patch, we have no grounds to object. What would it take for us to respect Jax's or Marco's decisions the same way?"

"They'd have to be adults."

"But we could file articles of incorporation tomorrow, if we wanted to," he says. "What makes us so sure we shouldn't? Suppose one day Jax says to you he understands what he'd be getting into by accepting Binary Desire's offer, just like you with the job at Polytope. What would it take for you to accept his decision?"

She thinks for a moment. "I guess it would depend on whether or not I thought he was basing his decision on experience. Jax has never had a romantic relationship or held a job, and accepting Binary Desire's offer would mean doing both, potentially forever. I'd want him to have had some experience with those matters before making a decision where the consequences are so permanent. Once he's had that experience, I suppose I couldn't really object."

"Ah," says Derek, nodding. "I wish I'd thought of that when I was talking to Marco." It would mean modifying the digients into sexual beings, but without the intention of selling them; another expense for the users' group, even after they got Neuroblast ported. "That's going to take a long time, though."

"Sure, but there's no hurry to make the digients sexual. Better to wait until we can do it properly."

Better to set an older age of majority than risk setting it too young. "And until then, it's up to us to look after them."

"Right! We have to put their needs first." Ana looks grateful for the agreement, and he's glad he can provide it. Then frustration returns to her face. "I just wish Kyle understood that."

He searches for a diplomatic response. "I'm not sure anyone can, if they haven't spent the time we have," he says. It's not intended as a criticism of Kyle; it's what he sincerely believes.

9

A month has passed since Binary Desire's presentation, and Ana is in the private Data Earth with a few of the Neuroblast digients, awaiting the arrival of visitors. Marco tells Lolly about the latest episode of his favorite game drama, while Jax practices a dance he's choreographed.

"Look," he says.

Ana watches him rapidly cycle through a sequence of poses. "Remember, when they get here, you have to talk about what you built."

"I know, you said and said already. I stop dancing soon they here. Just having fun."

"Sorry, Jax. I'm just nervous."

"Watch me dancing. Feel better."

She smiles. "Thanks, I'll try that." She takes a deep breath and tells herself to relax.

A portal opens and two avatars walk through. Jax promptly stops dancing, and Ana walks her avatar over to greet the visitors. The on-screen annotations identify them as Jeremy Brauer and Frank Pearson.

"I hope you didn't have any trouble getting in," says Ana.

"No," says Pearson, "the logins you gave us worked fine."

Brauer is looking around. "Good old Data Earth." His avatar pulls on the branch of a shrub and then lets go, watching the way it sways. "I remember how exciting it was when Daesan first released it. It was state of the art."

Brauer and Pearson work for Exponential Appliances, maker of household robots. The robots are examples of old-fashioned AI; their skills are programmed rather than learned, and while they offer some real convenience, they aren't conscious in any meaningful sense. Exponential regularly releases new versions, advertising each one as being a step closer to the consumer's dream of AI: a butler that is utterly loyal and attentive from the moment it's switched on. To Ana this upgrade sequence seems like a walk to the horizon, providing the illusion of progress while never actually getting any closer to the goal. But consumers buy the robots, and they've given Exponential a healthy balance sheet, which is what Ana's looking for.

Ana isn't trying to get the Neuroblast digients jobs as butlers; it's obvious that Jax and the others are too willful for that type of work. Brauer and Pearson don't even work for the commercial division of the company; instead, they're part of the research division, the reason that Exponential was founded. The household robots are Exponential's way of funding its efforts to conjure up the technologist's dream of AI: an entity of pure cognition, a genius unencumbered by emotions or a body of any kind, an intellect vast and cool yet sympathetic. They're waiting for a software Athena to spring forth fully grown, and while it'd be impolite for Ana to say she thinks they'll be waiting forever, she hopes to convince Brauer and Pearson that the Neuroblast digients offer a viable alternative.

"Well, thank you for coming out to meet me," says Ana.

"We've been looking forward to it," says Brauer. "A digient whose cumulative running time is longer than the life span of most operating systems? You don't see that very often."

"No, you don't." Ana realizes that they came more for nostalgia's sake than to seriously entertain a business proposal. Well, so be it, as long as they're here.

Ana introduces them to the digients, who then give little demonstrations of projects they've been working on. Jax shows a virtual contraption he's built, a kind of music synthesizer that he plays by dancing. Marco gives an explanation of a puzzle game he's designed, one that can be played cooperatively or competitively. Brauer is particularly interested in Lolly, who shows them a program she's been writing; unlike Jax and Marco, who built their projects using toolkits, Lolly is writing actual code. Brauer's disappointment is evident when it becomes clear that Lolly is just like any other novice programmer; it's clear he was hoping her digient nature had given her a special aptitude for the subject.

After they've talked with the digients for a while, Ana and the visitors from Exponential log out of Data Earth and switch to videoconferencing.

"They're terrific," says Brauer. "I used to have one, but he never got much beyond baby talk."

"You used to have a Neuroblast digient?"

"Sure, I bought one as soon as they came out. He was an instance of the Jax mascot, like yours. I named him Fitz, kept him going for a year."

This man had a baby Jax once, she thinks. Somewhere in storage is a baby version of Jax that knows this man as his owner. Aloud, she says, "Did you get bored with him?"

"Not so much bored as aware of his limitations. I could see that the Neuroblast genome was the wrong approach. Sure Fitz was smart, but it would take forever before he could do any useful work. I've got to hand it to you for sticking with Jax for so long. What you've achieved is impressive." He makes it sound like she's built the world's largest toothpick sculpture.

"Do you still think Neuroblast was the wrong approach? You've seen for yourself what Jax is capable of. Do you have anything comparable at Exponential?" It comes out more sharply than she intended.

Brauer's reaction is mild. "We're not looking for human-level AI; we're looking for superhuman AI."

"And you don't think that human-level AI is a step in that direction?"

"Not if it's the sort that your digients demonstrate," says Brauer. "You can't be sure that Jax will ever be employable, let alone become a genius at programming. For all you know, he's reached his maximum."

"I don't think he has—"

"But you don't know for certain."

"I know that if the Neuroblast genome can produce a digient

like him, it can produce one as smart as you're looking for. The Alan Turing of Neuroblast digients is just waiting to be born."

"Fine, let's suppose you're right," says Brauer; he's clearly indulging her. "How many years would it take to find him? It's already taken you so long to raise the first generation that the platform they run on has become obsolete. How many generations before you come up with a Turing?"

"We won't always be restricted to running them in real time. At some point there'll be enough digients to form a self-sufficient population, and then they won't be dependent on human interaction. We could run a society of them at hothouse speeds without any risk of them going feral, and see what they produce." Ana's actually far from confident that this scenario would produce a Turing, but she's practiced this argument enough times to sound like she believes it.

Brauer isn't convinced, though. "Talk about a risky investment. You're showing us a handful of teenagers and asking us to pay for their education in the hopes that when they're adults, they'll found a nation that will produce geniuses. Pardon me if I think there are better ways we could spend our money."

"But think about what you're getting. The other owners and I have devoted years of our attention to raising these digients. Porting Neuroblast is cheap compared with what it'd cost to hire people to do that for another genome. And the potential payoff is exactly what your company's been looking for: programming geniuses working at high speed, bootstrapping themselves to superhuman intelligence. If these digients can invent games now, just imagine what their descendants could do. And you'd make money off every one of them."

Brauer is about to reply when Pearson interjects, "Is that

why you want Neuroblast ported? To see what superintelligent digients might invent one day?"

Ana sees Pearson scrutinizing her and decides there's no point in trying to lie. "No," she says. "What I want is for Jax to have a chance at a fuller life."

Pearson nods. "You'd like Jax to be a corporation one day, right? Have some sort of legal personhood?"

"Yes, I would."

"And I'll bet Jax wants the same thing, right? To be incorporated?"

"For the most part, yes."

Pearson nods again, his suspicions confirmed. "That's a deal breaker for us. It's nice that they're fun to talk to, but all the attention you've given your digients has encouraged them to think of themselves as persons."

"Why is that a deal breaker?" But she knows the answer already.

"We aren't looking for superintelligent employees, we're looking for superintelligent products. You're offering us the former, and I can't blame you; no one can spend as many years as you have teaching a digient and still think of it as a product. But our business isn't based on that kind of sentiment."

Ana has been pretending it wasn't there, but now Pearson has stated it baldly: the fundamental incompatibility between Exponential's goals and hers. They want something that responds like a person, but isn't owed the same obligations as a person, and that's something she can't give them.

No one can give it to them, because it's an impossibility. The years she spent raising Jax didn't just make him fun to talk to, didn't just provide him with hobbies and a sense of humor. They were what gave him all the attributes Exponential is looking for:

fluency at navigating the real world, creativity at solving new problems, judgment you could entrust with an important decision. Every quality that made a person more valuable than a database was a product of experience.

She wants to tell them that Blue Gamma was more right than it knew: experience isn't merely the best teacher; it's the only teacher. If she's learned anything raising Jax, it's that there are no shortcuts; if you want to create the common sense that comes from twenty years of being in the world, you need to devote twenty years to the task. You can't assemble an equivalent collection of heuristics in less time; experience is algorithmically incompressible.

And even though it's possible to take a snapshot of all that experience and duplicate it ad infinitum, even though it's possible to sell copies cheaply or give them away for free, each of the resulting digients would still have lived a lifetime. Each one would have once seen the world with new eyes, have had hopes fulfilled and hopes dashed, have learned how it felt to tell a lie and how it felt to be told one.

Which means each one would deserve some respect. Respect that Exponential can't afford to give.

Ana makes one final attempt. "These digients could still make money for you as employees. You could—"

Pearson shakes his head. "I appreciate what you're trying to do, and I wish you the best of luck, but it's not a good match for Exponential. If these digients were going to be products, the potential profits might be worth the risk. But if all they're going to be is employees, that's a different situation; we can't justify such a large investment for so little return."

Of course not, she thinks. Who could? Only someone who's a fanatic, someone who's motivated by love. Someone like her.

· · ·

Ana is sending a message to Derek about the failed meeting with Exponential when the robot body comes to life. "How meeting go?" asks Jax, but he can read her expression well enough to answer the question himself. "Is my fault? They not like what I show them?"

"No, you did great, Jax. They just don't like digients; I made a mistake in thinking I could change their minds."

"Worth trying," says Jax.

"I suppose it was."

"You okay?"

"I'll be fine," she assures him. Jax gives her a hug and then walks the body back to the charging platform and returns to Data Earth.

Sitting at her desk, staring at a blank screen, Ana contemplates the user group's remaining options. As far as she can tell, there's only one: working for Polytope and trying to convince them that the Neuroblast engine is worth porting. All she has to do is wear the InstantRapport patch and join their experiment in industrialized caregiving.

Whatever else one might say about Polytope, the company understands the value of real-time interaction in a way that Exponential does not. Sophonce digients might be content to be left alone in a hothouse, but that's not a viable shortcut if you want them to become productive individuals. Someone is going to have to spend time with them, and Polytope recognizes that.

Her objection is to Polytope's strategy for getting people to spend that time. Blue Gamma's strategy had been to make the digients lovable, while Polytope is starting with unlovable digients and using pharmaceuticals to make people love them.

It seems clear to her that Blue Gamma's approach was the right one, not just more ethical but more effective.

Indeed, maybe it was too effective, considering the situation she's in now: she's faced with the biggest expense of her entire life, and it's for her digient. It's not what anyone at Blue Gamma expected, all those years ago, but perhaps they should have. The idea of love with no strings attached is as much a fantasy as what Binary Desire is selling. Loving someone means making sacrifices for them.

Which is the only reason Ana's considering working for Polytope. Under any other circumstances, she'd be insulted by the offer of a job that required the use of InstantRapport: she has as much experience working with digients as anyone in the world, yet Polytope is implying that she can't be an effective trainer without pharmaceutical intervention. Training digients—like training animals—is a job, and a professional can do her job without having to be in love with a particular assignment.

At the same time, she knows the difference that affection can make in the training process, how it enables patience when patience is needed most. The idea that such affection can be manufactured isn't appealing, but she can't deny the realities of modern neuropharmacology: if her brain is flooded with oxytocin every time she's training Sophonce digients, it's going to have an effect on her feelings toward them whether she wants it to or not.

The only question is whether that's something she can tolerate. She's confident that the InstantRapport patch won't distract her from taking care of Jax; no Sophonce digient is going to displace Jax in her affections. And if working for Polytope is the best chance of getting Neuroblast ported, she's willing to do it.

Ana just wishes Kyle understood; she has always made it clear that Jax's welfare comes first, and up until now Kyle has never had a problem with that. She doesn't want their relationship to end because of this job, but she's been with Jax longer than she's been with any boyfriend; if it comes down to it, she knows whom she'll choose.

10

The message from Ana about the failed meeting is short, but to Derek it conveys plenty. He's heard the tone in her voice when she has talked about this possibility before, so he knows she's preparing herself to accept Polytope's job offer.

This is Ana's last-ditch attempt to get Neuroblast ported, nothing more. No one likes the idea, but she's an adult; she's weighed the costs and benefits and made her decision. If she's willing to do it, the least he can do is be supportive.

Except that he can't. Not when there's an alternative: accepting Binary Desire's offer.

After his earlier conversation with Marco and Polo, Derek privately contacted Jennifer Chase to ask her if the digients' desire to be incorporated wouldn't render them unsuitable for Binary Desire's purposes. She told him that Binary Desire's customers will be free to file articles of incorporation on the copies they've purchased. In fact, if their feelings toward their digients become as strong as Binary Desire hopes, she expects that many of them will do so. It's the right answer as far as he's concerned, but part of him hoped they'd give the wrong one, providing him with a clear reason to refuse their proposal. Instead, the decision remains his to make. His, and Marco's.

He's thought about the argument Ana articulated, about the digients not being competent to accept Binary Desire's offer because of their lack of experience with romantic relationships and jobs. The argument makes sense if you think of the digients as being like human children. It also means that as long as they're confined to Data Earth, as long as their lives are so radically sheltered, they'll never become mature enough to make a decision of this magnitude.

But perhaps the standards for maturity for a digient shouldn't be as high as they are for a human; maybe Marco is as mature as he needs to be to make this decision. Marco seems entirely comfortable thinking of himself as a digient rather than a human. It's possible he doesn't fully appreciate the consequences of what he's suggesting, but Derek can't shake the feeling that Marco in fact understands his own nature better than Derek does. Marco and Polo aren't human, and maybe thinking of them as if they were is a mistake, forcing them to conform to his expectations instead of letting them be themselves. Is it more respectful to treat him like a human being, or to accept that he isn't one?

Under other circumstances this would be an academic question, something he could postpone for later discussion, but instead it ties directly into the decision he is facing here and now. If he accepts Binary Desire's offer, there'll be no need for Ana to take the job at Polytope, so the question becomes: Is it better for Marco to have his brain chemistry altered than for Ana to alter hers?

Ana knows what she'd be getting into by agreeing to it, more so than Marco does. But Ana is a person, and no matter how amazing he thinks Marco is, he values Ana more. If one of them has to undergo neurological manipulation, he doesn't want it to be her.

On his screen Derek brings up the contract that Binary Desire sent. Then he calls Marco and Polo over in their robot bodies.

"Ready sign contract?" asks Marco.

"You know you shouldn't do this if it's just to help the others," says Derek. "You should do it because it's what you want to do." Then he wonders if that's really true.

"You not need keep asking me," says Marco. "I feel same as before, want do this."

"What about you, Polo?"

"Yes, agree."

The digients are willing, even eager, and perhaps that should be enough to settle the matter. But then there are the other considerations, purely selfish ones.

If Ana takes the job with Polytope, it will create a rift between her and Kyle, one that Derek might benefit from. It's not an admirable thought, but he can't pretend it hasn't occurred to him. Whereas if he accepts Binary Desire's offer, the rift created will be between him and Ana; it'll ruin his chances of ever getting together with her. Can he give that up?

Maybe he never had a chance with Ana; maybe he's been fooling himself for all these years. In which case he'll be better off if he lets go of that fantasy, if he frees himself from yearning for something that'll never happen.

"What you waiting for?" asks Marco.

"Nothing," says Derek.

With the digients watching, he signs the contract from Binary Desire and sends it to Jennifer Chase.

"When I go to Binary Desire?" asks Marco.

"We'll take a snapshot of you after I get a countersigned copy of the contract," he replies. "Then we'll send it to them."

"Okay," says Marco.

As the digients talk excitedly about what this means, Derek thinks about what to say to Ana. He can't tell her he's doing it for her, of course. She'd feel horribly guilty if she thought he was sacrificing Marco for her benefit. This is his decision, and it's better that Ana put the blame on him.

. . . .

Ana and Jax are playing Jerk Vector, a racing game that Ana recently added to Data Earth; they pilot their hovercars across a landscape as hilly as egg-crate foam. Ana manages to gain enough velocity within a basin that she can jump across a nearby ravine, while Jax doesn't make it, and his hovercar tumbles spectacularly to the bottom.

"Wait me catch up," he says over the intercom.

"Okay," Ana says, and sets her hovercar in neutral. While she's waiting for Jax to ascend the switchback trail along the ravine wall, she switches to another window to check her messages. What she sees startles her.

Felix has sent a message to the entire user group, triumphantly beginning a countdown until humanity's first contact with the Xenotherians. Initially Ana wonders if she's misunderstanding Felix because of his eccentric use of language, but a couple of messages from others in the user group confirm that the Neuroblast port is under way, and Binary Desire is paying for it. Someone in the user group has sold their digient as a sex toy.

Then she sees a message saying that Derek was the one, that he sold Marco. She's about to post a reply saying that it can't be true, but she stops herself. Instead, she switches back to the Data Earth window.

"Jax, I've got to make a call. Why don't you practice jumping the ravine for a while?"

"You become sorry," says Jax. "I beat you next race."

Ana switches the game into practice mode so Jax can try

jumping the ravine again without having to climb up from the bottom each time he misses. Then she opens a videophone window and calls Derek.

"Tell me it's not true," she says, but one look at his face confirms that it is.

"I didn't mean for you to find out this way. I was going to call you, but—"

Ana's so astonished she can barely find the words. "Why did you do it?" Derek hesitates so long that she says, "Was it for the money?"

"No! Of course not. I just decided that Marco's arguments made sense, and that he was old enough to choose."

"We talked about that. You agreed that it was better to wait until he had more experience."

"I know. But then I—I decided I was being overly cautious."

"Overly cautious? You're not letting Marco risk scraping his knee; Binary Desire is going to perform brain surgery on him. How can you be too cautious about that?"

He pauses, and then says, "I realized it was time to let go."

"Let go?" As if the idea of protecting Marco and Polo were some childish fancy he'd outgrown. "I didn't know you thought of it that way."

"I didn't either, until recently."

"Does this mean you don't plan on incorporating Marco and Polo someday?"

"No, I still plan to do that. I just won't be as—" Again he hesitates. "Fixated."

"Not as fixated." Ana wonders how well she knew Derek at all. "Good for you, I guess."

He looks hurt by that, which is fine with her. "It's good for everyone," he says. "The digients get access to Real Space—"

"I know, I know."

"Really, I think it's for the best," he says, but he doesn't seem to believe it himself.

"How can it be for the best?" she asks. Derek doesn't say anything, and she just stares at him.

"I'll talk to you later," says Ana, and closes the phone window. Thinking about the ways Marco might be used—without ever realizing that he's being used—makes her heart break. You can't save them all, she reminds herself. But it never occurred to her that Marco might be one of those at risk. She assumed Derek felt the same way she does, that he understood the need to make sacrifices.

In her Data Earth window she can see Jax gleefully piloting his hovercar up and down slopes like a kid on a trackless roller-coaster. She doesn't want to tell him about the deal with Binary Desire right now; they would have to discuss what it means for Marco, and she doesn't have the energy for that conversation. For the moment, all she wants to do is watch him and, tentatively, try to get used to the idea that the Neuroblast port is actually under way. It's a peculiar sensation. She can't call it relief, because of the cost entailed, but it's undeniably a good thing that this enormous obstacle to Jax's future has been removed, and she didn't have to take the job with Polytope to do it. It'll be months before the port is finished, but the time will pass quickly now that the destination is known. Jax will be able to enter Real Space, see his friends again, and rejoin the rest of the social universe.

Not that the future will be all smooth sailing. There is still an endless series of obstacles ahead, but at least she and Jax will have a chance to tackle them. Briefly, Ana indulges herself, fantasizing about what might happen if they succeed.

She imagines Jax maturing over the years, both in Real Space and in the real world. Imagines him incorporated, a legal person, employed and earning a living. Imagines him as a participant in the digient subculture, a community with enough money and skills to port itself to new platforms when the need arises. Imagines him accepted by a generation of humans who have grown up with digients and view them as potential relationship partners in a way that members of her generation will never be able to. Imagines him loving and being loved, arguing and compromising. Imagines him making sacrifices, some hard and some made easy because they're for a person he truly cares about.

A few minutes pass, and Ana tells herself to stop daydreaming. There's no guarantee that Jax is capable of any of those things. But if he's ever going to get the chance to try them, she has to get on with the job in front of her now: teaching him, as best she can, the business of living.

She initiates the game's shutdown procedure and calls Jax on the intercom. "Playtime's over, Jax," she says. "Time to do your homework."

DACEY'S PATENT AUTOMATIC NANNY

FROM THE CATALOG ACCOMPANYING THE EXHIBITION
*LITTLE DEFECTIVE ADULTS—ATTITUDES TOWARD CHIL-
DREN FROM 1700 TO 1950;* NATIONAL MUSEUM OF PSY-
CHOLOGY, AKRON, OHIO

THE AUTOMATIC NANNY WAS THE CREATION OF REGINALD
Dacey, a mathematician born in London in 1861. Dacey's original interest was in building a teaching engine; inspired by the
recent advances in gramophone technology, he sought to con-
vert the arithmetic mill of Charles Babbage's proposed Analyti-
cal Engine into a machine capable of teaching grammar and
arithmetic by rote. Dacey envisioned it not as a replacement for
human instruction but as a laborsaving device to be used by
schoolteachers and governesses.

For years Dacey worked diligently on his teaching engine,
and even the death of his wife, Emily, in childbirth in 1894 did
little to slow his efforts.

What changed the direction of his research was his discovery,
several years later, of how his son, Lionel, was being treated by

the nanny, a woman known as Nanny Gibson. Dacey himself had been raised by an affectionate nanny, and for years assumed that the woman he'd hired was treating his son in the same way, occasionally reminding her not to be too lenient. He was shocked to learn that Nanny Gibson routinely beat the boy and administered Gregory's Powder (a potent and vile-tasting laxative) as punishment. Realizing that his son actually lived in terror of the nanny, Dacey immediately fired her. He carefully interviewed several prospective nannies afterward and was surprised to learn of the vast range in their approaches to child-rearing. Some nannies showered their charges with affection, while others applied disciplinary measures worse than Nanny Gibson's.

Dacey eventually hired a replacement nanny, but regularly had her bring Lionel to his workshop so he could keep her under close supervision. This must have seemed like paradise to the child, who demonstrated nothing but obedience in Dacey's presence; the discrepancy between Nanny Gibson's accounts of his son's behavior and his own observations prompted Dacey to begin an investigation into optimal child-rearing practices. Given his mathematical inclination, he viewed a child's emotional state as an example of a system in unstable equilibrium. His notebooks from the period include the following: "Indulgence leads to misbehavior, which angers the nanny and prompts her to deliver punishment more severe than is warranted. The nanny then feels regret, and subsequently overcompensates with further indulgence. It is an inverted pendulum, prone to oscillations of ever-increasing magnitude. If we can only keep the pendulum vertical, there is no need for subsequent correction."

Dacey tried imparting his philosophy of child-rearing to a series of nannies for Lionel, only to have each report that the child was not obeying her. It appears not to have occurred to him that Lionel might behave differently with the nannies than with Dacey himself; instead he concluded that the nannies were too temperamental to follow his guidelines. In one respect he concurred with the conventional wisdom of the time, which held that women's emotional nature made them unsuitable parents; where he differed was in thinking that too much punishment could be just as detrimental as too much affection. Eventually he decided that the only nanny that could adhere to the procedures he outlined would be one he built himself.

In letters to colleagues, Dacey offered multiple reasons for turning his attention to a mechanical nursemaid. First, such a machine would be radically easier to construct than a teaching engine, and selling it offered a way to raise the funds needed to perfect the latter. Second, he saw it as an opportunity for early intervention: by putting children in the care of machines while they were still infants, he could ensure they didn't acquire bad habits that would have to be broken later. "Children are not born sinful, but become so because of the influence of those whose care we have placed them in," he wrote. "Rational child-rearing will lead to rational children."

It's indicative of the Victorian attitude toward children that at no point does Dacey suggest that children should be raised by their parents. Of his own participation in Lionel's upbringing, he wrote, "I realize that my presence entails risk of the very dangers I wish to avoid, for while I am more rational than any woman, I am not immune to the boy's expressions of delight or dejection. But progress can only occur one step at a time, and even if it is too late for Lionel to fully reap the benefits of my work, he understands its importance. Perfecting this machine means other parents will be able to raise their children in a more rational environment than I was able to provide for my own."

For the manufacture of the Automatic Nanny, Dacey contracted with Thomas Bradford & Co., maker of sewing and laundry machines. The majority of the Nanny's torso was occupied by a spring-driven clockwork mechanism that controlled the feeding and rocking schedule. Most of the time, the arms formed a cradle for rocking the baby. At specified intervals, the machine would raise the baby into feeding position and expose an India-rubber nipple connected to a reservoir of infant formula. In addition to the crank handle for winding the mainspring, the Nanny had a smaller crank for powering the gramophone player used to play lullabies; the gramophone had to be unusually small to fit within the Nanny's head, and only custom-stamped discs could be played on it. There was also a foot pedal near the Nanny's base used for pressurizing the waste pump, which provided suction for the pair of hoses leading from the baby's rubber diaper to a chamber pot.

The Automatic Nanny went on sale in March 1901, with the following advertisement appearing in the *Illustrated London News*:

Do not leave your child in the care of a woman whose character you know nothing about. Embrace the modern practice of scientific child-rearing by purchasing

---

DACEY'S PATENT AUTOMATIC NANNY
· ·

The ADVANTAGES of this UNIQUE SUBSTITUTE
for a nanny are:

· It teaches your baby to adhere to a precise schedule of feeding and sleeping.

· It soothes your baby without administering stupefying narcotics.

· It works night and day, requires no separate quarters, and cannot steal.

· It will not expose your child to disreputable influences.

Consider these testimonials from customers:

"Our child is now perfectly behaved and a delight to be near."   —Mrs. Menhenick, Colwyn Bay.

"An immeasurable improvement over the Irish girl we previously employed. It is a blessing for our household."
                    —Mrs. Hastings, Eastbourne.

"I wish I had been raised by one myself."
                    —Mrs. Godwin, Andoversford.

THOMAS BRADFORD & CO.
68, FLEET-STREET, LONDON;
AND MANCHESTER

It is worth noting that, rather than promoting the raising of rational children, the advertising preys on parents' fears of untrustworthy nursemaids. This may have just been shrewd marketing on the part of Dacey's partners at Thomas Bradford & Co., but some historians think it reveals Dacey's actual motives for developing the Automatic Nanny. While Dacey always described his proposed teaching engine as an assistive tool for governesses, he positioned the Automatic Nanny as a complete replacement for a human nanny. Given that nannies came from the working class while governesses typically came from the upper class, this suggests an unconscious class prejudice on Dacey's part.

Whatever the reasons for its appeal, the Automatic Nanny enjoyed a brief period of popularity, with more than one hundred and fifty being sold within six months. Dacey maintained that the families that used the Automatic Nanny were entirely satisfied with the quality of care provided by the machine, although there is no way to verify this; the testimonials used in the advertisements were likely invented, as was customary at the time.

What is known for certain is that in September 1901, an infant named Nigel Hawthorne was fatally thrown from an Automatic Nanny when its mainspring snapped. Word of the child's death spread quickly, and Dacey was faced with a deluge of families returning their Automatic Nannies. He examined the Hawthornes' Nanny and discovered that the mechanism had been tampered with in an attempt to enable the machine to operate longer before needing to be rewound. He published a full-page ad in which—while trying not to blame the Hawthorne parents—he insisted that the Automatic Nanny was entirely safe if operated properly, but his efforts were in vain. No one would entrust their child to the care of Dacey's machine.

To demonstrate that the Automatic Nanny was safe, Dacey boldly announced that he would entrust his next child to the machine's care. If he had successfully followed through with this, he might have restored public confidence in the machine, but Dacey never got the chance because of his habit of telling prospective wives of his plans for their offspring. The inventor framed his proposal as an invitation to partake in a grand scientific undertaking and was baffled that none of the women he courted found this an appealing prospect.

After several years of rejection, Dacey gave up on trying to sell the Automatic Nanny to a hostile public. Concluding that society was not sufficiently enlightened to appreciate the benefits of machine-based childcare, he likewise abandoned his plans to build a teaching engine, and resumed his work on pure mathematics. He published papers on number theory and lectured at Cambridge until his death in 1918, during the global influenza pandemic.

The Automatic Nanny might have been completely forgotten were it not for the publication of an article in the *London Times* in 1925 titled "Mishaps of Science." It described in derisive terms a number of failed inventions and experiments, including the Automatic Nanny, which it labeled "a monstrous contraption whose inventor surely despised children." Reginald's son, Lionel Dacey, who by then had become a mathematician himself and was continuing his father's work in number theory, was outraged. He wrote a strongly worded letter to the newspaper demanding a retraction, and when it refused, he filed a libel suit against the publisher, which he eventually lost. Undeterred, Lionel Dacey began a campaign to prove that the Automatic Nanny was based on sound and humane child-rearing principles, self-publishing a book about his father's theories on raising rational children.

Lionel Dacey refurbished the Automatic Nannies that had been in storage on the family estate, and in 1927 offered them for commercial sale again, but was unable to find a single buyer. He blamed this on the British upper class's obsession with status; because household appliances were now being marketed to the middle class as "electric servants," he claimed upper-class families insisted on hiring human nannies for appearance's sake, whether they provided better care or not. Those who worked with Lionel Dacey blamed it on his refusal to update the Automatic Nanny in any way; he ignored one business adviser's recommendation to replace the machine's spring-driven mechanism with an electric motor and fired another who suggested marketing it without the Dacey name.

Like his father, Lionel Dacey eventually decided to raise his own child with the Automatic Nanny, but rather than look for a willing bride, he announced in 1932 that he would adopt an infant. He did not offer any updates in the following years, prompting a gossip columnist to suggest that the child had died at the machine's hands, but by then there was so little interest in the Automatic Nanny that no one ever bothered to investigate.

The truth regarding the infant would never have come to light if not for the work of Dr. Thackery Lambshead. In 1938 Lambshead was consulting at the Brighton Institute of Mental Subnormality (now known as Bayliss House) when he encountered a child named Edmund Dacey. According to admission records, Edmund had been successfully raised using an Automatic Nanny until the child was two years old, the age at which Lionel Dacey felt it appropriate to switch him to human care. He found that Edmund was unresponsive to his commands, and shortly afterward a physician diagnosed the child as "feeble-minded." Judging such a child an unsuitable subject for demonstrating the Nanny's efficacy, Lionel Dacey committed Edmund to the Brighton Institute.

What prompted the institute's staff to seek Lambshead's opinion was Edmund's diminutive stature: although he was five, his height and weight were those of the average three-year-old. The children at the Brighton Institute were generally taller and healthier than those at similar asylums, a reflection of the fact that the institute's staff did not follow the still-common practice of minimal interaction with the children. In providing affection and physical contact to their charges, the nurses were preventing the condition now known as psychosocial dwarfism, in which emotional stress reduces a child's levels of growth hormones and which was prevalent in orphanages at the time.

The nurses quite reasonably assumed that Edmund Dacey's delayed growth was the result of substituting the Automatic Nanny's mechanical care for actual human touch and expected him to gain weight under their care. But after two years as a resident at the institute, during which the nurses had showered attention on him, Edmund had scarcely grown at all, prompting the staff to look for an underlying physiological cause.

Lambshead hypothesized that the child was indeed suffering from psychosocial dwarfism but of a uniquely inverted variety: what Edmund needed was not more contact with a person, but more contact with a machine. His small size was not the result of the years he spent under the care of the Automatic Nanny; it was the result of being deprived of the Automatic Nanny after his father felt he was ready for human care. If this theory was correct, restoring the machine would cause the boy to resume normal growth.

Lambshead sought out Lionel Dacey to acquire an Automatic Nanny. He gave an account of the visit in a monograph written many years later:

[Lionel Dacey] spoke of his plans to repeat the experiment with another child as soon as he could ensure that the child's mother was of suitable stock. His feeling was that the experiment with Edmund had failed only because of the boy's "native imbecility," which he blamed on the child's mother. I asked him what he knew of the child's parents, and he answered, rather too forcefully, that he knew nothing. Later on I visited the orphanage from which Lionel Dacey had adopted Edmund, and learned from their records that the child's mother was a woman named Eleanor Hardy, who previously worked as a maid for Lionel Dacey. It was obvious to me that Edmund is in fact Lionel Dacey's own illegitimate son.

Lionel Dacey was unwilling to donate an Automatic Nanny to what he considered a failed experiment, but he agreed to sell one to Lambshead, who then arranged to have it installed in Edmund's room at the Brighton Institute. The child embraced the machine as soon as he saw it, and in the days that followed he would play happily with toys as long as the Nanny was nearby. Over the next few months the nurses recorded a steady increase in his height and weight, confirming Lambshead's diagnosis.

The staff assumed that Edmund's cognitive delays were congenital in nature and was content as long as he was thriving physically and emotionally. Lambshead, however, wondered if the consequences of the child's bond with a machine might be more far ranging than anyone suspected. He speculated that Edmund had been misdiagnosed as feebleminded simply because he paid no attention to human instructors and that he might respond better to a mechanical instructor. Unfortunately he had no way to test this hypothesis; even if Reginald Dacey had successfully completed his teaching engine, it would not have provided the type of instruction that Edmund required.

It was not until 1946 that technology advanced to the necessary level. As a result of his lectures on radiation sickness, Lambshead had a good relationship with scientists working at Chicago's Argonne National Laboratory and was present at a demonstration of the first remote manipulators, mechanical arms designed for the handling of radioactive materials. He immediately recognized their potential for Edmund's education and was able to acquire a pair for the Brighton Institute.

Edmund was thirteen years old at this point. He had always been indifferent to attempts by the staff to teach him, but the mechanical arms immediately captured his attention. Using an intercom system that emulated the low-fidelity audio of the original Automatic Nanny's gramophone, nurses were able to get Edmund to respond to their voices in a way they hadn't when speaking to him directly. Within a few weeks, it was apparent that Edmund was not cognitively delayed in the manner previously believed; the staff had merely lacked the appropriate means of communicating with him.

With news of this development Lambshead was able to persuade Lionel Dacey to visit the institute. Seeing Edmund demonstrate a lively curiosity and inquisitive nature, Lionel Dacey realized how he had stunted the boy's intellectual growth. From Lambshead's account:

> He struggled visibly to contain his emotion at seeing what he had wrought in pursuit of his father's vision: a child so wedded to machines that he could not acknowledge another human being. I heard him whisper, "I'm sorry, Father."
>
> "I'm sure your father would understand that your intentions were good," I said.
>
> "You misunderstand me, Dr. Lambshead. Were I any other scientist, my efforts to confirm his thesis would have been a testament to his influence, no matter what my results. But because I am Reginald Dacey's son, I have

disproved his thesis twice over, because my entire life has been a demonstration of the impact a father's attention can have on his son."

Immediately after this visit, Lionel Dacey had remote manipulators and an intercom installed in his house and brought Edmund home. He devoted himself to machine-mediated interaction with his son until Edmund succumbed to pneumonia in 1966. Lionel Dacey passed away the following year.

The Automatic Nanny seen here is the one purchased by Dr. Lambshead to improve Edmund's care at the Brighton Institute. All the Nannies in Lionel Dacey's possession were destroyed upon his son's death. The National Museum of Psychology thanks Dr. Lambshead for his donation of this unique artifact.

THE TRUTH OF FACT,
THE TRUTH OF FEELING

WHEN MY DAUGHTER NICOLE WAS AN INFANT, I READ AN essay suggesting that it might no longer be necessary to teach children how to read or write, because speech recognition and synthesis would soon render those abilities superfluous. My wife and I were horrified by the idea, and we resolved that, no matter how sophisticated technology became, our daughter's skills would always rest on the bedrock of traditional literacy.

It turned out that we and the essayist were both half correct: now that she's an adult, Nicole can read as well as I can. But there is a sense in which she has lost the ability to write. She doesn't dictate her messages and ask a virtual secretary to read back to her what she last said, the way that essayist predicted; Nicole subvocalizes, her retinal projector displays the words in her field of vision, and she makes revisions using a combination of gestures and eye movements. For all practical purposes, she can write. But take away the assistive software and give her nothing but a keyboard like the one I remain faithful to, and she'd have difficulty spelling out many of the words in this very sentence. Under those specific circumstances, English becomes a bit like a second language to her, one that she can speak fluently but can only barely write.

It may sound like I'm disappointed in Nicole's intellectual achievements, but that's absolutely not the case. She's smart and dedicated to her job at an art museum when she could be earning more money elsewhere, and I've always been proud of her accomplishments. But there is still the past me who would have been appalled to see his daughter lose her ability to spell, and I can't deny that I am continuous with him.

It's been more thirty years since I read that essay, and in that period our lives have undergone countless changes that I couldn't have predicted. The most catastrophic one was when Nicole's mother, Angela, declared that she deserved a more interesting life than the one we were giving her and spent the next decade crisscrossing the globe. But the changes leading to Nicole's current form of literacy were more ordinary and gradual: a succession of software gadgets that not only promised but in fact delivered utility and convenience, and I didn't object to any of them at the times of their introduction.

So it hasn't been my habit to engage in doomsaying whenever a new product is announced; I've welcomed new technology as much as anyone. But when Whetstone released its new search tool Remem, it raised concerns for me in a way none of its predecessors did.

Millions of people, some my age but most younger, have been keeping lifelogs for years, wearing personal cams that capture continuous video of their entire lives. People consult their lifelogs for a variety of reasons—everything from reliving favorite moments to tracking down the cause of allergic reactions—but only intermittently; no one wants to spend all their time formulating queries and sifting through the results. Lifelogs are the most complete photo album imaginable, but like most photo albums, they lie dormant except on special occasions. Now Whetstone aims to change all of that; they claim Remem's algorithms can search the haystack by the time you've finished saying "needle."

Remem monitors your conversation for references to past events and then displays video of that event in the lower-left corner of your field of vision. If you say "Remember dancing the conga at that wedding?" Remem will bring up the video. If the person you're talking to says "The last time we were at the beach," Remem will bring up the video. And it's not only for use when speaking with someone else; Remem also monitors your subvocalizations. If you read the words "the first Szechuan restaurant I ate at," your vocal cords will move as if you're reading aloud, and Remem will bring up the relevant video.

There's no denying the usefulness of software that can actually answer the question "Where did I put my keys?" But Whetstone is positioning Remem as more than a handy virtual assistant: they want it to take the place of your natural memory.

. . .

It was the summer of Jijingi's thirteenth year when a European came to live in the village. The dusty harmattan winds had just begun blowing from the north when Sabe, the elder who was regarded as chief by all the local families, made the announcement.

Everyone's initial reaction was alarm, of course. "What have we done wrong?" Jijingi's father asked Sabe.

Europeans had first come to Tivland many years ago, and while some elders said one day they'd leave and life would return to the ways of the past, until that day arrived it was necessary for the Tiv to get along with them. This had meant many changes in the way the Tiv did things, but it had never meant Europeans living among them before. The usual reason for Europeans to come to the village was to collect taxes for the roads they had built; they visited some clans more often because the people refused to pay taxes, but that hadn't happened in the Shangev clan. Sabe and the other clan elders had agreed that paying the taxes was the best strategy.

Sabe told everyone not to worry. "This European is a missionary; that means all he does is pray. He has no authority to punish us, but our making him welcome will please the men in the administration."

He ordered two huts built for the missionary, a sleeping hut and a reception hut. Over the course of the next several days everyone took time off from harvesting the Guinea corn to help lay bricks, sink posts into the ground, weave grass into thatch for the roof. It was during the final step, pounding the floor, that the missionary arrived. His porters appeared first, the boxes they carried visible from a distance as they threaded their way between the cassava fields; the missionary himself was the last to appear, apparently exhausted, even though he carried nothing. His name was Moseby, and he thanked everyone who had worked on the huts. He tried to help, but it quickly became clear that he didn't know how to do anything, so eventually he just sat in the shade of a locust-bean tree and wiped his head with a piece of cloth.

Jijingi watched the missionary with curiosity. The man opened one of his boxes and took out what at first looked like a block of wood, but then he split it open and Jijingi realized it was a tightly bound sheaf of papers. Jijingi had seen paper before; when the Europeans collected taxes, they gave paper in return so that the village had proof of what they'd paid. But the paper that the missionary was looking at was obviously of a different sort and must have had some other purpose.

The man noticed Jijingi looking at him and invited him to come closer. "My name is Moseby," he said. "What is your name?"

"I am Jijingi, and my father is Orga of the Shangev clan."

Moseby spread open the sheaf of paper and gestured toward it. "Have you heard the story of Adam?" he asked. "Adam was the first man. We are all children of Adam."

"Here we are descendants of Shangev," said Jijingi. "And everyone in Tivland is a descendant of Tiv."

"Yes, but your ancestor Tiv was descended from Adam, just as my ancestors were. We are all brothers. Do you understand?"

The missionary spoke as if his tongue were too large for his mouth, but Jijingi could tell what he was saying. "Yes, I understand."

Moseby smiled and pointed at the paper. "This paper tells the story of Adam."

"How can paper tell a story?"

"It is an art that we Europeans know. When a man speaks, we make marks on the paper. When another man looks at the paper later, he sees the marks and knows what sounds the first man made. In that way the second man can hear what the first man said."

Jijingi remembered something his father had told him about old Gbegba, who was the most skilled in bushcraft. "Where you or I would see nothing but some disturbed grass, he can see that a leopard had killed a cane rat at that spot and carried it off," his father said. Gbegba was able to look at the ground and know what had happened even though he had not been present. This art of the Europeans must be similar: those who were skilled in interpreting the marks could hear a story even if they hadn't been there when it was told.

"Tell me the story that the paper tells," he said.

Moseby told him a story about Adam and his wife being tricked by a snake. Then he asked Jijingi, "How do you like it?"

"You're a poor storyteller, but the story was interesting enough."

Moseby laughed. "You are right, I am not good at the Tiv language. But this is a good story. It is the oldest story we have. It was first told long before your ancestor Tiv was born."

Jijingi was dubious. "That paper can't be so old."

"No, this paper is not. But the marks on it were copied from older paper. And those marks were copied from older paper. And so forth many times."

That would be impressive, if true. Jijingi liked stories, and older stories were often the best. "How many stories do you have there?"

"Very many." Moseby flipped through the sheaf of papers, and Jijingi could see each sheet was covered with marks from edge to edge; there must be many, many stories there.

"This art you spoke of, interpreting marks on paper; is it only for Europeans?"

"No, I can teach it to you. Would you like that?"

Cautiously, Jijingi nodded.

. . .

As a journalist, I have long appreciated the usefulness of lifelogging for determining the facts of the matter. There is scarcely a legal proceeding, criminal or civil, that doesn't make use of someone's lifelog, and rightly so. When the public interest is involved, finding out what actually happened is important; justice is an essential part of the social contract, and you can't have justice until you know the truth.

However, I've been much more skeptical about the use of lifelogging in purely personal situations. When lifelogging first became popular, there were couples who thought they could use it to settle arguments over who had actually said what, using the video record to prove they were right. But finding the right clip of video often wasn't easy, and all but the most determined gave up on doing so. The inconvenience acted as a barrier, limiting the searching of lifelogs to those situations in which effort was warranted, namely situations in which justice was the motivating factor.

Now with Remem, finding the exact moment has become easy, and lifelogs that previously lay all but ignored are being scrutinized as if they were crime scenes, thickly strewn with evidence for use in domestic squabbles.

I typically write for the news section, but I've written feature stories as well, and so when I pitched an article about the potential downsides of Remem to my managing editor, he gave me the go-ahead. My first interview was with a married couple whom I'll call Joel and Deirdre, an architect and a painter, respectively. It wasn't hard to get them talking about Remem.

"Joel is always saying that he knew it all along," said Deirdre, "even when he didn't. It used to drive me crazy, because I couldn't get him to admit he used to believe something else. Now I can. For example, recently we were talking about the McKittridge kidnapping case."

She sent me the video of one argument she had with Joel. My retinal projector displayed footage of a cocktail party; it's from Deirdre's point of view, and Joel is telling a number of people, *"It was pretty clear that he was guilty from the day he was arrested."*

Deirdre's voice: *"You didn't always think that. For months you argued that he was innocent."*

Joel shakes his head. *"No, you're misremembering. I said that even people who are obviously guilty deserve a fair trial."*

"That's not what you said. You said he was being railroaded."

"You're thinking of someone else; that wasn't me."

"No, it was you. Look." A separate video window opened up, an excerpt of her lifelog that she looked up and broadcast to the people they've been talking with. Within the nested video, Joel and Deirdre are sitting in a café, and Joel is saying, *"He's a scapegoat. The police needed to reassure the public, so they arrested a convenient suspect. Now he's done for."* Deidre replies, *"You don't think there's any chance of him being acquitted?"* and Joel answers, *"Not unless he can afford a high-powered defense team, and I'll bet you he can't. People in his position will never get a fair trial."*

I closed both windows, and Deirdre said, "Without Remem, I'd never be able to convince him that he changed his position. Now I have proof."

"Fine, you were right that time," said Joel. "But you didn't have to do that in front of our friends."

"You correct me in front of our friends all the time. You're telling me I can't do the same?"

Here was the line at which the pursuit of truth ceased to be an intrinsic good. When the only persons affected have a personal relationship with each other, other priorities are often more important, and a forensic pursuit of the truth could be harmful. Did it really matter whose idea it was to take the vacation that turned out so disastrously? Did you need to know which partner was more forgetful about completing errands the other person requested? I was no expert on marriage, but I knew what marriage counselors said: pinpointing blame wasn't the answer. Instead, couples needed to acknowledge each other's feelings and address their problems as a team.

Next I talked to a spokesperson from Whetstone, Erica Meyers. For a while she gave me a typically corporate spiel about the benefits of Remem. "Making information more accessible is an intrinsic good," she said. "Ubiquitous video has revolutionized law enforcement. Businesses become more effective when they adopt good record-keeping practices. The same thing happens to us as individuals when our memories become more accurate: we get better, not just at doing our jobs, but at living our lives."

When I asked her about couples like Joel and Deirdre, she said, "If your marriage is solid, Remem isn't going to hurt it. But if you're the type of person who's constantly trying to prove that you're right and your spouse is wrong, then your marriage is going to be in trouble whether you use Remem or not."

I conceded that she may have a point in this particular case. But, I asked her, didn't she think Remem created greater opportunities for those types of arguments to arise, even in solid marriages, by making it easier for people to keep score?

"Not at all," she said. "Remem didn't give them a scorekeeping mentality; they developed that on their own. Another couple could just as easily use Remem to realize that they've both misremembered things and become more forgiving when that sort of mistake happens. I predict the latter scenario will be the more common one with our customers as a whole."

I wished I could share Erica Meyers's optimism, but I knew that new technology doesn't always bring out the best in people. Who hasn't wished they could prove that their version of events was the correct one? I could easily see myself using Remem the way Deirdre did, and I wasn't at all certain that doing so would be good for me. Anyone who has wasted hours surfing the Internet knows that technology can encourage bad habits.

. . .

Moseby gave a sermon every seven days, on the day devoted to resting and brewing and drinking beer. He seemed to disapprove of the beer drinking, but he didn't want to speak on one of the days of work, so the day of beer brewing was the only one left. He talked about the European god and told people that following his rules would improve their lives, but his explanations of how that would do so weren't particularly persuasive.

But Moseby also had some skill at dispensing medicine, and he was willing to learn how to work in the fields, so gradually people grew more accepting of him, and Jijingi's father let him visit Moseby occasionally to learn the art of writing. Moseby offered to teach the other children as well, and for a time Jijingi's age-mates came along, mostly to prove to one another that they weren't afraid of being near a European. Before long the other boys grew bored and left, but because Jijingi remained interested in writing, and his father thought it would keep the Europeans happy, he was eventually permitted to go every day.

Moseby explained to Jijingi how each sound a person spoke could be indicated with a different mark on the paper. The marks were arranged in rows like plants in a field; you looked at the marks as if you were walking down a row, made the sound each mark indicated, and you would find yourself speaking what the original person had said. Moseby showed him how to make each of the different marks on a sheet of paper, using a tiny wooden rod that had a core of soot.

In a typical lesson, Moseby would speak and then write what

he had said: "When night comes I shall sleep." *Tugh mba a ile yo me yav.* "There are two persons." *Ioruv mban mba uhar.* Jijingi carefully copied the writing on his sheet of paper, and when he was done, Moseby would look at his paper.

"Very good. But you need to leave spaces when you write."

"I have." Jijingi pointed at the gap between each row.

"No, that is not what I mean. Do you see the spaces within each line?" He pointed at his own paper.

Jijingi understood. "Your marks are clumped together, while mine are arranged evenly."

"These are not just clumps of marks. They are . . . I do not know what you call them." He picked up a thin sheaf of paper from his table and flipped through it. "I do not see it here. Where I come from, we call them 'words.' When we write, we leave spaces between the words."

"But what are words?"

"How can I explain it?" He thought a moment. "If you speak slowly, you pause very briefly after each word. That's why we leave a space in those places when we write. Like this: How. Many. Years. Old. Are. You?" He wrote on his paper as he spoke, leaving a space every time he paused: *Anyom a ou kuma a me?*

"But you speak slowly because you're a foreigner. I'm Tiv, so I don't pause when I speak. Shouldn't my writing be the same?"

"It does not matter how fast you speak. Words are the same whether you speak quickly or slowly."

"Then why did you say you pause after each word?"

"That is the easiest way to find them. Try saying this very slowly." He pointed at what he'd just written.

Jijingi spoke very slowly, the way a man might when trying to hide his drunkenness. "Why is there no space in between *an* and *yom*?"

"*Anyom* is one word. You do not pause in the middle of it."

"But I wouldn't pause after *anyom* either."

Moseby sighed. "I will think more about how to explain what I mean. For now, just leave spaces in the places where I leave spaces."

What a strange art writing was. When sowing a field, it was best to have the seed yams spaced evenly; Jijingi's father would have beaten him if he'd clumped the yams the way Moseby clumped his marks on paper. But he had resolved to learn this art as best he could, and if that meant clumping his marks, he would do so.

It was only many lessons later that Jijingi finally understood where he should leave spaces and what Moseby meant when he said "word." You could not find the places where words began and ended by listening. The sounds a person made while speaking were as smooth and unbroken as the hide of a goat's leg, but the words were like the bones underneath the meat, and the space between them was the joint where you'd cut if you wanted to separate it into pieces. By leaving spaces when he wrote, Moseby was making visible the bones in what he said.

Jijingi realized that, if he thought hard about it, he was now able to identify the words when people spoke in an ordinary conversation. The sounds that came from a person's mouth hadn't changed, but he understood them differently; he was aware of the pieces from which the whole was made. He himself had been speaking in words all along. He just hadn't known it until now.

. . .

The ease of searching that Remem provides is impressive enough, but that merely scratches the surface of what Whetstone sees as the product's potential. When Deirdre fact-checked her husband's previous statements, she was posing explicit queries to Remem. But Whetstone expects that, as people become accustomed to their product, queries will take the place of ordinary acts of recall, and Remem will be integrated into their very thought processes. Once that happens, we will become cognitive cyborgs, effectively incapable of misremembering anything; digital video stored on error-corrected silicon will take over the role once filled by our fallible temporal lobes.

What might it be like to have a perfect memory? Arguably the individual with the best memory ever documented was Solomon Shereshevskii, who lived in Russia during the first half of the twentieth century. The psychologists who tested him found that he could hear a series of words or numbers once and remember it months or even years later. With no knowledge of Italian, Shereshevskii was able to quote stanzas of *The Divine Comedy* that had been read to him fifteen years earlier.

But having a perfect memory wasn't the blessing one might imagine it to be. Reading a passage of text evoked so many images in Shereshevskii's mind that he often couldn't focus on what it actually said, and his awareness of innumerable specific examples made it difficult for him to understand abstract concepts. At times, he tried to deliberately forget things. He wrote down numbers he no longer wanted to remember on slips of paper and then burned them, a kind of slash-and-burn approach to clearing out the undergrowth of his mind, but to no avail.

When I raised the possibility to Whetstone's spokesperson, Erica Meyers, that a perfect memory might be a handicap, she had a ready reply. "This is no different from the concerns people used to have about retinal projectors," she said. "They worried that seeing updates constantly would be distracting or overwhelming, but we've all adapted to them."

I didn't mention that not everyone considered that a positive development.

"And Remem is entirely customizable," she continued. "If at any time you find it's doing too many searches for your needs, you can decrease its level of responsiveness. But according to our customer analytics, our users haven't been doing that. As they become more comfortable with it, they're finding that Remem becomes more helpful the more responsive it is."

But even if Remem isn't constantly crowding your field of vision with unwanted imagery of the past, I wonder if there aren't issues raised simply by having that imagery be perfect.

"Forgive and forget" goes the expression, and for our idealized magnanimous selves, that is all you needed. But for our actual selves the relationship between those two actions isn't so straightforward. In most cases we have to forget a little bit before we can forgive; when we no longer experience the pain as fresh, the insult is easier to forgive, which in turn makes it less memorable, and so on. It's this psychological feedback loop that makes initially infuriating offenses seem pardonable in the mirror of hindsight.

What I feared was that Remem would make it impossible for this feedback loop to get rolling. By fixing every detail of an insult in indelible video, it could prevent the softening that's needed for forgiveness to begin. I thought back to what Erica Meyers said about Remem's inability to hurt solid marriages. Implicit in that assertion was a claim about what qualified as a solid marriage. If someone's marriage was built on—as ironic as it might sound—a cornerstone of forgetfulness, what right did Whetstone have to shatter that?

The issue wasn't confined to marriages; all sorts of relationships rely on forgiving and forgetting. My daughter, Nicole, has always been strong-willed; rambunctious when she was a child, openly defiant as an adolescent. She and I had many furious arguments during her teen years, arguments that we have mostly been able to put behind us, and now our relationship is pretty good. If we'd had Remem, would we still be speaking to each other?

I don't mean to say that forgetting is the only way to mend relationships. While I can no longer recall most of the arguments Nicole and I had—and I'm grateful that I can't—there's one argument I remember very clearly, because it spurred me to be a better father.

It was when Nicole was sixteen, a junior in high school. It had been two years since her mother, Angela, had left, probably the two hardest years of both our lives. I don't remember what started the argument—something trivial, no doubt—but it escalated, and before long Nicole was taking her anger at Angela out on me.

"You're the reason she left! You drove her away! You can leave, too, for all I care. I sure as hell would be better off without you." And to demonstrate her point, she stormed out of the house.

I knew it wasn't premeditated malice on her part—I don't think she engaged in much premeditation in anything during that phase of her life—but she couldn't have come up with a more hurtful accusation if she'd tried. I'd been devastated by Angela's departure, and I was constantly wondering what I could have done differently to keep her.

Nicole didn't come back until the next day, and that night was one of soul-searching for me. While I didn't believe I was responsible for her mother leaving us, Nicole's accusation still served as a wake-up call. I hadn't been conscious of it, but I realized that I had been thinking of myself as the greatest victim of Angela's departure, wallowing in self-pity over just how unreasonable my situation was. It hadn't even been my idea to have children; it was Angela who'd wanted to be a parent, and now she had left me holding the bag. What sane world would leave me with sole responsibility for raising an adolescent girl? How could a job that was so difficult be entrusted to someone with no experience whatsoever?

Nicole's accusation made me realize her predicament was worse than mine. At least I had volunteered for this duty, albeit long ago and without full appreciation for what I was getting into. Nicole had been drafted into her role, with no say whatsoever. If there was anyone who had a right to be resentful, it was her. And while I thought I'd been doing a good job of being a father, obviously I needed to do better.

I turned myself around. Our relationship didn't improve overnight, but over the years I was able to work myself back into Nicole's good graces. I remember the way she hugged me at her college graduation, and I realized my years of effort had paid off.

Would those years of repair have been possible with Remem? Even if each of us could have refrained from throwing the other's bad behavior in their face, the opportunity to privately rewatch video of our arguments seems like it could be pernicious. Vivid reminders of the way she and I yelled at each other in the past might have kept our anger fresh and prevented us from rebuilding our relationship.

. . .

Jijingi wanted to write down some of the stories of where the Tiv people came from, but the storytellers spoke rapidly, and he wasn't able to write fast enough to keep up with them. Moseby said he would get better with practice, but Jijingi despaired that he'd ever become fast enough.

Then one summer a European woman named Reiss came to visit the village. Moseby said she was "a person who learns about other people" but could not explain what that meant, only that she wanted to learn about Tivland. She asked questions of everyone, not just the elders but young men, too, even women and children, and she wrote down everything they told her. She didn't try to get anyone to adopt European practices; where Moseby had insisted that there were no such things as curses and that everything was God's will, Reiss asked about how curses worked and listened attentively to explanations of how your kin on your father's side could curse you while your kin on your mother's side could protect you from curses.

One evening Kokwa, the best storyteller in the village, told the story of how the Tiv people split into different lineages, and Reiss had written it down exactly as he told it. Later she had recopied the story using a machine she poked at noisily with her fingers, so that she had a copy that was clean and easy to read. When Jijingi asked if she would make another copy for him, she agreed, much to his excitement.

The paper version of the story was curiously disappointing. Jijingi remembered that when he had first learned about writing, he'd imagined it would enable him to see a storytelling performance as vividly as if he were there. But writing didn't do that. When Kokwa told the story, he didn't merely use words; he used the sound of his voice, the movement of his hands, the light in his eyes. He told you the story with his whole body, and you understood it the same way. None of that was captured on paper; only the bare words could be written down. And reading just the words gave you only a hint of the experience of listening to Kokwa himself, as if one were licking the pot in which okra had been cooked instead of eating the okra itself.

Jijingi was still glad to have the paper version and would read it from time to time. It was a good story, worthy of being recorded on paper. Not everything written on paper was so worthy. During his sermons Moseby would read aloud stories from his book, and they were often good stories, but he also read aloud words he had written down just a few days before, and those were often not stories at all, merely claims that learning more about the European god would improve the lives of the Tiv people.

One day, when Moseby had been eloquent, Jijingi complimented him. "I know you think highly of all your sermons, but today's sermon was a good one."

"Thank you," said Moseby, smiling. After a moment, he asked, "Why do you say I think highly of all my sermons?"

"Because you expect that people will want to read them many years from now."

"I don't expect that. What makes you think that?"

"You write them all down before you even deliver them. Before even one person has heard a sermon, you have written it down for future generations."

Moseby laughed. "No, that is not why I write them down."

"Why, then?" He knew it wasn't for people far away to read them, because sometimes messengers came to the village to deliver paper to Moseby, and he never sent his sermons back with them.

"I write the words down so I do not forget what I want to say when I give the sermon."

"How could you forget what you want to say? You and I are speaking right now, and neither of us needs paper to do so."

"A sermon is different from conversation." Moseby paused to consider. "I want to be sure I give my sermons as well as possible. I won't forget what I want to say, but I might forget the best way to say it. If I write it down, I don't have to worry. But writing the words down does more than help me remember. It helps me think."

"How does writing help you think?"

"That is a good question," he said. "It is strange, isn't it? I do not know how to explain it, but writing helps me decide what I want to say. Where I come from, there's a very old proverb: *Verba volant, scripta manent*. In Tiv you would say, 'Spoken words fly away, written words remain.' Does that make sense?"

"Yes," Jijingi said, just to be polite; it made no sense at all. The missionary wasn't old enough to be senile, but his memory must be terrible and he didn't want to admit it. Jijingi told his age-mates about this, and they joked about it among themselves for days. Whenever they exchanged gossip, they would add, "Will you remember that? This will help you," and mimic Moseby writing at his table.

On an evening the following year, Kokwa announced he would tell the story of how the Tiv split into different lineages. Jijingi brought out the paper version he had, so he could read the story at the same time Kokwa told it. Sometimes he could follow along, but it was often confusing because Kokwa's words didn't match what was written on the paper. After Kokwa was finished, Jijingi said to him, "You didn't tell the story the same way you told it last year."

"Nonsense," said Kokwa. "When I tell a story it doesn't change, no matter how much time passes. Ask me to tell it twenty years from today, and I will tell it exactly the same."

Jijingi pointed at the paper he held. "This paper is the story you told last year, and there were many differences." He picked one he remembered. "Last time you said, 'The Uyengi captured the women and children and carried them off as slaves.' This time you said, 'They made slaves of the women, but they did not stop there: they even made slaves of the children.'"

"That's the same."

"It is the same story, but you've changed the way you tell it."

"No," said Kokwa, "I told it just as I told it before."

Jijingi didn't want to try to explain what words were. Instead he said, "If you told it as you did before, you would say 'The Uyengi captured the women and children and carried them off as slaves' every time."

For a moment Kokwa stared at him, and then he laughed. "Is this what you think is important, now that you've learned the art of writing?"

Sabe, who had been listening to them, chided Kokwa. "It's not your place to judge Jijingi. The hare favors one food, the hippo favors another. Let each spend his time as he pleases."

"Of course, Sabe, of course," said Kokwa, but he threw a derisive glance at Jijingi.

Afterward, Jijingi remembered the proverb Moseby had mentioned. Even though Kokwa was telling the same story, he might arrange the words differently each time he told it; he was skilled enough as a storyteller that the arrangement of words didn't matter. It was different for Moseby, who never acted anything out when he gave his sermons; for him, the words were what was important. Jijingi realized that Moseby wrote down his sermons not because his memory was terrible but because he was looking for a specific arrangement of words. Once he found the one he wanted, he could hold on to it for as long as he needed.

Out of curiosity, Jijingi tried imagining he had to deliver a sermon and began writing down what he would say. Seated on the root of a mango tree with the notebook Moseby had given him, he composed a sermon on *tsav*, the quality that enabled some men to have power over others, and a subject which Moseby hadn't understood and had dismissed as foolishness. He read his first attempt to one of his age-mates, who pronounced it terrible, leading them to have a brief shoving match, but afterward Jijingi had to admit his age-mate was right. He tried writing out his sermon a second time and then a third before he became tired of it and moved on to other topics.

As he practiced his writing, Jijingi came to understand what Moseby had meant: writing was not just a way to record what someone said; it could help you decide what you would say before you said it. And words were not just the pieces of speaking; they were the pieces of thinking. When you wrote them down, you could grasp your thoughts like bricks in your hands and push them into different arrangements. Writing let you look at your thoughts in a way you couldn't if you were just talking, and having seen them, you could improve them, make them stronger and more elaborate.

. . .

Psychologists make a distinction between semantic memory—knowledge of general facts—and episodic memory, or recollection of personal experiences. We've been using technological supplements for semantic memory ever since the invention of writing: first books, then search engines. By contrast, we've historically resisted such aids when it comes to episodic memory; few people have ever kept as many diaries or photo albums as they did ordinary books. The obvious reason is convenience; if we wanted a book on the birds of North America, we could consult one that an ornithologist has written, but if we wanted a daily diary, we had to write it for ourselves. But I also wonder if another reason is that, subconsciously, we regarded our episodic memories as such an integral part of our identities that we were reluctant to externalize them, to relegate them to books on a shelf or files on a computer.

That may be about to change. For years parents have been recording their children's every moment, so even if children weren't wearing personal cams, their lifelogs were effectively already being compiled. Now parents are having their children wear retinal projectors at younger and younger ages so they can reap the benefits of assistive software agents sooner. Imagine what will happen if children begin using Remem to access those lifelogs: their mode of cognition will diverge from ours because the act of recall will be different. Rather than thinking of an event from her past and seeing it with her mind's eye, a child will subvocalize a reference to it and watch video footage with her physical eyes. Episodic memory will become entirely technologically mediated.

An obvious drawback to such reliance is the possibility that people might become virtual amnesiacs whenever the software crashes. But just as worrying to me as the prospect of technological failure was that of technological success: How will it change a person's conception of herself when she's only seen her past through the unblinking eye of a video camera? Just as there's a feedback loop in softening harsh memories, there's also one at work in the romanticization of childhood memories, and disrupting that process will have consequences.

The earliest birthday I remember is my fourth; I remember blowing out the candles on my cake, the thrill of tearing the wrapping paper off the presents. There's no video of the event, but there are snapshots in the family album, and they are consistent with what I remember. In fact, I suspect I no longer remember the day itself. It's more likely that I manufactured the memory when I was first shown the snapshots, and over time, I've imbued it with the emotion I imagine I felt that day. Little by little, over repeated instances of recall, I've created a happy memory for myself.

Another of my earliest memories is of playing on the living room rug, pushing toy cars around, while my grandmother worked at her sewing machine; she would occasionally turn and smile warmly at me. There are no photos of that moment, so I know the recollection is mine and mine alone. It is a lovely, idyllic memory. Would I want to be presented with actual footage of that afternoon? No; absolutely not.

Regarding the role of truth in autobiography, the critic Roy Pascal wrote, "On the one side are the truths of fact, on the other the truth of the writer's feeling, and where the two coincide cannot be decided by any outside authority in advance." Our memories are private autobiographies, and that afternoon with my grandmother features prominently in mine because of the feelings associated with it. What if video footage revealed that my grandmother's smile was in fact perfunctory, that she was actually frustrated because her sewing wasn't going well? What's important to me about that memory is the happiness I associate with it, and I wouldn't want that jeopardized.

It seemed to me that continuous video of my entire childhood would be full of facts but devoid of feeling, simply because cameras couldn't capture the emotional dimension of events. As far as the camera was concerned, that afternoon with my grandmother would be indistinguishable from a hundred others. And if I'd grown up with access to all the video footage, there'd have been no way for me to assign more emotional weight to any particular day, no nucleus around which nostalgia could accrete.

And what will the consequences be when people can claim to remember their infancy? I could readily imagine a situation where, if you ask a young person what her earliest memory is, she will simply look baffled; after all, she has video dating back to the day of her birth. The inability to remember the first few years of one's life—what psychologists call childhood amnesia—might soon be a thing of the past. No more would parents tell their children anecdotes beginning with the words "You don't remember this because you were just a toddler when it happened." It'll be as if childhood amnesia is a characteristic of humanity's childhood, and in ouroboric fashion, our youth will vanish from our memories.

Part of me wanted to stop this, to protect children's ability to see the beginning of their lives filtered through gauze, to keep those origin stories from being replaced by cold, desaturated video. But maybe they will feel just as warmly about their lossless digital memories as I do about my imperfect, organic memories.

People are made of stories. Our memories are not the impartial accumulation of every second we've lived; they're the narrative that we assembled out of selected moments. Which is why, even when we've experienced the same events as other individuals, we never constructed identical narratives: the criteria used for selecting moments were different for each of us, and a reflection of our personalities. Each of us noticed the details that caught our attention and remembered what was important to us, and the narratives we built shaped our personalities in turn.

But, I wondered, if everyone remembered everything, would our differences get shaved away? What would happen to our sense of self? It seemed to me that a perfect memory couldn't be a narrative any more than unedited security-cam footage could be a feature film.

. . .

When Jijingi was twenty, an officer from the administration came to the village to speak with Sabe. He had brought with him a young Tiv man who had attended the mission school in Katsina-Ala. The administration wanted to have a written record of all the disputes brought before the tribal courts, so they were assigning each chief one of these youths to act as a scribe. Sabe had Jijingi come forward, and to the officer he said, "I know you don't have enough scribes for all of Tivland. Jijingi here has learned to write; he can act as our scribe, and you can send your boy to another village." The officer tested Jijingi's ability to write, but Moseby had taught him well, and eventually the officer agreed to have him be Sabe's scribe.

After the officer had left, Jijingi asked Sabe why he hadn't wanted the boy from Katsina-Ala to be his scribe.

"No one who comes from the mission school can be trusted," said Sabe.

"Why not? Did the Europeans make them liars?"

"They're partly to blame, but so are we. When the Europeans collected boys for the mission school years ago, most elders gave them the ones they wanted to get rid of, the layabouts and malcontents. Now those boys have returned, and they feel no kinship with anyone. They wield their knowledge of writing like a long gun; they demand their chiefs find them wives, or else they'll write lies about them and have the Europeans depose them."

Jijingi knew a boy who was always complaining and looking for ways to avoid work; it would be a disaster if someone like him had power over Sabe. "Can't you tell the Europeans about this?"

"Many have," Sabe answered. "It was Maisho of the Kwande clan who warned me about the scribes; they were installed in Kwande villages first. Maisho was fortunate that the Europeans believed him instead of his scribe's lies, but he knows of other chiefs who were not so lucky; the Europeans often believe paper over people. I don't wish to take the chance." He looked at Jijingi seriously. "You are my kin, Jijingi, and kin to everyone in this village. I trust you to write down what I say."

"Yes, Sabe."

Tribal court was held every month, from morning until late afternoon for three days in a row, and it always attracted an audience, sometimes one so large that Sabe had to demand everyone sit to allow the breeze to reach the center of the circle. Jijingi sat next to Sabe and recorded the details of each dispute in a book the officer had left. It was a good job; he was paid out of the fees collected from the disputants, and he was given not just a chair but a small table, too, which he could use for writing even when court wasn't in session. The complaints Sabe heard were varied—one might be about a stolen bicycle, another might be about whether a man was responsible for his neighbor's crops failing—but most had to do with wives. For one such dispute, Jijingi wrote down the following:

> Umem's wife Girgi has run away from home and gone
> back to her kin. Her kinsman Anongo has tried to con-
> vince her to stay with her husband, but Girgi refuses, and
> there is no more Anongo can do. Umem demands the

return of the £11 he paid as bridewealth. Anongo says he has no money at the moment, and moreover that he was only paid £6.

Sabe requested witnesses for both sides. Anongo says he has witnesses, but they have gone on a trip. Umem produces a witness, who is sworn in. He testifies that he himself counted the £11 that Umem paid to Anongo.

Sabe asks Girgi to return to her husband and be a good wife, but she says she has had all that she can stand of him. Sabe instructs Anongo to repay Umem £11, the first payment to be in three months when his crops are salable. Anongo agrees.

It was the final dispute of the day, by which time Sabe was clearly tired. "Selling vegetables to pay back bridewealth," he said afterward, shaking his head. "This wouldn't have happened when I was a boy."

Jijingi knew what he meant. In the past, the elders said, you conducted exchanges with similar items: if you wanted a goat, you could trade chickens for it; if you wanted to marry a woman, you promised one of your kinswomen to her family. Then the Europeans said they would no longer accept vegetables as payment for taxes, insisting that it be paid in coin. Before long, everything could be exchanged for money; you could use it to buy everything from a calabash to a wife. The elders considered it absurd.

"The old ways are vanishing," agreed Jijingi. He didn't say that young people preferred things this way, because the Europeans had also decreed that bridewealth could only be paid if the woman consented to the marriage. In the past, a young woman might be promised to an old man with leprous hands and rotting teeth and have no choice but to marry him. Now a woman could marry the man she favored, as long as he could afford to pay the bridewealth. Jijingi himself was saving money to marry.

Moseby came to watch sometimes, but he found the proceedings confusing, and often asked Jijingi questions afterward.

"For example, there was the dispute between Umem and Anongo over how much bridewealth was owed. Why was only the witness sworn in?" asked Moseby.

"To ensure that he said precisely what happened."

"But if Umem and Anongo were sworn in, that would have ensured they said precisely what happened, too. Anongo was able to lie because he was not sworn in."

"Anongo didn't lie," said Jijingi. "He said what he considered right, just as Umem did."

"But what Anongo said wasn't the same as what the witness said."

"But that doesn't mean he was lying." Then Jijingi remembered something about the European language, and understood Moseby's confusion. "Our language has two words for what in your language is called 'true.' There is what's right, *mimi,* and what's precise, *vough.* In a dispute the principals say what they consider right; they speak *mimi.* The witnesses, however, are sworn to say precisely what happened; they speak *vough.* When Sabe has heard what happened he can decide what action is *mimi* for everyone. But it's not lying if the principals don't speak *vough,* as long as they speak *mimi.*"

Moseby clearly disapproved. "In the land I come from, everyone who testifies in court must swear to speak *vough,* even the principals."

Jijingi didn't see the point of that, but all he said was "Every tribe has its own customs."

"Yes, customs may vary, but the truth is the truth; it doesn't change from one person to another. And remember what the Bible says: 'the truth shall set you free.'"

"I remember," said Jijingi. Moseby had said that it was knowing God's truth that had made the Europeans so successful. There was no denying their wealth or power, but who knew what was the cause?

. . .

In order to write about Remem, I felt it was only fair that I try it out myself. The problem was that I didn't have a lifelog for it to index; typically I only activated my personal cam when I was conducting an interview or covering an event. But I've certainly spent time in the presence of people who kept lifelogs, and I could make use of what they'd recorded. While all lifelogging software has privacy controls in place, most people also grant basic sharing rights: if your actions were recorded in their lifelog, you have access to the footage in which you're present. So I launched an agent to assemble a partial lifelog from the footage others had recorded, using my GPS history as the basis for the query. Over the course of a week, my request propagated through social networks and public video archives, and I was rewarded with snippets of video ranging from a few seconds in length to a few hours: not just security-cam footage but excerpts from the lifelogs of friends, acquaintances, and even complete strangers.

The resulting lifelog was of course highly fragmentary compared with what I would have had if I'd been recording video myself, and the footage was all from a third-person perspective rather than the first person that most lifelogs have, but Remem was able to work with that. I expected that coverage would be thickest in the later years, simply due to the increasing popularity of lifelogs. It was somewhat to my surprise, then, that when I looked at a graph of the coverage, I found a bump in the coverage more than a decade ago. Nicole had been keeping a lifelog since she was a teenager, so an unexpectedly large segment of my domestic life was present.

I was initially a bit uncertain of how to test Remem, since I obviously couldn't ask it to bring up video of an event I didn't remember. I figured I'd start out with something I did remember. I subvocalized, "The time Vince told me about his trip to Palau."

My retinal projector displayed a window in the lower-left corner of my field of vision: I'm having lunch with my friends Vincent and Jeremy. Vincent didn't maintain a lifelog either, so the footage was from Jeremy's point of view. I listened to Vincent rave about scuba diving for a minute.

Next I tried something that I only vaguely remembered. "The dinner banquet when I sat between Deborah and Lyle." I didn't remember who else was sitting at the table and wondered if Remem could help me identify them.

Sure enough, Deborah had been recording that evening, and with her video I was able to use a recognition agent to identify everyone sitting across from us.

After those initial successes, I had a run of failures, not surprising, considering the gaps in the lifelog. But over the course of an hour-long survey of past events, Remem's performance was generally impressive.

Finally it seemed time for me to try Remem on some memories that were more emotionally freighted. My relationship with Nicole felt strong enough now for me to safely revisit the fights we'd had when she was young. I figured I'd start with the argument I remembered clearly and work backward from there.

I subvocalized, "The time Nicole yelled at me 'You're the reason she left.'"

The window displays the kitchen of the house we lived in when Nicole was growing up. The footage is from Nicole's point of view, and I'm standing in front of the stove. It's obvious we're fighting.

"You're the reason she left. You drove her away! You can leave, too, for all I care. I sure as hell would be better off without you."

The words were just as I remembered them, but it wasn't Nicole saying them.

It was me.

My first thought was that it must be a fake, that Nicole had edited the video to put her words into my mouth. She must have noticed my request for access to her lifelog footage and concocted this to teach me a lesson. Or perhaps it was a film she had created to show her friends, to reinforce the stories she told about me. But why was she still so angry at me that she would do such a thing? Hadn't we gotten past this?

I started skimming through the video, looking for inconsistencies that would indicate where the edited footage had been spliced in. The subsequent footage showed Nicole running out of the house, just as I remembered, so there wouldn't be signs of inconsistency there. I rewound the video and started watching the preceding argument.

Initially I was angry as I watched, angry at Nicole for going to such lengths to create this lie, because the preceding footage was all consistent with me being the one who yelled at her.

Then some of what I was saying in the video began to sound queasily familiar: complaining about being called to her school again because she'd gotten into trouble, accusing her of spending time with the wrong crowd. But this wasn't the context in which I'd said those things, was it? I had been voicing my concern, not berating her. Nicole must have adapted things I'd said elsewhere to make her slanderous video more plausible. That was the only explanation, right?

I asked Remem to examine the video's watermark, and it reported the video was unmodified. I saw that Remem had suggested a correction in my search terms: where I had said "the time Nicole yelled at me," it offered "the time I yelled at Nicole." The correction must have been displayed at the same time as the initial search result, but I hadn't noticed. I shut down Remem in disgust, furious at the product. I was about to search for information on forging a digital watermark to prove this video was faked, but I stopped myself, recognizing it as an act of desperation.

I would have testified, hand on a stack of Bibles or using any oath required of me, that it was Nicole who'd accused me of being the reason her mother left us. My recollection of that argument was as clear as any memory I had, but that wasn't the only reason I found the video hard to believe; it was also my knowledge that—whatever my faults or imperfections—I was never the kind of father who could say such a thing to his child.

Yet here was digital video proving that I had been exactly that kind of father. And while I wasn't that man anymore, I couldn't deny that I was continuous with him.

Even more telling was the fact that for many years I had successfully hidden the truth from myself. Earlier I said that the details we choose to remember are a reflection of our personalities. What did it say about me that I put those words in Nicole's mouth instead of mine?

I remembered that argument as being a turning point for me. I had imagined a narrative of redemption and self-improvement in which I was the heroic single father, rising to meet the challenge. But the reality was . . . what? How much of what had happened since then could I take credit for?

I restarted Remem and began looking at video of Nicole's graduation from college. That was an event I had recorded myself, so I had footage of Nicole's face, and she seemed genuinely happy in my presence. Was she hiding her true feelings so well that I couldn't detect them? Or if our relationship had actually improved, how had that happened? I had obviously been a much worse father fourteen years ago than I'd thought; it would be tempting to conclude I had come further to reach where I currently was, but I couldn't trust my perceptions anymore. Did Nicole even have positive feelings about me now?

I wasn't going to try using Remem to answer this question; I needed to go to the source. I called Nicole and left a message saying I wanted to talk to her and asking if I could come over to her apartment that evening.

· · ·

It was a few years later that Sabe began attending a series of meetings of all the chiefs in the Shangev clan. He explained to Jijingi that the Europeans no longer wished to deal with so many chiefs and were demanding that all of Tivland be divided into eight groups they called septs. As a result, Sabe and the other chiefs had to discuss whom the Shangev clan would join with. Although there was no need for a scribe, Jijingi was curious to hear the deliberations and asked Sabe if he might accompany him, and Sabe agreed.

Jijingi had never seen so many elders in one place before; some were even-tempered and dignified like Sabe, while others were loud and full of bluster. They argued for hours on end.

In the evening after Jijingi had returned, Moseby asked him what it had been like. Jijingi sighed. "Even if they're not yelling, they're fighting like wildcats."

"Who does Sabe think you should join?"

"We should join with the clans that we're most closely related to; that's the Tiv way. And since Shangev was the son of Kwande, our clan should join with the Kwande clan, which lives to the south."

"That makes sense," said Moseby. "So why is there disagreement?"

"The members of the Shangev clan don't all live next to one another. Some live on the farmland in the west, near the Jechira clan, and the elders there are friendly with the Jechira elders. They'd like the Shangev clan to join the Jechira clan, because then they'd have more influence in the resulting sept."

"I see." Moseby thought for a moment. "Could the western Shangev join a different sept from the southern Shangev?"

Jijingi shook his head. "We Shangev all have one father, so we should all remain together. All the elders agree on that."

"But if lineage is so important, how can the elders from the west argue that the Shangev clan ought to join with the Jechira clan?"

"That's what the disagreement was about. The elders from the west are claiming Shangev was the son of Jechira."

"Wait, you don't know who Shangev's parents were?"

"Of course we know! Sabe can recite his ancestors all the way back to Tiv himself. The elders from the west are merely pretending that Shangev was Jechira's son because they'd benefit from joining with the Jechira clan."

"But if the Shangev clan joined with the Kwande clan, wouldn't your elders benefit?"

"Yes, but Shangev was Kwande's son." Then Jijingi realized what Moseby was implying. "You think our elders are the ones pretending!"

"No, not at all. It just sounds like both sides have equally good claims, and there's no way to tell who's right."

"Sabe's right."

"Of course," said Moseby. "But how can you get the others to admit that? In the land I come from, many people write down their lineage on paper. That way we can trace our ancestry precisely, even many generations in the past."

"Yes, I've seen the lineages in your Bible, tracing Abraham back to Adam."

"Of course. But even apart from the Bible, people have recorded their lineages. When people want to find out whom they're descended from, they can consult paper. If you had paper, the other elders would have to admit that Sabe was right."

That was a good point, Jijingi admitted. If only the Shangev clan had been using paper long ago. Then something occurred to him. "How long ago did the Europeans first come to Tivland?"

"I'm not sure. At least forty years ago, I think."

"Do you think they might have written down anything about the Shangev clan's lineage when they first arrived?"

Moseby looked thoughtful. "Perhaps. The administration definitely keeps a lot of records. If there are any, they'd be stored at the government station in Katsina-Ala."

A truck carried goods along the motor road into Katsina-Ala

every fifth day, when the market was being held, and the next market would be the day after tomorrow. If he left tomorrow morning, he could reach the motor road in time to get a ride. "Do you think they would let me see them?"

"It might be easier if you have a European with you," said Moseby, smiling. "Shall we take a trip?"

·   ·   ·

Nicole opened the door to her apartment and invited me in. She was obviously curious about why I'd come. "So what did you want to talk about?"

I wasn't sure how to begin. "This is going to sound strange."

"Okay," she said.

I told her about viewing my partial lifelog using Remem and seeing the argument we'd had when she was sixteen that ended with me yelling at her and her leaving the house. "Do you remember that day?"

"Of course I do." She looked uncomfortable, uncertain of where I was going with this.

"I remembered it, too, or at least I thought I did. But I remembered it differently. The way I remembered it, it was you who said it to me."

"Me who said what?"

"I remembered you telling me that I could leave for all you cared, and that you'd be better off without me."

Nicole stared at me for a long time. "All these years, that's how you've remembered that day?"

"Yes, until today."

"That'd almost be funny if it weren't so sad."

I felt sick to my stomach. "I'm so sorry. I can't tell you how sorry I am."

"Sorry you said it, or sorry that you imagined me saying it?"

"Both."

"Well, you should be! You know how that made me feel?"

"I can't imagine. I know I felt terrible when I thought you had said it to me."

"Except that was just something you made up. It actually *happened* to me." She shook her head in disbelief. "Fucking typical."

That hurt to hear. "Is it? Really?"

"Sure," she said. "You're always acting like you're the victim, like you're the good guy who deserves to be treated better than you are."

"You make me sound like I'm delusional."

"Not delusional. Just blind and self-absorbed."

I bristled a little. "I'm trying to apologize here."

"Right, right. This is about you."

"No, you're right, I'm sorry." I waited until Nicole gestured for me to go on. "I guess I am . . . blind and self-absorbed. The reason it's hard for me to admit that is that I thought I had opened my eyes and gotten over that."

She frowned. "What?"

I told her how I felt like I had turned around as a father and rebuilt our relationship, culminating in a moment of bonding at her college graduation. Nicole wasn't openly derisive, but her expression caused me to stop talking; it was obvious I was embarrassing myself.

"Did you still hate me at graduation?" I asked. "Was I completely making it up that you and I got along then?"

"No, we did get along at graduation. But it wasn't because you had magically become a good father."

"What was it, then?"

She paused, took a deep breath, and then said, "I started seeing a therapist when I went to college." She paused again. "She pretty much saved my life."

My first thought was, Why would Nicole need a therapist? I pushed that down and said, "I didn't know you were in therapy."

"Of course you didn't; you were the last person I would have told. Anyway, by the time I was a senior, she had convinced me that I was better off not staying angry at you. That's why you and I got along so well at graduation."

So I had indeed fabricated a narrative that bore little resemblance to reality. Nicole had done all the work, and I had done none.

"I guess I don't really know you."

She shrugged. "You know me as well as you need to."

That hurt, too, but I could hardly complain. "You deserve better," I said.

Nicole gave a brief, rueful laugh. "You know, when I was younger, I used to daydream about you saying that. But now . . . well, it's not as if it fixes everything, is it?"

I realized that I'd been hoping she would forgive me then and there, and then everything would be good. But it would take more than my saying sorry to repair our relationship.

Something occurred to me. "I can't change the things I did, but at least I can stop pretending I didn't do them. I'm going to use Remem to get an honest picture of myself, take a kind of personal inventory."

Nicole looked at me, gauging my sincerity. "Fine," she said. "But let's be clear: you don't come running to me every time you feel guilty over treating me like crap. I worked hard to put that behind me, and I'm not going to relive it just so you can feel better about yourself."

"Of course." I saw that she was tearing up. "And I've upset you again by bringing all this up. I'm sorry."

"It's all right, Dad. I appreciate what you're trying to do. Just . . . let's not do it again for a while, okay?"

"Right." I moved toward the door to leave, and then stopped. "I just wanted to ask . . . if it's possible, if there's anything I can do to make amends . . ."

"Make amends?" She looked incredulous. "I don't know. Just be more considerate, will you?"

And that's what I'm trying to do.

.   .   .

At the government station there was indeed paper from forty years ago, what the Europeans called assessment reports, and Moseby's presence was sufficient to grant them access. They were written in the European language, which Jijingi couldn't read, but they included diagrams of the ancestry of the various clans, and he could identify the Tiv names in those diagrams easily enough, and Moseby had confirmed that his interpretation was correct. The elders in the western farms were right, and Sabe was wrong: Shangev was not Kwande's son; he was Jechira's.

One of the men at the government station had agreed to type up a copy of the relevant page so Jijingi could take it with him. Moseby decided to stay in Katsina-Ala to visit with the missionaries there, but Jijingi came home right away. He felt like an impatient child on the return trip, wishing he could ride the truck all the way back instead of having to walk from the motor road. As soon as he had arrived at the village, Jijingi looked for Sabe.

He found him on the path leading to a neighboring farm;

some neighbors had stopped Sabe to have him settle a dispute over how a nanny goat's kids should be distributed. Finally, they were satisfied, and Sabe resumed his walk. Jijingi walked beside him.

"Welcome back," said Sabe.

"Sabe, I've been to Katsina-Ala."

"Ah. Why did you go there?"

Jijingi showed him the paper. "This was written long ago, when the Europeans first came here. They spoke to the elders of the Shangev clan then, and when the elders told them the history of the Shangev clan, they said that Shangev was the son of Jechira."

Sabe's reaction was mild. "Whom did the Europeans ask?"

Jijingi looked at the paper. "Batur and Iorkyaha."

"I remember them," he said, nodding. "They were wise men. They would not have said such a thing."

Jijingi pointed at the words on the page. "But they did!"

"Perhaps you are reading it wrong."

"I am not! I know how to read."

Sabe shrugged. "Why did you bring this paper back here?"

"What it says is important. It means we should rightfully be joined with the Jechira clan."

"You think the clan should trust your decision on this matter?"

"I'm not asking the clan to trust me. I'm asking them to trust the men who were elders when you were young."

"And so they should. But those men aren't here. All you have is paper."

"The paper tells us what they would say if they were here."

"Does it? A man doesn't speak only one thing. If Batur and Iorkyaha were here, they would agree with me that we should join with the Kwande clan."

"How could they, when Shangev was the son of Jechira?" He pointed at the sheet of paper. "The Jechira are our closer kin."

Sabe stopped walking and turned to face Jijingi. "Questions of kinship cannot be resolved by paper. You're a scribe because Maisho of the Kwande clan warned me about the boys from the mission school. Maisho wouldn't have looked out for us if we didn't share the same father. Your position is proof of how close our clans are, but you forget that. You look to paper to tell you what you should already know, here." Sabe tapped him on his chest. "Have you studied paper so much that you've forgotten what it is to be Tiv?"

Jijingi opened his mouth to protest, when he realized that Sabe was right. All the time he'd spent studying writing had made him think like a European. He had come to trust what was written on paper over what was said by people, and that wasn't the Tiv way.

The assessment report of the Europeans was *vough*; it was exact and precise, but that wasn't enough to settle the question. The choice of which clan to join had to be right for the community; it had to be *mimi*. Only the elders could determine what was *mimi*; it was their responsibility to decide what was best for the Shangev clan. Asking Sabe to defer to the paper was asking him to act against what he considered right.

"You're right, Sabe," he said. "Forgive me. You're my elder, and it was wrong of me to suggest that paper could know more than you."

Sabe nodded and resumed walking. "You are free to do as you wish, but I believe it will do more harm than good to show that paper to others."

Jijingi considered it. The elders from the western farms would undoubtedly argue that the assessment report supported their position, prolonging a debate that had already gone too long. But more than that, it would move the Tiv down the path of regarding paper as the source of truth; it would be another stream in which the old ways were washing away, and he could see no benefit in it.

"I agree," said Jijingi. "I won't show this to anyone else."

Sabe nodded.

Jijingi walked back to his hut, reflecting on what had happened. Even without attending a mission school, he had begun thinking like a European; his practice of writing in his notebooks had led him to disrespect his elders without his even being aware of it. Writing helped him think more clearly, he couldn't deny that, but that wasn't good enough reason to trust paper over people.

As a scribe, he had to keep the book of Sabe's decisions in tribal court. But he didn't need to keep the other notebooks, the ones in which he'd written down his thoughts. He would use them as tinder for the cooking fire.

. . .

We don't normally think of it as such, but writing is a technology, which means that a literate person is someone whose thought processes are technologically mediated. We became cognitive cyborgs as soon as we became fluent readers, and the consequences of that were profound.

Before a culture adopts the use of writing, when its knowledge is transmitted exclusively through oral means, it can very easily revise its history. It's not intentional, but it is inevitable; throughout the world, bards and griots have adapted their material to their audiences and thus gradually adjusted the past to suit the needs of the present. The idea that accounts of the past shouldn't change is a product of literate cultures' reverence for the written word. Anthropologists will tell you that oral cultures understand the past differently; for them, their histories don't need to be accurate so much as they need to validate the community's understanding of itself. So it wouldn't be correct to say that their histories are unreliable; their histories do what they need to do.

Right now each of us is a private oral culture. We rewrite our pasts to suit our needs and support the story we tell about ourselves. With our memories we are all guilty of a Whig interpretation of our personal histories, seeing our former selves as steps toward our glorious present selves.

But that era is coming to an end. Remem is merely the first of a new generation of memory prostheses, and as these products gain widespread adoption, we will be replacing our malleable organic memories with perfect digital archives. We will have a record of what we actually did instead of stories that evolve over repeated tellings. Within our minds, each of us will be transformed from an oral culture into a literate one.

It would be easy for me to assert that literate cultures are better off than oral ones, but my bias should be obvious, since I'm writing these words rather than speaking them to you. Instead I will say that it's easier for me to appreciate the benefits of literacy and harder to recognize everything it has cost us. Literacy encourages a culture to place more value on documentation and less on subjective experience, and overall I think the positives outweigh the negatives. Written records are vulnerable to every kind of error, and their interpretation is subject to change, but at least the words on the page remain fixed, and there is real merit in that.

When it comes to our individual memories, I live on the

opposite side of the divide. As someone whose identity was built on organic memory, I'm threatened by the prospect of removing subjectivity from our recall of events. I used to think it could be valuable for individuals to tell stories about themselves, valuable in a way that it couldn't be for cultures, but I'm a product of my time, and times change. We can't prevent the adoption of digital memory any more than oral cultures could stop the arrival of literacy, so the best I can do is look for something positive in it.

And I think I've found the real benefit of digital memory. The point is not to prove you were right; the point is to admit you were wrong.

Because all of us have been wrong on various occasions, engaged in cruelty and hypocrisy, and we've forgotten most of those occasions. And that means we don't really know ourselves. How much personal insight can I claim if I can't trust my memory? How much can you? You're probably thinking that, while your memory isn't perfect, you've never engaged in revisionism of the magnitude I'm guilty of. But I was just as certain as you, and I was wrong. You may say, "I know I'm not perfect. I've made mistakes." I am here to tell you that you have made more than you think, that some of the core assumptions on which your self-image is built are actually lies. Spend some time using Remem, and you'll find out.

But the reason I now recommend Remem is not for the shameful reminders it provides of your past; it's to avoid the need for those in the future. Organic memory was what enabled me to construct a whitewashed narrative of my parenting skills, but by using digital memory from now on, I hope to keep that from happening. The truth about my behavior won't be presented to me by someone else, making me defensive; it won't even be something I'll discover as a private shock, prompting a reevaluation. With Remem providing only the unvarnished facts, my image of myself will never stray too far from the truth in the first place.

Digital memory will not stop us from telling stories about ourselves. As I said earlier, we are made of stories, and nothing can change that. What digital memory will do is change those stories from fabulations that emphasize our best acts and elide our worst, into ones that—I hope—acknowledge our fallibility and make us less judgmental about the fallibility of others.

Nicole has begun using Remem as well and discovered that her recollection of events isn't perfect, either. This hasn't made her forgive me for the way I treated her—nor should it, because her misdeeds were minor compared with mine—but it has softened her anger at my misremembering my actions, because she realizes it's something we all do. And I'm embarrassed to admit that this is precisely the scenario Erica Meyers predicted when she talked about Remem's effects on relationships.

This doesn't mean I've changed my mind about the downsides of digital memory; there are many, and people need to be aware of them. I just don't think I can argue the case with any sort of objectivity anymore. I abandoned the article I was planning to write about memory prostheses; I handed off the research I'd done to a colleague, and she wrote a fine piece about the pros and cons of the software, a dispassionate article free from all the soul-searching and angst that would have saturated anything I submitted. Instead, I've written this.

The account I've given of the Tiv is based in fact, but isn't precisely accurate. There was indeed a dispute among the Tiv in 1941 over whom the Shangev clan should join with, based on differing claims about the parentage of the clan's founder, and administrative records did show that the clan elders' account of their genealogy had changed over time. But many of the specific details I've described are invented. The actual events were more complicated and less dramatic, as actual events always are, so I have taken liberties to make a better narrative. I've told a story in order to make a case for the truth. I recognize the contradiction here.

As for my account of my argument with Nicole, I've tried to make it as accurate as I possibly could. I've been recording everything since I started working on this project, and I've consulted the recordings repeatedly when writing this. But in my choice of which details to include and which to omit, perhaps I have just constructed another story. In spite of my efforts to be unflinching, have I flattered myself with this portrayal? Have I distorted events so they more closely follow the arc expected of a confessional narrative? The only way you can judge is by comparing my account against the recordings themselves, so I'm doing something I never thought I'd do: with Nicole's permission, I am granting public access to my lifelog, such as it is. Take a look at the video, and decide for yourself.

And if you think I've been less than honest, tell me. I want to know.

THE GREAT SILENCE

THE HUMANS USE ARECIBO TO LOOK FOR EXTRATERREStrial intelligence. Their desire to make a connection is so strong that they've created an ear capable of hearing across the universe.

But I and my fellow parrots are right here. Why aren't they interested in listening to our voices?

We're a nonhuman species capable of communicating with them. Aren't we exactly what humans are looking for?

. . .

The universe is so vast that intelligent life must surely have arisen many times. The universe is also so old that even one technological species would have had time to expand and fill the galaxy. Yet there is no sign of life anywhere except on Earth. Humans call this the Fermi Paradox.

One proposed solution to the Fermi Paradox is that intelligent species actively try to conceal their presence, to avoid being targeted by hostile invaders.

Speaking as a member of a species that has been driven nearly to extinction by humans, I can attest that this is a wise strategy.

It makes sense to remain quiet and avoid attracting attention.

.   .   .

The Fermi Paradox is sometimes known as the Great Silence. The universe ought to be a cacophony of voices, but instead it is disconcertingly quiet.

Some humans theorize that intelligent species go extinct before they can expand into outer space. If they're correct, then the hush of the night sky is the silence of a graveyard.

Hundreds of years ago, my kind was so plentiful that the Río Abajo Forest resounded with our voices. Now we're almost gone. Soon this rain forest may be as silent as the rest of the universe.

.   .   .

There was an African gray parrot named Alex. He was famous for his cognitive abilities. Famous among humans, that is.

A human researcher named Irene Pepperberg spent thirty years studying Alex. She found that not only did Alex know the words for shapes and colors, he actually understood the concepts of shape and color.

Many scientists were skeptical that a bird could grasp abstract concepts. Humans like to think they're unique. But eventually Pepperberg convinced them that Alex wasn't just repeating words, that he understood what he was saying.

Out of all my cousins, Alex was the one who came closest to being taken seriously as a communication partner by humans.

Alex died suddenly, when he was still relatively young. The evening before he died, Alex said to Pepperberg, "You be good. I love you."

If humans are looking for a connection with a nonhuman intelligence, what more can they ask for than that?

. . .

Every parrot has a unique call that it uses to identify itself; biologists refer to this as the parrot's "contact call."

In 1974, astronomers used Arecibo to broadcast a message into outer space intended to demonstrate human intelligence. That was humanity's contact call.

In the wild, parrots address each other by name. One bird imitates another's contact call to get the other bird's attention.

If humans ever detect the Arecibo message being sent back to Earth, they will know someone is trying to get their attention.

. . .

Parrots are vocal learners: we can learn to make new sounds after we've heard them. It's an ability that few animals possess. A dog may understand dozens of commands, but it will never do anything but bark.

Humans are vocal learners, too. We have that in common. So humans and parrots share a special relationship with sound. We don't simply cry out. We pronounce. We enunciate.

Perhaps that's why humans built Arecibo the way they did. A receiver doesn't have to be a transmitter, but Arecibo is both. It's an ear for listening, and a mouth for speaking.

. . .

Humans have lived alongside parrots for thousands of years, and only recently have they considered the possibility that we might be intelligent.

I suppose I can't blame them. We parrots used to think

humans weren't very bright. It's hard to make sense of behavior that's so different from your own.

But parrots are more similar to humans than any extraterrestrial species will be, and humans can observe us up close; they can look us in the eye. How do they expect to recognize an alien intelligence if all they can do is eavesdrop from a hundred light-years away?

.   .   .

It's no coincidence that "aspiration" means both hope and the act of breathing.

When we speak, we use the breath in our lungs to give our thoughts a physical form. The sounds we make are simultaneously our intentions and our life force.

I speak, therefore I am. Vocal learners, like parrots and humans, are perhaps the only ones who fully comprehend the truth of this.

.   .   .

There's a pleasure that comes with shaping sounds with your mouth. It's so primal and visceral that, throughout their history, humans have considered the activity a pathway to the divine.

Pythagorean mystics believed that vowels represented the music of the spheres, and chanted to draw power from them.

Pentecostal Christians believe that when they speak in tongues, they're speaking the language used by angels in heaven.

Brahman Hindus believe that by reciting mantras, they are strengthening the building blocks of reality.

Only a species of vocal learners would ascribe such importance to sound in their mythologies. We parrots can appreciate that.

. . .

According to Hindu mythology, the universe was created with a sound: "om." It is a syllable that contains within it everything that ever was and everything that will be.

When the Arecibo telescope is pointed at the space between stars, it hears a faint hum.

Astronomers call that the cosmic microwave background. It's the residual radiation of the Big Bang, the explosion that created the universe fourteen billion years ago.

But you can also think of it as a barely audible reverberation of that original "om." That syllable was so resonant that the night sky will keep vibrating for as long as the universe exists.

When Arecibo is not listening to anything else, it hears the voice of creation.

. . .

We Puerto Rican parrots have our own myths. They're simpler than human mythology, but I think humans would take pleasure from them.

Alas, our myths are being lost as my species dies out. I doubt the humans will have deciphered our language before we're gone.

So the extinction of my species doesn't just mean the loss of a group of birds. It's also the disappearance of our language, our rituals, our traditions. It's the silencing of our voice.

. . .

Human activity has brought my kind to the brink of extinction, but I don't blame them for it. They didn't do it maliciously. They just weren't paying attention.

And humans create such beautiful myths; what imaginations

they have. Perhaps that's why their aspirations are so immense. Look at Arecibo. Any species who can build such a thing must have greatness within them.

My species probably won't be here for much longer; it's likely that we'll die before our time and join the Great Silence. But before we go, we are sending a message to humanity. We just hope the telescope at Arecibo will enable them to hear it.

The message is this:

You be good. I love you.

OMPHALOS

LORD, I PLACE MYSELF IN YOUR PRESENCE, AND ASK YOU to shine your light into my heart as I look back upon this day, so that I may see more clearly your grace in everything that has happened.

Right now I'm content and grateful for such a satisfying day, but it didn't begin auspiciously. My mood was poor when my aeroplane arrived this morning. As I was looking around the terminal for the cabstand, a man thought I was lost and tried to come to my rescue. He told me Chicagou was no place for a woman traveling alone, and I replied that I had managed well enough in Mongolia and that I doubted Chicagou could be any worse. Forgive me, Lord, for being sharp to a man who sought only to assist me. I ask for your help in being patient with those who believe women helpless.

I admit, I wasn't exactly looking forward to stopping here. It's been so long since I wrote the book that my attention has moved on to other things, and in the last month I've been entirely focused on preparing for the Arisona dig. After Dr. Janssen's electric mailgram, all I could think about was those spearpoints and what they might tell us. When my publisher arranged for me to give a public lecture here, I thought he was just taking advantage of my travel plans, getting me to promote the book without paying for the aeroplane ticket, and it felt more like a delay than anything else.

My mood improved after I got to the hotel and was met by an assistant from the theater where I was to speak. At first, when she told me how much she was looking forward to my lecture, I thought she was simply being polite, but then she spoke in some detail about how my book had given her a renewed appreciation for the work that scientists did, and I realized her enthusiasm was unfeigned. Hearing such a response from a reader was gratifying, but more important, it was a reminder that education is just as important a part of an archaeologist's job as fieldwork. Thank you, Lord, for gently showing me how self-absorbed I was to regard the public lecture as a chore.

I had a light supper in the hotel restaurant and then proceeded to the theater. It was by far the biggest audience I've had for one of my lectures; men and women crowded the hall like puffins on a beach. I knew better than to imagine the turnout was a reflection of my popularity; the name "Dorothea Morrell" on a poster has never been a major draw. They came because the Atacama mummies are being sent on a fund-raising tour around the country, and their first stop is here in Chicagou. Archaeology is on everyone's mind right now, and I was incidentally benefiting from that. But that was fine with me; I was happy to have such a large audience, no matter what the reason.

I began my lecture by discussing the growth rings of a tree trunk, and how the thickness of each ring depends on the rainfall during that year of the tree's growth, so that a succession of narrow rings indicated a period of drought. I explained that by counting back from the year a tree was felled, we can compile a chronology of weather patterns going back many decades, beyond the memory of any person living. The past has left its traces on the world, and we only have to know how to read them.

Then I described the technique of cross-dating: matching the pattern of growth rings across different trees. I offered an example where we see an identical sequence of thick and thin rings in two pieces of wood: in one case it's near the center of a recently felled tree, whereas in another it's near the perimeter of a piece of timber found in an old building. We know those trees' life spans overlapped; the former was a sapling when the latter was mature, but they experienced the same sequence of abundant and scarce rain. We can use the growth rings in the older tree to extend our record of weather patterns further into the past. Thanks to cross-dating, we're no longer limited to the life span of any individual tree.

I told the audience that archaeologists have examined the timbers from older and older buildings, matching the patterns of growth rings along the way. Even without the benefit of written records, we knew that the timbers in the top of Trier Cathedral in Germany came from trees cut in the year 1074, while those in the base came from trees cut in 1042, by examining the growth rings they contained. And it didn't stop there, I told them; there were even older timbers we could use, like the pilings in the Roman bridge at Cologne and the beams that reinforced ancient salt mines at Bad Nauheim. Every timber served as a volume in a history written by nature itself, an almanac of yearly rainfall reaching back to the birth of Christ.

Then I told them that going back further was trickier. It meant finding tree trunks preserved in bogs, beams excavated from archaeological digs, even large pieces of charcoal found in the firepits of cave dwellers. I explained that it was like assembling a jigsaw puzzle; sometimes we found many pieces that fit with one another, but we didn't know where they belonged until we found the piece that connected them to our main chronology. Over time we filled in the gaps, until our unbroken record of growth rings became five thousand years long, then seven thousand years. I told them how thrilling it was to examine a piece of wood and know that the tree it came from was felled eight thousand years before the present.

But even that thrill can't compare to that inspired by examining samples of wood a few centuries older. Because in those tree trunks, there's a point at which the growth rings stop. Counting back from the present, the oldest growth ring was formed eight thousand nine hundred and twelve years ago. There are no growth rings before that, I told them, because that is the year you created the world, Lord. In the center of every tree of that era is a circle of perfectly clear and homogeneous wood, and the diameter of that ringless area indicates the size of the tree at the moment of creation. Those are primordial trees, created directly by your hand rather than grown from seedlings.

I told them that the absence of growth rings in these tree sections is just as significant as the absence of navels in the Atacama mummies. In fact, the tree sections tell us things that the human remains, skeletal or mummified, do not. Without the growth-ring chronology, we would have no way of knowing when those primordial humans appeared; their bodies tell us that humanity was created all over the world, but the tree sections tell us exactly when it happened.

Then I told them that, while trees without growth rings and men without navels are wondrous and surprising, they are also logically necessary. To help them understand why, I asked them to consider the alternative. What would it mean, Lord, if you had created primordial trees with growth rings all the way to their centers? It would mean that you had created evidence of summers and winters that never took place. That would be a deception, no different than if you had given a primordial man a scar on his brow as a remnant of an injury suffered during a childhood he never experienced. And to support that fabricated memory, you would have to create the graves of the parents who raised the man during his fictitious childhood. Those parents would surely have mentioned their own parents, so you would have to create graves for the grandparents as well, Lord. In order to be consistent, you would fill the ground with the bones of countless generations past, so many that no matter how deeply we dig, every spadeful of soil we turn would disturb the grave of an ancestor. The Earth would be nothing except a boneyard of infinite extent.

Obviously, I said, that's not the world we live in. The world we see around us cannot be infinitely old, so it must have had a beginning, and it's only logical that when we look closely enough, we discover confirmation of that beginning. Trees without growth rings and men without navels attest to our reasoning. But more than that, I told them, they provide us with spiritual reassurance.

I asked them to imagine what it would be like if we lived in a world where, no matter how deeply we dug, we kept finding traces of an earlier era of the world. I asked them to imagine being confronted with proof of a past extending so far back that the numbers lost all meaning: a hundred thousand years, a million years, ten million years. Then I asked, wouldn't they feel lost, like a castaway adrift on an ocean of time? The only sane response would be despair.

I told them that we are not so adrift. We have dropped an

anchor and struck bottom; we can be certain that the shoreline is close by, even if we can't see it. We know that you made this universe with a purpose in mind; we know that a harbor awaits. I told them that our means of navigation is scientific inquiry. And, I said, this is why I am a scientist: because I wish to discover your purpose for us, Lord.

They applauded when I had finished speaking, and I admit that I took pleasure from that. Forgive me for my pride, Lord. Help me to remember that all the work I do—whether it is excavating bones in the desert or giving lectures to the public—is not for my own glory, but for yours. Let me never forget that my task is to show others the beauty of your works and in doing so bring them closer to you.

Amen.

. . .

Lord, I place myself in your presence, and ask you to shine your light into my heart as I look back upon this day, so that I may see more clearly your grace in everything that has happened.

Today was filled with reminders of your majesty, for which I am grateful, but it has also troubled me. It began with the breakfast I had with cousin Rosemary and her husband, Alfred. I don't see Rosemary very often, but I always enjoy the time we spend together. Thank you, Lord, for giving me at least one relative who thinks archaeology is a suitable profession for a woman, and who does not ask me when I'm going to marry or have children.

After Rosemary had given me the latest news about her side of the family, she revealed she had an additional motive for meeting me for breakfast. "I bought a relic last week, but Alfred thinks it's a fake," she said.

"It's because of the price she paid," explained Alfred. "'If it's too good to be true, it probably isn't.' That's my motto."

"We were hoping you could settle the matter for us," said Rosemary, and I told them I'd be happy to take a look at it. When we had finished eating, she went to the front desk to retrieve a parcel that she'd left with the clerks there, and we found an unoccupied seating area in a corner of the hotel lobby.

Inside the box, wrapped in a yard of muslin, was the femur of a deer, immensely old but in an excellent state of preservation, and I could immediately see that it wasn't an ordinary one. The bone lacked an epiphyseal line, the remnant of the growth plate where new cartilage is added as a juvenile's bones lengthen into an adult's. The femur had never been shorter than it was now; the deer it had come from had never been a fawn. It was the femur of a primordial deer, created at its adult size by your hand, Lord.

I told Rosemary and Alfred that it was real; she was triumphant and he was sheepish, both muting their reactions because I was there, but I could tell they'd be discussing it at length later. Rosemary thanked me, and I told her it was no trouble; but where, I asked, had she purchased it?

"I went to see the mummy exhibit. You're probably used to seeing things like that, but I thought it was spectacular. Anyway, there's a gift shop accompanying the tour. It's mostly postcards and books about the mummies, but there were also some relics for sale. Clamshells and mussel shells, of course, but some unusual items, too: bones like this one, abalone shells."

That caught my attention. Was she certain there were abalone shells?

"Definitely," she said. "I've shopped for relics before, and I've never seen an abalone shell. I had to ask the dealer about it. I was tempted to get it just for the novelty, but you can't see the lines."

I understood what she meant. The shells of ordinary clams and mussels have concentric growth rings like those of a tree. But the shells of a primordial bivalve are preternaturally smooth near their centers; only at their margins do they exhibit rings, each indicating a year of growth after creation. Such shells are the most popular relics among collectors; they're not too expensive because they're relatively common, but they display clear evidence of being made directly by your hand, Lord. By contrast, an abalone is a univalve, and the growth layers of its shell are only visible by drilling a hole and examining it with a microscope. To the naked eye, the shell of a primordial abalone is indistinguishable from that of any other abalone.

But that wasn't why I was surprised to hear of one being sold in a gift shop; it was that I knew of only one place where primordial abalone shells had been discovered, and I couldn't see how they could have come to be for sale at all. So after I finished my visit with Rosemary and Alfred, I took the bus to the church where the Atacama mummies were being exhibited.

There was a long line of visitors outside, and I suppose I could have gone directly to the gift shop and bypassed the main exhibit altogether. But contrary to what Rosemary assumed, I had never actually examined the mummy of a primordial human. I've read scholarly papers about the mummies, of course, and perused the accompanying photograms, but before today that was as close as I had come to an actual mummy. So although I had misgivings about the tour itself, I decided to buy a ticket and wait in the exhibit line.

As I stood in line, I overheard two people standing behind me talk about the mummies. A boy, maybe ten years old, asked his mother if it was a miracle that these bodies had remained intact since creation. His mother said no, and explained that they'd been preserved by an extraordinarily arid environment. She told the child, quite correctly, that so little rain falls on Chile's Atacama Desert that the hoofprints of mules remain visible fifty years later, and such conditions prevented any bodies buried there from decaying.

I found this very heartening to hear, because many people are so quick to classify events as miraculous that it devalues the word. It's that type of thinking that leads people to look to the mummies for a cure when medicine can't provide one, and even if the Church no longer makes claims about the healing power of relics, it doesn't do enough to dissuade the desperate. Among the ticket holders were one blind person and two confined to wheelchairs, all presumably hoping that proximity to one miracle could induce another. I pray that their suffering might be lessened, Lord, but I follow the secular consensus that there has been exactly one verified miracle—the creation of the universe—and all of us are precisely equidistant from it.

I must have waited in line for an hour before reaching the mummies, but that's an estimate I made in retrospect, because seeing them was such a profound experience that I forgot all about the wait. There were two, both male, each in its own temperature-and-humidity-controlled display case. Their skin looked as delicate as the paper of a wasp's nest, while simultaneously seeming to be stretched across their skulls as tight as a drum skin; I imagined that a slight jostling would cause it to tear. Both mummies wore guanaco hides around their pelvises, but nothing else; they lay recumbent on the reed mats they'd been buried with, their abdomens fully exposed.

I've handled the skeletal remains of primordial humans

before, Lord, and as wondrous as it is to hold a cranium that has no sutures or a femur that has no epiphyseal line, it frankly cannot compare with the experience of seeing a body that lacks a navel. The difference lies, I think, in the fact that we are not conscious of the detailed structure of our own bones, so it requires some anatomical knowledge to recognize what distinguishes a primordial skeleton. But we are all conscious of having a navel, so seeing a torso without one induces awe of a more visceral, even intimate, variety.

When I left the exhibit area, I overheard the boy and his mother behind me again. The mother was leading the child in prayer, and they thanked you, Lord, for ensuring that the mummies were discovered by Church archaeologists rather than secular ones, because now they were being exhibited to the public instead of being hidden in the back rooms of a museum, where only select scientists could see them. I was less heartened to hear this. It's not because I disagree with her, precisely. On this question, I'm of two minds.

I appreciate how powerful an experience it is to see the mummies directly, and this tour will bring tens or hundreds of thousands of people closer to you, Lord, by giving them that experience. But as a scientist, I feel that preservation of the tissue is the highest priority. No matter what pains the Church is taking, exhibiting these mummies across the country is bound to cause more deterioration than if they were stored in a museum. Who knows what techniques for analyzing soft tissues will be developed in the future? Biologists believe they are close to identifying the particles of inheritance through which organisms transmit their characteristics to their offspring; perhaps one day they'll be able to read the information those particles carry. When that day arrives, we could have access to your original blueprint for the human species, uncorrupted by time. A discovery like that would bring all of humanity closer to you, Lord, but it requires us to be patient and not damage the tissue in the meantime.

In any case, I proceeded to the gift shop, where a number of visitors were lined up to purchase postcards. While waiting for the salesman to become available, I looked at the display case of relics; just as Rosemary had said, there were abalones among the various more conventional shells for sale. I had wondered if the gift shop would claim the abalone shells came from Chile along with the mummies, but in fact the card describing the shells said they were found on Santa Rosa Island off the coast of Alta California. It said they were found at the bottom of middens, the trash heaps of prehistoric communities.

Once there was a lull in the visitors making purchases, the gift shop's salesman came to attend to me. Perhaps he was accustomed to people being put off by the shells' origins in trash heaps, so he explained how that enhanced their status. "Not only do these come from primordial shellfish, but they were actually handled by primordial humans. Men made directly by God held these in their hands."

I told him I was curious about the abalone shells; had they been found by Church archaeologists, like the mummies were?

"These were donated by a private collector. He provided the information that's on the cards."

I asked him if I could get the name of the collector, and he asked why I wanted to know. That was when I introduced myself and explained that I was an archaeologist; he told me his name was Mr. Dahl. I said that the only excavations on Santa Rosa Island were funded by the University of Alta California. Any and all recovered relics became part of the collections of the university's museums, so there should be no primordial abalone shells in the hands of private collectors.

"I didn't know that about abalone shells," he said. "If I had, I would've asked more questions. Are you suggesting these were stolen?"

I told him that I couldn't be certain, and that there might be an innocent explanation for it, but I'd be very interested in hearing what that was.

Mr. Dahl was obviously concerned. "We've received donations from private collectors in the past, and there's never been an issue with provenance." He looked through a ledger and then wrote down for me the name and address of the donor: a Mr. Martin Osborne, at a post-office box in San Francisco. "He sent a large selection shortly before the tour began, and asked that the items be priced inexpensively so that everyday people could afford them. It was such a generous sentiment that I agreed, even though it meant fewer funds raised for Yosemeti Cathedral. Would he do that if he had stolen them from a museum?"

I told him I didn't know. I thanked him for his help and told him I would write to him once I had verified the source of Osborne's donated relics; I suggested that, to avoid further complications, he might not want to sell any more of them until he had heard from me, and he agreed.

Now I confess that what I did next was to lie. Forgive me, Lord, but I couldn't think of any other way to meet this Mr. Osborne if he's in fact guilty of theft. I have sent an electric mailgram to Mr. Osborne, claiming to be Mr. Dahl, saying that I believe the relics he donated were stolen and I'm shipping them back to him immediately. I've also prepared a package addressed to Mr. Osborne, which will travel via train to San Francisco. I have exchanged my aeroplane tickets so that, rather than taking the flight to Arisona tomorrow, I will leave on the same train as my package. Once I'm in San Francisco, all I have to do is watch the post office and question whoever picks up the package. If he can't explain how he acquired the relics, I'll report him to the authorities. Then I'll take the train south to Los Angeles, and from there I can make arrangements to get to the Arisona dig.

I know how unorthodox this is. If Mr. Osborne had provided a residential address, I could simply knock on his door. The fact that he's using a post-office box not only makes it difficult to confront him, but leads me to think that subterfuge is justified. I hope I'm not leaping to conclusions.

Guide me toward the proper course of action, Lord. I recognize that my desire to seek answers, while necessary in scientific endeavors, is not always welcome outside of it. Help me to know when it's appropriate to keep looking and when it's better to ignore my doubts. Let me always be inquisitive, but never be suspicious.

Amen.

.   .   .

Lord, I place myself in your presence, and ask you to shine your light into my heart as I look back upon this day, so that I may see more clearly your grace in everything that has happened.

Just as I feared, the relics in the gift shop were indeed stolen. But I don't want to focus on that to the exclusion of everything else; today gave me many reasons to think of you, and I shouldn't ignore them.

My first full day in San Francisco began well; thank you for a good night's rest in a hotel bed. The days of train travel took their toll; or, should I say, the nights. I've always had trouble sleeping on trains, so they'll always be my least favorite form of travel. I would much rather cross a desert in a motorcar and sleep under the stars at night.

San Francisco is a city where no one can forget your presence, Lord. The moment I left my hotel, a petitioner asked me for a donation for Yosemeti Cathedral. Presumably they're outside every hotel, targeting visitors from out of town because every local resident has long since reached the point of fatigue. I didn't donate, but I did admire the paintings on the sandwich boards next to the petitioner. There were some lovely depictions of what the cathedral will look like when it's completed. I was particularly impressed by one that showed the main gallery illuminated by the setting sun. I've read that the gallery will be a thousand feet high from floor to ceiling, and the painting did a good job of conveying the scale.

No one can deny, Lord, that you've sculpted a landscape of great beauty on the surface of the Earth. I've been fortunate enough to have visited three continents, and I've seen cliffs of chalk, canyons of sandstone, pillars of basalt; all spectacular. But for me, the knowledge that they're no more than a decorative façade tempers my appreciation; perhaps it is my scientific mind-set that makes me want to look deeper. I have more reverence for the granite that lies just beneath the surface of all those features, the ocean of stone that the Earth is actually made of. So it's when I see those places where the granite is exposed, where the true essence of the Earth is visible, that I feel a more profound connection to your handiwork.

The Yosemeti Valley is one of those places, and I wish I could have visited it a century ago, when it was pristine and untouched. I've seen photograms of the rock formation from before they began hollowing it out, and it was magnificent. I don't mean to criticize the archdiocese's decision. Or perhaps I do. Forgive me, Lord. I know the Yosemeti Cathedral will be awe inspiring when it's completed, and I hope it happens within my lifetime. It will no doubt bring countless people closer to you. I just happen to think that the sight of the granite peak itself could have done so just as well.

Is it wrong of me to question whether the construction of cathedrals is, as we approach the twenty-first century, the best use of countless millions of dollars and the effort of generations of people? I agree that a project lasting longer than a human life span provides its participants with aspirations beyond the temporal. I even understand the motivation for carving a cathedral out of the Earth's substrate, to create a testament to both human and divine architecture. But for me, science is the true modern cathedral, an edifice of knowledge every bit as majestic as anything made of stone. It fulfills all the goals that Yosemeti Cathedral does and more, and I wish more people appreciated that.

Perhaps I'm merely envious of the Church's ability to raise money; forgive me for that, Lord. They are trying to celebrate your glory, Lord, just as we in the scientific community are, so I cannot disagree with them too strenuously. Our commonalities are more important than our differences.

I went to the post office where Martin Osborne received his mail and sat on a bench at a bus stop across the street. I had sealed the package with colored tape so I'd be able to recognize it easily when he left the post office, so I waited and watched. I felt conspicuously awkward as people arrived and got on buses while I continued to sit there. An hour passed, and then another, and more than once I wondered if I had gone about this in the wrong way. I am more accustomed to hunting for bones than for living prey, Lord; I know very little about stalking or camouflage.

At last I saw the package that I had prepared. I had almost missed it, because I had been expecting to see a man, but instead a young woman had carried it out and set it down on the curb while she hailed a cab. She was young, no more than eighteen, and maybe younger; too young to be an employee of the museum. At first I thought she must be an accomplice of Martin Osborne, perhaps someone he'd inveigled into his scheme, but then I realized that I was being a chauvinist just as much as the men whose preconceptions constantly irritate me.

I approached her and asked if she was "Martin Osborne." She hesitated for a long moment and then, accepting that she'd been caught, said, "Yes, I am. Did you send the mailgram?" I told her I did. I'd been prepared to hurl fiery accusations at the brigand I expected to find, but faced with a young woman, I was uncertain how to proceed. I introduced myself, and she said her name was Wilhelmina McCullough. The surname was familiar, and struck by a sudden suspicion, I asked if she was related to Nathan McCullough. She answered, "He's my father."

That made things clear; the girl was the daughter of the director of the University of Alta California's Museum of Natural Philosophy in Oakland. None of the staff would question the presence of the director's daughter in the storerooms.

She asked me, "I take it this means this package doesn't actually contain the relics?" I told her it didn't. She picked it up and dropped it in a nearby trash container. "So now that you've found me, what do you want?"

I said that for a start, she could explain to me why she had stolen from her father's museum.

She said, "I'm not a thief, Dr. Morrell. Thieves steal for their personal benefit. I took the relics for God's benefit."

I asked her why, if she wanted to support the construction of Yosemeti Cathedral, had she asked that the relics be sold at modest prices. She said, "You think I was trying to raise money for the cathedral? I don't care about that at all. What I wanted was for as many people as possible to be able to appreciate the relics. I would've handed them out for free, but who'd believe they were real if I did? I couldn't sell them myself, so I donated them to someone who could."

I said that people could appreciate the relics by visiting the museum.

"No one could see the relics I took; they were gathering dust in cabinets. It makes no sense for the university to collect so many things it can't display."

I told her that all museum curators wish they were able to display more of their collection. I told her that they rotate through their collections.

She responded by saying, "There are plenty of items that will never go on display," and I couldn't deny that. She pulled an item from her purse; it was a primordial clamshell, with a smooth section surrounded by growth rings. "I show this to people when I talk to them about God, and everyone who sees it has been impressed. Think of how many people could have their faith strengthened by the relics that sit in the back rooms of the museum. I'm trying to put them to good use."

I asked her how long she had been taking relics from the museum, and she said she had only begun recently. "People's faith will be tested soon, and some of them will need reassurance. That's why it's important for the relics to be available. They'll dispel people's doubts."

I asked her what kind of test of faith was coming. She said,

"There's a paper that's about to be published; I know about it because my father was asked to review it. When people read it, a lot of them will lose their faith."

I asked her if the paper had precipitated a crisis of faith in her, and she was dismissive. "My faith is absolute," she said. "My father's, on the other hand . . ."

The idea that her father might be experiencing a crisis of faith seemed incredible to me; as a scientist, he was the last person to have reason to doubt. I asked her what kind of paper it was, and she said, "Astronomy."

I admit, Lord, that I've never had much regard for astronomy; it has always struck me as the dullest of the sciences. The life sciences are seemingly limitless; every year we discover new species of plants and animals and gain a deeper appreciation of your ingenuity in creating the Earth. By contrast, the night sky is just so finite. All five thousand eight hundred and seventy-two stars were cataloged in 1745, and not another has been found since then. Whenever astronomers peer at one more closely, they confirm that it's identical in size and composition to every other, and to what end? It's the essential nature of stars that they have so few characteristics; they're the backdrop against which the Earth stands out, reminding us of how special we are. Choosing to study them has always felt a bit like choosing to taste the plate that food is served on.

So it doesn't completely surprise me that an astronomy paper might cause people to lose sight of what's important, although I would have expected such a reaction from a layperson rather than a scientist. I asked Wilhelmina what was in the paper, and she said, "Nonsense." I asked her to elaborate, but all she would say was that it was a theory designed to instill doubt. "And all based on something someone saw in a telescope!" she said.

"Every relic I gave away was a piece of evidence you can hold in your hand. You know it tells the truth because you can feel it." She brought her clamshell to my hand and pushed my thumb back and forth across the border between the smooth and ringed areas of its shell. "How can anyone have doubts about that?"

I told Wilhelmina I would have to speak to her parents about what she had done. She seemed unconcerned. "I won't apologize for bringing people closer to God. I know I've broken rules in doing so, but it's the rules that need to be changed, not my behavior."

I told her that people couldn't simply disobey rules just because they disagreed with them, because society would cease to function if everyone did that.

"Don't be silly," she said. "You lied when you sent that mailgram as Mr. Dahl. Was that because you believe we should all be free to lie? Of course not. You thought about the situation and concluded that lying was justified. You're prepared to take responsibility for what you did, aren't you? Well, so am I. That's what society needs us to do, not to follow rules without thinking."

I wish I had her confidence when I was her age. Indeed, I wish I had her confidence right now. It's only when I'm doing fieldwork that I am certain I am following your will, Lord. When it comes to matters such as this, there is always some uncertainty in my mind.

"My father is in Sacramento today," Wilhelmina said. "If you want to speak with him, you can come by our house tomorrow morning before nine." She gave me her address.

I told her she had better be there as well, and she looked insulted. "Of course I'll be there. I'm not ashamed of what I've done. Weren't you listening?"

Tomorrow I go to speak with Dr. and Mrs. McCullough. This

has not turned out at all the way I expected when I left Chicagou. I was preparing to bring a criminal to justice, and instead I have to inform parents about their child's misbehavior. Or, I should say, their daughter's misbehavior. She is neither child nor criminal, but I'm uncertain as to what she is. Had she been a criminal, I would know better where I stand. Instead I'm just perplexed.

Help me to understand other people's positions, Lord, even when I don't share them. At the same time, grant me the strength to not ignore wrongdoing simply because it is committed by someone who is well intentioned. Let me be compassionate while remaining true to my convictions.

Amen.

. . .

Lord, I'm frightened by what I've heard today. I need your guidance desperately. Please help me make sense of what has happened.

I rode the ferry to Oakland today and from there hired a cab to the address that Wilhelmina had given me. A housekeeper opened the door. I introduced myself and told her that I needed to speak to the McCulloughs regarding their daughter, Wilhelmina. A minute later they appeared. "Are you one of Mina's teachers?" asked Dr. McCullough.

I explained that I am an archaeologist with Boston's Museum of Natural Philosophy. Mrs. McCullough recognized my name. "You write those popularizations," she said. "How is it that you're acquainted with our daughter?" I suggested that we speak inside. Both of them turned to look at Wilhelmina, who was standing on the stairs behind them, and they let me in.

Once we were in Dr. McCullough's study, I described how I

came to suspect that relics were being taken from the museum's storerooms, and how I discovered Wilhelmina was behind it. Dr. McCullough turned to Wilhelmina and asked if it was true. "Yes, it is," she declared, with neither shame nor belligerence.

Dr. McCullough was plainly incredulous. "Why on earth would you do such a thing?"

"You know why," she said. "To remind people of what you've forgotten."

His face grew red, and he said, "Go to your room. We will discuss this later."

"I want to discuss it now," she said. "You can't keep denying—"

"Do as your father tells you," said Mrs. McCullough. Wilhelmina left reluctantly, and then Dr. McCullough turned to me.

"Thank you for bringing this to my attention," he said. "You can be assured that nothing else from the university's collection will leave the premises."

I told him I appreciated his saying that, but I wanted to know what had prompted Wilhelmina's actions. She seemed to be acting in reaction to something he had said or done. Was that true?

"That's no concern of yours," he said. "We'll deal with this as a private family matter."

I told Dr. McCullough that it wasn't my intention to pry, but the theft of property might legitimately be a concern of the museum's board of trustees, and I needed a more detailed explanation in order to be comfortable with not informing them. I asked him whether, if our positions were reversed, he would accept an explanation like the one he had given me. He glared at me so severely that if I'd been a subordinate of his, I might have left the matter alone. I wasn't, though, so it seemed like we were at an impasse.

Then Mrs. McCullough said to him, "Tell her about the paper, Nathan. She came all this way, and besides, everyone will know soon enough."

Dr. McCullough relented. "Very well, then," he said. He went to his desk and picked up a manuscript. "I was asked to review a paper for publication in the journal *Natural Philosophy*." He handed the manuscript to me, and I saw the title was "On the Relative Motion of the Sun and the Luminiferous Aether." I have only a layperson's understanding of the aether, the medium that carries light waves: I know that, just as a shout carries farther when traveling with the wind than against it, the speed of light varies relative to the Earth's own motion through the aether. I said as much to Dr. McCullough.

"Your understanding is correct, as far as it goes. However, detailed measurements suggest that the variations in the speed of light are not caused solely by the Earth's motion around the Sun. Instead, there appears to be a steady aetheric wind across our solar system as a whole. Most physicists believe this has no significance, but the astronomer Arthur Lawson proposes an alternate explanation: he suggests that the Sun is not actually at rest, but is in motion relative to the aether, which is itself at rest."

That seemed a bit like observing an incessant wind blowing across the desert and concluding that the desert must be in motion while the atmosphere was still. Dr. McCullough anticipated my objection, saying, "Yes, of course, it sounds topsy-turvy, but bear with me. Lawson hypothesizes that there is another star whose motion relative to the Sun is the same as the aetheric wind. Such a star would be stationary with respect to the luminiferous aether, and therefore truly be at absolute rest.

"Astronomers have only recently begun mapping the proper motions of stars, but they have detected some broad patterns, so

Lawson began looking at the section of the sky where the stars' velocities are similar to that of the aetheric wind. He found several stars whose motions are close to it, but none that match it exactly.

"Then he happened across 58 Eridani, a star in the constellation Eridanus. Based on its Doppler shift, Lawson measured 58 Eridani to be moving toward us at a speed of several thousand miles per second. That would be extraordinary in and of itself, but later measurements showed that its motion wasn't consistent. The star was alternately moving toward us and then away from us, again at several thousand miles per second."

I said that obviously some sort of measurement error must be responsible.

"Of course that was his first assumption. But after ruling out every source of error he could think of, Lawson asked astronomers at another observatory to take a look; they confirmed his findings. Together they determined that 58 Eridani's motion varied with a period of exactly twenty-four hours. Lawson believes it is moving in a circle."

I asked if it was in orbit around a larger body, and he said an object traveling in that manner couldn't possibly be gravitationally bound. It defies everything we know about celestial mechanics. I asked if he thought it qualified as miraculous, whether this was finally unambiguous evidence of your ongoing, active intervention in the universe, Lord.

"It certainly does," said Dr. McCullough. "But the significance of the miracle is the real question. What does this marvel tell us about God's design?

"Lawson offers an interpretation. He suggests that 58 Eridani is actually orbiting a smaller body too small for us to detect, a planet the size of the Earth. The star is moving in such a way as

to provide a day-and-night cycle of twenty-four hours for a stationary planet. He believes that it constitutes a geocentric solar
system.

"He goes on to suggest that the planet that 58 Eridani is orbiting is stationary relative to the luminiferous aether, meaning
that it's the sole object in the universe that is at absolute rest. On
that planet, and only on that planet, would the speed of light be
precisely the same no matter which direction it was traveling.
And although there's no way to detect life on that planet, Lawson
suggests the planet is inhabited, and that its inhabitants are the
reason God created the universe."

I was speechless for a moment. Then I asked how Lawson explained the existence of humanity and life on Earth.
Dr. McCullough took the manuscript from my hands, flipped
through the pages until he found the section he was looking for,
and then handed it back to me.

Reading, I saw that Lawson offered three hypotheses for the
presence of humanity. The first was that humanity was the result
of a separate act of creation, an experiment or test performed
as rehearsal for the main undertaking. The second was that the
creation of humanity was an unintended side effect, a kind of
"sympathetic vibration" induced because of our solar system's
similarity to 58 Eridani. The third was that humanity on Earth
was in fact the main undertaking, and life on 58 Eridani was
the rehearsal or side effect. He rejected this last one as unlikely,
because if we assume that miracles are signs of your attention,
Lord, then a continuous miracle like a star orbiting a planet must
be a clear indicator of what you consider most important.

Lawson concluded his paper by acknowledging that many of
his conclusions were necessarily speculative, and he invited other
hypotheses that fit the observations just as well or better. As I

stared at the page, I tried to come up with an alternate explanation, but couldn't think of any. Then I looked up at McCullough, who nodded as if I were a student arriving at the correct answer.

"It's a compelling theory," he said sourly. "And it becomes more so when you consider that it solves many unanswered questions. The multiplicity of languages, for example."

I realized he was correct. Why are the languages of the world so different? Philologists have struggled to reconcile their variety with the age of the Earth and the rate at which languages diverge. If you had imbued all the primordial humans with knowledge of a common tongue, Lord, we'd expect the world's languages to all bear a family resemblance, like the Indo-European ones. But the vastly greater differences between languages of the world means there must have been more than a dozen completely unrelated languages spoken immediately after creation. We have long wondered why you would have done that, Lord. But if the disparate populations of primordial humans had each invented language independently, then there was no puzzle to be solved; the multiplicity of languages was accidental rather than by design.

"So now you know," said Dr. McCullough. "The paper will be published soon, and everyone will read it. I wanted to recommend that it be rejected, but I couldn't find any grounds for doing so. My commitment to scientific practice made me approve it." He scowled. "But what if the entire practice of science is founded on a false premise? When I was a boy I used to wish that God had given primordial men the gift of writing, because they would've been able to record the dates on which new stars appeared in the night sky. Then we'd know precisely how far away each star was, because we'd know—to the day—when each one's light first reached the Earth. But men didn't invent writing until long after the emergence of the stars, so astronomers are forced to use more indirect means to deduce their distances. My teachers told me that God wanted us to reason things out for ourselves. But what if that's not true? What if"—his voice cracked—"what if God had no intentions about us at all?"

This was the crisis of faith that Wilhelmina had referred to. I clumsily tried to offer some reassurance, saying that this was an enormously confounding discovery, but we could still retain our faith in God. Dr. McCullough shouted, "Then you understand nothing!"

His wife touched his hand, and he grasped hers, struggling to contain his feelings. The two of them were silent for a while. Then Mrs. McCullough turned to me and said, "We had a son, older than Mina by ten years. His name was Martin. He died of influenza."

I told them how sorry I was. I recalled that "Martin" was the name Wilhelmina had used when donating the relics.

Dr. McCullough said, "You are childless, so you can't comprehend the pain caused by losing a son."

I told him he was correct and said that now I realized why this discovery must be especially difficult for the two of them.

"Do you really?" he asked.

I told him what I surmised: that the only thing that had made his son's death bearable was the knowledge that it was part of a greater plan. But if humanity is not in fact the focus of your attention, Lord, then there is no such plan, and his son's death was meaningless.

Dr. McCullough remained stone-faced, but his wife nodded. "I've enjoyed your books, Dr. Morrell," she said. "They remind me of the things Nathan said when I was a student of his, before we married. In his lectures he talked about how scientific inquiry provided the strongest foundation for faith. He said, 'Personal convictions may waver, but the physical world cannot be denied,' and I believed him. So when Nathan threw himself into his research after Martin's death, it wasn't just for his solace, but for mine, too."

"And I was successful," said Dr. McCullough quietly. "I found wave oscillations within the Sun, the echoes of the initial compression God used to initiate the gravitational collapse responsible for its heat and light."

"It was like finding God's fingerprints on our world," said Mrs. McCullough. "At the time, it provided all the reassurance we could have asked for."

"But now I wonder if it proves anything," he said. "All stars must have wave oscillations within them; there's nothing that sets us apart. Nothing science has discovered carries any meaning."

I told him that science can be a salve to our wounds, but that shouldn't be the only reason we pursue it. I said we have a duty to search for the truth.

"Science is not just the search for the truth," he said. "It's the search for purpose."

And I had no response. I had always assumed those were one and the same, but what if they aren't?

I don't know what to think now. It frightens me to imagine that you have never been listening at all.

. . .

Dear Rosemary,

The last few weeks have been very difficult for me, more so than I expected. I am writing to let you know that I have temporarily left the Arisona dig.

As I told you in my last letter, I thought I would be able to participate in the dig because, even with all that had happened, I believed my affinity for the physical work of archaeology would carry me through. As it turned out, it wasn't as easy to carry on as I expected. The doubts sown by Lawson's discovery have been gnawing at my mind like rodents. A few days ago it reached the point that, as I was removing a spearpoint from the soil matrix, I thought, What does this matter? Everything we're doing here is irrelevant. I had to stop working for fear that I might smash an ancient artifact with a hammer out of frustration. That was when I knew I had to leave the dig. I don't know if there was a real risk of me doing that, but the mere fact of it crossing my mind told me I was not in a fit state of mind to work there.

I have taken residence in a rental cabin about an hour away from the dig. I couldn't explain to anyone why I was leaving, since I feel it would be inappropriate for me to talk publicly about Lawson's paper before it's published. Perhaps that contributed to my feeling of isolation while I was there, but I think the greater cause was that I feel estranged from God. I need time to decide what I should do next.

You asked whether the Church oughtn't be disturbed by the discovery just as much as the secular scientific community, and to that I would say yes, they ought to be. But the Church as an institution has always been able to derive strength from the evidence when it's useful and ignore it when it's not. Take the story of Adam and Eve. The Church was willing to admit it could not be literally true after skeletons of primordial humans were found around the world, but they insisted the story retained foundational importance as an allegory. And you and I and every other woman continue to live in Eve's shadow, for no reason except custom. So I expect that they will be able to explain away this discovery in a similar fashion and use it to advocate for the same values they always have.

I suppose one could argue that the idea of polygenism has been around for centuries, so it didn't come as a surprise when archaeological findings confirmed it. Which is true. Church scientists have long struggled to explain how a single couple could populate the Earth so quickly, so they must have privately contemplated alternative theories before they were forced to change their official stance. By contrast, I have never heard a serious argument that humanity was not the purpose of creation before Lawson's paper. So perhaps Church scientists will be just as taken aback as I was, before their loyalty to doctrine reasserts itself.

The problem for me as a secular scientist is that my faith has always been, first and foremost, shaped by the evidence. I admit that I didn't previously appreciate the importance of astronomy in understanding our station, but now I do. And if we take as our premise that humanity was the reason for creation, then that should be reflected in the skies above just as much as in the earth beneath our feet. If humanity is the central fact of the universe, if our species is the omphalos, then a close examination of the celestial sphere should confirm that privileged status. Our solar system should be the fixed point against which all else is moving; our Sun should be at absolute rest. If the evidence doesn't support that premise, then we must ask where our commitment truly lies.

I understand, Rosemary, if this doesn't disturb you or Alfred the way it does me. I don't know how most people will react when Lawson's discovery becomes widely known. Wilhelmina McCullough anticipated that others would respond the way her father did, and in my case she was correct. I wish this didn't affect me so deeply. Would that we could choose the things that trouble us, but we can't.

But if you find that this does disturb you, know that you can discuss your apprehensions with me, whatever form they take. While each of us must find our own way forward through this forest of doubt, it is only with the support of others that we'll be able to do so.

With much love, your cousin,
Dorothea

· · ·

Lord, perhaps you don't hear my prayers. But I've never prayed with the expectation that it would affect your actions; I prayed with the expectation that it would affect mine. So I pray now, for the first time in two months, because even if you're not listening, I need the clarity of thought that prayer provides.

I left the dig because I feared that Lawson's discovery rendered the whole enterprise meaningless. The reason the spearpoints that Dr. Janssen discovered were so exciting was that enough of the shafts remain that we thought we might be able to use growth rings to precisely identify the years in which they were fashioned. If we could identify trends in stone-knapping technique, we hoped to learn if knappers' expertise grew or waned in the first generations after creation, and from there draw deductions about what your intentions were regarding human knowledge, Lord. But that was based on the assumption that the primordial humans were the most direct expression of your will. If humanity's creation wasn't deliberate on your part, then whatever skills primordial humans possessed tell us nothing about your intentions. Their endowments would have been purely accidental.

Since I've been here at the cabin, I have spent a lot of time thinking about how much the primordial humans knew. They couldn't have come into being with minds as blank as newborn infants, because they'd have rapidly starved to death in such a scenario. Even tiger cubs must be taught how to hunt by their mothers. There's no way that humans could have, from first principles, learned how to hunt for food before they perished. The primordial humans must have possessed some knowledge of hunting and constructing shelters. Was that one of the experiments you conducted, Lord? Determining the minimum set of skills necessary for the species to survive? Or perhaps it was just another unintended side effect, a faint echo of whatever information you imbued the primordial inhabitants of 58 Eridani with.

There is another piece of information, just as vital as survival skills, that I've assumed the primordial humans knew from the moment they drew breath: that they were created for a reason. The possibility that they didn't know this is something I haven't been able to stop thinking about. Rather than being filled with pride and ambition, they must have been afraid and confused during their first few days. I've tried to imagine what it must have been like to awaken fully formed, possessing certain skills but without a past to remember, lost in a world of amnesiacs. It seems terrifying to me, even more terrifying than what I've experienced these last few weeks.

And it raises another question. Why did the primordial humans set about building civilization, if not out of a desire to fulfill divine purpose? Avoiding cold and hunger would motivate them to secure necessities, but why did they advance beyond those? Why did they begin inventing all the art and technology that has made humanity what it is today, if not to carry out your will, Lord?

I don't know, but I have formed a theory.

Archaeology may not be as exact a science as physics, but it relies on physics for its foundations. Physical law is what makes it possible to study the past; examine the state of the universe closely enough, and we can infer its state a moment earlier in time. Each moment follows inexorably from the previous one and is followed inexorably by the next, links forged in a causal chain.

But the moment of creation is where all causal chains end; inference can lead us back to this moment and no further. That is why the creation of the universe is a miracle: because what happened in that moment was not a necessary consequence of what preceded it. That primordial clamshell that Wilhelmina keeps with her is indeed proof of something: not of God's plans for humanity, but of the existence of miracles. That border where the growth rings end marks the limit of physical law's explanatory power. And that is something we can take inspiration from.

Because I think there are events of another category that are likewise not fixed in a causal chain: acts of volition. Free will is a kind of miracle; when we make a genuine choice, we bring about a result that cannot be reduced to the workings of physical law. Every act of volition is, like the creation of the universe, a first cause.

If we had no evidence for the miracle of creation, we might think physical law was sufficient to explain every phenomenon in the cosmos, leading us to conclude that our own minds were nothing more than natural processes. But we know that there is more to what we observe than physical law can encompass; miracles happen, and human choices are surely among them.

I believe the primordial humans made a choice. They found themselves in a world full of possibilities but with no guidance as to what to do. They didn't do what we would have expected, which is to merely survive; instead, they sought to improve themselves so that they might become masters of their world.

We scientists are in a similar situation. The evidence has always been there for us to find: the trees without growth rings, the mummies without navels, the motion of 58 Eridani. It is up to us what we do with that. We have always seen it as determinative of the value of our lives, but that wasn't inevitable. We chose to do that, which means we can choose to do otherwise.

I've devoted my life to studying the wondrous mechanism that is the universe, and doing so has given me a sense of fulfillment. I've always assumed that this meant that I was acting in accordance with your will, Lord, and your reason for making me. But if it's in fact true that you have no purpose in mind for me, then that sense of fulfillment has arisen solely from within myself. What that demonstrates to me is that we as humans are capable of creating meaning for our own lives.

I don't claim that this will be an easy path. I have nothing to offer the McCulloughs except my hope that they will be able to make sense of their lives despite the absence of their son. But our lives have often been difficult even when we believed there was a divine plan, and we've persevered. If we have only ever been on our own, then our successes in spite of that are proof of our capabilities.

So I will return to the Arisona dig, Lord, whether it is under your watchful eye or not. Even if humanity is not the reason for which the universe was made, I still wish to understand the way it operates. We human beings may not be the answer to the question *why,* but I will keep looking for the answer to *how.*

This search is my purpose; not because you chose it for me, Lord, but because I chose it for myself.

Amen.

ANXIETY IS THE DIZZINESS OF FREEDOM

NAT COULD HAVE USED A CIGARETTE, BUT COMPANY POL-icy forbade smoking in the store, so all she could do was get more and more nervous. Now it was a quarter to four, and Morrow still hadn't returned. She wasn't sure how she'd explain things if he didn't get back in time. She sent him a text asking where he was.

A chime sounded as the front door opened, but it wasn't Morrow. A guy with an orange sweater came in. "Hello? I have a prism to sell?"

Nat put her phone away. "Let's take a look at it."

He came over and put the prism on the counter; it was a new model, the size of a briefcase. Nat slid it around so she could see the numeric readout at one end: the activation date was only six months ago, and more than 90 percent of its pad was still avail-able. She unfolded the keyboard to reveal the display screen, tapped the ONLINE button, and then waited. A minute went by.

"He might have run into some traffic," said Orange Sweater uncertainly.

"It's fine," said Nat.

After another minute the ready light came on. Nat typed

> Keyboard test.

A few seconds later a reply came back:

> Looks good.

She switched to video mode, and the text on the screen was replaced by a grainy image of her own face looking back at her.

Her parallel self nodded at her and said, "Mic test."

"Loud and clear," she replied.

The screen reverted to text. Nat hadn't recognized the necklace her paraself had been wearing; if they wound up buying the prism, she'd have to ask her where she got it. She looked back at the guy with the orange sweater and quoted him a price.

His disappointment was obvious. "Is that all?"

"That's what it's worth."

"I thought these things got more valuable over time."

"They do, but not right away. If this was five years old, we'd be having a different conversation."

"What about if the other branch has something really interesting going on?"

"Yeah, that'd be worth something." Nat pointed at his prism. "*Does* the other branch have something interesting going on?"

"I . . . don't know."

"You'll have to do the research yourself and bring it to us if you want a better offer."

Orange Sweater hesitated.

"If you want to think it over and come back later, we're always here."

"Can you give me a minute?"

"Take your time."

Orange Sweater got on the keyboard and had a brief typed exchange with his paraself. When he was done, he said, "Thanks, we'll be back later." He folded the prism up and left.

The last customer in the store had finished chatting and was ready to check out. Nat went to the carrel he'd been using, checked the data usage on the prism, and carried it back to the storeroom. By the time she had finished ringing him up, the three customers with four o'clock appointments had arrived, including the one who needed the prism Morrow had with him.

"Just a minute," she told them, "and I'll get you checked in." She went to the storeroom and brought out the prisms for the two other customers. She had just set them up in their carrels when Morrow came through the front door, elbows splayed as he carried a big cardboard carton. She met him at the counter.

"You're cutting it close," she whispered, glaring at him.

"Yeah, yeah, I know the schedule."

Morrow took the oversize box into the storeroom and came out with the prism. He set it up in a carrel for the third customer with seconds to spare. At four o'clock, the ready lights on all three prisms came on, and all three customers began chatting with their paraselves.

Nat followed Morrow into the office behind the front counter. He took a seat at the desk as if nothing had happened. "Well?" she asked. "What took you so long?"

"I was talking to one of the aides at the home." Morrow had just come back from seeing one of their customers. Jessica Oehlsen was a widow in her seventies with few friends and whose only son was more of a burden than a comfort. Almost a year ago she'd started coming in once a week to talk with her paraself; she always reserved one of the private booths so she could use voice chat. A couple months ago she had fractured her hip in a bad fall, and now she was in a nursing home. Since she couldn't come to the store, Morrow brought the prism to her every week so she could continue her regular conversations; it was a violation of SelfTalk's company policy, but she paid him for the favor. "He filled me in about Mrs. Oehlsen's condition."

"What about it?"

"She's got pneumonia now," said Morrow. "He said it happens a lot after a broken hip."

"Really? How does a broken hip lead to pneumonia?"

"According to this guy, it's because they don't move around a lot and they're zonked on oxy, so they never take a deep breath. Anyway, Mrs. Oehlsen's definitely got it."

"Is it serious?"

"The aide thinks she'll be dead within a month, two tops."

"Wow. That's too bad."

"Yeah." Morrow scratched his chin with his blunt, square fingertips. "But it gave me an idea."

That was no surprise. "So what is it this time?"

"I won't need you on this one. I can handle it by myself."

"Fine by me. I've got enough to do."

"Right, you've got a meeting to go to tonight. How's that going?"

Nat shrugged. "It's hard to tell. I think I'm making progress."

.   .   .

Every prism—the name was a near acronym of the original designation, "Plaga interworld signaling mechanism"—had two LEDs, one red and one blue. When a prism was activated, a quantum measurement was performed inside the device, with two possible outcomes of equal probability: one outcome was indicated by the red LED lighting up, while the other was indicated by the blue one. From that moment forward, the prism allowed information transfer between two branches of the universal wave function. In colloquial terms, the prism created two newly divergent timelines, one in which the red LED lit up and one in which the blue one did, and it allowed communication between the two.

Information was exchanged using an array of ions, isolated in magnetic traps within the prism. When the prism was activated and the universal wave function split into two branches, these ions remained in a state of coherent superposition, balanced on a knife's edge and accessible to either branch. Each ion could be used to send a single bit of information, a yes or a no, from one branch to the other. The act of reading that yes/no caused the ion to decohere, permanently knocking it off the knife's edge and onto one side. To send another bit, you needed another ion. With an array of ions, you could transmit a string of bits that encoded text; with a long-enough array, you could send images, sound, even video.

The upshot was that a prism wasn't like a radio connecting the two branches; activating one didn't power up a transmitter whose frequency you could keep tuning into. It was more like a notepad that the two branches shared, and each time a message was sent, a strip of paper was torn off the top sheet. Once the notepad was exhausted, no more information could be exchanged and the two branches went on their separate ways, incommunicado forever after.

Ever since the invention of the prism, engineers had been working to add more ions to the array and increase the size of the notepad. The latest commercial prisms had pads that were a gigabyte in size. That was enough to last a lifetime if all you were exchanging was text, but not all consumers were satisfied with that. Many wanted the ability to have a live conversation, preferably with video; they needed to hear their own voice or see their own face looking back at them. Even low-resolution, low-frame-rate video could burn through a prism's entire pad in a matter of hours; people tended to use it only occasionally, relying on text or audio-only communications most of the time in order to make their prism last for as long as possible.

. . .

Dana's regular four o'clock appointment was a woman named Teresa. Teresa had been a client for just over a year; she had sought out therapy primarily because of her difficulty in maintaining a long-term romantic relationship. Dana had initially thought her issues stemmed from her parents' divorce when she was a teenager, but now she suspected that Teresa was prone to seeking better alternatives. In their session last week, Teresa had told her that she had recently run into an ex-boyfriend of hers; five years ago she had turned down a marriage proposal from him, and now he was happily married to someone else. Dana expected that they would continue talking about that today.

Teresa often started her sessions with pleasantries, but not this time. As soon as she sat down she said, "I went to Crystal Ball during my lunch break today."

Already suspecting the answer, Dana asked, "What did you ask them about?"

"I asked them if they could find out what my life would look like if I had married Andrew."

"And what did they say?"

"They said maybe. I hadn't realized how it worked; a man

there explained it to me." Teresa didn't ask if Dana was familiar with it. She needed to talk it through, which was fine; she was often able to untangle her thoughts that way with only slight prompting from Dana. "He said that my decision to marry Andrew or not didn't cause two timelines to branch off, that only activating a prism does that. He said they could look at the prisms they had that had been activated in the months before Andrew proposed. They would send requests to the parallel versions of Crystal Ball in those branches, and their employees would look up the parallel versions of me and see if any of them were married to him. If one of me was, they could interview her and tell me what she said. But he said there was no guarantee that they'd find such a branch, and it cost money just to send the requests, so they would have to charge me whether they found one or not. Then, if I want them to interview the parallel version of me, there'd be a separate charge for that. And because they'd be using prisms that are five years old, everything would be expensive."

Dana was glad to hear that Crystal Ball had been honest about their claims; she knew there were data brokers out there that promised results they couldn't deliver. "So what did you do?"

"I didn't want to do anything without talking to you first."

"Okay," said Dana, "let's talk. How did you feel after the consultation?"

"I don't know. I hadn't considered the possibility that they might not be able to find a branch where I said yes to Andrew. Why wouldn't they be able to find a branch like that?"

Dana considered trying to lead Teresa to the answer herself, but decided it wasn't necessary. "It could mean that your decision to reject him wasn't a close call. It may have felt like you were on the fence, but in fact you weren't; your decision to turn him down was based on a deep feeling, not a whim."

Teresa looked thoughtful. "That might be a good thing to know. I wonder if I ought to just have them do the search first. If they don't find a version of me that married Andrew, then I can just stop."

"And if they do find a version that married Andrew, how likely is it that you'll ask them to interview her?"

She sighed. "A hundred percent."

"So what does that tell you?"

"I guess it tells me that I shouldn't have them do the search unless I'm sure I want to know the answer."

"And do you want to know the answer?" asked Dana. "No, let's put it another way. What would you like the answer to be, and what are you afraid it might be?"

Teresa paused for a minute. Eventually she said, "I guess what I'd like to find out is that a version of me married Andrew and then divorced him because he wasn't the right guy for me. What I'm afraid of finding out is that a version of me married him and is now blissfully happy. Is that petty of me?"

"Not at all," said Dana. "Those are perfectly understandable feelings."

"I suppose I just have to decide if I'm willing to take the risk."

"That's one way to think about it."

"What's another?"

"Another would be to consider whether anything you learn about the other branch would actually be helpful. It could be that nothing you find out about some other branch will change your situation here in this branch."

Teresa frowned as she thought it over. "Maybe it wouldn't

change anything, but I'd feel better knowing that I had made the right decision." She went silent, and Dana waited. Then Teresa asked, "Do you have other clients who've gone to data brokers?"

Dana nodded. "Many."

"In general, do you think it's a good idea to use one of these services?"

"I don't think there's a general answer to that. It depends entirely on the individual."

"And you're not going to tell me whether or not I should do it."

Dana smiled. "You know that's not my role."

"I know, I just figured it couldn't hurt to ask." After a moment, Teresa said, "I've heard that some people become obsessed with prisms."

"Yes, that can happen. I actually facilitate a support group for people whose prism use has become an issue for them."

"Really?" Teresa seemed briefly tempted to ask for details, but instead she said, "And you're not going to warn me away from using Crystal Ball's services?"

"Some people have issues with alcohol, but I'm not going to advise my clients to never take a drink."

"I suppose that makes sense." Teresa paused, and then asked, "Have you ever used one of these services yourself?"

Dana shook her head. "No, I haven't."

"Have you ever been tempted?"

"Not really."

She looked at Dana curiously. "Don't you ever wonder if you made the wrong choice?"

I don't have to wonder; I know. But aloud Dana said, "Of course. But I try to focus on the here and now."

. . .

The two branches connected by a prism start out as perfectly identical except for the result of the quantum measurement. If a person has resolved to base a huge decision on the measurement—"If the blue LED lights up, I will detonate this bomb; otherwise, I will disarm it"—then the two branches will diverge in an obvious manner. But if no one takes any action as a result of the measurement, how much will the two branches diverge? Can a single quantum event by itself lead to visible changes between the two branches? Is it possible for broader historical forces to be studied using prisms?

These questions had been a matter of debate ever since the first demonstration of communication with a prism. When prisms with pads about a hundred kilobytes in size were developed, an atmospheric scientist named Peter Silitonga conducted a pair of experiments to settle the matter.

At the time, a prism was still a large array of laboratory equipment that used liquid nitrogen for cooling, and Silitonga required one for each of his planned experiments. Before activating them he made a number of arrangements. First he recruited volunteers in a dozen countries who were not currently pregnant but were trying to conceive children; in one year's time, the couples who'd successfully had a child agreed to have a twenty-one-loci DNA test performed on their newborns. Then he activated the first of his prisms, typing the keyboard command that sent a photon through a polarization filter.

Six months later, he scheduled a software agent to retrieve weather reports from around the globe in one month's time. Then he activated the second of his prisms, and waited.

. . .

Nat liked that, no matter what the issue was, support-group meetings always had coffee. She didn't care so much whether the coffee was good or bad; what she appreciated was that holding the cup gave her something to do with her hands. And even though this support group's location wasn't the nicest she'd ever seen—a pretty typical church basement—the coffee was usually really good.

Lyle was at the coffeemaker pouring himself a cup as Nat walked up. "Hey there," he said. He handed her the cup he had just filled and started pouring another for himself.

"Thanks, Lyle." Lyle had been attending the group just a little longer than Nat had, about three months. Ten months ago he'd been offered a new job and couldn't decide whether he should accept it. He'd bought a prism and used it as a coin flip: blue LED accepts the offer, red LED rejects it. The blue LED had lit up in this branch, so he took the new job while his paraself stayed at his existing job. For months they both felt happy with their situations. But after the initial novelty of the new job wore off, Lyle found himself disenchanted with his duties, while his paraself got a promotion. Lyle's confidence was shaken. He pretended he was happy when communicating with his paraself, but he was struggling with feelings of envy and jealousy.

Nat found them a couple of empty chairs next to each other. "You like sitting up front, right?" she asked.

"Yeah, but you don't have to if you don't want to."

"It's fine," she said. They sat and sipped their coffee while waiting for the meeting to start.

The group's facilitator was a therapist named Dana. She was

young, no older than Nat, but seemed to know what she was doing. Nat could have used someone like her in her previous groups. Once everyone was seated, Dana said, "Does anyone want to start us off today?"

"I'll go," said Lyle.

"Okay, tell us about your week."

"Well, I looked up the Becca here." Lyle's parallel self had been seeing a woman named Becca for months, after a chance meeting at a bar.

"Bad idea, bad idea," said Kevin, shaking his head.

"Kevin, please," said Dana.

"Sorry, sorry."

"Thanks, Dana," said Lyle. "I messaged her, I told her why I was messaging her, I sent her a photo of my paraself and her paraself together, and I asked if I could take her out for coffee. She said sure."

Dana nodded for him to continue.

"We met on Saturday afternoon, and at first we seemed to hit it off. She laughed at my jokes, I laughed at hers, and I was thinking, I'll bet this is just how it went when my paraself met her. I felt like I was living my best life." He looked embarrassed.

"And then it went all wrong. I was saying how great it was to meet her, and how I felt like things were turning around for me, and before I knew it I told her how using the prism had screwed things up for me. I talked about how jealous I was of my paraself for having met parallel Becca, how I was always second-guessing myself now, and on and on. And I could hear how pathetic I sounded as I was saying it. I knew I was losing her, so out of desperation I . . ." He hesitated, and then said, "I offered to let her borrow my prism so she could talk with parallel Becca, and that Becca could tell this one what a great guy I could be. You can imagine how well that went over. She was polite, but she made it clear that she didn't want to see me again."

"Thanks for sharing that, Lyle," said Dana. She addressed the rest of the group. "Does anyone want to say anything in response?"

This was an opportunity, but Nat wasn't going to jump in right away. It'd be best if the other group members spoke first.

Kevin started. "Sorry about my earlier remark. I didn't mean that you were dumb for trying it. What I was thinking was it sounded like something I would do, and because of that, I had a bad feeling about how it was going to turn out. I'm sorry it didn't work out better for you."

"Thanks, Kevin."

"And really, it's not a bad idea. The two of you have got to be compatible if your paraselves are a couple."

"I agree with Kevin that the two of you are compatible," said Zareenah. "But the mistake that all of us keep making is that, when we see our paraselves experiencing good fortune, we think we're entitled to the same good fortune."

"I don't think I'm entitled to Becca," said Lyle. "But she's looking for someone, just like I am. If we're compatible, shouldn't that count for something? I know I made a bad first impression, but I feel like our compatibility should be a reason for her to overlook that."

"It'd be nice if she did, but she's under no obligation to do that."

"Yeah," said Lyle grudgingly. "I see what you're saying. I just feel so . . . I know I say this all the time, but I feel envious. Why am I like this?"

Now seemed like a good time. Nat said, "Something happened to me recently that I think might be similar to what Lyle's going through?"

"Go ahead," said Dana.

"Okay, I've got this hobby where I make jewelry, mostly earrings. I have a little online store where people can buy them; I don't fill the orders myself, I just upload the designs and this company fabs them and mails them to customers." That part was all true, which was good in case anyone wanted to look at her store. "My paraself was just telling me that some influencer happened across one of our designs, and posted about how she loved them, and in the last week my paraself has sold hundreds of earrings. She actually saw someone at a coffee shop who was wearing the earrings.

"The thing is, the design that got all the attention wasn't one she made after I activated the prism; it's one from before. Those exact same earrings are for sale in my store in this branch, but no one's buying them here. She's making money for something we did before our branches diverged, but I'm not. And I resented her for it. Why is she so lucky and I'm not?" Nat saw some others nodding in sympathy.

"And I realized, this didn't feel the same as when I see other people sell a lot of jewelry in their online stores. This is different." She turned to face Lyle. "I don't think I'm an envious person by nature, and I don't think you are, either. We're not always wanting what other people have. But with a prism, it's not other people, it's you. So how can you not feel like you deserve what they have? It's natural. The problem isn't with you, it's with the prism."

"Thanks, Nat. I appreciate that."

"You're welcome."

Progress. That was definitely progress.

. . . .

Set up a rack of billiard balls and execute a flawless break. Imagine the table has no pockets and is frictionless, so the balls just keep rebounding, never coming to a stop; how accurately can you predict the path of any given ball as it collides against the others? In 1978, the physicist Michael Berry calculated that you could predict only nine collisions before you would need to account for the gravitational effect of a person standing in the room. If your initial measurement of a ball's position is off by even a nanometer, your prediction becomes useless within a matter of seconds.

The collisions between air molecules are similarly contingent and can be affected by the gravitational effect of a single atom a meter away. So even though the interior of a prism is shielded from the external environment, the result of the quantum measurement that takes place when the prism is activated can still exert an effect on the outside world, determining whether two oxygen molecules collide or whether they drift past each other. Without anyone intending it, the activation of the prism inevitably gives rise to a difference between the two branches generated. The difference is imperceptible at first, a discrepancy at the level of the thermal motion of molecules, but when air is turbulent, it takes roughly a minute for a perturbation at the microscopic level to become macroscopic, affecting eddies one centimeter in diameter.

For small-scale atmospheric phenomena, the effects of perturbations double in size every couple of hours. In terms of prediction, that means that an error one meter wide in your initial measurements of the atmosphere will lead to an error a kilometer wide in your prediction of the weather on the following day.

At larger scales, the propagation of errors slows down due to factors like topography and the stratification of the atmosphere, but it doesn't stop; eventually errors on the kilometer scale become errors hundreds or thousands of kilometers in size. Even if your initial measurements were so detailed that they included data about every cubic meter of the Earth's atmosphere, your prediction of the future weather would cease to be useful within a month's time. Increasing the resolution of the initial measurements has a limited benefit; because errors propagate so rapidly at the small scale, starting with data about every cubic centimeter of the atmosphere would prolong the accuracy of the prediction by only a matter of hours.

The growth of errors in weather prediction is identical to the divergence between the weather in the branches on opposite sides of a prism. The initial perturbation is the difference in the collision of oxygen molecules when the prism is activated, and within a month, the weather around the globe is different. Silitonga confirmed this when he and his parallel self exchanged weather reports one month after activating a prism. The weather reports were all seasonally appropriate—there was no location that experienced winter in one branch and summer in the other—but beyond that they were essentially uncorrelated. Without anyone making an effort, the two branches had diverged visibly on a worldwide scale.

After Silitonga published these results, in a paper titled "Studying Atmospheric Upscale Error Propagation with the Plaga Interworld-Signaling Mechanism," historians engaged in heated debates over the extent to which weather could affect the course of history. Skeptics acknowledged that it could affect individuals' daily lives in various ways, but how often were the outcomes of history-making events decided by the weather? Silitonga didn't participate in the debates; he was waiting for his other, yearlong prism experiment to conclude.

. . .

There were times when the clients came in just the right order, and Wednesday afternoons were like that for Dana. The afternoon began with one of her most demanding clients, a man who asked her to make all his decisions for him, whined when she wouldn't, and blamed her whenever he eventually did take an action. So it was a relief to see Jorge immediately afterward, a breath of fresh air to clear out her office. The issues he was dealing with weren't the most interesting she'd ever seen, but she liked having him as a client. Jorge was funny and kind, and always well-intentioned; he was tentative about the therapeutic process, but they'd been making steady progress on his poor self-image and the negative attitudes that were holding him back.

Four weeks ago there had been an incident. Jorge's manager at work was a mean-spirited tyrant who belittled everyone who worked for him; one of the ongoing themes of Dana's sessions with Jorge was helping him to ignore his manager's insults. One day, Jorge had lost his temper and punctured all four tires of his manager's car when he was alone in the parking lot. Enough time had passed that it seemed like there was no risk of him getting caught, and while part of him wanted to pretend that it had never happened, part of him still felt terrible about what he'd done.

They began their session with some small talk; Dana got the sense that Jorge had something he wanted to say. She looked at him expectantly, and he said, "After our session last week, I went to one of those prism brokers, Lydoscope."

Dana was surprised. "Really? What for?"

"I wanted to see how many versions of me acted the same way I did."

"Tell me more."

"I asked them to send questions to six versions of me. Since it's such a recent departure point, it was cheap, so I asked for video. This morning they sent me a bunch of video files, recordings of what my paraselves said."

"And what did you learn?"

"None of my paraselves have punctured their manager's tires. All of them said they've fantasized about it. One came really close on the same day that I did it, but he stopped himself."

"What do you think that means?"

"It means that my puncturing his tires was a freak accident. The fact that I did it doesn't say anything important about me as a person."

Dana knew of people using prisms in a similar way, but it was usually someone justifying their actions by pointing out they might have done something worse. She hadn't encountered this particular version of it before, where the defense was based on their parallel selves behaving better. She certainly hadn't expected it from Jorge. "So you think your paraselves' behavior is a reflection on you?"

"The branches they checked, they were all ones where the departure point was just a month before the incident. That means that those paraselves were just the same as me; they hadn't had time to become different people."

She nodded; he was right about that. "Do you think the fact that you vandalized your manager's car is canceled out by the fact that your paraselves didn't?"

"Not canceled out, but it's an indicator of the type of person I am. If all of my paraselves had punctured his tires, that would indicate something significant about my personality. That's something Sharon would need to know about." Jorge hadn't told his wife about what he'd done; he'd been too ashamed. "But the fact that they didn't means that I'm fundamentally not a violent person, so telling Sharon about what happened would give her the wrong idea."

Getting him to tell his wife everything was something they'd have to build up to. "So how do you feel, now that you've gotten this information?"

"Relief, I suppose," said Jorge. "I was worried about what it meant that I had done that. But now I'm not so worried."

"Tell me more about that feeling of relief."

"I feel like . . ." Jorge fidgeted in his chair as he searched for the words. Eventually he said, "I guess I feel like I got the results of a medical test back, and I'm in the clear."

"Like you might have been sick, but it turns out you're not."

"Yes! It was nothing serious. It's not something that's going to be a recurring thing with me."

Dana decided to take a chance. "So let's think of it as a medical test. You had some symptoms that might have indicated something serious, like cancer. But it turns out you don't have cancer."

"Right!"

"Of course it's great that you don't have cancer. But you still had those symptoms. Isn't it worth figuring out what it was that gave you those symptoms?"

Jorge looked blank. "If it's not cancer, what does it matter?"

"Well, it could be something else, something it'd help you to know about."

"I got the answer I needed." He shrugged. "That's good enough for now."

"Okay, that's fine," said Dana. No sense in pushing the issue. She was sure he'd get there eventually.

. . .

It's a commonly held belief that you would have been born in any branch where your parents met and had children, but no one's birth is inevitable. Silitonga intended his yearlong experiment to show how the act of conception was highly contingent on circumstances, including the day's weather.

Ovulation is a gradual and regulated process, so the same egg cell emerges from the follicle no matter whether it's raining or shining that day. The sperm cell that reaches that egg, however, is like a winning Ping-Pong ball siphoned from a lottery drum as it rotates; it's the result of utterly random forces. Even if the external circumstances surrounding an act of intercourse appear identical in the two branches, it takes only an imperceptible discrepancy to cause one spermatozoon to fuse with the ovum rather than another. Consequently, as soon as weather patterns are visibly different in two branches, all instances of fertilization are affected. Nine months later, every mother around the globe is giving birth to a different infant in each of the two branches. This is immediately evident when the child is a boy in one branch and a girl in the other, but it remains true even when the children are the same sex. The newly christened Dylan in one branch is not the same as the Dylan in the other; the two are siblings.

This is what Silitonga demonstrated when he and his parallel self exchanged the DNA tests of infants born a year after activating a prism, in a paper titled "The Effect of Atmospheric Turbulence on Human Conception." He had used a different prism from the one in his "Error Propagation" paper to avoid the question of whether the publication of that experiment's results had somehow created divergences that wouldn't have otherwise occurred. At the time of these children's conceptions, there had been no communication at all between the two branches. Every child had a different chromosomal makeup than their counterpart in the other branch, and the only possible cause had been the outcome of a single quantum measurement.

Some people still argued that the broader course of history wouldn't change between the two branches, but it became a more difficult case to make. Silitonga had shown that the smallest change imaginable would eventually have global repercussions. For a hypothetical time traveler who wanted to prevent Hitler's rise to power, the minimal intervention wasn't smothering the baby Adolf in his crib; all that was needed was to travel back to a month before his conception and disturb an oxygen molecule. Not only would this replace Adolf with a sibling, it would replace everyone his age or younger. By 1920 that would have composed half of the world's population.

. . .

Morrow had started working at SelfTalk around the same time as Nat, so neither had been an employee back when the company was thriving. When prisms were something only corporations could afford, people were happy to go to a store to communicate with parallel versions of themselves. Now that it was possible for people to buy their own prisms, SelfTalk had only a few locations left, and their customers were mostly teenagers whose parents didn't let them use prisms or senior citizens who were unsophisticated enough that they still found the idea of paraselves a novelty.

Nat had been content to keep her head down, but Morrow

had always had plans. He was promoted to store manager after coming up with a way to get new customers. Every time they got a new prism, he checked the accident reports from a month after a prism's activation date and sent targeted advertisements to the people involved. They were often unable to resist the chance to get a glimpse of their lives if things had gone differently. None of them became long-term customers—most of them were depressed by what they learned—but they were a reliable way of generating revenue from every new prism acquired.

At the nursing home, Morrow waited just outside the door to Mrs. Oehlsen's room while she talked to her paraself. Now they were using video for their conversations instead of text; she knew she didn't have long left, so there was no point in conserving the prism's pad for later. This made things difficult for the parallel Mrs. Oehlsen, though, who was now actually watching a version of herself die. Their conversation was strained—Morrow had left a microphone in the room so he could listen to them through an earpiece—although the dying Mrs. Oehlsen didn't seem to notice.

When they were done, Mrs. Oehlsen raised her voice slightly to tell Morrow to come back in. "How did your conversation go?" he asked.

"Fine," she said. Her breathing was labored. "If there's one person you can talk to without pretense, it's your own self."

Morrow lifted the prism from the overbed table and repacked it into the carton. "Mrs. Oehlsen, if you don't mind, I'd like to suggest something."

"Go ahead."

"You've said you don't know anyone who really deserves your money. If you really feel that way, maybe you ought to give the money to your paraself."

"You can do that?"

Confidence was the key to selling any lie. "Money is just another form of information," he said. "We can transmit it through a prism the same way that we transmit audio or video information."

"Hmm, that's an interesting idea. I know she'd put it to better use than my son would." Her face puckered slightly as she thought about him. "How would I go about that? Would I ask my lawyer to adjust my will?"

"You could, but it will take some time before your estate is settled, and you might want to transfer the money sooner rather than later."

"Why is that?"

"There's a new law that goes into effect next month." He pulled out his phone and showed her an article he had dummied up. "The government wants to discourage people from moving money out of this timeline, so they're imposing a fifty-percent tax on fund transfers to other timelines. If you send the money before the law goes into effect, you can avoid that tax." He could see from her expression that the idea appealed to her. "SelfTalk could handle it for you right away."

"Make the arrangements," she said. "We'll do it when you visit next week."

"I'll have everything ready," said Morrow.

When he got back to SelfTalk, Morrow used the prism to send a message to his parallel self, asking him to play along. The two of them would tell the parallel Mrs. Oehlsen that this one was becoming delusional from the pain medication, believing that she had sent money across the prism, and it would be better to humor her in her remaining days. That would probably suffice, but if necessary, they could always put an end to the video conversations altogether by saying that another client had unexpectedly exhausted the prism's pad.

Once that was done, Morrow began setting up the dummy account to receive the funds. He wasn't expecting a fortune from this; Mrs. Oehlsen presumably had some money saved, but she wasn't wealthy. The big score would come, if they were lucky, from Nat's support group.

As part of his job for SelfTalk, Morrow maintained a list of support groups for people struggling with their prisms. He knew some people in those groups would wind up selling their prisms, so he'd regularly go to the churches and community centers where those groups met and put up flyers: WE'LL BUY YOUR PRISM; TOP DOLLAR PAID. Three months ago Morrow had been stapling a flyer to a bulletin board when a couple of support-group members were standing nearby, cups of coffee in their hand, chatting before the room opened up. Morrow could hear them talking.

"Do you ever wonder if you ruined someone else's life by activating your prism?"

"What do you mean?"

"Like, maybe someone might die in a car crash in the other branch but not in this one, and all because you activated the prism."

"Now that you mention it, you remember that car crash in Hollywood a few months back? In my paraself's branch, Scott died in that crash instead of Roderick."

"That's exactly the sort of thing I mean. You activating the prism had a huge impact on someone else's life. Do you ever think about that?"

"Not really. Maybe I'm too self-absorbed, but I'm usually thinking about my own life."

The guy had been talking about a celebrity couple, pop singer Scott Otsuka and movie star Roderick Ferris. They'd been en route to a movie premiere when their limousine had been hit by a drunk driver; Roderick had been killed, and Scott was left a grieving widower. But this guy's prism connected to a branch where Scott had been the one who was killed and Roderick was the survivor.

That prism could be worth a lot of money, but Morrow couldn't just go up to him and offer to buy it. So he had sent Nat into the group to pretend she was someone wanting to kick her prism habit. The guy's name was Lyle, and her job was to make friends with him. Nothing sexual—Morrow knew better than to ask her to do that—just a support-group buddy, someone he liked and trusted. That way she could gently nudge him in the direction of giving up his prism. And when he was ready, Nat would tell him she was ready to get rid of hers, too, and she knew someone who was paying good prices for used prisms, so how about the two of them sell theirs together? And then she'd bring Lyle to SelfTalk, where Morrow would buy both of their prisms.

Then Morrow would arrange a visit with Scott Otsuka and offer to sell him a prism that let him talk with his dead husband.

· · ·

No prism would ever allow communication to a branch that had split off prior to its moment of activation, so there'd be no reports from branches where Kennedy hadn't been assassinated or where the Mongols had invaded western Europe. By the same token, there were no fortunes to be made by patenting inventions gleaned from branches where technological progress had taken a different route. If there were going to be any practical benefits gained from using a prism, they would have to derive from subsequent divergences, not earlier ones.

Occasionally, random variations made it possible to avert an accident: once, when a passenger plane crashed, the FAA notified its counterpart in another branch, which was able to ground its version of the plane and perform a closer inspection, identifying a component in the hydraulic system that was on the verge of failing. But there was nothing to be done about accidents caused by human error, which were different in every branch. Nor was it possible to send advance notice of natural disasters: a hurricane in one said nothing about the likelihood of a hurricane in another, while earthquakes happened simultaneously in every branch, so no early warning was possible.

An army general purchased a prism because he thought he'd be able to use a branch as a supremely realistic military simulation: he intended to have his parallel self make an aggressive move in the other branch so they could see what the response was. He discovered the flaw in this plan as soon as he communicated with his parallel self, who intended to use him in exactly the same way. Every branch was of paramount importance to its inhabitants; no one was willing to act as a guinea pig for anyone else.

What prisms did offer was a way to study the mechanisms of historical change. Researchers began comparing news headlines across branches, looking for discrepancies and then investigating their causes. In some cases the divergence arose from an explicitly random event, such as a wanted fugitive being arrested during a traffic stop. In other cases the divergence was the result of an individual choosing different actions in two branches, in which case researchers would request an interview, but if the person was a public figure, they rarely offered details on why they had made the choice they did. For cases that didn't fall into those categories, the researchers had to comb through the news stories from the preceding weeks to try to identify the causes of the discrepancy, which usually led to scrutinizing the stochastic jitters of the stock market or social media.

Then the researchers would continue to monitor the news over the following weeks and months to see how the divergences grew over time. They looked for a classic "for want of a nail, a kingdom was lost" scenario, where the ripples expanded steadily but in an intelligible manner. Instead what they found were other small discrepancies, unrelated to the one they'd originally discovered; the weather was instigating changes everywhere, all the time. By the time a significant political divergence was observed, it was difficult to ascertain what the cause had been. The problem was exacerbated by the fact that every study had to end once a prism's pad was exhausted; no matter how interesting any particular divergence might be, the connection between branches was always temporary.

In the private sector, entrepreneurs realized that while the information obtained from prisms had limited instrumental value, it was something that could be sold as content to consumers. A new kind of data broker emerged: a company would exchange news about current events with its parallel versions and sell the information to subscribers. Sports news and celebrity gossip were the easiest to sell; people were often just as interested in what their favorite stars did in other branches as in what they did in their own. Hard-core sports fans collected information from multiple branches and argued about which team had the best overall performance and whether that was more important than their performance in any individual branch. Readers compared different versions of novels published in different branches, with the result that authors faced competition from pirated copies of books they might have written. As prisms with larger pads were developed, the same thing began happening with music, and then film.

. . .

At the first meeting she attended, Nat had been incredulous at the things its attendees talked about: a man obsessively worried that his paraself was having more fun than he was, a woman trapped in a spiral of doubt because her paraself voted for a different candidate than she did. Were these the sorts of things regular people thought of as problems? Waking up covered in your own vomit; having to fuck your dealer because you couldn't scrape together enough cash: those were real problems. Nat had momentarily fantasized about telling everyone in the group they should just get over themselves, but of course she didn't, and not just because it would have blown her cover. She was in no position to judge these people. So what if they felt sorry for themselves? Better to wallow in self-pity over nothing than to have actually screwed up your life.

Nat had moved out here to get a fresh start, away from the people and places that could trigger a relapse. The job at SelfTalk wasn't great, but it was good to earn an honest paycheck, and she mostly liked hanging out with Morrow. His side hustles had been fun; she'd always been good at that sort of thing, and she told herself that it helped keep her from relapsing, because the pleasure of conning people was a safe substitute for getting high. Lately, though, Nat had begun to feel that she was just fooling herself about that. Even if she wasn't spending the money on drugs, these little scams would probably lead her back to using again. It'd be better for her to get away from all of it; she had to find a different job, away from Morrow, and that probably meant relocating again. But she needed money to do that, so she had to keep working with Morrow before she'd be able to not work with him anymore.

Zareenah was talking. "My niece is a senior in high school, and for the last few months it's been college application season. This week they heard back, and she did pretty well; she was accepted to three schools. I was feeling good about it until I was chatting with my paraself.

"It turns out that my paraself's niece got accepted to Vassar, which was her first choice. But here in this branch, that's one of the schools that rejected my niece. Everything different between our two branches is a result of my activating the prism, right? So I'm the cause of my niece getting rejected. I'm to blame."

"You're assuming that if you hadn't activated the prism, your niece would have gotten accepted," said Kevin. "But that's not necessarily true."

Zareenah started tearing apart a tissue she held in her hands, a habit of hers when talking about herself. "But that means my paraself did something to help her niece, something I didn't do in this branch. So I'm to blame through my inaction."

"You're not to blame," said Lyle.

"But everything different is because of my prism."

"That doesn't mean it's your fault."

"How can it not be?"

At a loss, Lyle turned to Dana for help. Dana asked Zareenah, "Aside from Vassar, were there any other differences in the acceptances and rejections that your niece and her paraself got?"

"No, the rest are the same."

"So we can assume that your niece's overall application package was equally strong in both branches."

"Yes," she said firmly. "She's a smart girl, and nothing I do is going to change that."

"So let's speculate for a minute. Why would Vassar accept your niece in the other branch but not in this one?"

"I don't know," said Zareenah.

Dana looked around the room. "Does anyone else have any ideas?"

Lyle said, "Maybe the admissions officer in this branch was having a bad day when he reviewed her application."

"And what might have caused him to have a bad day?"

Nat had to feign interest, so she participated. "Maybe someone cut him off in traffic that morning."

"Or he dropped his phone in the toilet," said Kevin.

"Or both," said Lyle.

To Zareenah, Dana said, "Are any of those foreseeable consequences of actions you took?"

"No," admitted Zareenah. "I guess not."

"They're just random results of the weather being different between the two branches. And anything can cause the weather to be different. If we looked, I'm sure we could find a hundred people whose prisms connect a branch where your niece was rejected. If the same thing happens in branches where you acted differently, then you aren't the cause."

"But I still feel like it's my fault."

Dana nodded. "We like the idea that there's always someone responsible for any given event, because that helps us make sense of the world. We like that so much that sometimes we blame ourselves, just so that there's someone to blame. But not everything is under our control, or even anyone's control."

"I can see it's not a rational response, but I feel it anyway," said Zareenah. "I think I'm prone to feeling guilty about my sister . . ." She paused. "Because of our history."

"Do you want to talk about that?" asked Dana.

Zareenah hesitated, and then went on. "Years ago, when we were teenagers, we both studied dance, but she was much better than me. She got an audition to attend Juilliard, but I was so jealous that I sabotaged her."

Now this was interesting: legitimately bad behavior. Nat hadn't heard anything like this in the group before, but she was careful not to lean forward too eagerly.

"I put caffeine in her water bottle because I knew that would throw her off. She didn't get accepted." Zareenah put her face in her hands. "I feel like I can never make up for what I've done. You probably can't relate to that."

A pained look crossed Dana's face, but she quickly rearranged her expression. "We've all made mistakes," she said. "Believe me, I've made my share. But there's a difference between accepting responsibility for our actions and taking the blame for random misfortunes."

Nat studied Dana as she spoke. Dana's face had returned to its usual calm acceptance, but her momentary loss of composure had caught Nat's attention. She'd never seen that in a group facilitator before. The one time she heard a facilitator in rehab recount his past, it was a guy who was so practiced at it that his story sounded like part of a sales pitch. It made her curious: What had Dana done that she felt so guilty about?

. . .

As prisms with larger pads became available, data brokers began offering personal research services for people who wanted to learn about the other paths their lives might have taken. This was a much riskier venture than selling news from other branches, for a couple reasons. First, it might take years before the divergences had grown large enough to be interesting, and the brokers had to stockpile prisms, activating them but not exchanging any information, saving their pads for use later. Second, it required a higher level of cooperation between the parallel versions of the company. If customer Jill wanted to know about her parallel selves, several versions of the company would have to do research in their branches, but Jill could only pay the version in her branch; there was no way for money to be shared across branches. The hope was that cross-branch cooperation would enable every version of a company to get paying customers in their branch, and over time this would work to everyone's advantage: a form of reciprocal altruism between all of the company's parallel versions.

Predictably, some individuals became depressed after learning that their parallel selves had enjoyed successes that they themselves hadn't. For a time there was concern that these private queries would gain a reputation as a product that made buyers unhappy. However, most people decided that they liked more things about their life than they did about their parallel selves' lives, and so concluded that they had made the right decisions. While this was likely just confirmation bias, it was common enough that personal research services remained a profitable business for data brokers.

Some people avoided the data brokers entirely, afraid of what they might learn, while others became obsessed with them. There were married couples where one person fell into the former category while the other fell into the latter, which often led to divorce. Data brokers made various attempts to expand their customer base, but rarely met with success. The product that was most successful at winning over naysayers was one aimed at those who had lost a loved one: the data brokers would find a branch where the person was still alive and forward their social-media updates, so the bereaved could see the life their loved one might have lived. This practice only solidified the most common criticism offered by pundits: that data brokers were promoting unhealthy behavior in their customers.

. . .

Nat expected that Morrow would be satisfied for a while given the success of his plan with Mrs. Oehlsen. The woman had transferred some money into a dummy account a couple weeks ago, and her parallel self had bought the story about confusion from the pain meds. Now that Mrs. Oehlsen had passed away, everything was wrapped up tidily. But instead of being content with that, Morrow now seemed more eager than ever for a bigger score.

They were in the office at SelfTalk eating tacos that Morrow had brought from a food truck two blocks away when he raised the topic. "Where are we with Lyle?" he asked.

"I'm making progress," said Nat. "I can tell he's thinking that he'd be happier without a prism."

Morrow finished his taco and drained his can of soda. "We can't just sit around waiting for him to decide to give up his prism."

Nat frowned at him. "'Just sit around'? You think that's what I've been doing?"

He waved a hand at her. "Take it easy, I didn't mean anything by it. But it's no good for us if he hangs on to that prism for years. We need to make him want to get rid of it."

"I know, and that's exactly what I've been working on."

"I was thinking about something more concrete."

"Like what?"

"I know a guy, he works with a crew doing identity theft. I could ask him to target Lyle, ruin his credit. After that, Lyle really won't want to hear about how well his paraself is doing."

Nat grimaced. "Is that the sort of thing we're doing now?"

He shrugged. "If there were a way to make Lyle's parallel life look better, I'd be fine with that, but that's not an option. The only thing we can do is make his life here look worse."

A plea based on squeamishness wouldn't sway Morrow; she needed a more pragmatic argument. "You don't want to make him so miserable that he holds on to the prism as his only connection to a happy life."

That seemed to work. "You've got a point there," he admitted.

"Give me a few more meetings before you do that."

Morrow crumpled up his paper food tray and empty soda can and tossed them into the wastebasket. "All right, we'll try it your way for a while longer. But you've got to speed things up."

She nodded. "I have an idea."

. . .

Dana was a little surprised when Nat announced to the group that she had sold her prism; in previous meetings she hadn't gotten the feeling that Nat was ready to make the leap, although she knew it wasn't always possible to anticipate these things. Nat seemed to be happy with her decision, but that was typical; everyone felt good when they first quit. She did notice that Nat very subtly checked Lyle's reaction to her announcement, something that Dana had seen her doing before. It didn't appear that Nat's interest was romantic, or if it was, she wasn't pursuing it, maybe so as to not complicate things while she worked on her own issues.

At the next meeting Nat talked for longer than usual, describing the ways she felt her attitude had improved since giving up the prism. While she wasn't overly effusive, Dana was a little concerned that she might have unrealistic expectations and was setting herself up for a fall. Kevin expressed a similar sentiment, somewhat indelicately, and he seemed to be motivated more by envy than compassion; he'd been in the group much longer than Nat, and in all that time had made only modest progress. Fortunately, Nat didn't become defensive; she said that she understood that getting rid of her prism hadn't magically solved all the problems in her life. Then the group spent the rest of the meeting focusing on Kevin and what he'd been going through in the last week, without Dana having to steer them at all.

She was feeling pretty pleased about both the group and herself afterward, but her good mood didn't last long. She had just taken the coffeemaker back to the church kitchen and was locking up the meeting room when Vinessa showed up.

"Hey Dana."

"Vinessa? What are you doing here?"

"I looked for you at your office," Vinessa explained, "but you weren't there, so I figured I'd try here."

"What's up?"

"It's about the money."

Of course it was; Vinessa had decided to go back to school and had asked Dana for help with the tuition. "What about it?"

"I need it now. The enrollment period is closing this week."

"This week? The last time we talked about this, you were saying this fall."

"Yeah, I know, but I decided that the sooner I started, the better. So can you get me the money this week?"

Dana hesitated, thinking about how she would have to rearrange her budget.

"Are you changing your mind?"

"No—"

"Because I took you at your word before, and I made plans based on that. But if you're changing your mind, say so."

"No, no, I can get it to you. I'll send it to you tomorrow, okay?"

"Great, thanks. You won't be sorry, I promise. I'm going to make it work this time."

"I know you will."

The two of them stood there awkwardly for a moment, and then Vinessa left. As Dana watched her walk away, she wondered what was the right word to describe their relationship.

Back in high school they'd been best friends. They spent all their time together, confided in each other, reduced each other to tears laughing. More than that, Dana had admired the way Vinessa didn't care what anyone thought, how she refused to be boxed in; she got good grades because it was easy for her, and then openly mocked the teachers until they had no choice but to give her detention. Sometimes Dana wished she could have been as brave, but she was too comfortable with the role of teacher's pet to do anything that might jeopardize that.

Then came the field trip to Washington, D.C. The two of them had planned to host a party in their hotel room for their last evening in the city, but there was the problem of what to do if a teacher knocked on the door: alcohol was too hard to hide, marijuana too easy to smell. Instead they collected Vicodin from their parents' medicine cabinets, leftovers from Dana's father's gum surgery and Vinessa's mother's hysterectomy, enough for them and their friends.

What they hadn't counted on was that one of the teachers had borrowed a key card from housekeeping to do surprise room checks. The very first night, Ms. Archer came in just as the two of them were recounting their stash, two dozen pills arranged in neat rows across the top of the dresser.

"What in the world is going on here?"

They both stood there for a long moment, mute as statues. Dana could see all her future plans evaporating like morning mist.

"Neither of you have anything to say?"

That was when she said it. "They're Vinessa's."

And Vinessa looked at her, more shocked than anything else. She could have denied it, but they both knew it wouldn't change anything, that Dana would be believed and Vinessa wouldn't. There was a moment when Dana could have taken back what she said, when she could have confessed the truth, but she didn't.

Vinessa was suspended. When she returned to school, she pointedly ignored Dana, for which Dana could hardly blame her, but that wasn't the end of it. Angry at the world, she began acting out: shoplifting, staying out all night, coming to school drunk or stoned, and hanging out with kids who did the same. Her grades plummeted, and her chances of getting into a good college vanished. It was as if, before that night, Vinessa had been balanced on a knife's edge; she could have become either what society considered a good girl or a bad girl. Dana's lie had pushed her off the edge, onto the side of being bad, and with that label the course of Vinessa's life had taken a different direction.

They lost touch after that, but Dana ran into her several years later. Vinessa told her she forgave her, said she understood why Dana had done it. Now, after some time in jail and a stint in rehab, she was trying to get her life back on track; she wanted to take classes at a community college, but she couldn't afford the tuition on her own, and her parents had given up on her. Dana had immediately offered to help.

That first attempt hadn't been a success; Vinessa had discovered that she couldn't engage with college on an emotional level and dropped out. Later on she had tried to start her own business online, and asked Dana for some money to help her get off the ground. That hadn't worked out, either; she had misjudged the expenses involved. Now she had an idea for another venture, but she wasn't asking Dana for money for it. Vinessa's plan was to take the classes needed for her to draw up a sound business proposal, which she would present to potential investors. And so now she was asking Dana for tuition money again.

Dana knew Vinessa was taking advantage of her feelings of guilt, but it didn't matter. Dana was guilty. She owed her.

.   .   .

Nat was coming out of the restroom when she heard Dana talking to someone just around the corner, in the hallway. Nat stopped, leaned against the wall, and held her phone up to her ear as camouflage. Then she slid over until she could eavesdrop: someone was getting money out of Dana, but it wasn't clear what the situation was. Was this woman running some kind of scam? Nat told herself she ought to find out more, just to make sure that there weren't any surprises that could affect what she and Morrow were doing, but mostly she was just curious.

She went outside and caught up with the woman. "Excuse me, but do you know Dana?"

The woman eyed her suspiciously. "Why do you want to know?"

"I'm in a support group that she facilitates. I was just about to leave when I saw you two talking. I couldn't hear what you were saying, but it looked like you were angry with her. I was just wondering if you had been in a group she facilitated, or been a patient of hers, and had a bad experience with her. I don't mean to pry, I'm just wondering if there's anything I ought to know about Dana."

The woman chuckled. "That's an interesting question. What kind of group are you in?"

"It's for people who have issues with using prisms," said Nat. At the dismissive look on the woman's face, Nat decided to play a hunch. "I used to be in NA before, though."

She gave a single nod. "But Dana wasn't your facilitator for that, was she?"

"No."

"Good, because I wouldn't trust her with that. For that prism stuff, though, I'm sure she's fine. You've got nothing to worry about."

"Can you tell me why you wouldn't trust her for an NA group?"

She considered it, and then shrugged. "Sure, why not. Drinks are on you."

They went to a nearby bar. The woman's name was Vinessa, and Nat bought her a Maker's Mark while sticking with a cranberry and soda for herself. Nat told a sanitized version of her history of drug use, one that could plausibly dovetail with her cover in the support group; she didn't think Vinessa would mention this conversation to Dana, but it couldn't hurt to be careful. Once she was satisfied with Nat's cred, Vinessa started talking about her own past; she explained that she'd had all the potential in the world when she was in high school, that she'd been on the path to a prestigious college and a charmed life. It all came to an end when her best friend had betrayed her, selling her out to protect her own prospects. Ever since then Vinessa had been traveling a hard road, a road that she was getting off only now.

"Which is why I wouldn't want her for an NA group. You can't trust her not to turn you in."

"Everything that happens in those groups is supposed to be confidential," said Nat.

"So is a secret between best friends!" Some other people in the bar turned to look at them. Vinessa resumed at a regular speaking volume, "It's not like she's the worst person I've ever met; at least she has the decency to feel bad about what she did. But there are people you can count on for anything, and then there are people you can count on only for some things, and you've got to know who's who."

"You still see her, though."

"Well, like I said, Dana's good for some things. My point is she's not good for everything. I learned that the hard way."

Then Vinessa started talking about her plans to start her own business. Nat didn't ask her about the money that she was getting from Dana, but she could tell it wasn't a deliberate scam. Vinessa was just using Dana, offering her a chance to atone for her sins by providing financial support for Vinessa's latest venture. Nat thanked Vinessa and promised she wouldn't mention their conversation to anyone, and then headed home.

Nat used to be like Vinessa, always blaming someone else for her problems. For years she believed it was her parents' fault that she was arrested for breaking and entering, because if they hadn't changed the locks on their house, she wouldn't have had

to break in to find something she could sell for drug money. It
had taken a long time for Nat to take responsibility for the things
she did. Clearly Vinessa hadn't gotten there yet, and maybe it was
because in Dana she had found someone willing to accept the
blame. Dana had done something shitty to Vinessa, no doubt
about it, but that was years ago. If Vinessa hadn't gotten her act
together by now, it was her own fault, not Dana's.

.   .   .

When prisms became affordable to individual consumers, retailers initially advertised them as a private alternative to visiting
a data broker. They targeted new parents, encouraging them
to buy one now, activate it, and store it until their child was
an adult, at which point the child could see how her life might
have gone differently. This approach won a few customers, but
not nearly the numbers that retailers had hoped for. Instead, it
turned out that when people were able to buy prisms themselves,
they found uses for them beyond exploring scenarios of "what
might have been."

A popular use of a prism was to enable collaboration with
yourself, increasing your productivity by dividing the tasks on a
project between your two versions; each of you did one half the
job, and then you shared the results. Some individuals tried to
buy multiple prisms so that they'd be part of a team consisting
solely of versions of themselves, but not all the parallel selves
were in direct contact with each other, which meant that information needed to be relayed from one to another, consuming the
prisms' pads faster. A number of projects came to an abrupt end
because someone had underestimated their data usage, exhaust-
ing the prism before the work done in one branch could be transmitted, leaving it forever inaccessible.

More than data brokers, the availability of private prisms had an enormous impact on the public imagination; even people who never used prisms found themselves thinking about the enormous role that contingency played in their lives. Some people experienced identity crises, feeling that their sense of self was undermined by the countless parallel versions of themselves. A few bought multiple prisms and tried to keep all their parallel selves in sync, forcing everyone to maintain the same course even as their respective branches diverged. This proved to be unworkable in the long term, but proponents of this practice simply bought more prisms and repeated their efforts with a new set of parallel selves, arguing that any attempt to reduce their dispersal was worthwhile.

Many worried that their choices were rendered meaningless because every action they took was counterbalanced by a branch in which they had made the opposite choice. Experts tried to explain that human decision-making was a classical rather than quantum phenomenon, so the act of making a choice didn't by itself cause new branches to split; it was quantum phenomena that generated new branches, and your choices in those branches were as meaningful as they ever were. Despite such efforts, many people became convinced that prisms nullified the moral weight of their actions.

Few acted so rashly as to commit murder or other felonies; the consequences of your actions still fell on you in this branch, not any other. But there was a shift in behavior that, while falling short of a mass outbreak of criminality, was readily discernible by social scientists. Edgar Allan Poe had used the phrase "the imp of the perverse" to describe the temptation to do the wrong thing simply because you could, and for many people the imp had become more persuasive.

· · ·

Not for the first time, Nat wished there were some way to tell how Lyle felt about his prism, some visible gauge of her progress. A month had gone by since her gambit of announcing she had given up her prism, and while she knew Lyle was closer to giving his up than when she started, she had no way of telling how much longer it would be. Another month? Another six months? Morrow's patience would run out soon, and then they'd have to try something more drastic.

Once everyone was seated, Lyle volunteered to go first. He turned to Dana. "When I first started attending this group, you said one of the goals was to have a healthy relationship with your paraself."

"One of the possible goals, yes," said Dana.

"The other day I was talking to this guy who goes to the same gym I go to, and he seems to have that. He says he and his paraself are friends, they exchange tips that they've learned, they encourage each other to do better. It sounded amazing."

Nat was immediately alert. Was Lyle resolving to make that his goal? That would be a disaster. If he was set on that, even Morrow's plan wouldn't be enough to get him to sell his prism.

"And I realized that I will never, ever have that kind of relationship with my paraself. So I've decided that I'm going to get rid of my prism."

Nat was so relieved that for a moment she thought it must have been obvious to the others, but no one noticed. Zareenah asked Lyle, "Did you talk it over with your paraself?"

"Yeah. At first he suggested we just take a break for a while but still hang on to our prisms. I had thought about doing that before, because then I could show him when things were going better for me. But a couple meetings back, Nat mentioned that she didn't need to prove anything to anyone. I think that keeping my prism would just keep me in that mind-set, wanting to prove something. So I told my paraself that, and he understood. We're going to sell our prisms."

Kevin said, "Just because your relationship with your paraself isn't perfect doesn't mean you have to give it up. That's like saying if your marriage isn't fairy-tale happy all the time, you don't want to be married at all."

"I don't think it's like that," said Zareenah. "Maintaining your marriage is a lot more important than maintaining your relationship with your paraself. Everyone got by just fine before prisms were invented."

"But is getting rid of your prism going to be what everyone in this group is expected to do? First Nat, now you. I don't know if I want to give up my prism."

"Don't worry, Kevin," said Dana. "You get to choose what your goal is. Not everyone has to have the same one."

The group spent some more time reassuring Kevin and discussing the validity of different ways of living with prisms. When the meeting was over, Nat went to talk to Lyle. "I think you're making the right decision," she told him.

"Thanks, Nat. You definitely helped me make it."

"I'm glad." Now came the crucial part. Nat was surprised by how nervous she felt. As casually as she could, she said, "You know what, you should sell your prism at the same place I sold mine. They'll give you and your paraself a good price."

"Really? What's it called?"

"SelfTalk, on Fourth Street."

"Oh yeah, I think I saw a flyer of theirs around here."

"Yeah, that's where I got their name, too. If you want some

moral support when you sell it, I can go with you, and afterward we can go get coffee or something."

Lyle nodded. "Sure, let's do that."

And just like that, the plan was right on track. "How about Sunday?" she said.

· · ·

Nat was waiting outside of SelfTalk for Lyle to arrive. She knew there was a chance he had changed his mind, but he showed up right on time and had the prism with him. It was a little anticlimactic to finally see it; here was what she and Morrow had been working toward for months, but it didn't look any different from any other late-model prism, just a blue aluminum briefcase. Nat was suddenly struck by how the situation was both extraordinary and surprisingly mundane: each prism was like something out of a fairy tale, a bag containing a door to another world, and yet most of those worlds weren't particularly interesting, most of those doors weren't especially valuable. It was only because this one might reunite a prince with his beloved that it was precious.

"Still ready to do this?" she asked.

"One hundred percent," said Lyle. "I checked with my paraself this morning, and he's still on board. He should be at his version of SelfTalk right now."

"Great. Let's go."

They went inside, and Morrow was at the counter. "Can I help you?" he asked.

Lyle took a deep breath. "I'd like to sell this prism."

Morrow did the usual, checking the keyboard, the video camera, the microphone. This was the biggest variable in their plan: they couldn't be sure who was working the counter on the other side of the prism, who was going to make parallel Lyle an offer.

It was very likely parallel Morrow or parallel Nat, in which case things would be fine; even though they had no idea what the plan was, they would follow this Morrow's lead. But there was always the chance that someone else was working the counter at Self-Talk in the other branch, which might make things complicated.

Nat saw that Morrow kept typing longer than the hardware check would require, which was a good sign. Morrow was telling the person on the other end to trust him, to pay parallel Lyle more than market price for the prism and act as if it were perfectly normal, that he would explain later. Fortunately Lyle had no idea of how long a prism inspection usually took.

Morrow made his offer, and then Lyle briefly conferred with his paraself. Since they had already agreed to sell their prisms, they weren't talking about the price; just a final farewell. Nat made sure not to exchange looks with Morrow while they waited, but she wasn't sure where she ought to look. It didn't make sense to stare at Lyle, so she just looked out the front window.

Finally Lyle handed the prism over and took his payment. Once it was done, Nat asked him, "How do you feel?"

"Kind of sad, kind of relieved."

"Let's go get some coffee."

They chatted for a while at the coffee shop. Afterward they hugged goodbye, and she told him she'd see him at the next meeting. Her plan was to attend one more meeting and then announce that she felt like she didn't need to go to the meetings anymore.

When she got back to SelfTalk, it was a half hour before closing time, and there were only a couple of customers left in the store. She found Morrow in his office, typing on Lyle's prism. "You're just in time," he said. "I'm on with my paraself." He gestured for her to look at the screen as he typed.

Hey bro.

You want to tell me why I just
paid so much for this prism?

Car crash, six months ago, Scott
Otsuka and Roderick Ferris.
Who survived in your branch?

Roderick Ferris.

Here it was Scott Otsuka.

Got it! Great find, bro!

Yeah, it's your lucky day.
Here's what you have to do next.

Morrow had already found a printed copy of a six-month-old
newspaper whose headline said Roderick Ferris died in the car
crash while Scott Otsuka lived. Parallel Morrow's job now was
to find a printed newspaper in his branch that covered the same
crash, the one in which Otsuka died while Ferris lived. They
scheduled a time a few days from now when they would con-
verse again.

Morrow folded up the keyboard and put the prism on a shelf
at the rear of the storeroom. He grinned at Nat when he came
back into the office. "You didn't think we'd pull it off, did you?"

She'd had her doubts, and even now she could hardly believe
it. "We haven't pulled it off yet," she said.

"The hard part's done. The rest is going to be easy." He
laughed. "Cheer up, you're going to be rich."

"I suppose I am." Which was worrying in itself; for an addict, a giant windfall could trigger a relapse just as easily as a traumatic event.

As if he were reading her mind, Morrow said, "You worried about falling back into old habits? I could hold your money for you, keep it safe so you don't spend it on the wrong things."

Nat gave a little laugh. "Thanks, Morrow, but I think I'll just take my share."

"Just trying to be helpful."

Nat wondered about the version of herself on the opposite side of the prism. She and that parallel self had been the same person up until just under a year ago, when the prism had been activated. Now Nat was going to be rich, while her parallel self wasn't. Parallel Morrow was going to be rich, but he wasn't the type to share the money with parallel Nat. Not that she particularly deserved any of it; parallel Nat hadn't gone to the support-group meetings, hadn't done any of the work. Parallel Morrow hadn't done any work, either; he was just lucky enough to have been working the counter when they made contact. If parallel Nat had been working the counter at that moment, she would probably have to split things with parallel Morrow—he was the boss—but she'd still be making a lot of money for being in the right place at the right time. So much came down to luck.

Someone had come in the front door, a man in his forties wearing a windbreaker, so Nat went to the front counter. "Can I help you?"

"Is there a guy named Morrow here?"

Morrow came out of the office. "I'm Morrow."

The man stared at him. "I'm Glenn Oehlsen. You stole twenty thousand dollars from my mother."

Morrow looked mystified. "There's been a mistake. I was helping your mother stay in touch with her paraself—"

"Yeah, and you convinced her to give away her money. That money belonged to me!"

"It belonged to your mother," said Morrow. "She could do whatever she wanted with it."

"Well, I'm here now, and I want it back."

"I don't have the money, it's been transferred into the other branch."

Oehlsen's face twisted with contempt. "Don't give me that, I know you can't send money into another timeline. I'm not an idiot!"

"If you give me a few days, I can see if your mother's paraself would be willing to return—"

"Fuck that noise." Oehlsen pulled a pistol out of his jacket and aimed it at Morrow. "Give me the money!"

Morrow and Nat raised their hands. "Okay, let's relax," said Morrow.

"I'll relax once you give me the money."

"I don't have what you're looking for."

"Bullshit!"

From her vantage point Nat could tell that a customer in one of the carrels had seen what was happening and was calling the police. "There's some cash in the register," she said. "You can have that."

"I'm not a goddamned robber, I just want what's mine. What this guy cheated out of my mother." With his free hand, Oehlsen pulled his phone out and put it on the counter. "Now you take yours out," he said to Morrow.

Slowly, Morrow took out his phone and laid it next to Oehlsen's.

Oehlsen tapped open the digital wallet on his phone. "Now you're going to make a transfer. Twenty thousand dollars."

Morrow shook his head. "No."

"You think I'm joking?"

"I'm not paying you," he said.

Nat looked at him incredulously. "Just—"

"Shut up," said Morrow with a glare. He returned his attention to Oehlsen. "I'm not going to pay you."

Oehlsen was clearly flustered. "You think I won't do it?"

"I think you don't want to go to jail."

"You work with prisms. You know there's some timeline where I shoot you right now."

"Yeah, but I don't think this is the one."

"If it's going to happen anyway, why shouldn't I be the one to do it?"

"You kill me, you're the one that goes to jail. And like I said, you don't want that."

Oehlsen stared at him for a minute. Then he lowered the pistol, picked up his phone, and walked out of the store.

Nat and Morrow both let out enormous sighs of relief. "Jesus Christ, Morrow," said Nat. "What the fuck were you thinking?"

Morrow smiled weakly. "I knew he didn't have it in him."

"When a guy is holding a gun on you, you do what he says." Nat realized her heart was racing; she tried some deep breathing to slow it down. Her shirt was soaked with sweat. "I better check on the customers—" Oehlsen was standing in the doorway again.

"Fuck it," he said, "what difference does it make?" He raised the pistol, shot Morrow in the face, and walked away.

· · ·

The police picked Glenn Oehlsen up a few miles away. Officers questioned Nat, the customers who were in the store, and an executive who came from SelfTalk's main office. Nat told the officers she had no idea what Morrow had been up to, and they seemed to believe her. She admitted to the executive that she knew Morrow had been taking a prism out of the store and visiting Jessica Oehlsen at the nursing home, and was reprimanded for failing to report a violation of company policy. The next day a temporary store manager arrived; he ordered an inventory of all the prisms in the store and established new procedures for checking them in and out of the storeroom, but Nat had already taken home the prism that Morrow had bought from Lyle.

At the next scheduled meeting with parallel Morrow, Nat got on the keyboard:

Hey bro.

> This isn't Morrow. This is Nat.

Hey Nat. Why are you on the prism?

> We've had problems here. Morrow's dead.

What? Are you serious?

> He ran a scam on a woman named Jessica Oehlsen. Her son Glenn came in here and shot him. I don't know if you're running a scam on her in your branch, but if you are, back off. Her son's unstable.

> Shit. That's fucked up.

> You're telling me. So what
> do you want to do now?

There was a long pause. Eventually a reply appeared on the screen.

> We can still go ahead with the deal. You'll
> have to take care of things on your end
> by yourself. Think you can handle that?

Nat thought about it. Selling the prism to Scott Otsuka would mean going to Los Angeles, a bus ride of several hours each way. There would probably have to be a preliminary meeting before the actual sale could take place, which would mean at least two trips.

> I can handle it.

For the first time, Nat wasn't acting as the buyer; she was the seller. She would have to provide evidence of what made her prism valuable. Nat and parallel Morrow exchanged photos of their respective printed newspapers; these were harder to forge than screenshots of the newspaper websites.

Now she had to contact someone who worked for Scott Otsuka, explain what she was offering, and send the photo as proof.

. . .

Ornella had worked as Scott's personal assistant for ten years, well before he met and married Roderick. Roderick's assistant had moved to France a couple years ago, and while he got someone to accompany him when he was filming on location or doing a publicity tour, when Roderick was at home Ornella worked as assistant for both of them. Until six months ago, when a drunk driver had changed everything. Now she worked just for Scott again.

Before the car crash, Ornella had never paid much attention to prisms. She knew that Scott's fans circulated pirated copies of other versions of his songs, but he had never listened to any of them, so she hadn't, either; the same was true of Roderick and his films. But ever since the car crash, it seemed like she was barraged by advertisements from prism data brokers: "Subscribe now and be the first to see the movies Roderick Ferris would have made if he had lived."

And then there were the offers from fans who owned prisms and wanted to give them to Scott. They knew from interviews that Scott and Roderick hadn't owned a prism, and while it would have been easy for Scott to buy one from a data broker, a lot of his fans wanted to connect with him, to be the one who eased his pain. Ornella knew Scott had thought about finding a prism; he would have given anything to see Roderick alive again. But the problem was obvious: in every one of those branches where the car crash hadn't happened and his husband was still alive, his paraself was there, too. Scott would be a grieving widower intruding upon a happily married couple, a reminder that disaster could strike out of nowhere, a specter at the feast. That wasn't what he wanted. If Scott were going to see a parallel Roderick, it couldn't be as an object of pity or dread.

This newest offer was different: a prism connecting to a branch where there was no parallel Scott, only a grieving Roderick. This was something Scott might be interested in. She wasn't going to mention it to him without making sure it was a legitimate offer first, though.

Ornella had asked an expert to examine the image she'd received, of course. He'd told her it wasn't an obvious forgery, but he could easily create one just as good, so by itself the image wasn't proof of anything. She told the seller that she wanted to talk to the Ornella in the other branch first, so they arranged a time when that could happen.

She was a little surprised when the seller arrived. She had assumed "Nat" was a man, but it was a woman who showed up at the front gate carrying a prism. Nat was thin and could have been pretty if she tried, but she had a certain sadness about her. Ornella's years of working for Scott had given her a lot of experience identifying opportunists, but she didn't get that sense from Nat, at least not right off the bat.

"I want to be clear," Ornella told her when she came in. "You're not going to see Scott today. He's not even in the house. If I'm satisfied by what I see, then we'll schedule another appointment."

"Of course, that's what I figured," said Nat. She seemed almost apologetic about what she was doing.

Ornella had her set up the prism on a coffee table. At first Nat had a text conversation with the person on the other side, and then she switched to video and slid the prism over to Ornella. A face appeared on the screen, but it wasn't a parallel version of Nat, it was a man, lean and lanky. An opportunist. "Who are you?" she asked.

"Name's Morrow." He stepped away and then the screen was filled by another version of herself. Ornella could see that the room in the background was the same one she was in now, and she recognized the outfit her parallel self was wearing, too.

"Is this for real?" she asked, tentatively. "Roderick is alive in your branch?"

Her parallel self looked like she could hardly believe it, either. "He is. And Scott's alive in yours?"

"Yes."

"I have a few questions."

"The same ones I have, probably." The two Ornellas exchanged information about the car crash. It had happened the same way in both branches: same movie premiere, same drunk driver. Just a different survivor.

They agreed that Ornella would talk to Scott, and her parallel self would talk to Roderick. Assuming both of them were open to the possibility, the Ornellas scheduled a date next week for them to try the prisms and decide if they wanted to buy them.

"Now let's talk about the price," said Ornella.

"We're not talking price now," Morrow said firmly, from the other side. "After your bosses have tried the product, I'll name a price. Either you pay it, or we walk."

Which was a sensible strategy; assuming Scott and Roderick wanted to buy, they'd be in no mood to haggle. It was clear that this Morrow was the one running the show. "Okay," said Ornella. "We'll talk then." She slid the prism back to Nat, who conferred briefly with Morrow before closing it up.

"I guess that's it," said Nat. "I'll be back next week."

"Fine," said Ornella. She accompanied Nat to the front door and let her out. As Nat began walking down the steps, Ornella asked, "How is it that I'm working with you on this?"

Nat turned around. "Say what?"

"My paraself is working with a guy named Morrow. Why am I working with you instead of a version of Morrow?"

The woman sighed. "Long story."

. . .

Nat got herself a cup of coffee and took her seat. This was her second meeting since getting the prism from Lyle; last week she'd been planning on announcing that she wasn't going to be coming back, but she had wound up hardly saying anything at all. So she had had to attend at least one more and say that she was going to take a break from the meetings; people would wonder if she simply stopped.

Dana smiled at the group and said, "Who wants to start us off today?"

Without intending to, Nat found herself speaking, just as Lyle began saying something as well. Both of them stopped.

"You go," said Nat.

"No, you should go," said Lyle. "I don't think you've ever started off a meeting before."

Nat realized that he was right. What had come over her? She opened her mouth, but for once she couldn't think of a good lie. Eventually, she said, "A guy I work with, I guess you'd call him my supervisor, he was killed recently. Murdered, actually."

The group was shocked, with assorted "Oh my Gods" being murmured.

"Do you want to tell us about your relationship with him?" asked Dana.

"Yeah," asked Kevin. "Was he a friend?"

"Kind of," Nat admitted. "But that's not why it's been on my mind. I know this isn't a grief support group . . . I guess I brought this up because I wanted your take on something."

"Of course," said Dana. "Go ahead."

"I keep thinking about the randomness of this murder. I don't mean the killer picked him at random. I mean, when he had the gun pointed at my supervisor, he said that some version of him was going to pull the trigger, so why shouldn't it be him? We've all heard that line before, but I never paid any attention to it. But now I'm wondering, are the people who say that actually right?"

"That's a good question," said Dana. "I agree that we've all heard people make similar claims." She addressed the group. "Does anyone have any thoughts on that? Do you think that every time someone makes you angry, there's a branch where you pick up a gun and shoot the guy?"

Zareenah spoke up. "I've read that there's been an increase in crimes of passion since prisms became popular. Not an enormous one, but statistically significant."

"Yeah," said Kevin, "which is why the theory can't be true. The fact that there's been an increase, even a small one, disproves the theory."

"How do you figure?" asked Zareenah.

"Branches are generated by any quantum event, right? Even before we had prisms, branches were still splitting off constantly; we just didn't have access to any of them. If it were true that there's *always* a branch where you pick up a gun and shoot someone on a whim, then we should have seen the same number of random murders every day before the prism was invented as we saw every day after. The invention of prisms wouldn't cause more of those murders to line up in this particular branch. So if we're seeing more people killing one another since prisms became popular, it can't be because there's always a branch where you pick up a gun."

"I follow your reasoning," said Zareenah, "but then what's causing the rise in murders?"

Kevin shrugged. "It's like a suicide fad. People hear about other people doing it, and it gives them ideas."

Nat thought about it. "That proves that the argument can't be right, but it doesn't explain why it's wrong."

"If you know the theory's wrong, why do you need more?"

"I want to know whether my decisions matter!" That came out more emphatically than she intended. Nat took a breath, and then continued. "Forget about murder; that's not the kind of thing I'm talking about. But when I have a choice to do the right thing or the wrong thing, am I always choosing to do both in different branches? Why should I bother being nice to other people, if every time I'm also being a dick to them?"

There was some discussion among the members for a while, but eventually Nat turned to Dana. "Can you tell me what you think?"

"Sure," said Dana. She paused to gather her thoughts. "In general, I think your actions are consistent with your character. There might be more than one thing that would be in character for you to do, because your behavior is going to vary depending on your mood, but there are a lot more things that would be utterly out of character. If you're someone who's always loved animals, there isn't a branch where you kick a puppy just because it barked at you. If you're someone who's always obeyed the law, there's no branch where you suddenly rob a convenience store instead of going into work in the morning."

Kevin said, "What about branches that diverged when you were a baby and your life took a totally different course?"

"I don't care about that," said Nat. "I'm asking about branches where I, having lived the life I led, am faced with a choice."

"Kevin, we can talk about bigger divergences later, if you want," said Dana.

"No, that's fine. Proceed."

"Okay, so let's imagine you're in a situation where you have a couple options, and either course of action would be consistent with your character. For example, suppose a cashier has given you too much change, and you can either give it back or just keep it. Suppose you could see yourself doing either of those, depending on the kind of day you're having. In that case, I'd say it's entirely possible that there's a branch where you keep the extra change, as well as a branch where you give it back."

Nat realized there probably weren't any branches out there where she gave back the extra change. For as long as she could remember, if she was having a good day, getting extra change would have just made it a better day.

Kevin asked, "So does that mean it doesn't matter if we act like jerks?"

"It matters to the person in this branch that you're acting like a jerk to," said Zareenah.

"But what about globally? Does being a jerk in this branch increase the percentage of jerkish behavior across all branches?"

"I'm not sure about the math," said Dana. "But I definitely think that your choices matter. Every decision you make contributes to your character and shapes the kind of person you are. If you want to be someone who always gives the extra money back to the cashier, the actions you take now affect whether you'll become that person.

"The branch where you're having a bad day and keep the extra change is one that split off in the past; your actions can't affect it anymore. But if you act compassionately in this branch, that's still meaningful, because it has an effect on the branches that will split off in the future. The more often you make compassionate choices, the less likely it is that you'll make selfish choices in the future, even in the branches where you're having a bad day."

"That sounds good, but—" Nat thought about how years of acting a certain way could wear ruts in a person's brain, so that you would keep slipping into the same habits without trying to. "But it's not easy," said Nat.

"I know it's not," said Dana. "But the question was, given that we know about other branches, whether making good choices is worth doing. I think it absolutely is. None of us are saints, but we can all try to be better. Each time you do something generous, you're shaping yourself into someone who's more likely to be generous next time, and that matters.

"And it's not just your behavior in this branch that you're changing: you're inoculating all the versions of you that split off in the future. By becoming a better person, you're ensuring that more and more of the branches that split off from this point forward are populated by better versions of you."

Better versions of Nat. "Thanks," she said. "That's what I was looking for."

. . .

Ornella had known it would be awkward when Nat and Scott met, but it was even more so than she expected. Scott had hardly spoken to anyone who wasn't a family member or close friend in months and was out of practice at wearing his public face; the prospect of seeing Roderick alive again was making him particularly anxious. As for Nat, she seemed distant, which was not what Ornella had expected from someone who stood to make a lot of money in the next few minutes.

Nat set the prism up on the coffee table again. Ornella switched it to video and saw Morrow's face; then it was her parallel self, who looked as nervous as she felt. For a moment Ornella had an impulse to call the whole thing off, afraid that

Scott would only be hurt more, but she knew they couldn't pass up this opportunity. She gestured for Scott to sit down on the couch next to her at the same time that her parallel self gestured to someone offscreen, and then Ornella turned the prism so that it faced Scott.

On the screen was a face that was doubly familiar, first because it was Roderick and second because his face was worn from months of grief, the same pattern of wear that Ornella saw on Scott's face every day. Scott and Roderick must have had the same reaction because simultaneously they started to cry, and never before had Ornella felt so strongly that these two men were meant to be together, the way that each one could look into the other's face and see himself.

Scott and Roderick started talking, their words overlapping. Ornella didn't want strangers to hear what they said, and stood up. "Can we give them some privacy?"

The woman, Nat, nodded and made to leave the room, but Ornella heard Morrow on the other side of the prism speak up. "They can have all the private conversations they want once the prisms are theirs. But first they have to buy them."

At the same time, the two Ornellas asked, "How much?"

Morrow named a figure. Ornella saw Nat react, as if the number was higher than she expected.

Scott and Roderick didn't hesitate. "Pay them."

Ornella took Scott's hand and looked at him, wordlessly asking, Are you sure about this? He squeezed her hand and nodded. Earlier they had talked about the finiteness of what the prism offered. No matter how much he and Roderick tried to conserve, the amount of data left on its pad wouldn't last the rest of their lives. They wouldn't be satisfied with just text; they would want to hear each other's voices and see each other's faces, so the pad would eventually run out, and then they'd have to say goodbye. Scott had been willing to go ahead with it; any extra time they had together was worth it, as far as he was concerned, and when the end came, at least it wouldn't come as a surprise.

Ornella stood and turned to Nat. "Come with me and I'll issue the payment." She could hear her parallel self telling Morrow the same thing. The screen shifted away from Roderick's face to Morrow's, and then the screen went dark; he wasn't going to let his prism out of his sight until the money was in his account.

Nat, by contrast, was content to leave her prism on the table with Scott. She looked at him awkwardly for a moment, and then said, "I'm very sorry for your loss."

"Thank you," Scott said, wiping away tears.

Nat followed Ornella into the room where she had her desk. Ornella unlocked her work phone and opened the digital wallet. She and Nat exchanged their account numbers and then laid their phones next to each other on the desk. Ornella entered the dollar amount and hit SEND. Nat's phone acknowledged the offered transfer, but Nat didn't touch the ACCEPT button.

"I suppose Scott has a lot of fans who would have given him that prism for free," said Nat, staring at the screen.

Ornella nodded, although Nat wasn't looking at her. "Yes," she said. "He absolutely does."

"There are probably people who aren't even fans of his who would have done the same."

"Probably." Ornella was about to say that there were still good Samaritans in the world, but didn't want to offend Nat by implying she wasn't one of them. After a long moment, Ornella said, "Since the money's right there, do you mind if I make a personal observation?"

"Go ahead."

"You're not like Morrow."

"How do you mean?"

"I understand why he's doing this." How could she put this tactfully? "He sees a grieving person as an opportunity to make a profit."

Nat gave a reluctant nod. "Yeah, he does."

"But you're not like that. So why are you doing this?"

"Everyone needs money."

Ornella felt emboldened enough to be frank. "If you don't mind me saying it, there are better ways of making money than this."

"I don't mind. I've been thinking the same thing myself."

Ornella wasn't sure what she should say. Eventually, she said, "Scott's happy to pay you for what you've done. But if you wouldn't feel good about taking the money, no one says you have to."

Nat's finger hovered over the button.

. . .

For the past several weeks, Dana had made sure that in her sessions with Jorge she didn't bring up the vandalism incident. Instead they talked about his efforts to recognize his own good qualities and ignore what other people might or might not think of him. She felt they were making progress and thought that she might be able to broach the topic in the near future.

So she was surprised when Jorge began a session by saying, "I've been wondering if I should go back to Lydoscope and ask them to contact my paraselves again."

"Really? Why?"

"I want to know if they've acted out since the last time I checked."

"Was there anything that prompted this?"

Jorge described a recent interaction with his manager. "And I felt really angry, like I wanted to smash things. And that made me think about what we talked about before, that it was like I had gotten the results of a medical test when I went to Lydoscope. I started thinking that maybe the test wasn't sensitive enough."

"And if you learn that your paraselves have acted out recently, then that would mean there's something serious that the first test didn't pick up?"

"I don't know," said Jorge. "Maybe."

Dana decided to push him a little on this. "Jorge, I want to suggest something. Even if your paraselves haven't acted on their anger recently, maybe it's worth thinking about what happened here in this branch."

"But how can I know if it was a freak accident or not unless I check my paraselves?"

"It was obviously out of character for you," said Dana. "There's no question about that. But it was still something you did. You, not your paraselves."

"You're saying I'm terrible."

"That is absolutely not what I'm saying," she assured him. "I know you're a good person. But even a good person can get angry. You got angry and you acted on it. That's okay. And it's okay to acknowledge that you have that side of your personality."

Jorge sat silently for a minute, and Dana worried that she had pushed him too far. Then he said, "Maybe you're right. But isn't it important that it was out of character for me, instead of being something typical for me?"

"Of course it is. But even if you were acting out of character, you have to take responsibility for your actions."

A look of fear crossed his face. "You mean I have to tell my manager what I did?"

"I'm not talking about legal responsibility," Dana reassured him. "I don't care whether your manager ever finds out. What I mean by taking responsibility is admitting to yourself what you did, and taking it into consideration when deciding what you do in the future."

He sighed. "Why can't I just forget that this ever happened?"

"If I genuinely thought you'd be happier forgetting that it ever happened, I'd be fine with that. But the fact that you've spent so much energy on this indicates that it's bothering you."

Jorge looked down, and nodded. "You're right. It has been." He looked back up at her. "So what should I do now?"

"How would you feel about talking to Sharon about what happened?"

He paused for a long time. "I suppose . . . if I also tell her about how my paraselves didn't do the same things, then maybe she'd know that it wasn't something fundamental about me. Then she wouldn't get the wrong idea."

Dana allowed herself a tiny smile; he'd achieved a breakthrough.

. . .

A new town, a new apartment; Nat hadn't found a new job yet, but it was early yet. It had been easy to find an NA meeting to attend, though. Originally she had wanted to go to the prism support group one last time and tell them everything, but the more she thought about it, the more she was sure that doing so would have been purely for her own benefit, not anyone else's. Lyle was in a good place now; he wouldn't appreciate learning that she'd had ulterior motives the whole time they'd known each other. Same for the rest of the group. Better for them to keep thinking that the Nat they knew was the real Nat.

Which was why she was now at an NA meeting. It was bigger than the prism support group—prisms would never be able to match drugs in terms of appeal—and it was the usual mix: people you'd never suspect were addicts and people who completely looked the part. She had no idea whether this group was hard core about working the steps or submitting to a higher power. She wasn't even sure she wanted to attend meetings regularly; she was just going to play it by ear.

The first person to speak was a man who described waking up from an overdose to realize that his thirteen-year-old daughter had had to give him an injection of Narcan. It wasn't easy to listen to, but Nat found something vaguely comforting about being back in a group of people whose experiences she could relate to. A woman spoke next, and then another man; neither recounted anything particularly harrowing, which was a relief. Nat didn't want to speak immediately after anyone with a horror story.

The group leader was a soft-spoken man with a salt-and-pepper beard. "I see some new faces here tonight. Would you like to say something to the group?"

Nat raised her hand, introduced herself. "I haven't been to one of these in a few years. I've been able to stay clean without them. But some things happened to me recently . . . it's not that I felt I needed a meeting to keep me from relapsing, but I've been thinking about stuff, and guess I wanted a place to talk."

Nat was silent for a while—it had been a long time since she'd done anything like this—but the group leader could tell she had more to say and he waited patiently. Eventually she continued, "There are people I've hurt that I'll probably never be able to make amends to. They'll never give me the chance, and I can't blame them. But I suppose, at some level, that made me think that if I wasn't able to do right by them, the ones I'd hurt the most, then it didn't really matter whether I was nice to other people or not. So I stayed clean, but I would still lie, I would still cheat. Nothing terrible, nothing that hurt anyone the way I did when I was using. I just looked out for myself, and I never really thought much about it.

"But recently I had this . . . this opportunity to do something actually nice for another person. It wasn't anyone I had wronged, just someone who was hurting. It would have been easy for me to behave the way I always have. But I imagined what a better person might do, and I did that instead.

"I feel good about what I did, but it's not like I deserve a medal or anything. Because there are other people for whom being generous comes easily, without a struggle. And it's easy for them because in the past they made a lot of little decisions to be generous. It was hard for me because I've made a lot of little decisions to be selfish in the past. So I'm the reason it's hard for me to be generous. That's something I need to fix. Or that I want to fix. I'm not sure if this is the right group for that, but this is the first place I thought of."

"Thank you," said the group leader. "You are absolutely welcome to attend these meetings."

The other new person, a young man who looked like he'd just graduated from high school, introduced himself and started talking. Nat turned to him to listen.

．　．　．

There was a package waiting for her when Dana got home. Once she was in her apartment, she opened it and found a personal tablet inside; no retail packaging, just an adhesive note stuck to the screen: "For Dana." She checked the wrapping, but there was no name or address for the sender.

Dana turned the tablet on; the only icons on the screen were half a dozen video files, each labeled with her name followed by a sequence of numbers. She tapped the first one to watch it, and the screen filled with a low-resolution image of her face. But it wasn't her, it was a parallel version of her, talking about her past.

"Ms. Archer came into our room and found us counting the pills. She asked us what was going on, and for a second I froze. Then I said they were mine, that Vinessa hadn't known anything about them. She was suspicious, because I'd never been in trouble before, but I convinced her. Eventually I got suspended from school, but it didn't turn into as big a deal as it could have; they put me on probation, so if I stayed out of trouble, it wouldn't go on my permanent record. I knew it would have been much worse for Vinessa because of the way the teachers felt about her.

"But Vinessa started avoiding me, and when I finally asked her why, she told me she felt guilty every time she saw me. I told her she didn't have to feel guilty and that I wanted to hang out with her, but she said I was just making it worse. I got angry at her; she got angry at me. She started spending time with these other girls who were constantly getting into trouble, and everything went downhill from there. She was caught dealing on school grounds, she was expelled, and she was in and out of jail all the time after that.

"And I keep thinking, if I hadn't said the pills were mine, everything would be different. If I had let Vinessa take her share of the blame, there wouldn't have been that wedge to drive us apart. We would have been in it together, she wouldn't have started hanging out with those troubled girls, and her life would have gone in a completely different direction."

What the hell? Fingers trembling, she tapped on the second video.

Another Dana: "One of the teachers came into our room just as we were counting the pills. I confessed everything immediately; I told her that Vinessa and I had stolen them from our parents so we could have a party. Eventually the school suspended us and put us on probation; I think they wanted to do something worse to Vinessa, but they had to punish us both equally.

"Vinessa was furious at me. She said I should have told the teacher we just found the pills, that someone must have slipped them into our bag at the airport, and we were about to tell a teacher about them. She said they wouldn't have been able to pin anything on us. But because I had confessed, she was on probation and the teachers who hated her could take her down at any time. She wasn't going to give them that power over her. As soon as our suspensions were over, Vinessa came into school drunk. After she did that a few times, the school expelled her, and she started getting arrested.

"And I keep thinking, if only I hadn't confessed, everything would be different. That close call would have been enough to warn Vinessa away from getting into real trouble. She only started acting out because she was angry at me. If it weren't for that, she would have gotten into a good college, and her life would have gone in a completely different direction."

The other videos made no mention about being caught with the pills, but they still followed a recognizable pattern. In one, Dana felt guilty about introducing Vinessa to a boy who got her addicted to drugs. In another, it was a successful shoplifting incident that emboldened Vinessa to attempt more dramatic thefts. All these Vinessas getting stuck in patterns of self-destructive behavior. All these Danas blaming themselves for it, no matter what actions they took.

If the same thing happens in branches where you acted differently, then you aren't the cause.

She had lied about the pills being Vinessa's, but her lie wasn't what pushed Vinessa off the edge, what turned her into a delinquent. That was the direction Vinessa was always going to move in, no matter what anyone else did. And Dana had spent years and thousands of dollars trying to make amends for what she'd done, trying to fix Vinessa's life. Maybe she didn't need to do that anymore.

Dana took a look at the metadata on the video files. Each file included information about the prism it had come from; the prisms had activation dates that were fully fifteen years in the past.

Fifteen years was how long it had been since she and Vinessa had gone on that field trip. Data brokers were just getting started then, and the prisms of the time had much-smaller pads than modern ones. She was surprised that any data brokers still had prisms of that vintage, let alone ones with enough data left in their pads to transmit video. Those were the most valuable prisms that data brokers owned, and transmitting these videos had probably exhausted their pads.

Who would have paid for this? It must have cost a fortune.

STORY NOTES

....

"THE MERCHANT AND THE ALCHEMIST'S GATE"
Back in the mid-1990s the physicist Kip Thorne was on a book tour, and I heard him give a talk in which he described how you could—in theory—create a time machine that obeyed Einstein's theory of relativity. I found it absolutely fascinating. Movies and television have encouraged us to think of time machines as vehicles you ride in, or else some kind of teleporter that beams you to different era. But what Thorne described was more like a pair of doors, where anything that goes in or comes out of one door will come out or go into the other door a fixed period of time later. Several questions raised by vehicular or transporter-style time machines—what about the movement of the Earth, why haven't we seen visitors from the future yet—were answered by this type of time machine. Even more interesting was the fact that Thorne had performed some mathematical analysis indicating that you couldn't change the past with this time machine, and that only a single, self-consistent timeline was possible.

Most time-travel stories assume that it's possible to change the past, and the ones in which it's not possible are often tragic. While we can all understand the desire to change things in our past, I wanted to try writing a time-travel story where the inability to do so wasn't necessarily a cause for sadness. I thought that a Muslim setting might work, because acceptance of fate is one of the basic articles of faith in Islam. Then it occurred to me that the recursive nature of time-travel stories might mesh well with the "Arabian Nights" convention of tales within tales, and that sounded like an interesting experiment.

"EXHALATION"

This story has two very different inspirations. The first was a short story by Philip K. Dick called "The Electric Ant," which I read as a teenager. In it the protagonist goes to a doctor for a routine visit and is told, to his utter surprise, that he's actually a robot. Later on, he opens up his own chest and sees a spool of punch tape that's slowly unwinding to produce his subjective experience. That image of a person literally looking at his own mind has always stayed with me.

The second was the chapter in Roger Penrose's book *The Emperor's New Mind* in which he discusses entropy. He points out that there's a sense in which it's incorrect to say we eat food because we need the energy it contains. The conservation of energy means that it is neither created nor destroyed; we are radiating energy constantly, at pretty much the same rate that we absorb it. The difference is that the heat energy we radiate is a high-entropy form of energy, meaning it's disordered. The chemical energy we absorb is a low-entropy form of energy, meaning it's ordered. In effect, we are consuming order and generating disorder; we live by increasing the disorder of the universe. It's only because the universe started in a highly ordered state that we are able to exist at all.

The idea is simple enough, but I had never seen it expressed that way until I read Penrose's explanation. I wanted to see if I could convey that idea in fictional form.

"WHAT'S EXPECTED OF US"

There's a sketch by Monty Python about a joke that's so funny that anyone who hears or reads it dies laughing. It's an example of an old trope that has acquired the name "the motif of harmful sensation": the idea that you could die simply by hearing or seeing something. Or, depending on the version, by understanding something; in the Monty Python sketch, English speakers could safely recite the German version of the joke as long as they didn't understand what they were saying.

Most versions of this trope involve some element of the supernatural; for example, horror fiction often features cursed books that drive people mad. I was wondering if a nonsupernatural version of this might be possible, and it occurred to me that a truly convincing argument that life was pointless might qualify. It's not something that would work instantaneously; the argument would take time to fully sink in, but that just means it would spread further as people repeated it to others while they mulled it over.

The safeguard against this, of course, is that even an airtight argument won't convince everyone who hears it. Arguments are simply too abstract to sway most people. A physical demonstration, on the other hand, would be much more effective.

"THE LIFECYCLE OF SOFTWARE OBJECTS"

Science fiction is filled with artificial beings who, like Athena out of the head of Zeus, spring forth fully formed, but I don't believe consciousness actually works that way. Based on our experience with human minds, it takes at least twenty years of steady effort to produce a useful person, and I see no reason that teaching an artificial being would go any faster. I wanted to write a story about what might happen during those twenty years.

I was also interested in the idea of emotional relationships between humans and AIs, and I don't mean humans becoming infatuated with sex robots. Sex isn't what makes a relationship real; the willingness to expend effort maintaining it is. Some lovers break up with each other the first time they have a big argument; some parents do as little for their children as they can get away with; some pet owners ignore their pets whenever they become inconvenient. In all of those cases, the people are unwilling to make an effort. Having a real relationship, whether with a lover or a child or a pet, requires that you be willing to balance the other party's wants and needs with your own.

I've read stories in which people argue that AIs deserve legal rights, but in focusing on the big philosophical question, there's a mundane reality that these stories gloss over. It's similar to the way movies always depict love in terms of grand romantic gestures when, over the long term, love also means working through money problems and picking dirty laundry off the floor. So while achieving legal rights for AIs would be a major step, another milestone that would be just as important is people putting real effort into their individual relationships with AIs.

And even if we don't care about them having legal rights, there's still good reason to treat conscious machines with respect. You don't have to believe that bomb-sniffing dogs deserve the right to vote to recognize that abusing them is a bad idea. Even if all you care about is how well they can detect bombs, it's in your best interest that they be treated well. No matter whether we want AIs to fill the role of employees, lovers, or pets, I suspect they will do a better job if, during their development, there were people who cared about them.

Finally, let me quote Molly Gloss, who gave a speech in which she talked about the impact that being a mother had on her as a writer. Raising a child, she said, "puts you in touch, deeply, inescapably, daily, with some pretty heady issues: What is love and how do we get ours? Why does the world contain evil and pain and loss? How can we discover dignity and tolerance? Who is in power and why? What's the best way to resolve conflict?" If we want to give an AI any major responsibilities, then it will need good answers to these questions. That's not going to happen by loading the works of Kant into a computer's memory; it's going to require the equivalent of good parenting.

"DACEY'S PATENT AUTOMATIC NANNY"

In general I'm incapable of writing a story around a specified theme, but on rare occasions it works out. Jeff VanderMeer was editing an anthology built around museum exhibits of imaginary artifacts: artists would create illustrations of the artifacts, and writers would provide descriptive text to accompany them. The artist Greg Broadmore proposed the idea of an "automatic nanny," a "subrobotic machine, designed to look after an infant," and that felt like something I could work with.

The behaviorist psychologist B. F. Skinner designed a special crib for his daughter, and there's a persistent myth that she grew up psychologically damaged and eventually committed suicide. It's completely false; she grew up healthy and happy. On the other hand, consider the psychologist John B. Watson, known as the founder of behaviorism. He advised parents, "When you are tempted to pet your child, remember that mother love is a dangerous instrument," and he shaped views on child-rearing for the first half of the twentieth century. He believed that his approach was in the best interests of the child, but all of his own children suffered from depression as adults, with more than one attempting suicide and one succeeding.

"THE TRUTH OF FACT, THE TRUTH OF FEELING"

Back in the late 1990s I heard a presentation about the future of personal computing, and the speaker pointed out that one day it would be possible to keep a permanent video recording of every moment of your life. It was a bold claim—at the time, hard disc space was too expensive to use for storing video—but I realized he was right: eventually, you'd be able to record everything. And even though I didn't know what form it would take, I felt certain this would have a profound impact on the human psyche. Intellectually we are aware that our memories are fallible, but rarely do we have to confront it. What would it do to us to have a truly accurate memory?

Every few years, I would be reminded of this question and think about it again, but I never made any headway on building a story around it. Memoirists have written eloquently about the malleability of memory, and I didn't want to simply rehash what they've already said. Then I read Walter Ong's *Orality and Literacy*, a book about the impact of the written word on oral cultures; while some of the stronger claims in the book have come under question, I still found it eye-opening. It suggested to me that there might be a parallel to be drawn between the last time a technology changed our cognition and the next time.

"THE GREAT SILENCE"

There are actually two pieces titled "The Great Silence," only one of which can fit in this collection. This requires a little explanation.

Back in 2011 I was a participant in a conference called "Bridge the Gap," whose purpose was to promote dialogue between the arts and the sciences. One of the other participants was Jennifer Allora, half of the artist duo Allora & Calzadilla. I was completely unfamiliar with the kind of art they created—hybrids of performance art, sculpture, and sound—but I was fascinated by Jennifer's explanation of the ideas they were engaged with.

In 2014 Jennifer got in touch with me about the possibility of collaborating with her and her partner, Guillermo. They wanted to create a multiscreen video installation about anthropomorphism, technology, and the connections between the human and nonhuman worlds. Their plan was to juxtapose footage of the radio telescope in Arecibo with footage of the endangered Puerto Rican parrots that live in a nearby forest, and they asked if I would write subtitle text that would appear on a third screen, a fable told from the point of view of one of the parrots, "a form of interspecies translation." I was hesitant, not only because I had no experience with video art, but also because fables aren't what I usually write. But after they showed me a little preliminary footage I decided to give it a try, and in the following weeks we exchanged thoughts on topics like glossolalia and the extinction of languages.

The resulting video installation, titled "The Great Silence," was shown at Philadelphia's Fabric Workshop and Museum as part of an exhibition of Allora & Calzadilla's work. I have to admit that when I saw the finished work, I regretted a decision I made earlier. Jennifer and Guillermo had previously invited me to visit the Arecibo Observatory myself, but I had declined because I didn't think it was necessary for me to write the text. Seeing footage of Arecibo on a wall-sized screen, I wished I had said yes.

In 2015, Jennifer and Guillermo were asked to contribute to a special issue of the art journal *e-flux* as part of the fifty-sixth Venice Biennale, and they suggested publishing the text from our collaboration. I hadn't written the text to stand alone, but it turned out to work pretty well even when removed from its intended context. That was how "The Great Silence," the short story, came to be.

"OMPHALOS"

What we now call young-earth creationism used to be common sense; up until the 1600s, it was widely assumed that the world was of recent origin. But as naturalists began looking at their environment more closely, they found clues that called this assumption into question, and over the last four hundred years, those clues have multiplied and interlocked to form the most definitive rebuttal imaginable. What would the world have to look like, I wondered, for it to confirm that original assumption?

Some aspects were easy to imagine: trees without growth rings, skulls without sutures. But when I started thinking about the night sky, answering the question became significantly harder. Much of modern astronomy is premised on the Copernican principle, the idea that we are not at the center of the universe and are not observing it from a privileged position; this is pretty much the opposite of young-earth creationism. Even Einstein's theory of relativity, which presupposes that physics should look the same no matter how fast you're moving, is an outgrowth of the Copernican principle. It seemed to me that if humanity really were the reason the universe was made, then relativity shouldn't be true; physics should behave differently in different situations, and that should be detectable.

"ANXIETY IS THE DIZZINESS OF FREEDOM"

In discussions about free will, a lot of people say that for an action of yours to be freely chosen—for you to bear moral responsibility for that action—you must have had the ability to do something else under exactly the same circumstances. Philosophers have argued endlessly about what exactly this means. Some have pointed out that when Martin Luther defended his actions to the church in 1521, he reportedly said, "Here I stand, I can do no other," i.e., he couldn't have done anything else. But does that mean we shouldn't give Luther credit for his actions? Surely we don't think he would be worthier of praise if he had said, "I could have gone either way."

Then there's the many-worlds interpretation of quantum mechanics, which is popularly understood to mean that our universe is constantly splitting into a near-infinite number of differing versions. I'm largely agnostic about the idea, but I think its proponents would encounter less resistance if they made more modest claims about its implications. For example, some people argue that it renders our decisions meaningless, because whatever you do there's always another universe in which you make the opposite choice, negating the moral weight of your decision.

I'm pretty confident that even if the many-worlds interpretation is correct, it doesn't mean that all of our decisions are canceled out. If we say that an individual's character is revealed by the choices they make over time, then, in a similar fashion, an individual's character would also be revealed by the choices they make across many worlds. If you could somehow examine a multitude of Martin Luthers across many worlds, I think you'd have to go far afield to find one that didn't defy the church, and that would say something about the kind of person he was.

ACKNOWLEDGMENTS

Thanks to everyone at the Sycamore Hill and Rio Hondo workshops for reading my early drafts. Thanks to Karen Joy Fowler, Molly Gloss, Daniel Abraham, Benjamin Rosenbaum, Meghan McCarron, Geoff Ryman, Moses Tsenongu, Richard Butner, and Christopher Rowe for their feedback on various stories. Thanks to Jennifer Allora and Guillermo Calzadilla for the invitation to collaborate. Thanks to Tim O'Connell for believing in this book, and to Kirby Kim for believing in me. And thanks to Marcia Glover, for everything.

PUBLICATION HISTORY

These stories were originally published as follows:

"The Merchant and the Alchemist's Gate," *Fantasy and Science Fiction,* and by Subterranean Press, 2007

"Exhalation," *Eclipse Two,* Night Shade Books, 2008

"What's Expected of Us," *Nature,* 2005

"The Lifecycle of Software Objects," Subterranean Press, 2010

"Dacey's Patent Automatic Nanny," *The Thackery T. Lambshead Cabinet of Curiosities,* Harper Voyage, 2011

"The Truth of Fact, the Truth of Feeling," *Subterranean Online,* 2013

"The Great Silence," *e-flux,* 2015

ALSO BY

TED CHIANG

STORIES OF YOUR LIFE AND OTHERS

Stories of Your Life and Others delivers dual delights of the very, very strange and the heartbreakingly familiar, often presenting characters who must confront sudden change—the inevitable rise of automatons or the appearance of aliens—with some sense of normalcy. With sharp intelligence and humor, Ted Chiang examines what it means to be alive in a world marked by uncertainty, but also by beauty and wonder. An award-winning collection from one of today's most lauded writers and the basis for the major motion picture *Arrival*, *Stories of Your Life and Others* is a contemporary classic.

Fiction